MW01138090

something like hail

Jay Bell Books
www.jaybellbooks.com

Did you buy this book? If so, thank you for putting food on our table! Making money as an independent artist isn't easy, so your support is greatly appreciated. Come give me a hug!

Did you pirate this book? If so, there are a couple of ways you can still help out. If you like the story, please take the time to leave a nice review somewhere, such as an online retail store (my preference), or on any blog or forum. Word of mouth is important for every book, so if you can recommend this book to friends with more cash to spare, that would be awesome too!

ISBN: 978-1548535087

Cover art by Andreas Bell: www.andreasbell.com

-=Books by Jay Bell=-

The *Something Like...* series

#1 Something Like Summer
#2 Something Like Autumn
#3 Something Like Winter
#4 Something Like Spring
#5 Something Like Lightning
#6 Something Like Thunder
#7 Something Like Stories - Volume One
#8 Something Like Hail
#9 Something Like Rain
#10 Something Like Stories - Volume Two
#11 Something Like Forever

The *Loka Legends* series

#1 The Cat in the Cradle
#2 From Darkness to Darkness

Other Novels

Kamikaze Boys
Hell's Pawn
Straight Boy

Other Short Stories

Language Lessons
Like & Subscribe

Something Like Hail

by Jay Bell

Foreword

Last year I embarked on a writing experiment with the working title of *Something Like Chance*. Together with my supporters on Patreon, I would write a few thousand words and then come up with three different directions in which the story could go. My patrons would then vote to steer the fate of the character they helped design. That character is Noah Westwood, whom you are about to meet, and what was intended to be a short story became a full-blown novel. Writing is normally a lonely job, so I loved the interactive nature of this project. Getting instant feedback as the novel progressed was gratifying too. Naturally many of the choices made weren't what I was initially hoping for, but I couldn't be more pleased with the end result. Readers who have stuck with me this deep into the series have a similar literary sensibility as I do, so you'll find that this book fits in nicely with the rest of the series. I owe a huge debt to the readers who participated in this experiment, not just for adding a creative spark to my work, but also for their ongoing support. You'll find their names listed below. I ask that you cast your eye over each, because without these people, there's a very real chance that I wouldn't have been able to pursue the dreams that I have.

Many thanks to each and every one of you for so generously accompanying me in my creative endeavors. I hope I've been able to repay some of your kindness through these stories. Much love to you all!

-Jay Bell
September, 2017

My eternal gratitude goes out to...

My summer saviors, whose hearts burn with a fiery passion for all things love:

Jack Becker and Bear Sayer
Daniel Bell
Daniel Bestmann
Kevin Bowling
Jonathan Brito
Cindy Clare
Alex Cook
Mark Edwards
Erego
Jeremy Eskelsen
Travis Falla
Tiffany Graham
Bryan Grasso-Shonka
Stephen Hurwitz
Jason Jermyn
Jim
A. Joseph
Leigh Juhlke
Eric King
Shaun King
Jonothon J. Laycock
Lucky Summer Light
David MacDonald
Marc Martinez
Marc Anthony Maestre

Susen McBeth
Jesse McCain
Jini McClelland
Eric LaMonte Meno
Robert Lucas
Stephanie Michelle
Lori Neville
Michael Oaks
Zara Park
Chantal de Pessemier
Ray Pond
Jose Reyes
Dicxy Roa
Jeffrey Roach
John Smeallie
Kathie Smestad
Anna Solomonov
Joanna Sowerby
Matt Tadros
Steve Thomas
Ian Thomson
Guillermo Tirimacco
Sean Tucker
Michael Wallace
David Wood

My autumn angels, who act as wise guardians for those who should need their guidance:

Jacob Allman
Josh Barronton
James Brown
Cory Byers
Marcelo Castaldeli
Ricky Castañeda
D. Damiano
Peter Elsesser
Zac Ford
Lena Grey
David Griffin
Sal Guenette
Chris Hedley and Kai Burton
Robert B. Helms
Christopher and Simon Hill
Aydrian Howard
Laura Jones
Ingrid Birgitta Karlsson
Raigo Kirss
Jerry Lowe
Ross MacDonald
John Neumann
Olivier Ochin
Joie Olayiwola
Josh Oliff
Courtney Owen
Scott Page
Denis Polunin
Ben Pound
Dominic Romano
Kevenn T. Smith & Ray Caspio
Jamie Snow
Zachary Staback
Sydnie Wheeler
Tasha Wolfe

My winter warriors, whose cool demeanor is a comfort in any crisis:

Jeffrey Bledsoe
Ryan Cores
Maura Curtiss
Lucas Dantas de Paula
Corey Dobbs
EJG2
Hunter Faulkner
Gareth Foot
Erika Friedman
Ryan Hagel
Boomer Hatami
Mario Hinterhoelzl
A. Hudson
Tarah Jean
Reto Jordi
Tom Kerry
Brendan L
Daniel Lohse
Chaz Lutz
Jens Möller
Cade Nethercott
Trung Nguyen and Chandler Johnson
Phil and Pieter
Paul Rhind
Matthew Richards
Melvin Rivas
Ray Rogers
Alex Rojas
Rey Rosado
John Sheu
Lux St. Vilus
James and Jon Stewart
Christie Taylor
Michael Thompson
Dayle Walsh
Vincent van Zon and Peter Smithuis
Yin

Part One
Austin, 2015

Chapter One

This is a contract. A promise to rise up like a phoenix and find my way back to a normal life. Sure, I've been through some hard times. I'm one substance abuse problem away from hitting bottom, but I'm still young, and my mom always insisted that I'm smart. Now I'll prove that I really am. No more excuses. I'll use my head—use my whole body if need be—to finally escape the streets. My life fell apart years ago. Nothing will stop me from putting it back together again. I hereby swear to myself, for what that's worth, to uphold this promise. Signed on today's date...

Noah Westwood stood outside the production studio, palms sweaty as he tucked the homemade contract into his back pocket. His heart was pounding. He tried to blame this on the heat and the physical exertion it had taken to get there. The bus had brought him only part of the way. Once on the edge of Austin, he started walking. Few cars passed him on the road. Probably because there wasn't much to see out here except overgrown lots marked with worn realty signs that declared the potential of the land. Only a few of these lots had been developed and were now populated with office buildings. Or an industrial village, as one entrance was optimistically labeled. The parking spots were mostly empty, the purpose of each business vague. None more so than his destination. The studio building was large, appearing like a warehouse. No cheerful landscaping greeted him, nor did any windows provide an impression of the interior. All he could see was a massive silent structure, a scattering of cars out front, and a door. He approached, unsure if this was the correct destination until he read the sign: **Studio Maltese**

Okay. Right place. Now he just hoped it was the right time. Noah wiped his hands on his jeans, wishing he had nicer clothes to wear. Then again, a suit would have baked him alive after such a long walk. He would be better off wishing for a car, a garage to park it in, and a house filled with every comfort. If he'd had any of that, Noah wouldn't be here. Nor would he be quite so desperate. After taking a few deep breaths for courage, he pushed open the door.

The interior was as drab as the exterior. A long poorly-lit hallway, dotted by a number of doors, led to an elevator. He focused on this as he walked forward. Noah needed to speak to the man in charge, and that person would most likely be found on the top floor. He had nearly reached the elevator when a man with a large belly blocked his path. He wore a beige shirt with cloth patches on the shoulders that asserted his position.

"What can I do for you?" the security guard asked, hands on his belt.

"Hi!" Noah said, doing his best to sound friendly. He casually checked the security guard's name tag. "How are you today, Dave?" He had heard that saying someone's name helped to establish rapport. In theory. In practice…

The security guard's mustache tilted as he smirked. He didn't bother answering the question, instead repeating his own. "What can I do for you today, *sir*?"

That "sir" was firm enough to assure Noah that if he didn't get to the point soon, he would be asked to leave. "I'm here to see Mr. Maltese."

"There's nothing on the books today," Dave replied.

It took Noah a second to understand what he meant. "I don't have an appointment. All I need is five minutes of his time."

The security guard looked him up and down. "Are you selling something? Looking for work?"

"Five minutes," Noah said again. "Please."

Dave sighed and pulled out his phone. He tapped it and held it to his ear, pinning Noah down with a stare, even as he spoke. "Someone here to see you. Doesn't have an appointment. Won't say why. Uh-huh." He lowered the phone and pointed to one corner of the hallway. "Turn around and look up there."

Noah did what he was told, discovering a camera mounted high in one corner. He smiled and waved, hoping that a little cheerfulness would earn him access.

"Okay," Dave said. "Yep. I understand."

Noah turned back around to see that the security guard had put away the phone and now wore a determined expression.

"Marcello is very busy today," Dave said. "Go home, give us a call, and set up a time."

"I really need to talk to him," Noah said.

Dave puffed up his chest. "Not without an appointment."

He hadn't come all this way just to fail! Nor was he about to break the folded contract in his back pocket. It might not be legally binding, but he had given his word, and that still meant something to him. "Can I make an appointment while I'm here?" he asked, stalling for time. He casually eyed the surroundings. No way would he get the elevator doors open and closed again before he was stopped, but he *did* see stairs off to one side.

"Don't try anything funny," Dave said, picking up on his intent. "Call for an appointment. The big boss man will see you when he can."

"Okay," Noah said, nodding in agreement. "You're right." He started to turn away, then spun around. He feinted to the left, like he was going to plow right through the security guard. The man braced. Noah launched instead toward the right, bolted past Dave, and hit the door to the stairwell. He said a silent prayer that it would be unlocked, stomach sinking when it didn't budge. Then he tried pulling instead of pushing. The door swung open.

Noah felt fingertips swipe the back of his shirt as he resumed running and took the stairs two at a time. He might not be an athlete, but he was in better shape than Dave. The stairs wound around not once but twice before they came to an end on the next flight. That ground floor sure had high ceilings! He risked a look back as he pushed through this door, seeing no sign of pursuit, but he could hear thudding footsteps steadily nearing.

He turned his attention to the new hallway he found himself in, this one much nicer than the one downstairs. Not only was it properly lit, but decorative palms flanked a window further down. Less pleasing was the number of options. Any of the closed doors lining the hall could belong to Marcello. Noah didn't have time to check every room, but he did slow enough to read the signs next to each door as he passed them:

Archives
Randall Lockard
Jameson Belmont
Finances
Restrooms

He was tempted to duck into that last one to hide, but it wouldn't help. Dave would find him eventually, and Noah still wouldn't have won the audience he sought. A shout from behind sent him running again. He whizzed past door after door without having a chance to read the signs. Marcello could be at the end of the hall. The door next to those nice plants and natural daylight.

That made sense, right? Noah sprinted for it and blindly pushed his way inside, not having any options left.

The office beyond was on the corner of the building, perhaps facing the back, because he hadn't noticed any windows from the street. Here they defined the room. The space was large, a table and two chairs off to one side, and in the center, a desk surface mostly empty aside from a framed photo and a razor-thin laptop. A man sat behind this, broad-shouldered and scowling.

"Who the hell are you?" the man grumbled.

"Noah," he panted in response. "Noah Westwood. Are you him? Are you Marcello?"

Before the man could respond, a hand clamped around Noah's arm.

"That's it!" Dave shouted. "You can either come quietly or I'll break your neck. Which is it gonna be?"

"I'd go with him," said the man behind the desk. "Dave was a championship wrestler in college."

As if to demonstrate this, Dave pinned one of Noah's arms behind his back. He ignored the discomfort, making one last plea. This man might not be Marcello, but only someone important had an office like this. "I need to speak with Mr. Maltese," he said. "Please! It's important!"

The man let out a heavy sigh, then held up his hand just as Noah was being dragged away. "Hold on. What's going on here?"

"Sorry, Nathaniel," Dave said. "This punk thinks he doesn't need an appointment to talk to the boss man. Thought he would bust in rather than wait."

"Why?" Nathaniel responded.

"I need Marcello's help," Noah blurted out.

"I bet you do," Nathaniel said, but he nodded to Dave. "Let go of him. I'll take care of this."

"Are you sure? I can stick around and—"

"He doesn't look very tough," Nathaniel said. "Or dangerous. Go on. It's fine."

Noah gasped in relief when he was released, glaring at Dave as he left. Probably not fair, considering the guy was just doing his job, but Noah's pride was hurting. His arm too. He turned his attention forward again. "Thank you." He walked closer to offer his hand. "I'm Noah."

Nathaniel didn't budge. "What do you want?"

Noah let his hand drop, since it was being ignored. "I'd like to talk to Marcello, please. I mean… Mr. Maltese."

"About?"

Noah hesitated. He didn't know who he was dealing with, and that made him reluctant to speak.

Nathaniel studied him. Then he sighed, picked up his phone, and held it to his ear. "Hey," he said. "I've got a kid here who insists on talking to you personally. Goes by Noah. You know him?" Eyes traveled over his body. "Red hair, green eyes. Mm-hm. I got the same impression. What? I'm not going to… Fine!" The phone was lowered again. "Take off your shirt."

Noah stared. "What?"

"Take off your shirt. Or at least lift it up."

Maybe they were worried he had a gun tucked in his jeans. He took the shirt's hem and lifted it, revealing his waist.

"All the way up," Nathaniel insisted.

Or maybe they thought he was wired. Noah lifted the shirt to his neck, fully exposing his torso before he let the fabric drop again.

Nathaniel raised the phone to his ear. "Body is average at best."

"Hey!" Noah protested, but it went unnoticed.

"I agree," Nathaniel said, addressing Marcello again. "Will do." He set down the phone and considered for it a moment before speaking. "Look, if you really want to be a model, get into shape, or better yet, find an agent. Right now, we're not interested."

Noah's mouth fell open. "I'm not here because I want to be a model!"

Nathaniel's jaw clenched in response. "Then you either tell me why you're here, or get out. I've got better things to do than play guessing games."

Noah wasn't in the mood for charades either, but his purpose here was illegal. From what he understood, that part of the business was secret and not openly advertised. He also knew that Studio Maltese wasn't just a front. They really did hire models—the respectable kind—and produce high-profile advertisements. That's not the job he was after, but how to discreetly broach the subject? Unless that's what Nathaniel was attempting.

"When you say model," Noah tried. "Do you mean model or *model*?"

"They sound the same to me," Nathaniel grumped. Then he seemed to understand, leaning back in his chair slowly, expression guarded. "You're interested in movies."

"No," Noah said. He knew about those as well, but that would be too much. Too permanent. "The other thing."

"Dating?"

"Exactly!" He felt happy they had finally gotten there.

Nathaniel didn't look so pleased. "Do you have a reference?"

"Sorry?"

"A reference," Nathaniel repeated. "Who sent you here?"

Oh. In other words, how did he know about the escort service? That was complicated. Noah was loath to say the person's name, so he scrambled to find a different one. Someone who would know the same information and could get him where he needed to be. "Tim Wyman."

That did the trick. Nathaniel sat upright. "Tim?"

"Yeah," he said, praying he had gotten the last name right. Was it Tim Wyatt instead? No. He had heard it said often enough. Noah was certain.

"Seriously?"

Uh oh. What choice did he have but to stick with his story? He nodded.

Nathaniel considered him, then looked at the door. "And this is why you felt the need to bust in here like your life depended on it? Because you're interested in *that* sort of work?"

Noah would have swallowed if he had any pride left. "Can I talk to Marcello now?"

"I think you'd better." Nathaniel said, sounding exasperated. He picked up his phone again and turned around in his chair, voice a low murmur that Noah couldn't hear. After a short discussion, Nathaniel hung up the phone and stood. "Come with me."

Noah was led back down the hallway to the elevator. He wondered if he was being shown to the exit. Tim's last name might be Wyatt after all. Once they were in the elevator, Nathaniel punched a code into a keypad, the doors closed, and the little box moved.

"Are we going up?" he asked, not hiding his surprise.

Nathaniel looked over at him. "I'm guessing you took the stairs. They don't go to the third floor."

"I didn't know there was one."

"It's just an addition built onto the roof."

He tried to picture what awaited him there. A rooftop garden where Marcello pruned exotic plants while overseeing his criminal empire? He certainly didn't expect such a large and luxurious space. The lush carpets strewn about the stone floor, and the wet bar that occupied one wall, made it resemble a living room. On the opposite side of this, near the windows, two couches faced each other, separated by a low coffee table. The desk at the far end of the room was cluttered with files, papers, knickknacks, and a large monitor. An imposing man sat behind this, already eyeing him critically. Just an elaborate office then. Nothing so dramatic as a rooftop garden, but Marcello still would have made a great Bond villain.

Nathaniel led the way and stopped when they reached the couches. There he sat. Noah looked to him for guidance. When none came, he proceeded to the desk. Marcello didn't rise to meet him, or offer his hand. His gaze was appraising. Perhaps he was deciding if Noah was hot enough for the job. Marcello was basically what Noah had imagined: old, overweight, and dressed in a conservative suit. Exactly the kind of client he could expect to entertain. Those dark eyes though, they were shrewd! Noah had a hard time meeting them, but he forced himself to as he held out a hand.

"Hello," he said. "It's an honor to finally meet you. I'm Noah."

"You've caused quite a stir," Marcello said, standing finally. His voice was husky, his palm warm. "Let's start from the beginning. Why are you here?"

Noah glanced over his shoulder to where Nathaniel still sat.

"Don't worry about him," Marcello said reassuringly. "He finds this sort of business tedious. I doubt he'll take in a word of it. Speak freely."

"I want to work for you," Noah said. "As an escort."

"The direct approach!" Marcello sat and gestured at one of the chairs. "Please. Make yourself comfortable."

Noah did so, trying to position himself in a way that was sexually appealing. He spread his legs wide and angled himself so he could put one arm on the back of the chair. He wasn't sure what to do with the other arm. He moved it around a few times, finally placing a hand behind his head.

Marcello was busy taking a tablet computer from a drawer, but when he looked up, he did a double take. "Everyone has their own definition of comfortable," he said. "Are you sure that's yours?"

Noah shifted, cheeks burning as he adopted his normal sitting pose. For whatever reason, this seemed to make more of an impression.

"Lovely," Marcello said. "I do wish I was still capable of blushing. That's the problem with being shameless. I can't remember the last time I felt the youthful flushing of cheeks. Then again, that depends on which cheeks we are referring to and to whom they belong. Tell me, what is it precisely that an escort does?"

"An escort has sex with other people," Noah answered, glad his face was already red. "For money."

"Incorrect. That would be prostitution, which is illegal. An escort provides company to gentlemen with specialized needs. Men who appreciate discretion. That definition is specific to the business I run. I want to be very clear on all points. One: You will *not* exchange sexual favors for monetary rewards. Two: We cater to clients who demand exceptional care and quality. Three: The work done here is not to be discussed with anyone, not friends, lovers, or spouses. Not even your mother. Do you feel you can handle all of that?"

"Yes," Noah said, already wondering how much of it was true. He didn't really want to have sex with complete strangers, but he was pretty sure Marcello only pretended his business didn't involve that for legal reasons. "If you would just give me a chance, sir, you won't be disappointed."

"Everyone deserves a chance," Marcello said, sliding the tablet toward him. "You can begin by filling this out."

On the screen was what looked like a very normal job application, although without a section for previous employment. The only equivalent was a blank field asking for a reference. He entered the same name he had used on Nathaniel. Tim Wyman. The rest of the application didn't require dishonesty, although one question tripped him up. "I don't have a phone."

"None at all?" Marcello asked. "There isn't a single number where you can be reached?"

There was, but Noah wasn't about to give it out. "I'll get one," he said. "I promise."

Marcello looked him over again, but not in a way that felt sexual. He barely glanced at the tablet when it was handed back. Instead he motioned to Nathaniel, who approached to take it before asking for his ID and Social Security card. Once Noah had relinquished these, Nathaniel returned to the elevator and left with the tablet.

"Alone at last!" Marcello said, shooting him a wink.

Were they going to do it now? Noah assumed that's how it worked. Marcello would try out all of his boys personally before passing them around for money. Noah wondered—not for the first time—if he could really go through with this. He supposed the test began now. "What do you want me to do?" he asked.

"Talk," Marcello said. "Tell me how you know Tim."

Great. Noah struggled to remember useful details about him. He knew one story in particular, but it wouldn't earn him any love. Instead he resorted to inventing things again, even though it went against his instinct. "I met him at a party."

"A party?"

"A club."

"Ah," Marcello said, as if this made more sense. "Go on."

"We danced together," Noah said.

"Did he extend the invitation?"

"Yes. He bought me a drink first. We talked a little, but mostly he just wanted to dance. I did too."

"You like to dance?"

"Yes," he said truthfully. "I'm pretty good. Tim was impressed enough that he mentioned your... business."

Marcello smiled. "How thoughtful of him. And how did the evening end?"

"We just talked," Noah said. "I didn't go home with him."

"Even when Tim asked you to?"

"He didn't," Noah said, suspecting the question was meant to trick him. "I think he might have been in a relationship with someone at the time."

"Perhaps," Marcello said. "How long ago was this? You can't be more than..."

"I'm twenty-two. This was over a year ago. Tim probably doesn't even remember me. He was a little tipsy." Noah felt proud. Was he a genius or what? This way, if they asked Tim and he didn't remember, they would just assume it was too long ago or he had been too drunk to recall.

"Do you have much experience with men?"

Noah shrugged. "The normal amount."

Marcello nodded. "I was fifteen when I lost my virginity. I felt desperate to, as most boys do. Hormones alone didn't drive me. I longed for transformation. In my mind, the single obstacle on the path to becoming a man was that treasured experience. Circumstances had forced me to grow up quickly and become independent, but regardless, I still felt hounded by a missing credential, that no matter my achievements, I wouldn't attain adult status until I found someone willing to share a bed with me. When I did—well, the experience wasn't a complete disappointment. I spent days afterwards deluding myself that I had changed, when in truth, I was the same person as before. Becoming a man has nothing to do with sticking your dick inside of someone else. If only maturity was a gift so easily given."

"I feel mature enough for this job," Noah said, not understanding the point of the story.

"Good. What I found a greater challenge was the relationship I entered into with this man. Another first for me. I gave him my heart, and everything else I had to offer, and my reward was many months of happiness, swiftly followed by betrayal. When I first found evidence of his infidelity, I couldn't believe it. I refused to! I gave him the benefit of the doubt, and not wanting to insult him by asking directly, I started digging. My shovel soon struck something hard and unyielding. A lie. Then another. And another! I discovered that the pleasant little world I had been living in was constructed from equal parts illusion and delusion. *That's* when I changed. I had expected it to happen when I lost my virginity, that I would become a new person and be able to draw a line between then and now. Before and after. Accepting that my boyfriend was a liar allowed me to do just that. I've never been capable of blind faith since. Having the wool pulled over my eyes once was enough for me. Do you understand?"

Noah nodded. He understood perfectly. His entire ruse had been seen through. "I'm sorry."

"As I said, everyone deserves a chance, sometimes two, but listen carefully to what I say next. If you ever lie to me again, even once, we're finished. I can become your greatest friend or your worst enemy. Think carefully about which you would prefer. Now then, what are you doing here?"

"I'm hungry," Noah said, having to force the words out of a tight throat. "I used the last five bucks I had to take the bus here. I'm broke and I need a quick solution. I tried going to a temp service, but I don't have any real employment history. I've tried fast food places too, and maybe I'm just unlucky, but I can't seem to catch a break and I'm tired. I've got nothing. That's what I'm trying to say. I've got nothing and I know you can change that."

Marcello didn't react to this outpouring of emotion. He simply moved on to the next question, the one Noah had been dreading. "Who really told you about me? Tim Wyman possesses many desirable traits, but a passion for dancing is not among them. I've seen his husband drag him onto the dance floor, Tim kicking and screaming the entire way. Or maybe that's simply how he dances. Regardless, he is never a willing participant, and he certainly didn't ask you to do him the honor."

"I won't lie," Noah said, "but if I told you the truth, you wouldn't speak to me anymore. That's why I wasn't honest. I don't want to be judged by how I got here. I know I'm in the worst position to say this right now, but you can trust me. I want... I *need* a clean slate. Give that to me, and I swear I'll make it up to you. Please."

Marcello locked eyes with him. "Would you care to know the true focus of my business? It isn't advertising, photography, or media production. Nor is it adult films or escorts. I'm successful because I place the highest value on information. That is what I deal in and what gives me an edge in all aspects of life. Whatever secrets you might possess, I *will* discover them."

"Then it's a race," Noah said, feeling brave.

"Meaning?"

"That I have until that long to prove myself. By the time you find out the truth about me, I'm hoping you'll have also seen that you can trust me. And that I can be valuable to you."

Marcello considered him. Then he chuckled, the sound warm and friendly. He perked up as the elevator doors opened again and Nathaniel stepped out. "Well?"

"Nothing of interest," came the reply.

"Nothing at all?" Marcello appeared delighted. "The plot thickens! Nathaniel is very thorough, you know."

Noah didn't, but he breathed out in relief anyway. "So? Have I got the job?"

Marcello's finger tapped against the desk. Then he opened another drawer and removed a checkbook. He filled out one page, then jotted something down on a post-it note. Both of these were handed to Noah. "You'll be paid fifty dollars an hour, assuming you make the cut. Considering the level of determination you've demonstrated today, I don't see that being an issue, so I'm paying the first ten hours in advance. Regardless, you'll report to the given address tomorrow for assessment and training. Best of luck to you, Noah Westwood. We'll meet again at the finish line."

With a trembling hand, Noah took the check and the note with the address on it, scarcely believing his good fortune. He thanked Marcello, who absentmindedly waved him away, attention already on other matters. Nathaniel led him out, walked him to the front door of the building, and held it open without saying a word. Noah stepped into a bright afternoon, the sun warming skin that had been chilled by air conditioning. He examined the check. Five hundred dollars! Not a solution to his problems, but it sure helped ease them. Feeling a spring in his step, he turned toward the street and began the long walk home.

Noah's feet started dragging half an hour into his walk. The sun beat at his back, drenching his shirt in sweat, and man was his throat parched! He wished he could turn back the clock to before he left the studio, just so he could ask to use the restroom and drink from the sink. Each time a car passed, he was tempted to stick out his thumb and hitchhike, but Noah worried that wouldn't be safe. How ironic! He was about to sleep with total strangers for money, and he thought hitchhiking was too dangerous? He hoped Marcello's business had a way of weeding out violent creeps.

Another car passed him, a silver sedan. Noah ignored it until the brake lights glowed and it pulled over to the side of the road. When he reached the car, he kept walking, unsure if it stopping was merely coincidence. The electric whirr of a window rolling down attracted his attention. The driver leaned over to be seen.

"Unless you lied about your address too," Nathaniel said, "you've got a long walk ahead of you."

"I know," Noah responded.

"Get in."

Was that an order? Was Nathaniel his boss now? He didn't understand how the hierarchy worked, but his feet were already moving toward relief. He got in the car and hunched forward so his sweaty back wouldn't get the seat wet.

Nathaniel looked him over, then drove on. "You headed home?"

"No. I need to go to the bank."

This was met with stony silence, but he could feel judgement anyway, like Noah had only done all of this for the money. And he had, but not out of greed.

A few blocks later, Nathaniel said, "Which one?"

Noah consulted the check. "Austin City Finance Union." The bank that had issued the check should allow him to cash it. He hoped, since he didn't have an account of his own.

The quiet interior had him on edge as they continued their journey. Noah kept wondering how the dynamics of this job would work, but he felt uneasy about asking Nathaniel for specifics. He decided to try anyway, if only to banish the awkward atmosphere. "Any idea how many hours I'll be able to work per week? The more the better."

"I don't know," Nathaniel said. "I don't want to know. He'll have to find someone else to take over that part of the business, because I find it distasteful."

"Hey, it's not my first choice either," Noah said, refusing to feel ashamed. "Things have been really messed up for me lately. Some of it is my fault, I'll admit that, but not all of it. I'm just trying to get back on my feet."

Nathaniel looked over at him, the grumpy expression finally absent. "I've been there," he said. "I've got nothing against you personally. Not yet, anyway, but I love Marcello, and I hate the idea of him being taken advantage of. I'll make sure that doesn't happen."

He loved Marcello? Were they a couple? "He seems more than capable of taking care of himself."

"You'd think, but he has his weaknesses, and sometimes people are lucky enough to stumble into them without realizing."

Noah wasn't sure what that meant either. All he could do was speak for himself. "I'm just trying to get by, and not at the expense of anyone else."

Nathaniel nodded, as if satisfied. He remained quiet the rest of the way to the bank, until they pulled into the parking lot. "Should I wait?" he asked.

"I'll be okay," Noah said. "Thanks."

He left the car and went inside, feeling scuzzy but in better condition than he would have been otherwise. Hell, if Nathaniel hadn't given him a ride, he probably would have arrived too late and the bank would have been closed, forcing him to wait until tomorrow. Noah went up to the counter, hoping to cash the check, but of course they gave him grief about not having an account. No big deal. He would need one if he was going to be earning money regularly. He opened a new account and kept a hundred dollars in cash.

After this business was concluded, he made a beeline for the nearest fast food joint. Noah ordered a triple cheese burger, fries, and a fountain drink that he refilled before leaving. Thoroughly stuffed, he felt as large as Marcello as he began his walk toward the homeless shelter, stopping at a grocery store along the way for white bread, peanut butter, and bananas. Those would help solve one of his biggest problems: lunch. The shelter provided breakfast and dinner, but the portions weren't always generous and he had a high metabolism. Considering that he was on his feet and walking most of the day, he needed all the calories he could get.

Noah felt optimistic when reaching Jerusalem. He knew from his Bible school days that the real Jerusalem was a place of pilgrimage. Whoever had named the shelter had a sense of humor, because he wasn't the only one who made a daily pilgrimage there, seeking a different kind of salvation. The weather was warm, the spring days long enough that beds wouldn't be in such high demand. He still had a chance.

The shelter was on a corner downtown. As was so often the case, the sidewalk was filled with people who loitered and begged. Some asked him for money on the way in. Normally he found that ironic. Today, with substantial money in his pocket, he felt guilty. He perked up again when he saw Edith working the front desk. She was an older woman, tall and gaunt, who spoke with a light accent. Something European, although Noah had never asked her about it, assuming that everyone did so and that she was probably sick of explaining. Edith was firm and efficient but always had a smile for him. That's more than he could say for the hulking man next to her, hairy arms contrasting with the cue ball head. Noah thought of him as the Bouncer. He ignored this man, focusing on Edith instead.

"Sorry I'm late," he said, already smelling that dinner was being prepared. "I'll get washed up and help."

"Hello to you too," Edith said, pretending to scold him. "If you're always rushing, the good things will never catch up to you." She often said weird things like that. Noah assumed they were common phrases in her home country and sounded more natural in her native tongue.

"Sorry," he said again. "It's been a busy day."

Edith noticed the small bag of groceries and looked pleased for him. "We're almost out of beds," she said.

Noah swallowed. He usually didn't like to ask until he had already helped out by volunteering. He preferred working in the kitchen. At times he did less pleasant things, like cleaning the restrooms. None of this was required, or even suggested. He simply didn't expect anything for free.

"Don't worry," Edith said. "I have your back!"

He smiled as she handed him a small square ticket. In handwriting, it had the date on it and the letter/number combination of B49. They really were almost out of beds! The shelter had two dorms—large rooms filled with nothing but places to sleep. Dorm A was the better of the two, since the beds were larger, some of them for couples or families to share. Dorm B was cramped full of bunk beds instead. The shelter also provided private rooms, about twenty of them. These could be rented for thirty dollars a week. On occasion he had been lucky enough to stay in one. Not because he had the money, but if one happened to be empty, Edith would let him use it. A perk of volunteering, he supposed. He was tempted to rent one now, but this new job still wasn't certain, and he had to work off the loan Marcello had paid him. Noah would be frugal with the money he had left until more came in.

"Thanks!" he said, holding up the ticket. "You're the best!"

She smiled at him. He would come back later to socialize.

Now that he had a bed, he was twice as eager to pull his weight. First he went to the lockers, stowing his food and wallet there. After a quick trip to the restroom to wash his face and hands, he reported to the kitchen. Another benefit of working hard was how much easier a good night's sleep came. When he saw that they were serving chili, he was especially eager for a deep slumber. Sharing a room with fifty people, most of them guys who had guts stuffed full of beans? He prayed that he would be unconscious before the farting began.

Chapter Two

Noah lay awake, staring at a dimly lit ceiling. He had managed six hours sleep out of sheer exhaustion. Being in the top bunk helped him feel secure, but whoever was beneath him was an alcoholic, the fumes strong enough that Noah could smell them now. The man had other issues too, judging from the way he kept mumbling to himself. Was the guy even asleep? Noah wasn't sure, but he was used to this. He often divided the homeless into three categories: the junkies, who were addicted to booze or drugs; the crazies, who had mental health issues; and the tragedies, who each had a story. Some people fit into two or all three categories. Noah had mostly managed to stay in the third. He had a story, a sad tale that had landed him on the streets. Occasionally he did feel like he was going crazy, and Noah had also tried escaping the world by getting wasted, but mostly he wanted to keep his wits about him, hoping it would help him find a way out.

Speaking of which, he had an appointment today. From the limited light, Noah estimated that the current time was around five in the morning. The shelter would open its doors again in an hour. Between nine in the evening and six in the morning, the building was on lockdown. From what he understood, this was mostly to reassure the local community that those staying here weren't to blame for any spike in crime, although on occasion the police still needed to be called in to remove someone violent, or paramedics let in to deal with an overdose. As a kid, he had never conceived of such things. Noah thought back to a more innocent time of swing sets, a baby blue bedroom, and sack lunches packed by his mother. Each day had ended with loving hands tucking him into a warm bed. God that seemed so far away now!

No sense in dwelling on the past. Noah quietly climbed down from the top bunk and went to the dorm entrance. This led to a common area, where two sets of eyes appraised him and looked away. The staff knew he wasn't trouble. Noah used the restroom, then went to his locker to gather his clothes. He owned one pair of jeans and four shirts. Most of his underwear and socks were in bad condition, but soon he would invest in new ones. Especially since lots of people would be seeing his underwear. Geez, what a notion!

With this in mind, he went to the laundry room and its machines. One set was huge and industrial, made for washing and drying sheets in bulk. Noah had run it a few times while volunteering. Another set, smaller like those he had grown up with, was free for the homeless to use. He checked, but as often was the case, both machines were filled. The two coin-operated machines were available, so he used them instead. That meant stripping down to his underwear and sitting there yawning himself awake, but he wanted clean clothes for today. Besides, the shelter had seen stranger sights.

Once his things were in the dryer, Noah took a shower, returning from it to put on clothes as warm as freshly baked bread. The shelter was more active now. Noah reported to the kitchen to help serve breakfast. After the meal, he left Jerusalem and went to the library, using the computer there to look up the address he was given. His appointment wasn't until eleven, which gave him plenty of time to walk to his destination. He took it easy, not wanting to be a sweaty mess when he got there. The chaos of downtown slowly shifted to a sleepy residential neighborhood along the way. Neither environment was the kind he had grown up in. His family's nearest neighbor had been on the next farm over, more than a mile away. That had always made him feel isolated. Noah tried to imagine being raised in the neighborhood he was walking through now. This one was older, the trees overgrown, the small houses worn with time. Surely he would have made friends with the kids next door, or maybe across the street. Noah would have been spoiled for choice! He liked this area, although he didn't fully understand what he was doing there. What had Marcello said? Assessment and training?

After reaching his destination and double-checking that he had the right address, Noah rang the bell. When the door swung open, the breath caught in his throat, because the person standing there was hot. Not just "Oh, he's a good-looking guy!" attractive, but more like bite-your-knuckles-and-try-not-to-squeal handsome. This was especially impressive considering the guy had just gotten out of bed, judging from the mussed brown hair sticking up on one side. All the man wore was a maroon bathrobe, the glimpses of tan skin alluring, but the face is what truly captivated Noah. The eyebrows were thick and black, the dark irises of his eyes nearly blending in with the pupils. His nose was perfection—not too big, not too small—the kind people in Hollywood paid plastic surgeons to create. And that mouth? It was begging to be kissed, the delightfully pink lips moving to say his name and making it sound better than it ever had before.

"Noah, right?"

He managed to squeak out something resembling a "yes."

"Cool. I'm Harold. Come on in."

Awesome! Please let "assessment" mean lots of making out, just to prove Noah knew how. The front door led directly to the living room, where a large couch and coffee table faced a flat-screen television mounted on the wall. He could see a dining room and kitchen beyond, and on one side, a hallway that probably led to bedrooms.

"Have a seat," Harold said, gesturing to the couch. "You caught me by surprise."

"This is when Marcello said I should—"

"Not your fault," Harold said, his voice dry, but in a way that Noah found appealing. "It was a late night. I slept in. Hey, you want coffee?"

"Sure!" While he wasn't crazy about the taste, coffee was a cheap way of warming up during the winter, so he had learned to tolerate it. Right now Harold could offer him chocolate-covered grasshoppers and Noah would have gleefully nodded his consent.

His host disappeared into the kitchen. Noah sat and looked around the room. He saw a shelf filled with movies, a tall paper lamp in one corner, and on the side-table next to the couch, a cherry-red bong. The room wasn't dirty, but it also couldn't be described as tidy.

"Here you go, my man!" Harold reappeared, placing two steaming mugs on the coffee table. Then he plopped down on the other end of the couch, one leg tucked beneath him that was covered in fine dark hairs. "You're the new guy, huh?"

"I guess so," Noah said, trying to sound assertive. He was here to prove himself after all.

Harold saluted, brown eyes sparkling. "Welcome to the GAC!"

Noah did the same and felt ridiculous. "GAC?"

"Gentlemen's Agreement Club. That's the name of the game. Ever done anything like this before?"

Noah briefly considered his past. He could think of at least one guy he'd gone home with just so he'd be off the streets but… "Nothing so official."

"In that case, you've got a lot to learn. Any burning questions?"

"Are you my pimp?"

"Ha!" Harold smiled, swoon-worthy dimples appearing in each cheek. "No. I'm just an escort like you. I'm experienced enough that I help Marcello with the new recruits. You don't have a pimp, by the way. You have an employer. There's a big difference."

Noah's cheeks flushed. "Right."

Harold looked him over, starting with and returning to his hair. "Man, we finally have a ginger again. You'll be in demand. For a while we made one of our guys dye his hair, but it wasn't exactly convincing, you know?"

This failed to boost Noah's self-esteem because if Harold was an escort, and he represented the level of hotness clients were used to and expecting, then he didn't think he'd be in demand for long.

Harold reached for his mug and took a few sips before setting it on the coffee table again. Then he inhaled and stood. "Okay. Let's take a better look at you."

Noah remained where he was and tried his best not feel insecure. Confidence was sexy. Like the kind radiating from Harold, who was still scrutinizing him.

"Up up up!" he said. "Are you always this quiet?"

"No," Noah said as he stood. "I'm just trying to figure out what's going on."

"Come join me over here."

Noah rose and went to the middle of the room. Then he laughed as Harold walked around him, like his dad used to do with cattle before buying them at auction.

"Cute smile," Harold said approvingly. "You've got a boy-next-door vibe going on. That'll do well. Take off your shirt."

Ugh. Noah did so, cursing himself for the fast food he'd eaten the day before, and the dinner he'd gorged on just a couple hours after that. Living on the streets should have given him a rail-thin body. Instead he packed away food at every opportunity, always worried about where the next meal was coming from and wanting to stay warm on nights when he was forced to rough it. Being skinny wasn't good for survival. He was average at best, just like Nathaniel had said, when his clients would surely want more. He could tell from Harold's neck alone that he was in good shape. Not ripped, but he probably had a great body beneath that robe.

"Okay," Harold said, "we can work with this."

"We can?" Noah said, not hiding his surprise.

"Yeah! You've got an authentic vibe. You feel real."

He wasn't sure what that meant, and he didn't have time to focus on it, because—

"Take off the rest."

"My clothes?" he spluttered.

"Yup," Harold said matter-of-factly. "I know you just got here, but that's how it'll be with some of these guys. You'll show up, and they'll want to get right to it. Most of them want companionship more than sex, but you've gotta get used to people telling you to get naked."

Fair enough. Noah sat on the edge of the table to remove his shoes, then stood and worked on his jeans. He shot a glance at Harold, noticing the intense scrutiny, and decided it was easiest to not look at him at all. The jeans came off first.

"Tighty whiteys!" Harold declared, sounding amused. "That's so perfect. Down they go!"

A second later, they dropped to his ankles. Noah left them there, hoping he'd be able to pull them back up soon.

Harold circled him again. "I was hoping you'd be uncut. That's always worth bonus points."

"Are you?" Noah shot back. If he wasn't allowed any privacy, why should the other guy be?

Harold grinned, attention moving back to his face but only briefly. "Wouldn't you like to know? Body hair is minimal. Do you manscape?"

"No." That required more privacy than the showers at the shelter provided.

"You're lucky then. We'll keep you this way. Nice and natural. You've got a great ass. Take off your socks."

"I'm not naked enough?"

"Nope. Some guys will be more interested in your feet than anything else."

Noah kicked his underwear away and raised each leg so he could remove his socks. That's when Harold got to his knees to inspect his feet. Awkward, because now his head was really close to Noah's dick. Not that Harold seemed interested. He asked him to lift each foot. All this time Noah had been fighting against getting an erection, but he was failing quickly. Harold's handsome face was mere inches away from his cock, the distance closing quickly as Noah got hard. Just before the head could brush against a tanned cheek, Harold looked up.

And stared.

"At least we know you won't have any trouble performing," he said. "You'd be surprised how many guys think they can do this, but when the time comes to… Damn! You're a grower!"

If there's one thing Noah had going for him, it was this. He had never thought his appearance would make him a good escort, but when most guys saw what he was packing, they tended to get excited.

Harold was no exception. "Hold that thought," he said, hopping up and rushing from the room. When he came back he was holding a ruler.

"Seriously?" Noah asked.

"It's a number we need for your profile," Harold said, shooting him a grin. "And besides, I'm curious. Looks like you're at full mast?"

If he wasn't already, he became rock hard when Harold reached down and grabbed Noah's dick so he could press the top of the ruler to it. He squeezed the head to get an exact measurement. "Just a smidge under eight inches," he said. "If anyone asks, you're eight exactly."

He let go and moved the ruler away. Noah was mortified to see a strand of precum dangling from the tip of his dick.

"You leak a lot?" Harold asked.

"Depends on the situation. And how long it's been."

"Good. Plenty of guys will appreciate that. You can put your clothes on again."

Noah scurried to dress, cheeks burning. He'd have to get used to this. He wasn't naïve. He understood that he would be doing all sorts of depraved things. He just never expected it to be with someone so hot.

"Okay," Harold said, all business now. "Here's the deal.

We've got a lot of ground to cover today. We need to hit a clinic to have you tested. We'll get your hair cut too. A pedicure is probably a good idea. You own any clothes better than what you're wearing?"

"No," he admitted.

Harold exhaled. "That might have to wait. I'll take a quick shower, then we'll get started."

"Does this mean I'm in?"

"Yeah, you're in!" Harold said, making it sound obvious. "Enjoy your coffee. I'll be right back."

Noah sat on the couch, thinking pure thoughts until his erection subsided. When he heard water running from elsewhere in the house, he stood and strolled around the living room, trying to learn more about Harold. The movies on display didn't tell him much, simply because he rarely had the luxury of seeing many, although in the winter he sometimes went to cheap afternoon matinees to escape the weather. Not often. That money was better spent on food.

He walked to the dining room and stopped dead in his tracks. The table there was large and could have easily sat eight, if not for the model railway that filled the surface. He moved closer, looking for the train and feeling puzzled when he couldn't find one. The model didn't even have tracks. Just little buildings, streets with cars, and people. Weird. He couldn't investigate further because he heard the water shut off.

Noah rushed back to the couch, taking repeated swigs of the coffee so it appeared like he had been seated there all this time. When Harold returned… Noah sighed. The guy had been handsome enough straight out of bed. Freshly groomed and showered? He was perfect. Maybe they should break out the ruler again. He was pretty sure he could make it past the eight-inch mark now.

"You okay?" Harold asked, misinterpreting the strained expression.

"I'm just ready to go," Noah answered truthfully enough.

"I like your enthusiasm," Harold said approvingly. "Some people treat this job like an easy way to make money. You gotta be passionate to succeed. Let me grab my shoes and I'm ready. Oh yeah, this is for you." He held out a small rectangular box.

Noah accepted it. The packaging was minimal, mostly white,

but the words on the side had him stunned. "A phone?"

Harold shrugged. "Marcello said you didn't have one. I know they can be a pain, but you'll need it to stay in touch with clients and get assignments."

Noah shook his head. "Thank you, but I can't accept this."

Harold chuckled. "You're strange. Ready to go?"

Soon they were in a car, cruising through Austin. What a way to travel! Noah looked out the window as they went, spotting sunbaked people lugging heavy backpacks that probably contained everything they owned. The person pushing a shopping cart down the sidewalk was definitely one of his kind. Noah felt like he was betraying them by being in a car, but that was his goal. All of this was a means of escape.

They arrived at a clinic, where Harold took care of all but the most basic paperwork. They didn't need to wait. Noah heard him utter "Studio Maltese" like a password. This earned them instant attention. Noah was examined in a way much less erotic than Harold had done earlier, his blood was drawn, and they moved on to the next location. And the next and the next, until Noah found himself with a full belly, freshly trimmed hair, and feet that were becoming as pretty as possible thanks to the woman who was working on them. He played with the new phone, Harold walking him through the setup while getting his own pedicure in the next chair over. Noah still wouldn't let himself consider the phone his own. He couldn't afford either the base price or the monthly payments to keep it active. Still, it was fun to finally get to mess with one.

"A guy could get used to this," Noah said gleefully.

"It's not always days this good," Harold replied. "Sometimes it's even better."

"And when it's not?"

Harold laughed. "Yeah, sometimes it's pretty freaking gross."

If they were alone he would have asked for details. Noah supposed he would find out eventually. The magical name of "Studio Maltese" was uttered again when it came time to pay. Shopping followed, which wasn't so fun. They went from store to store, Harold searching for something but unable to find it. He didn't seem interested in Noah's opinion either, being far too focused on his own vision to converse much. When they visited a store specializing in Western wear, only then did he relax.

"Finally!" Harold declared, holding up a blue and white checkered shirt. He was even happier when discovering one with red squares. "What do you think?"

"Those are ugly!" Noah replied. He wasn't worried about hurting Harold's feelings because he clearly possessed a better fashion sense. The clothes he wore were stylish—American Eagle or something like that. Noah was out of touch when it came to brands, but he knew what looked good, and this wasn't it. "Throw in a brown vest and I'll be a cowboy."

"You'll pull it off," Harold said, his confidence unwavering. "And then other guys will pull these off of you. Ha ha!"

Noah laughed despite hating the clothes. Stupid hot guy, robbing him of his free will! Even worse was—when trying on the hideous shirts—how he did his best to prove Harold right. Noah didn't step out of the dressing room with slumped shoulders and a miserable expression. Instead he really tried to make it work.

"Sold!" Harold declared.

A few pairs of classic Levi's jeans were added to the pile. They browsed belts with giant buckles, but thankfully even Harold thought this was a step too far. Once finished at the register—the total making Noah cringe—they walked into the parking lot, the sun low on the horizon.

"Question," Harold said, flustering him with that perfect smile. "I know it's been a full day, but if you've still got the energy..."

"What?" Noah asked, struggling to breathe.

"Do you want to go on a date with me?"

"A date?"

"Yeah. Dinner. What do you say?"

Noah swallowed, mouth dry. "Sounds good."

"Awesome!" Harold looked him over. "Small favor though. I want you to put on the new clothes."

Noah stifled a groan. "Do I have to?"

Another flawless smile, this time reinforced by dimples. "For me?"

Soon he was on the other side of Harold's car, using it as a shield from the busier half of the parking lot so he could change clothes. Noah felt like he was getting dressed for a rodeo. That brought back less-than-pleasant memories. As soon as he finished changing, Harold grabbed him by the arm.

"Over here. Quick! The sunset is perfect!"

Noah was dragged to one side of the store they had just left and pushed up against the brick wall.

"Stand there, just like that," Harold said, backing up.

Noah squinted against the sun, adjusting to the light until he could see Harold holding up his phone. Was he taking pictures?

"Done!"

"I wasn't ready yet," Noah said.

"I know. That made it even better." Harold jerked his head toward his car and started walking toward it again. "You'll have studio photos taken if you get that far, but for now, this will do."

"Wait," Noah said, hurrying to catch up. "Is this for a dating profile or whatever? There's a website?"

Harold nodded. "I call it The Menu, but yeah, there's—"

The stern faces of his parents appeared in his mind, grim and disappointed. "Is it public?"

Harold looked over at him. "It's an app these days, and you've gotta know where to find it. Closeted?"

"No. I just don't want anyone knowing."

"That you're an escort. I get it." Harold's expression had lost some of its brightness. Was he insulted? Did he actually feel proud of his occupation?

Noah got into the car, worried that he had ruined their relationship before it had a chance to begin. Conversation was minimal as they drove.

Harold loosened up again when they stood in the parking lot of a steakhouse. "Paradise! For us, anyway. Not so much for the poor cows. You hungry?"

"Always," Noah said, stomach growling as they entered.

The restaurant did indeed seem like paradise. He struggled to remember the last time he had eaten somewhere with waiters that wasn't a cheap diner. Was it with his parents? Or back when he was dating— Yup! Noah smiled. That had definitely been the last time. Both starving, they had dined and dashed, feeling so bogged down with food that he was sure they would be too slow and get caught.

"Been here before?" Harold asked from across the table, mistaking the reason for his smile.

"I don't think so. I'll take…" He turned his attention to the menu. "Everything!"

Harold laughed. "That might get expensive."

"About that," Noah said, trying to remember how much cash he had in his wallet. Enough to cover this meal? Maybe. But not the rest. "Are the clothes we bought going to come out of my paycheck?"

"Business expense," Harold said easily. "Don't worry about it."

"Wow, so we get to shop for clothes and it's covered?"

"Normally? No, but Marcello said to help you get set up, and that's what I'm doing. Our clients are going to love you."

"Are you sure?" Noah asked, letting his insecurity show.

They were interrupted by the server, who came to take their orders, but Harold stuck with the topic once she had gone. "You're a good-looking guy," he said. "More important than that, you're real."

"You said that earlier too. I don't get what you mean."

"Our clientele look for one of two things. Some of them want what they can't normally have. The guy on the magazine cover, or a lookalike from the boy band they obsess over. Toned muscles, flawless face—"

"In other words, you."

Harold's teeth flashed at the compliment. "The other side of the coin—and you'll find out how popular it can be—is clients wanting to feel like they're really with someone. Instead of a superhero they worship, they want a down-to-earth connection with another human being. That's so you. You're cute, don't sell yourself short in that way, but the way you get nervous, or how easily you blush..."

Noah's stupid cheeks demonstrated his point.

"Exactly!" Harold said, laughing happily. "I hope you never lose that because it's sweet. That's what I mean by being real. Guys in boy bands? Fashion models? They don't feel real. You do. You've got this country boy charm that people are going to love. That's what I'm trying to cultivate with your clothes and stuff."

Noah sighed. "You can take the boy from the small town, but you can't take the small town from the boy."

Harold leaned forward. "Really? So I was right?" He held up his hands to stave off an answer. Or like he was setting a scene. "I want you to tell me all about yourself. Ready? Go!"

"Oh. Okay. Well, I'm from a small town out west. Have you

heard of Fort Stockton? No? I'm not surprised. There's nothing out there. A bunch of oil pumps, but my family doesn't own any of those. We have a farm, mostly for cattle and fish. The land out there isn't great for growing things. Odessa is a little over an hour away. 'The big city.' That's how I thought of it whenever we went there."

"Loving it so far!" Harold said.

That was a weird response, but Noah pressed on. "My parents are Southern Baptists. When I was fourteen they caught me spooning with a guy friend. We weren't doing anything. I was so naïve back then that I didn't even know how sex worked. We were playing house. Way too old for that sort of thing, I know, but we were only goofing around. My friend thought it was funny. Me? I felt all sorts of things. My parents sat me down, and after asking a bunch of questions— Most gay people come out. I feel like I was diagnosed. It doesn't help that our family doctor was also our minister. We tried praying the gay away, but he also used medicine. I was put on testosterone briefly, which made me crazy. They tried antibiotics, antidepressants, all sorts of things. I still don't know what most of it was. The sad thing is, I was right there with them, wanting to find a cure."

"Jesus," Harold breathed.

"Yeah, him too. I tried talking to Jesus about it, not that he ever responded. This attempt to fix me went on for a couple of years. None of it was working, so I quit. I refused any treatments. I had been reading things on the internet—which we didn't have at home. No computer at all. We only had one television, and that was in the living room. I wasn't allowed to watch it alone. Anyway, when they taught us how to use computers at school and I discovered that the local library didn't censor search results, I started drawing my own conclusions. I learned that I didn't have to be ashamed of who I am or need to change myself. My parents disagreed. After enough arguments, they kicked me out. I was only sixteen and I've—" Been homeless ever since, except he didn't want his date to know that. "It's been a struggle."

Harold looked aghast. "Man… I'm so sorry!"

"It's fine," Noah replied. "Everyone has problems."

"Yeah, but that's especially rough. Think they'll ever come around?"

Noah shrugged. "My mom got a laptop. I'm hoping that'll change her mind the way it did mine."

"I hope so. Wow."

Their food arrived, but Harold didn't touch his.

Noah had no such reservations. He grabbed a knife and fork and dug in. After swallowing a few bites, he looked up. "What about you?"

"My parents are cool." Harold chuckled. "Old hippies. I haven't managed to shock them yet. Anyway, back on track, your story is a little intense. It's okay to be honest, but maybe hold back on the details unless someone really asks."

Noah's chewing slowed. Then he swallowed. "What?"

"When people ask about you. Getting right to the heart like that is going to bring them down. Sounds mean, I know, but most clients want to have a good time. Especially at first. There's room for the deep stuff later."

Noah felt his face turning red, but not from embarrassment this time. "You're not a client."

"No! Of course not. But we're practicing."

"We are?" He wanted to take the words back the second they slipped free. When Harold had asked if Noah wanted to go on a date earlier, he hadn't meant in the romantic sense. This was a training exercise. Why else would he need to wear the stupid outfit? Noah sat up instead of slouching, suddenly aware of his table manners.

"I wish I could go on a real date with you," Harold said generously. He too had picked up on the misunderstanding. "Man, wouldn't that be nice! Only downside to this line of work, it kind of requires you to stay single."

"I knew that," Noah said. "Sorry. I have a weird sense of humor."

"And I can be dense. My dad has been telling me that my entire life."

Noah managed a laugh, then shoved more food in his mouth. God this was awkward! He decided the only way to fix the situation was to prove how professional he could be. "I grew up in a small town called Fort Stockton. I'm a farm boy, and I liked that life, but when all my friends started chasing after girls instead of me, I decided the big city might have what I need."

"That's good!" Harold said. "Like I said, you don't have to lie or always censor yourself. It's just that most heart-to-hearts happen later in the evening. After a few drinks."

"Got it. What else should I know?"

"How to keep conversation going."

Harold left it at that, finally turning his attention to his food. Noah waited for him to say more, and when he didn't, realized this was another test.

"Tell me about yourself," Noah tried.

"Ugh. I'm boring. Twelve hours in the office each day and nearly as much on the weekends. All I do is work."

"What sort of work?"

"Computers. Honestly, if I have to think about my job for one second more, I'll go nuts."

Okay. Someone who didn't want to talk about his life. Noah knew that blabbing on and on about himself was rude so… "I read an article the other day about how they want to terraform Mars and make it a green planet. It's all theories and sci-fi right now, but could you imagine moving to another world?"

Harold crinkled his nose as if not interested. "Space travel?"

"Yeah! Just imagine… Moving to another town or state can broaden your horizons. A new country is an even bigger change, but an entirely different planet? Think of the potential! You could reinvent yourself. What would you be if you could start over from scratch?"

"All I know is computers…"

"Doesn't matter. Start with your name. Choose a different one."

Harold cracked a smile. "Emperor Llama."

Noah laughed. "And what's the first thing Emperor Llama does when he wakes up in the morning on Mars?"

Harold nodded approvingly. "You're good!"

"I'm still waiting for an answer."

Harold put on a thoughtful expression. "He eats an entire pie. All by himself. No forks or spoons. He just shoves his face right in and pigs out."

"They have pie here," Noah said. "I saw it on the menu. We could get one to go."

Harold raised an eyebrow. "Maybe we should. I'd like to see what you and our imaginary client do with it."

"Feel free to hire me sometime," Noah said coolly, when really the idea alone made him want to jump up and down while giggling. "So tell me more about you. I'm tired of Emperor Llama or whatever his real name is. Tell me about Harold."

"Now I'm on the spot, huh?"

Noah nodded. "For real. Enough practice."

Harold speared a steak fry with his fork but didn't bring it to his mouth. "I'm a homebody. I'll probably be one of those people who die in their house but nobody notices because I never leave. That's why I like this job. It forces me to go outside. I get to have interesting conversations, eat at fancy places, and never have to pay for anything." He leaned back and patted his stomach. "It even encourages me to stay in shape. Otherwise I would just sit at home and… do stuff."

"Build models?"

Harold groaned. "You saw those? Yeah, that's what I'm into. That and toking and watching TV. Like I said, boring."

"Why models? And how come there's not a train?"

Harold shook his head ruefully. "Check you out, getting me talking about myself. I usually avoid that."

"Don't you have to on dates?"

"Talk about myself?" Harold leaned across the table and whispered, "I lie through my teeth. Constantly." After reclining again he added, "Only on the clock though."

"Think I should do the same?"

Harold shrugged. "Honesty suits you better. People will respond to that. You'll do well. I'm glad you found your way to us. How'd you manage that anyway?"

"How did I find out about your secret clubhouse?"

Harold nodded. "Yeah. Tell me everything."

Noah considered him. Then he narrowed his eyes suspiciously. "You're only asking because Marcello wants to know, right?"

"Busted! You've got a five-hundred-dollar bounty on your head."

"I do?"

"Yup. Paid to the first person who discovers your deep dark secret."

Noah smiled. He liked that, feeling it made him more interesting. "Stop changing the subject. There's got to be more to you than models and your bong."

"The devil is in the details."

"My mom used to say that. Then again, she saw the devil in just about everything."

"I've been on some weird dates," Harold said, a twinkle in his eye, "But so far I've never had the devil in me. Unless you count Marcello, but that was just a finger. Or two."

Noah tried to picture this, a french fry halfway to his mouth. Then he put it down and started laughing. Harold did too.

The rest of the meal passed pleasantly enough. Harold coached him about the kinds of establishments where Noah would likely eat with his dates. Not which fork to use or anything, since clients would find his confusion endearing, but Harold mentioned which foods to avoid and taught him how to drink sparingly without appearing to do so. Getting really drunk on dates was a bad idea, apparently.

Once the bill was paid (another business expense) they drove back to Harold's place. Noah's pulse quickened again as they went inside. If the meal had been a training exercise, maybe what happened afterwards would be too.

"So what's next?" he asked, intentionally broaching the subject. "Naked photos?"

"Nah," Harold said, plopping down on the living room couch. "Why buy the cow when you get the milk for free? I know a lot of escort sites show what you get up front, but people are willing to pay extra to solve a mystery."

Noah didn't give up hope. "What about the bedroom? What sort of techniques do I need to know there?"

"You? Nothing. If you don't know what you're doing, it will only feed into your image. I've already seen that you don't have trouble getting it up. You'll be fine."

Better safe than sorry? he was tempted to suggest. Before he could, his pocket vibrated, which shocked him until he remembered the phone there. He pulled it out, seeing a text message on the lock screen. It contained a guy's name and phone number along with a date, time, and address.

"First assignment?" Harold asked, checking his own phone. "I've got mine for tomorrow. Chester Burgess, an easy one. Who's yours?"

"George Perry."

Harold made a choking noise. "For your first assignment? That can't be right." He craned to see Noah's screen, shaking his head when presented with the evidence. "Did you make Marcello mad or something?"

"Not that I know of. Why?"

"He usually starts new people out slowly. Maybe he got our assignments mixed up. Hey! We could switch. I don't mind."

Noah looked down at his phone again. Maybe this was a challenge from Marcello that he was expected to meet. Then again, he would be a lot less nervous knowing that his first foray into the world of escorts was with an easy client.

He shook his head. More crucial than showing Marcello he could do this was proving himself to Harold. Noah didn't want to disappoint him. "I've got this."

"You're sure?" Harold asked with concern.

How sweet!

"I'll be fine. Um… Any tips?"

Harold bit his bottom lip as he thought about it. "Yeah. You'll reach a point in the evening where you think George is trying to drug you. Don't worry. He's not. Hey! Speaking of which, wanna smoke up with me?"

Noah looked at the bong. He'd gotten high before and liked it, but when on the streets he needed to keep a clear head. Even sleeping at the shelter came with risks, and they had a strict policy about—

The shelter! Noah searched the room for a clock, then remembered the one on his phone. Fifty minutes past eight. Jerusalem went on lockdown at nine. If he didn't leave now, he wouldn't have anywhere to sleep for the night. "I gotta go," he said.

"Oh. Okay. Need a ride anywhere?"

"Yes!" he said gratefully. Otherwise he'd never make it in time. The only alternative would be calling a taxi, which was pricey and required a wait. They'd be cutting it close as is.

"Cool," Harold said. "Just give me a second."

A second turned into minutes as Harold used the restroom, then switched his slippers for shoes, chatting casually while doing so. Once they were seated in the car, Noah saw that only five minutes had gone by, but it sure felt like longer. He could only hope that Harold drove *really* fast.

He didn't. He kept talking, telling the story of his first assignment. Noah couldn't take in the details, too preoccupied with the minutes ticking by on his phone. Nine o'clock came and went, but the doors didn't usually close exactly when the hour changed. The shelter wasn't run that precisely.

Sirens sounded from behind. Noah turned in his seat to see.

Just an ambulance, but the car pulled over way before it was near.

"Hate to be whoever called them," Harold said. "Whenever I see an ambulance, I wonder what the emergency is and am thankful I've never ridden in one."

Great. Very thoughtful, but right now Noah had an emergency of his own. When they finally reached the shelter, it was five minutes past and the doors were still open. Noah hesitated, not wanting to reveal that he was staying there.

"What's my next turn?" Harold asked.

"Just a couple more blocks," Noah replied. He couldn't ask him to pull over here. Nothing around the shelter resembled a decent home, so he had Harold cruise to the nearest neighborhood and pull into an apartment complex.

"Right here is fine," Noah said, already reaching for the door handle.

The car stopped in the parking lot. "Cool. Hey, if you get nervous tomorrow and want to call me, just say you need to use the restroom." Harold chuckled. "That'll probably only work at the restaurant, but it doesn't matter. Find some other excuse if you've got to. You're not on your own, okay? I'll be there for you."

The words would have made his heart flutter under different circumstances. Noah simply didn't have time for them now. "Okay. Thanks. Bye!"

He was outside the vehicle too fast to hear a response. He couldn't exactly turn and run for the shelter though. Instead he walked toward one of the buildings, wishing he really did live there as he listened to Harold's car pull away. Once certain he was gone, Noah started sprinting. The bags of clothing they had bought were slowing him down, thwacking against him repeatedly as he ran. He stayed away from the main road, just in case Harold was stopped at a traffic light.

Only when Noah saw the back of the shelter did he hustle to the front of the building. The doors were closed. This meant more than them being locked. A metal gate barred the entrance, stoic and unsympathetic to his plight. He checked the time and saw it was twenty minutes past. Right now Edith or whoever was volunteering that night would be getting people settled, offering leftovers from the evening's meal, and doing everything to provide temporary comfort. They would be busy. Noah could rattle the gate or hammer on the back door, and even if the staff inside broke policy, he would still feel guilty standing there with shopping bags in his hands and money in his pocket.

He could find a cheap hotel. Once again, he worried about making the money last. If he earned fifty bucks an hour, and assuming tomorrow's date lasted no more than three, he would still be hundreds of dollars in debt thanks to the advance. He also wasn't sure how often he'd get assignments, or if he was expected to pay back the price of the phone. Best to hold on to his money for now.

Noah looked up and down the street, considering his options. He knew of another shelter that was seedier. He'd had bad experiences there, but it was worth a shot. After walking fifteen blocks, he discovered it was full. Fine. The weather wasn't so bad. Noah's phone informed him that it would be getting down to fifty degrees that night. Chilly, but nothing he couldn't handle, especially if he minimized his time outdoors. A fast food joint or a diner then. Noah had a long list of them in mind. Some were friendlier toward the homeless than others, tolerant toward those who made a cheap cup of coffee last for hours.

He walked to a diner not far away that didn't mind him taking advantage of their free-refill policy. The waitress recognized him enough to act surprised when he also ordered a piece of pie—his version of splurging. At least now he had a phone to distract him. Noah played with the settings, eventually reaching the contacts, which only consisted of two names: Marcello and Harold. At one time more people would have been listed there—friends he had grown up with, or parents and other relatives, although not many. Noah's family was small. Maybe for a reason. How many other members had been pushed away in the name of God, or had decided to keep their distance because of his parents' extreme beliefs?

Still… Two names only? He didn't know anyone else? A melancholy settled over Noah as he realized just how isolated he had become. Even after being kicked out of his home, he used to have friends. The first place he had driven to was San Antonio, because that's where he knew actual gay people. Twins, Rico and Tito. That friendship had started in an online chatroom and felt even warmer once continued in person. They didn't have much either, but they gave him all the time and sympathy he needed.

Noah would sleep in his car at night, or sometimes on the floor in their shared bedroom. For one night, he snuggled up in the actual bed, but only with Rico. Tito had been elsewhere, allowing Noah to discover just how amazing playing house could be. As upset as he'd been about his parents kicking him out, for a brief period he had felt happy. Happier! His fling with Rico was only that, but Noah moved on to another relationship and another city. Austin this time, and while things were complicated, for the most part they were good.

When he lost the car, *that's* when Noah cut himself off from everyone. Until then, he didn't really consider himself homeless. Not exactly. After he had felt forced to sell the car, when his only sleeping options became relying on the generosity of others or spending the night on secluded park benches, Noah had changed. He didn't like to ask for help, or for others to see him so helpless. Noah stopped visiting San Antonio, wanting to hide the truth and needing to be closer to the only man who had ever claimed to love him. What a joke! When had they last seen each other? Six months ago? More?

He was alone. The realization hit Noah hard, his eyes moving back to the names on his phone. He needed to reach out to someone. Anyone, and of his two options, he definitely liked one of them more than the other.

Hey, he texted. *Quick question.*

Shoot! Harold responded.

What kind of plan does this phone have? Do I need to worry about how much I use it?

Ha! Marcello doesn't know the meaning of moderation. You're on unlimited.

Bandwidth or…

Unlimited everything!

Nice! He smiled, feeling like someone now occupied the empty seat across from him. *What are you doing?*

I'm toasted, man. I feel like it's taking me an hour to write each line. Sorry.

You're doing fine.

Cool. What are you up to? Already in bed?

Noah looked around the diner, seeing only lonely souls like himself and one drunk couple who kept snorting with laughter. *Yeah. I'm nice and warm in my big ol' bed.*

And playing with your phone. Don't use it to surf porn!

Why not?

You need to save your strength, Harold replied. *You can't just blow a load anytime you want. That stuff is too valuable. White gold!*

Noah laughed out loud. *Gross!*

I'm not kidding. Better change the topic. I'm always a horndog when I'm high.

Something to keep in mind for the next time Harold asked if he wanted to smoke. *I guess I'll crash now,* Noah texted.

Don't be nervous about tomorrow. You'll do fine. You're fun to be around. That's the most important part. Aside from all the other stuff. ;)

You're fun to be around too, Noah typed. *I really like you. A lot.* Then he thought better, deleting the words and replacing them with, *Goodnight.*

Sweet dreams!

Noah finished his pie, sipped a refill of coffee until he felt he'd worn out his welcome, and stood. He left a tip on the table and paid at the counter. Then he used the restroom while still having the convenience of doing so, and afterwards, grimaced at the light mist when he went outside. Too bad his pack was in the locker at Jerusalem. No sleeping bag or coat. That brought back memories. He'd survived those first nights on the street. He would do so again, this time a little wiser. Noah walked to one of the larger parks, avoiding the sidewalks and benches that police were likely to check when patrolling. He found a cluster of trees far away from the city lights and pushed his way through the brush there. His skin was scratched by branches, but at least here the earth was dry. He debated between layering the new clothes to keep warm or using the shopping bags as a pillow. In the end he opted for the latter, eyes remaining open long after he pressed his cheek to a plastic bag.

Chapter Three

Noah awoke, skin damp with dew and muscles aching from sleeping on hard ground. His clothing wasn't exactly dry, but he felt optimistic despite shivering with cold. The day always offered more options than the night. Starting with breakfast and a shower at the shelter. He warmed up on the walk to Jerusalem, hoping for a friendly face behind the counter, but the Bouncer and another man he didn't know were on duty. Noah took advantage of the offered hospitality, then went to the public library to read. Having money was a luxury. He didn't need to spend time begging on the streets. He could continue his job search, which until now had been fruitless. Noah didn't possess an education. He had dropped out of high school, and if potential employers ever bothered calling him back, they probably hung up when realizing they had reached a homeless shelter. Now he had a phone of his own, and after a few weeks of proving himself as an escort, maybe Marcello would be willing to vouch for him. With a reference, Noah could land a day job and really get his life on track.

He used the note-taking feature of the phone to key in a rough plan, looking up cheap apartment rentals and average utility costs to create a budget. Noah was encouraged by the results. Even without a day job—if he was careful—he could do this. He would have to work hard and spend lightly, but he saw a way out.

With this in mind, he found himself eager for his first date. Noah freshened up at the shelter, taking another shower and visiting a nearby department store to spray on a few puffs of sample cologne. He left early for the address that had been provided, walking slowly and sticking to shade to avoid sweating, and arrived in a middle-class neighborhood. The kind with perfectly manicured lawns and sprinklers to nourish the thick emerald grass. Residents walked their dogs while wearing specialized athletic clothing, earbuds snaking down their necks and into pockets fitted especially for their phones. Noah wasn't sure if he envied or despised them. Considering he had his own phone now—earbuds included—maybe he was one step closer to joining their ranks.

George's house didn't stand out from the rest. Noah wouldn't have given it a second glance, had he not been sent there. The ranch-style home had a decent yard and a two-car garage with an American flag hanging over the driveway.

Noah checked his phone, relieved that he was right on time. He went up to the door and knocked, bracing himself for a really old guy, or maybe one who looked like a troll and drooled when he spoke. Instead he was greeted by a man just as average as his home. George Perry was a few inches shorter than Noah and heavy enough to have stomach paunch and the hint of a double chin. His blond hair was trimmed, his glasses two maroon-framed rectangles. Clean-shaven and wearing a blue dress shirt and matching tie, his appearance was presentable enough. Noah normally wouldn't consider someone in his forties as a potential mate, but he could do a lot worse.

"So you're my date for the evening, huh?" George said, offering his hand. "A redhead!"

"Yeah," Noah said, gripping a palm that was slightly sweaty. "You sound surprised."

"I didn't get any photos this time. Marcello said he was sending me a surprise."

"Oh." He felt his cheeks blushing. "I hope you're not disappointed."

"I hope *you're* not!" George said, laughing amiably. "Ready to go? I'm starving!"

Noah nodded, confused when George gestured that he should enter the house. As it turned out, he was only being led to the garage. Together they drove to an Indian restaurant, and there the evening progressed in a fashion much simpler than what Harold had coached him for. Noah didn't struggle to make conversation or keep it going. George did all the talking. He owned a construction business and seemed to love his job because he rambled on and on about it. He also liked traveling to other countries, stopping by local construction sites to see how things were done differently. Dinner lasted the better part of two hours. Noah enjoyed himself, not having experienced the cuisine before. George was excited to discover this and ordered small dishes for him to sample. They even had dessert and some sort of mango drink. Once the bill was paid, George leaned back in his chair, belly a little larger now, and smiled.

"You're a great kid," he said.

"Thanks for the meal," Noah replied. "That was amazing!"

George's smile widened. "Would you be interested in coming home with me?"

Did it matter if he wasn't? Noah had been hired for a very specific purpose. Dinner was just a preamble, but maybe part of that was pretending to be on a normal date. "Sounds great!"

George tossed his napkin on the table and got to his feet, looking pleased. Once in the car, they didn't drive straight back to his house. They cruised around, George taking them to a construction site he owned to proudly show it off. To Noah it looked like any other not-yet-finished building. A concrete foundation and steel frame were in place, surrounded by mounds of dirt and a few portable toilets. He made sure to act impressed anyway, asking questions and nodding with interest at the answers.

When they finally returned to George's house, it got a little weird.

"Care for something to drink?" George asked, but he didn't wait for a response. Instead he traipsed to the kitchen, returning with a tall glass of yellow liquid. Noah could smell what it was before it was handed to him. Pineapple juice.

"Thanks," he said, accepting it but not bringing it to his lips. "You aren't thirsty?"

George shook his head, still smiling. "I'm fine. Drink up!"

Highly suspicious, Noah was searching for an excuse not to drink when he remembered Harold's advice. It might seem like George was trying to drug him, but he'd been assured that wasn't the case. Noah took a sip. He didn't taste alcohol either.

"What kind of music do you like?" George asked, turning to a large stereo system.

"Anything," Noah responded. When country music filled the room, he wished he'd been more specific. Nothing made him think of his hometown like a twangy guitar and lyrics about lonely truckers.

"It's good, isn't it?" George asked, nodding at the juice. "Fresh from this morning. There's plenty more in the kitchen. Don't be shy."

The man sure liked his juice! Or wanted Noah to like it. Maybe this was part of some weird fetish. Noah had once seen an X-rated Japanese cartoon where the woman was— Well, it was way weirder than this, but maybe George had a thing for bellies bulging with juice. Noah emptied the glass, only slightly surprised when George refilled it. Then he patiently listened to a lecture about how industries change. Maybe there really was something in the juice, because Noah found aspects of the discussion interesting.

"So you see," George said, "wars might advance our technological capabilities, but natural disasters are what force the construction industry to evolve."

"That's really cool," Noah said, draining his glass of juice.

"Care for a refill?" George asked.

"No thanks," Noah said, shaking his head. "I really need to use the restroom."

"Right this way!"

George led him through the house to a small room that definitely didn't have a toilet. Only a bed and a shelf loaded with towels were inside. Strange. George wanted to get down to business? That was fine, but Noah wasn't kidding. He really had to— Oh.

"You're very handsome," George said, taking his hand.

"Thanks," Noah responded, his mind racing. How was this going to work?

George took his other hand. As they faced each other, Noah realized he wasn't into this. At all.

"Can I kiss you?" George asked.

"Sure."

George brought his face near, and their lips mashed together. Noah felt uncomfortable. He tried thinking of the money. That didn't do anything for him. He thought instead of his dreams. No dice. His dick remained dormant, a tiny slumbering serpent. How long before George noticed and was disappointed or offended? Already he was unbuttoning the checkered shirt Harold had picked out for him.

Harold.

Now there was something worth thinking about! George slid a hand inside the shirt to rub a nipple. Noah used this as an excuse to close his eyes. "That feels good," he said.

"Yeah? You like that?"

His eyes almost shot open again, because it was Harold's voice he heard. Noah kept them shut. He'd always had a good imagination. Not having access to television, video games, or the internet for most of his childhood, he had been forced to hone this skill. When he had played on the farm, the barn was his pirate ship and the fish pools his sea. Or he'd read books, letting the words become images in his mind. He could do this!

Noah opened his eyes, keeping them unfocused. The blurry form shifting in front of him and working on getting his jeans open, that was Harold! "Oh man…" he murmured, cock swelling in response. Then he stepped forward, no longer passive. He kissed George, touching his body, mind working overtime to convince him it was hard muscle he felt instead. He shoved George's hands away and tore at his clothes. He wanted Harold, needed the comfort of being close to someone physically again. Soon their bare chests were pressed together, Noah grinding his crotch against another. His cock needed more room. He undid the top button of his jeans, grabbed George's hand, and stuffed it down there.

"Wow! Oh wow," Harold was saying. Or was it George?

No matter. The pleasure was intense. Noah wanted to return the favor. Their pants came down and their cocks rubbed together. Then Noah fell to his knees, eager to taste, longing to please. He listened to the gasps, picturing Harold's lazy smile transformed by ecstasy, lips tense against bleached white teeth.

"I need more. I need you!"

Welcome words. Noah rose, walking forward and forcing Harold back back back until he bumped against the bed and tumbled into it. "I know what you need," Noah said, crawling in after him.

"You do?"

Noah nodded, bringing his dick to those lips, forcing them to part. They were tight and moist, causing him to moan as he inched himself in slowly, then out again. He did this repeatedly, teasingly, before he finally picked up the pace. Then he had to rein back, because it had been a long time since he'd found relief, making it all too easy to reach the threshold. Besides, he wasn't here to fulfill his own needs. Not in this way. Noah's eyes focused and he saw George instead of Harold sucking desperately on his cock. That made it easier to calm down. So how was he supposed to make this man's dreams come true? He couldn't just piss all over the bed. Could he?

The sheets around his bare knees felt a little weird. Noah reached down as casually as possible to touch them. One side had a rubbery coating. Waterproof? George had brought him in here for a reason. The floor was covered in linoleum, the room devoid of anything personal that could be ruined. That suggested it served one purpose.

Noah pulled out and got to his feet, standing on the mattress with one foot to either side of George. He remembered when someone had done the same to him, how huge and powerful he had appeared, especially with his cock swinging around. Lying in bed had provided one hell of a vantage point! George seemed to think so too, his face rapt with wonder.

"Piss on me," he pleaded.

"I'm not sure you deserve that," Noah said, buying for time.

"I do!" George responded. "I've worked hard. Really really hard!"

Noah's bladder hurt from holding back. He'd had to go bad enough when entering this room and that had been twenty—maybe thirty minutes ago. He pointed his cock at George, who opened his mouth eagerly. Okay. "Here it comes!" Noah said. Nothing happened. This wasn't a promise he could keep. Peeing on people wasn't acceptable! You didn't kill your neighbor, steal their stuff, or covet their wife. There might not be a commandment about not pissing on your fellow man, but maybe there should have been.

"Please give it to me!" George pleaded. "Soak me to the bone!"

Working on it. He could do this. Somehow. Noah closed his eyes, imagining it was Harold begging to get wet instead. No good. That made him want to pee even less. Then he tried a different tactic. Noah pictured a urinal. Not just a normal ceramic one but a giant steel trough like they had at stadiums. He imagined he had drunk too many beers while watching a game and had to piss so bad that it hurt. After stumbling to the restroom and up to the metal trough, he found relief at last.

He heard a splattering sound and opened his eyes. George was writhing in pleasure, lost in absolute bliss as a golden stream hit him right in the chest. "Yes!" he was declaring over and over again. "Oh yes!"

Noah adjusted his aim, moving backward to bring the stream

lower to where George was still pumping himself. This felt good! A little erotic, yeah, but mostly it was a relief to finally go. He was wondering if he could get away with spelling out his name when George spoke again.

"I'm so thirsty! Please!"

No sense in being squeamish at this point. Noah aimed higher, spraying him right in the mouth and held back laughter when the man started gargling. Then he was finally spent, and grateful for all the fruit juice he had consumed, because the smell of citrus helped mask a more natural odor.

"Give me the rest!" George pleaded. "Please! I'm really close!"

Was he serious? What was Noah supposed to do, run back to the kitchen and chug more juice?

"Those balls look full!" George panted, still pumping himself.

Oh. Duh! Noah joined him, returning to his previous fantasy. Harold was squirming beneath him on the mattress, muscles glistening with moisture from the tight pecs down to the narrow waist. Every inch of him was perfect, but it was his face that drove Noah wild. He wanted to stare at it, kiss it, hold it close to his own. He even wanted to…

Noah dropped to his knees, pointed his cock right at the handsome visage, and shot load after load, soaking it with his seed and marking it as his own. Then he shoved his dick in the open mouth, wanting just a little more pleasure. A minute later, he felt warm spurts blast against his lower back and ass.

"Sweet Jesus!" Harold breathed when Noah finally pulled out. "You make me feel twenty years old again!"

That's because he was in his twenties! Oh, right. Noah returned to reality. He was in a pee-soaked bed, an older guy beneath him squinting one eye shut against the white goo that threatened to invade. Not the easiest way to earn fifty bucks, but not the most difficult either.

"Mind grabbing a towel?" George said.

"Sure." Noah hurried to comply, wiping the come away from George's eye for him. He knew how bad it could burn otherwise.

"It's always the nice ones," George said with a laugh.

"What?" Noah asked, shaking his head. "That's what you wanted, isn't it?"

"Yes! Definitely. I just didn't expect you to get so aggressive!"

"Sorry," Noah said sheepishly.

"I hope you're not!" George continued grinning at him. "Let's hit the shower."

Thank goodness for that! With the heat of the moment over, Noah wanted to get away from the mess. They left the room and showered together, which felt comfortable. He figured it was impossible to feel bashful after doing something so intimate together. George was ridiculously happy, making them both an herbal tea after they were dry. They sipped these while sitting in the living room, wrapped in lush bathrobes that smelled freshly laundered.

George yawned and smacked his lips contentedly. "A bad thing about the construction industry is the early mornings. I'm about ready for bed. You could join me if you like."

"Oh," Noah said, not sure what to make of the offer.

George chuckled. "Don't worry, I have a real bed. Even I don't like to sleep in wet sheets." He rose, waving a hand. "Just relax and think about it. I'll get your check."

As soon as he'd left the room, Noah consulted his phone. Half past ten. The shelter was definitely closed, and he wasn't looking forward to sleeping rough another night. He also wasn't sure about staying with George. Noah might be used to bunking up with strangers at the shelter, but he didn't share a bed with them. Would it be rude to ask to sleep on the couch instead? Harold also had a couch. What if Noah found some excuse to stay there?

"Here you go!" George said, reappearing and holding out a check.

Noah took it, trying to be casual as he looked to see how much he had earned. A five followed by two zeros. That couldn't be right! They had met at six, and even if George rounded the time up, that was still only five hours spent together. He should be getting half this amount! "Thanks!" he said. "Are you sure this is right?"

"Too little?"

"Too much!"

George tsked and wagged a finger. "Never tell a client when he's made an offer that's too high."

"I guess I shouldn't," Noah said while laughing. This was great! It meant he had earned back his advance already.

"About my offer…" George said. "No pressure! Just tell me what you want."

"I should get back to my own place," Noah said. "Feed the cat."

For a second he imagined himself doing just that, opening the door to an apartment, a cranky orange tabby demanding his attention. He could make that dream come true. It meant more nights doing weird stuff like peeing on a guy, but he had made it through the experience unscathed.

"I didn't notice a car outside," George said. "Do you need a ride?"

Noah reconsidered him. He had wondered if the offer to spend the night came with ulterior motives, but maybe George was simply a nice guy. "That's really sweet of you, but I like to walk."

"Is that how you keep in shape? If so, maybe I should sell my car. I'll get your things." George fetched his clothes, presenting them in a neatly folded stack.

Noah decided to get changed there in the living room, letting his robe drop to the floor. This gave George an extra thrill. Then they walked to the front door. After a peck on the lips and a hug, they said goodnight.

Once Noah was outside in the evening air, he breathed in, feeling satisfied. His debt to Marcello was as good as paid and he had made someone happy in the process. Not bad! He strolled at a casual pace, barely wanting to admit his destination to himself. When he did, a smile appeared on his face.

Harold's house. It took him nearly an hour to get there, only to find the windows dark, but he didn't think Harold had gone to bed. Most likely he was still out on a date. What if the client invited him to stay the night like George had? That seemed likely. Who wouldn't want Harold sleeping next to them? Noah sat on the front stoop and decided not to worry about it too much. The shelter was already closed, so it was either hang out here or find another bush in a park.

He distracted himself by playing with his phone, his only concern the dwindling battery life. Before it ran out, a car pulled into the driveway. Noah hadn't paid much attention to it before, not one to care about such things, but he supposed it did look cool. The vehicle was a maroon two-door, the roof some sort of brown fabric, implying it was a convertible. Harold climbed out and eyed him over the top of the car. His expression was concerned. Noah stood. An excuse was ready on his lips, but it was Harold who rushed over to him.

"Are you okay?"

"Fine!" Noah said. "I just had a question about my check."

Harold's expression turned to confusion. "This isn't about George? Or the uh—"

"Pineapple juice?" Noah said with a smirk. "I'm all right. It was a little weird, but no biggie."

Harold reappraised him. "Wow. Most guys are freaked out after someone pisses on them."

"He didn't pee on me. I peed on him."

"Yeah, but afterwards… He didn't piss on you?"

"Nope!"

Harold blinked. "What the hell? He *always* pisses on me."

"You must have one of those faces."

Harold glared. Then he started laughing. "Get inside. The door's open. I never lock it."

"That doesn't sound safe," Noah said, allowing him to take the lead.

"If someone wants to break in, a locked door isn't going to stop them."

But it might slow them down enough for a neighbor to notice and call the police. Noah didn't bother correcting him, too happy that he was being invited inside. They went to the kitchen, Harold taking two Dr Pepper's from the refrigerator and handing him one. In the interior light, he could see how mussed Harold's hair was, his pale-gray dress shirt a little wrinkled.

"How did your night go?" Noah asked.

"Great! Chester is a sweetheart. You just have to make sure you're not there in the morning. You really seem like you're okay."

"I'm fine," Noah said, feeling proud that he had successfully completed his task and glad that Harold was so concerned for his welfare. "I think I've got the hang of it."

"What'd you want to know about the check?"

"Oh!" Noah set the soda on the counter and pulled out his wallet. "Am I supposed to give this to you or…"

"I'm not your pimp," Harold said with a wink. "Remember?"

"Then what do I do with it?"

"You're supposed to cash it!"

Noah shook his head, not understanding. "I thought all the money would go back to Marcello and I would get my cut later."

"Of your hourly rate."

"Huh?"

Harold took a swig, gaze steady. "You know it's illegal to have sex with people for money, right? Marcello doesn't want to get his hands dirty with that sort of thing, so officially, clients pay a booking fee based on how long they need companionship. That's your hourly rate, and yeah, Marcello takes a big cut. Any extra stuff is between you and the client, but you'll probably never need to negotiate. Not unless they want you to leave town or they have a special request. The members of the GAC know the drill. If something sexual happens, they're expected to tip generously or they won't be in the club for long."

Noah held up the check. "This is a tip?"

"Yup."

"And it's all mine?"

Harold grinned. "Yeah! What are you gonna spend it on?"

Noah was too cautious to celebrate just yet. "Marcello paid me an advance when I was hired, so maybe he's expecting me to give this to him."

"Oh." Harold looked uncertain. "I don't know. Let me ask." He pulled out his phone at the same time Noah felt his rumble.

"Speak of the devil." Noah read the lock screen. Marcello had sent him another message. Much like the one from the previous day, this included a name, time, and location. "New assignment."

"Who'd you get?" Harold asked, busy texting.

"Doug Francis."

Harold's head whipped up. "What?"

"Doug Francis," Noah repeated.

Harold scowled. "You know what? I'd better call Marcello about that check. Be right back."

He swept from the room, head shaking. Noah glanced back down at his phone, struggling to decipher from the minimal information what could be so upsetting. The name was innocent enough, as was the address. He looked to the kitchen door when he heard Harold's voice, which had grown momentarily loud.

"—fucked up—"

That's the only snippet he could understand.

When Harold returned to the kitchen, his face was flushed, but he was smiling. "No problem on the check. What you owe

Marcello will come out of your hourly wages. Whatever you get from clients…" He grimaced. "You'll have earned it, trust me."

He made it sound like the worst was yet to come.

"Oh-kay," Noah said, feeling uneasy. "Any pointers when it comes to Doug?"

The muscles of Harold's jaw clenched. "I didn't tell you about George because of the image we're working on."

"Innocent small-town boy."

"Right. With Doug, he doesn't want anyone to know what's coming. That's what he gets off on. So I can't tell you anything. Just make sure you choose a safe word that you won't forget."

Ah. Sadomasochism. Noah didn't find it appealing, but he wasn't concerned. As a kid, anytime he got into trouble meant being on the receiving end of his father's belt. Including the buckle. He doubted Doug could dish out anything more painful than that.

Harold looked miserable. "Sorry, man."

"It's fine," Noah said. "I'm tougher than I look."

"I hope so. Listen, I gotta take a shower."

"Oh. Okay. I'll head out."

"No! Stay and chill. It'll just be a second. Make yourself at home."

Short of a proposal, these were the words Noah wanted to hear most. Once he was alone, he did a happy dance. Then he strutted goofily from the kitchen into the dining area, where the little model village was set up. Noah turned on the light to see it better, trying to recognize details that might reveal if it was a recreation of Austin or somewhere else. The model's setting could have represented most states, although the little plastic people were nearly all male. And shirtless. Or wearing even less clothing! Noah bent over to examine a public pool and the tiny muscles on display. He hadn't known such figures existed!

When he heard the shower stop, he turned off the light and went to the couch. A Rubik's Cube on the coffee table caught his eye, so he grabbed it and started twisting the colorful rows, pretending to be into it even when Harold entered the room and spoke.

"That thing pisses me off!" he said, nodding at the cube. "Got it in my stocking last year. A lump of coal would have been better."

"Then why do you keep it?" Noah asked, glancing over

casually. Yes! The bathrobe was back! Just one layer of fluffy cotton between him and a naked body. He *loved* the bathrobe.

Harold plopped down on the couch. "I keep it because I plan on solving the fucker. The second I do, I'm going to take a hammer to it."

"I had one when I was a kid," Noah said. "All you have to do is peel the stickers off and put them back on again in the right order."

"Cheater." Harold elbowed him. "Hey, do you wanna smoke a bowl?"

Why not? Twenty minutes later they were laughing nonstop while watching a show called *Key & Peele* he had never heard of. Hell, he probably wouldn't recognize any television show these days, but it sure felt good to do something so normal. After cracking up through two episodes, Noah felt a little tired. The high made everything so cozy. He stretched and yawned. When his mouth tried to close again, a finger was in the way.

Harold laughed, pulling his hand free. "You're like that lion."

"Oh, *that* lion," Noah said teasingly.

"The one at the beginning of movies," Harold clarified. "He's always yawning too."

"He growls!"

"No way. There might have been a growling sound effect, but you can tell he's really yawning."

"Probably because of all the boring previews," Noah said, stifling another yawn.

"Tired?"

"Yeah. I didn't sleep so good last night."

"Lie down."

The couch wasn't that big. He looked over, ready to make a joke, when he noticed Harold patting his lap in invitation. Seriously? Noah wasn't about to turn that down! He flopped over, resting his head against the soft robe, the thighs beneath it strong. As erotic as that might be, it simply felt good being close to another person in that way. Someone he really liked. The hand resting on his shoulder was nice too.

Harold turned off the television and used his phone to conjure up music from speakers on a shelf. The song was mellow, a light electronic beat, the volume low enough that they could still converse comfortably.

"I'm glad you're doing okay," Harold said. "This job isn't for everyone."

"I bet." The events of the evening seemed distant and ludicrous now.

"What's your big need?"

"My what?"

"The reason why you're doing this," Harold pressed. "Are you putting yourself through college? Paying off debts? It's usually one or the other."

Noah chose his answer carefully. "I'm trying to get back on my feet. What about you?"

"I'm in it for the long haul. Can't say it's my dream job, because this isn't what I wanted to do when I was little. Could you imagine? Some little kid who can't wait to grow up and be an escort?"

"That would make a good *Key & Peele* sketch," Noah said with a chuckle. "How long have you been doing this now?"

"Years. I love it."

Noah turned his head to glance up at him. "Really?"

"Yeah! Usually I feel good about it. Take someone like George. Imagine him going on a first date. Should he be honest about his fetish and tell the other person during dinner?"

"No. Too soon."

"Exactly. Then you get weeks, months, maybe even years into a relationship, drop the bomb, and the other person freaks out and leaves. Or maybe they just refuse. We get a lot of guys like that. Some of them have a boyfriend who doesn't want to fulfill the fantasy. Others are into stuff that scares people away. So I feel good about helping them out. I'm either taking the burden off an unwilling partner or making someone feel less lonely."

"You make it sound noble."

"I don't mean to. It still gets really nasty, and I definitely love the money. This isn't charity work. But it's not like a real job either, you know? No office cubicle. No boss breathing down my neck."

"Marcello doesn't count?"

"He's okay," Harold said. "Usually. Sometimes he can be a real bastard. For the most part, you're in good hands."

He was in a good lap! Noah closed his eyes, a feeling of warm contentment spreading through him. "What about the future?" he murmured. "In forty years, are you still going to be doing this?"

"Sure! I'll put my best dentures in, pop some Viagra, and make my rounds in the old folks' home."

Noah smiled at the mental image. "Seriously."

"I'll have enough saved up by then to retire. Or to do something else I love. Just don't ask me what because I don't have a clue. What about you?"

"I plan on staying right here," Noah said, thoughts becoming abstract. He heard Harold snigger in response, felt the hand on his shoulder squeeze tighter, but the words spoken were too distant to understand. He wasn't too concerned with them, only wanting to sink deeper into the blissful darkness that cradled his consciousness.

Chapter Four

Noah was stretched out on the couch, a heavy quilt covering him to his neck. He blinked, watched dust motes float through a sunbeam of morning light, then forced himself to sit up. He was still in Harold's living room, but saw no sign of his host. Noah felt momentarily embarrassed for having passed out. Mostly he was glad for the solid night of sleep.

After using the restroom, he padded into the kitchen for a glass of water, noticing the time on the microwave. The hour was later than he expected, the day creeping closer to noon. He found a note on the counter. The handwriting was so messy that he could barely decipher it.

I'm out with my mom. It's her birthday! Help yourself to some cereal or whatever. If you need me tonight, just call or stop by.

An open invitation? Cool. Noah took advantage of the privacy to snoop, starting with the kitchen. He found health food in the refrigerator and cabinets. After helping himself to a bowl of granola with almond milk, he decided he wanted real food and prepared to leave. Before he did, he snuck down the hall to Harold's bedroom, which wasn't different than any other, but he committed the details of the bed (queen-sized, brown comforter, unmade) to memory for a future fantasy. Then he left the house.

The day was rainy, but he refused to let that get him down. Noah used his phone to locate the nearest branch of his bank. After walking there and depositing his check, he left again, nearly strolling into traffic while looking at his account statement. Nine hundred dollars! A little under that, actually, but holy shit! He felt filthy rich as he continued on his way to the shelter.

The doors to Jerusalem were open, two familiar faces sitting behind the reception desk. One was the Bouncer, stoic and frowning as always. The other was Edith, who wore her usual welcoming smile— No, scratch that! The older woman did *not* look pleased as she shot to her feet.

"Where have you been?" she demanded, her accent sounding German today. Or maybe it was the hissed anger giving him that impression. "Two nights now! Where?"

Noah's mouth moved as he grasped for an explanation. "I stayed with a friend."

Edith slowly sat back down again. "You are okay?"

"Yes," he said, deciding to inject a little humor. "I promise to call next time, Mom."

"This isn't funny," Edith said, matching the Bouncer's body language. "If you had a phone, I wouldn't have to worry."

"Actually..." he said, pulling it out of his pocket. "Do you really want me to call next time?"

Edith seemed concerned by this revelation. She quietly asked the Bouncer to watch things. Then she stood again, took Noah's arm, and led him deeper into the shelter. "What is going on? Where did you get that?"

"I have a job now," Noah said.

"Since when?"

"Two or three days."

"And they pay you in advance? Enough to get a phone?" She stopped in the hallway and turned to face him. "What have you gotten mixed up in? Drugs?"

"No!"

Edith's lips pressed together briefly. "Other things?"

Noah opened his mouth to protest again, but then realized that she probably meant prostitution, which is exactly what he was doing. "I'm fine," he stressed. "Really."

Edith's eyes closed. When she opened them again, they were pleading. "You need to be safe. Do you understand me?"

Safe in terms of sex? Or who he chose to be with? Either way... "I will. I promise."

"I'm glad you have a phone. Here." Edith took out her own, a model that was much older and dented around the edges. "I'll give you my number. If you don't make it here before the doors close, you can call me and I'll let you in. I'll save you a bed no matter the rules."

Noah shook his head. "I might not be here every night. I appreciate it, but I don't want to cost someone a bed." An idea occurred to him. "Actually, do you have any private rooms left?" Why not! He could definitely afford the thirty dollars a week.

Edith thought about it. "Mr. Carvajal hasn't paid in two weeks. All he does in there is drink. He thinks I don't smell it on him? Time for him to go. That's what he gets for touching my boobs!"

Noah laughed. "What?"

"Trying to touch my boobs," Edith amended.

"I won't try that, or drink in the room, I swear."

Edith nodded. "I'll get it ready for you. There's still a curfew, but if you're late, call me."

Noah's smile faltered. "Thanks, but if you're not working, I don't want to—"

"Then you call Pete instead."

"Pete?"

Edith pointed in the direction they had come. "My colleague."

The Bouncer? His name was Pete? Noah would have expected it to be Bruno or Dirk or something tougher-sounding.

Edith's expression remained earnest. "Okay?"

Noah nodded. "Okay."

She fussed over him more by making sure he had eaten. Noah was always up for more food, so after downing some leftovers she scrounged for him, he went to his locker, got fresh clothing, and took a shower. He decided another load of laundry was in order, just to make sure his work uniforms—as he was starting to consider them—were both as fresh as could be. Tonight he might be slow dancing with Doug, or cuddling with him, or slapping him in the face with a boiled hotdog while calling him Daddy. Lord only knew what he was in for, but Noah was determined to be presentable regardless.

"There you are!" Edith appeared in the laundry area just as he was folding his last shirt. "Are you ready for your room?"

"Yeah!"

Noah followed her to a stairwell that he normally ignored. Up the stairs were staff areas, storage units, and the doors to twenty rooms. He felt taller than usual as she walked him down the hall to number seven. A lucky number! Edith opened the door, presenting it to him and murmuring apologies about how it wasn't much.

Noah disagreed. The room had enough space for a twin-size bed, a small table with a chair, a narrow dresser, and a safe. Edith rattled off the rules: Nobody else was allowed in the room. No drinking or drugs. The room had to be cleaned once a week and open for inspection.

Noah eagerly agreed to all of this. A private room! He couldn't exactly invite anyone over and probably wouldn't even if allowed, but it felt good to have his own space.

Edith helped him set a new combination for the safe, which was small but would keep his wallet and other valuables secure. Then she handed him a key. And a letter.

"You received mail while you were gone."

"Oh." He took it from her, not needing to glance at the return address. Only one person ever wrote him. "Thanks," he said. "For everything."

"You are welcome." She hovered in the doorway. Did she want a hug? Noah was about to offer one when Edith shook her head and turned. "I'll let you get settled."

"Thank you," he said again.

She closed the door behind her. Noah spun to examine the room, a grin plastered on his face. Was he still homeless? A temporary room in a homeless shelter probably didn't count for much, but it felt awesome anyway. He went to the window. The view was a brick wall and an alley below. At least he could get fresh air if he craved it. Noah cracked open the window, then set the letter on the table. He went downstairs for his clothes, stuffing them in the dresser when he returned. He relocated his possessions from the locker too. Moving day!

He laughed to himself. Other people had to rent a truck. He only needed two arms and fifteen minutes to get the job done. Once he was finished, he kicked off his shoes, sat on the bed, and let himself bask in the feeling of security. And privacy! Such a thing had become incredibly rare. Normally he was either sitting in a library surrounded by others, or sleeping in a large crowded room, or out on the streets. The fear of wearing out his welcome, or the possibility of being forced to leave, always hung over his head. Not here. He could sit in this room for twenty-four hours and do nothing, and nobody would complain. Then again, he still had to eat and use the restroom. His new room didn't have a private bathroom. He would need to use the communal one downstairs.

This was definitely a step up regardless, and thanks to the two new names in his phone, he no longer had to worry about getting shut out at night. The only downside was that he had less of an excuse to crash on Harold's couch. Noah closed his eyes, remembering how that lap had felt as a pillow. Then he imagined Harold sharing this bed while cuddled up against him. Wouldn't that be nice?

Noah let himself enjoy the fantasy. It had been way too long since someone special was in his life. He opened his eyes and turned his head, looking to the letter on the table. Then he sighed, sat up, and reached for it. He felt no suspense as he opened the envelope. The letters were all the same these days. Needy, complaining, affectionate… His eyes widened as he reached the bottom.

Maybe I should just kill myself. Seriously. What's the point? I'm never going to see you again, am I?

Noah swallowed, feeling guilty. Then again, it's not like he could just walk there. Last time he had hitchhiked and— Ugh! Excuses. That's all they were. Noah had money now. Maybe he could use it to travel to Gatesville. No buses went there. He had looked into that before, but now that he had money…

He grabbed his phone, sending a quick text to Harold. *Have you ever rented a car?*

The response came a few minutes later. *Yeah! When mine was in the shop. Why?*

Would I need a credit card?

Definitely.

Okay. Thanks.

That should have been the end of it. Noah didn't have a credit card, and he couldn't imagine any company giving him one. Then Harold texted again.

Do you have one?

No point in denying it. *Nope.*

Wanna borrow my car? If you're driving to LA then no way. If you've got errands to run, then it's cool.

I need to visit— Noah hesitated. What were they now? They hadn't broken up officially but it was also impossible for them to date. *–a friend. He's not doing so well. He lives two hours away.*

Huh. Can you drive?

Yeah! LOL

Okay. Just let me know when.

Seriously? Could Harold get any nicer? "I freaking love you," Noah said out loud. Then he texted back. *Thanks! I'll pay whatever a rental would cost. How do I get a day off?*

Just text Marcello and say what day you need.

Simple as that? Noah nibbled his bottom lip. If he was honest, he didn't want to go to Gatesville. Then again, the letters were often dramatic, but suicide? He wouldn't be able to live with himself if something happened, so he sent a text to Marcello, asking for the next day off.

Take all the time you need, came the reply. *I'll mark you as decommissioned until I hear otherwise.*

What the hell? Noah needed one day off. That was all! *I'll be back that night. Before dinner. I'll make sure of it, so never mind. No time off needed.*

He waited for a response. It never came. Had he just ruined it all? Noah rolled his eyes, blaming himself, then the letter. He texted Marcello one more time in desperation. *I mean it. I want to work.*

Understood.

Finally! What was Marcello's problem? Noah was never going to ask for time off again, that was for sure!

Noah refused to let moody letters or dismissive text messages get him down. He went to a nearby dollar store, buying a few essentials for his room, such as a small trashcan and liners. Nothing frivolous aside from a scented candle, because Mr. Carvajal hadn't been the best-smelling guy. When he returned, he found a brochure about safe sex on the floor in front of his door, along with samples of lube and rows of condoms. He didn't have to guess who had left those there, but he was sure Edith meant well.

Then he got ready for his next date. Noah was hungry, but he avoided eating at the shelter. He would probably have dinner with his client, and it seemed unfair to take food from people less fortunate. He began his walk early, since this destination was farther away than the others had been. Nearly two hours! Maybe he should invest in a bike, or pay more attention to the bus system.

He was expecting another house, but instead arrived at an apartment complex on a busy road. Noah walked up the stairs to the third floor, five minutes late. A note was taped to the door, something dark hanging from the knob.

Put this on. Then knock.

That's all the note said. One look at the knob revealed that black cloth was draped over it. He lifted this, discovering it was a blindfold. Okay. Noah glanced around. He felt self-conscious, but once certain nobody was watching, he did as instructed. The blindfold was thick, obscuring his vision completely. No wonder Harold didn't like this guy. Things were weird already! He felt for the door, then knocked. It squeaked open almost instantly.

A hand grabbed his and pulled him inside. He listened as the door closed, multiple locks sliding into place.

"What's your safe word?" asked a gruff voice.

"Armadillo," Noah answered. "Sorry, but can I—"

He was reaching for the blindfold with his free hand when his arm was yanked behind his back, joined by the other, like he was about to be handcuffed. He shoved aside his concerns. S&M always involved restraints of some sort, didn't it?

"You don't do anything unless I tell you to," the voice said. He could only assume it was Doug. "Understood?"

"Okay."

His arms were yanked harder behind his back. It kind of hurt!

"Excuse me?"

"Yes, sir," Noah said, catching on.

"That's better. Now start walking."

The hands released him. Noah didn't move at first. He couldn't see! If he walked, he could—

"Now!" Doug barked.

Fine. Noah took one step at a time, feeling around with his hands and using the tip of his shoe to detect any obstacles.

"Better watch out!" Doug said. His voice sounded far away.

Was Noah meant to follow? He turned, moving toward where he thought he'd heard the voice. Something jabbed into his leg. A sharp corner. Judging from its height, the object was probably a coffee table. He heard laughter, the sound like a tire losing air. Doug was enjoying himself.

Noah tried to imagine the living room. If he was next to a coffee table, that meant a couch wasn't far away. Most people put their couch against a wall so…

He kept walking, managing ten steps before his hands touched books. He felt around them, detecting shelves.

"I'm getting bored," Doug said.

Noah reoriented on his voice. He found a clear path and walls to either side of him. A hallway! At least he wouldn't have to worry about furniture being in the way.

A dog started barking, the sound dangerously close. Noah

froze and gasped. He heard a chain being yanked, then a growl.

"Down, boy," Doug said. "We don't want to upset our guest."

A little late for that! This was freaky! "Where am I going exactly?" Noah asked.

"Did I tell you to speak?"

"No, but—"

"From now on you speak only when spoken to. Understood?"

Noah hesitated. He had pride, but it wouldn't serve him well in this situation, so he did his best to abandon it. "Yes, sir."

"That's better. Now take off your clothes."

Yay. Suddenly he missed George. Noah would prefer a friendly dinner followed by way too much pineapple juice over this any day. He took off his clothes, not feeling remotely sexy, and tried thinking dirty thoughts to get an erection. It didn't work.

"Very nice," Doug said. "I might just keep you."

What the hell did that mean?

"Now turn to the right. Walk! Keep going. Faster! FASTER!"

Noah did what he was told, making good progress until he collided with a wall, but at least his extended hands braced him somewhat. He turned around again. Hands snatched his wrists and lifted his arms. He could feel someone close to him and smell the stale stench of cigarette smoke. A leather cuff was lashed around one of Noah's wrists, then the other, until both were raised high above his head. He moved experimentally, hearing the rattle of metal above him. He didn't have much leeway. Noah could take a step forward but that was it. He was captive.

"You're very beautiful," Doug said, his breath on Noah's neck. "By the end of the night, you will have learned to serve me. Do you understand?"

"Yes, sir," Noah replied.

He felt cold fingers on his nipples. Then nothing. Noah was left there, arms above his head. It didn't take long before they started to ache. He squirmed, hoping to relieve them and maybe arouse Doug enough that something would finally happen.

"He's cute," a voice said. It didn't sound like Doug.

"Yeah. He'll bring us a lot of pleasure."

Another voice! What the hell? Just how many people were in this room? He struggled to remember if Harold or Marcello had said anything about group sex. Surely he would have been told in advance. He opened his mouth to speak, a rubber ball filling it before he could. Noah nearly spit it out. There wasn't a strap. That helped him calm down. For now, the ball in his mouth was a choice. He tried to remain calm and listened to the shuffling in the room, attempting to figure out how many people were present and where they stood. Would they only watch? Or would this turn into a gangbang? Could he take the abuse, find some pleasure in the experience, or would it only hurt?

He flinched as something brushed against his leg, cold and wet. What the fuck was that? Then he felt a huge object slide between his ass cheeks. A dildo, judging from the way it vibrated. If they thought that was going inside of him, he'd be shouting armadillo before even the tip made it in! Right now it was only pressing against his rectum, and it did feel kind of good. This ceased. The dildo pulled away and something hot seared the skin of his chest. Wax?

"I can make you feel pleasure," Doug said. "Or I can make you feel pain."

Pleasure! Noah was definitely a bigger fan of pleasure. The vibrating device returned, sliding between his ass cheeks again before it was pressed against his balls, then his dick. It felt good enough that he got hard. He heard laughter from what he imagined as a corner of the room. Simultaneous laughter. Definitely more than one person here! Noah almost spit out the ball in his mouth, but he hesitated.

Did it really matter? If some guys wanted to watch him get molested while he was tied up, maybe that was okay. Plenty of other people would see him naked over the coming nights. Part of Noah got off on the idea. He was rock hard, the vibrator making him drip. Let them stare!

Cold! This time on the tip of his dick. Was that ice? The vibrator was gone now, the sound having vanished. Noah was standing on carpet, but he thought he could hear footsteps moving away from him. Then a sliding noise, like a window opening. He was sure of it because now he heard cars outside and felt cool air on his skin. Could anyone see him? They were on the third floor, but the apartment complex consisted of multiple buildings. Maybe some old lady had been staring at her bird feeder and was now looking at him instead.

Noah's arms tingled, the blood having all but left them. He

couldn't stop wondering how many sets of eyes watched him. Were they taking photos? Video? He gasped as the ice cube returned, pressing against his chest and tracing a shape. Like a letter. *M.* Noah pulled back, trying to escape the sensation, but Doug—or whoever—persisted, spelling out another letter. *E.* Then an *A.* A gust of wind blew in through the window, chilling the drops of water running down his skin. Another letter, this time a *T.* That spelled *MEAT*! Charming. Noah almost wished he would be treated like a piece of meat instead of a science experiment. He was here to have sex, not… whatever this was. Just as he was getting used to the cold, hot wax scalded his skin, his stomach, and the base of his cock.

"Do you like it?" Doug whispered.

Noah shook his head. He did so instinctually.

"Fine." Doug sounded hurt. "I'll stop then. I won't touch you anymore. In fact, I think I'll make a phone call. Come on, boys."

Noah strained to listen. He definitely heard footsteps, and a door close. Then it was quiet. He remained hanging there, unsure of how much time was drifting by. His stomach growled. So much for dinner. Maybe he could trick Doug into force-feeding him when he came back. He *was* coming back. Wasn't he? Or was Doug still in the room and had only pretended to leave?

Noah spit out the rubber ball and waited to see if he would be reprimanded. When nothing happened, he tried speaking.

"Hello?"

No response. He was getting cold, air still blowing in from the window, so he tried removing the blindfold by turning his head to rub his face against his arm. He was making progress when he heard the door open. Then laughter. A warm deep chuckle.

"Who's there?" Noah asked.

A radio answered him by crackling, a female dispatcher rattling off a series of codes he didn't understand. The police! He felt momentary relief. They could help him! Or arrest him, since prostitution wasn't legal. Shit! He could pretend to be a victim, tell them that Doug had tricked him into this predicament, but that would mean explaining why he was there in the first place. If his presence was traced back to Marcello—or even worse, Harold—then they would get in trouble instead and possibly serve time.

Fuck! Noah's mind raced. Doug hadn't given him any money

yet. The bastard might be crazy enough to call the police, but he wasn't likely to incriminate himself. As of now, Noah hadn't done anything wrong. What could he be accused of? Breaking in before handcuffing and blindfolding himself? Then again, maybe Doug was friends with a police officer, or was one himself.

"Looks like someone caught me a big fish," a voice said, one that matched the deep chuckle he'd heard earlier.

Noah licked his lips, but not in a way that was seductive. "I heard a radio. Are you a police officer? Can you let me down?"

"I'm Officer Leroy," the voice responded. "I should arrest you. Or I could have a little fun and let you go. Which is it going to be?"

A cold hand slid beneath his balls, a finger pressing against his butthole. Noah tried not to react, but inside he was freaking out. He'd never bottomed before. A little finger play, yeah, but he was worried the cop would just shove it in dry and keep pounding until Noah bled or screamed or…

Maybe he could take it. If he forced himself to relax. Or he could try bargaining.

"I'll suck your dick," he said.

The hand pulled away. He heard the deep chuckle again, then sensed a body moving around him. Something hard wedged its way between his ass cheeks, pushing and probing. A nightstick? No way could he—

Cool liquid drizzled down his lower back, the night stick moving upward to capture some of it before sliding down between his cheeks again. Lube. That was good news, but Noah really *really* didn't want to lose his virginity to a stick that was designed for beating people.

"Stop," he said. "Please. I don't do stuff like that."

The nightstick kept probing.

"I can't take that," he said. "It'll hurt me."

The nightstick moved away, replaced by a finger. Okay, that wasn't so bad. After sliding in and out a few times, a second digit joined it. A hand reached around to play with him. Noah wasn't expecting that, but he was grateful, because it increased the pleasure he felt and made the fingers inside of him more bearable. He even felt himself getting closer. Then the fingers pulled out and something else pressed against him. This time it wasn't a nightstick. Noah clenched his jaw, hoping the officer wasn't too hung. While trying to imagine what was going on, he realized there was one crucial detail he didn't know.

"Are you wearing a condom?" he asked.

No answer.

This encounter could kill him! Especially since this was his first time. If something tore inside, and this creep had HIV, Noah could end up infected. Was that worth not getting arrested?

"Stop!" Noah said, squirming to get away from the man. "I mean it!"

Hands grabbed his hips.

"I have AIDS!" He wasn't proud of the lie, but if it helped… "If you stick your dick in me, you better be wearing a condom or you'll get it too. You know what? Fuck it! Arrest me! I don't care. I'm not doing this!"

The person behind him moved away, Noah going perfectly still in an effort to hear what was happening. Would he be set free? Or beaten and raped?

"Looks like someone caught me a big fish," the officer said. Again.

Noah thought he heard someone swear under their breath followed by a dull tapping noise. Was it the sound of someone poking at a touchscreen? Like the kind belonging to a phone?

The deep voice spoke again. "I'm going to make you come, boy. Blow a big load for me, and I might be forgiving."

Noah remained still, trying to figure out what was really happening. In particular, why the police officer would say something so strange twice in a row. Not only the same words, but the cadence was identical too. Like a recording. Then it all clicked into place. Doug wouldn't have invited the police here. Those spectators from earlier probably didn't exist either. He might not even have a dog. Noah had only heard those things and assumed they were real, but with the right setup, it wouldn't be too hard to fake them. That would be messed up and would definitely necessitate hiring an escort, because most people would call the real police after being put through an experience like this.

Feeling he now had the upper hand, Noah wanted to smile, but instead he put on a performance. "Look, I don't want any trouble, but you can't fuck me. I don't really have any STDs, but I also don't do that sort of thing. I'll suck your dick. Just please don't arrest me!"

The deep chuckle again. Then a finger returned to prod his ass. This time though, it remained one finger. The hand resumed jerking Noah off. Maybe that's all Doug wanted to do. Noah let himself get into it. Even if wrong and truly in danger, it was still easier to pretend the situation was all a ruse. And lose himself in the pleasure, because that finger was hitting him just right. Eventually he growled while his cock convulsed and shot repeatedly. He had no idea where his load landed. Nor did he have much time to relax. The chains above his head were lowered, but he remained captive.

"On your knees, boy."

That he could handle. Noah did as he was told, and a cock was shoved in his mouth. It wasn't long enough to gag him, but he put on a show anyway, making choking noises and gasping for air whenever the guy pulled out. He must have done well, because soon enough, warm liquid struck his face.

Noah could hear the other person panting, but it didn't sound as deep as the supposed police officer's voice had.

"Please let me go," he said. "I won't tell anyone what happened. I swear."

He listened to the other person move around the room. Then another recorded message was played.

"I'm going to set you free. Keep the blindfold on until I've left the room. After that, you've got five minutes to get out of here. Understand?"

"Yes, sir," he said, nodding eagerly.

The leather cuffs around his wrists were undone. Noah was tempted to pull off the blindfold to see the truth, but at this point, playing along was easier. He remained on his knees, listening to footsteps move away. Then he heard a voice, but again, it wasn't deep enough to match that of the officer.

"Five minutes."

As soon as the door clicked shut, Noah ripped off the blindfold. The room was sparse. A variety of sex equipment and some shelves surrounded him. The speakers weren't immediately obvious, but he spotted some mounted in the corners. Noah had seen Harold stream music from his phone to a distant wireless speaker at home. No reason Doug couldn't do the same.

Noah noticed his clothing in a pile just in front of him. He scrambled for it, eager to leave. He only paused to look at the check sitting on top of them. Four hundred bucks. He allowed himself a smile, certain now it had all been some twisted game. He had done pretty well! At least his ass hadn't been violated by a nightstick. He got dressed and patted his pockets, feeling his phone and wallet there. Then he left the room.

The apartment was large and nicely decorated, but he didn't linger. No sign of a dog, but at this point, he wasn't surprised. Noah was outside and walking down the street with time to spare. Once he was a few blocks away, he allowed himself to stop and look back. What a freak show! He had nothing against roleplay, but that had been weird. And sort of mean. If he hadn't figured out the truth, how would he be feeling right now? Violated? Humiliated?

He checked his phone, unsure of the time, and noticed two text messages. Both were from Harold. The first said, *Screw the rules! It's not real. You'll hear some weird stuff tonight but it's all fake. Remember that!*

Noah smiled. The text message had arrived too late to be useful, but he appreciated the intent. The next message was even better.

Text me as soon as you're done. Or call. I can give you a ride.

That would be nice! For more than one reason. Noah walked to the next major intersection, then sent the address to Harold along with a disclaimer that he didn't need to drive there at all if he was busy.

He wasn't. Harold showed up fifteen minutes later, pulling into a fast food parking lot and getting out of the car before Noah could get in. Harold's face was gaunt, like he expected the worst.

"I'm okay," Noah said. "It was freaky, but I figured it out."

"You didn't get my text message?"

"Not before I went in, but—"

"I'm sorry, man!" Appearing pained, Harold rushed forward and hugged Noah, which felt pretty excellent. "Are you sure you're okay?"

He was tempted to play it up, but that didn't seem fair. "I'm fine. I get why you don't like him. The guy is a creep."

Harold still looked pale as he gestured to the car. Noah climbed in, casually inhaling the scent of the interior. Soon they were cruising down the street, Harold's expression haunted.

Noah studied him. "I take it you had a bad experience with Doug?"

Harold nodded. "Yeah. Did you have sorority girls?"

"Huh?"

Harold glanced over at him. "What sort of stuff did you hear?"

"Oh! At first it was a group of guys. Later a police officer came in and made me do stuff for him. Sorority girls?"

"It sounds stupid, I know. They were laughing and toying with me, but that's not what freaked me out. I had never done anything like that before. Bondage, handcuffs… nothing. I was okay with the blindfold, but as soon as I was tied up, I freaked. One hundred percent panic. We didn't know it at the time, but I have cleithrophobia. That means I don't like being trapped. I guess no one does, but when it happens to me, I go mental. I couldn't even remember my safe word. That was the worst part. I went nuts and Doug loved it. Eventually I remembered, but by then I was crying and…" His voice seemed to lose strength. Harold shook his head. "I don't know."

Noah wanted to reach over and take his hand, just to comfort him, but he was worried it would also reveal his interest. "I'm sorry."

"It's fine," Harold said. Then his jaw clenched. "Actually, it's not! I hate Doug! I get along with most people, but he shouldn't be in the club. Or we should only send people to him who can act. Like, we'd tell them the truth ahead of time. Marcello and I keep arguing about that."

"Sorry," Noah said again. "I'll tell him I agree with you. Maybe it'll help."

Harold shot him a look of gratitude, his eyes lingering. Was he interested too? Or maybe not, because he said, "You've got something on your chin. Uh… I think it's dried come."

Noah's face flushed as he started rubbing at it. How embarrassing! Harold seemed to find it funny, which was worth it when the pain in his voice was replaced by mirth.

"I hope you didn't go into McDonald's while waiting for me! If you did, they probably wondered why you're covered in mayo."

"Laugh it up," Noah said, grinning at him.

"I will!" Harold's smile was bright, and best of all, shining in his direction. "Where to? Wanna hang out at my place?"

Definitely! But tonight was the first in a long while that Noah had a dedicated place to sleep, and he didn't want to make Edith angry or upset by not showing up again. "I have a busy day tomorrow. Sorry."

"Oh, right! You wanted to borrow the car. In that case, we'll stop at my place, I'll hop out, and you can take the car home with you."

Or Noah could forget about Edith's feelings and the dumb trip to Gatesville and spend the night with the most excellent guy in the world.

Maybe I should just kill myself. Seriously.

Ugh. Noah couldn't ignore that. Besides, he'd just been manhandled and splooged on by an absolute creep. Not the best time to make a move on Harold. "That would be great," he said lamely. "Thanks."

He wished the car ride had lasted longer, but in less time than he liked, they were standing in Harold's driveway.

"Just bring her back when you're done," Harold said, handing over the key. "Tomorrow, right?"

"Yeah," Noah said, not moving. "I really *really* appreciate it."

"No problem."

Noah still didn't budge. "I guess I'm too gross to hug right now."

Harold laughed. "I've been way grosser after a date. You will be too. Just you wait!"

Noah didn't like the sound of that, but his concerns were forgotten when strong arms wrapped around him and squeezed. If he didn't feel so repulsive, he would have tried his luck, but now definitely wasn't the time. He said goodbye and began the drive toward Jerusalem. Then he started worrying about the car getting vandalized and decided to park it at the apartment complex where he had pretended to live. That way, if Harold came looking for it, the fake story would hold up. He didn't like maintaining a lie. Noah knew he needed to switch genres. No more fiction. He wanted an apartment and all the normal stuff he pretended to have. Only then could his story and Harold's become one.

Chapter Five

Most people associated the open road with freedom. They left the city or suburbs behind, saw empty fields and yawning horizons, and assumed this meant they were no longer restricted. Noah felt differently. For him, returning to the country was a reminder of the oppressive environment of his youth—a small town where people entertained themselves by watching and criticizing each other. Sometimes you wanna go where everybody knows your name, but those who have actually been to such a place rarely want to stay for long. He greatly preferred the anonymity of city life where the hectic pace and constant noise made blending in easy. Few people in Austin cared that he was gay, or homeless, or even knew he existed. That was freedom!

Despite his love for the city, it did feel good to get away. Noah did some mental arithmetic, surprised by the results. Six years now. That's how long it had been since his parents had kicked him out. He'd been homeless ever since. That didn't always mean living on the streets, but the situation had never been easy. Even at the beginning, when he had stayed with the twins. Not having a home had robbed him of a sense of security. He *had* felt loved though, thanks to one man, and it wasn't Rico.

Noah drummed his fingers on the steering wheel as he drove, experiencing a curious mixture of excitement and dread. When he thought of how the relationship had ended, how crazy it had all gotten toward the end, he questioned the wisdom of making this trip. The only thing that kept him going was the very beginning of their story, which his mind drifted back to as he continued driving.

*

Rico wasn't as bright as his twin brother, but he did possess one talent: He always knew where the parties were. Noah certainly appreciated this. As a trio of gay seventeen-year-olds, they didn't have a lot of options. They couldn't go to a bar or dance club. Meeting guys online was too solitary and usually resulted in disappointment, so the alternative was to crash any party they could find. Even if it meant hours of driving. That was Noah's job. He had once ferried them all the way to Houston just to attend a lesbian wedding. They hadn't known anyone there, but the guests were too tipsy to notice when a few bottles of wine went missing, and as usual, Rico had gotten lucky, this time with the best man.

Tonight they were in Austin. Noah had no idea who owned the house, or which of the mingling people was the host. Normally that wouldn't bother him, but he was feeling lonely and conspicuous. Tito had found someone to debate with. The topic was mass surveillance in the United Kingdom, and terms like "Orwellian" and "Big Brother" were repeatedly bandied about. Noah couldn't keep up, so he didn't. Unfortunately, Rico had already found some muscle-bound oaf to lust after and was doing his best to seduce him. Noah had once experienced the same treatment and had loved every second of it. After their one night together, Rico had no longer been interested because, as he so eloquently put it, "Life is a box of chocolates shaped like dicks, and I want to eat every single one of them."

This left Noah standing there on his own, feeling increasingly awkward. And distracted, because his attention kept returning to the same person. The man was sitting on the couch, tucked into one corner of it. He wore tight jeans and a navy-blue hoodie that hugged his slim body. As per Noah's usual weakness, the face is what really drew him in. The man was beautiful. Noah wished he possessed the sort of poetry necessary to describe it because the basic facts were insufficient: pink lips, even features, and bright blue eyes. These things were true, but the allure went far beyond that. The man was pretty, a word normally reserved for women, but here it was perfectly suited. This person was masculine enough to stir Noah's hormones, but somehow, he was also pretty.

Noah sought excuses to look at the stranger from different angles, such as during a trip to the kitchen for more drinks or on the way back again. The man's hood was up, hiding his hair. Noah tried imagining all the colors it could be. Red like his own. Black like Rico or Tito's. Dirty brown, buzzed, or blond. He liked that last idea best. Golden hair to accompany the rest of the beauty that he couldn't tear his eyes away from.

He must have stared for the better part of an hour, but the scene never changed. The man remained alone on the couch. Once or twice, couples sat next to him briefly before moving on, but no one spoke to him or made a move. Why not? Did he stink?

Or were people too intimidated to approach?

"Hey!" Rico said, jostling into him. "Can I get the car keys?"

Noah pulled his attention away, noticing the muscular guy who had an arm around Rico's neck. Mission successful. "Where are you going?"

"Nowhere. We just need some privacy."

Noah rolled his eyes, dug in his pocket, and pulled out the key ring. "Just don't get any stains on the fabric, okay?"

"No promises!" Rico said, swiping the keys. Then he disappeared out the front door with his latest conquest.

Noah looked around, longing for companionship of his own.

"Are you devoid of logic?" Tito was snarling at his debate partner. "The only people who have anything to hide while in public are those committing crimes!"

Nope. Noah still wasn't interested in joining that conversation. He looked back at the couch. Would sitting on it be such a big deal? It wouldn't mean anything. That's what people did with couches. Maybe he and the guy would strike up a conversation. Maybe not. At least it would get him one step closer.

Before he could overthink it, Noah hurried forward. He exhaled theatrically as he sat, like it felt good to take a load off, and that moving to the couch was an act of pure necessity. An empty seat cushion separated him and the other guy, who definitely didn't smell bad. Noah's thrill at being closer was short lived, because from here it was difficult to look at the man. Doing so now meant turning his head, making his infatuation painfully obvious, but he couldn't help himself. Up close, the guy was even hotter. How was that possible?

The pink lips smirked, a blue iris moving to consider him. Then the head slowly turned in his direction. Noah's heart was pounding. The guy had noticed his stare, and stupid him hadn't looked away in time! Too late now. He felt frozen in place as the eyes moved over him. Noah was certain that his every flaw was magnified ten times over, that a look of disgust would appear on the pretty face before it turned away from him forever. Instead, once the inspection was completed, the head cocked slightly, as if asking a question.

"Hey," Noah managed to say. His voice was raspy, his breath strained.

The beautiful man slid a hand across the cushion, palm

rubbing the fabric. It stopped halfway to him and flipped over. An invitation? Noah reached out to take it—certain it was the bravest thing he had ever done. Their fingers intertwined, electricity or something similar shooting through his arm and into his body. Then those pink lips tugged upward as the man pulled on him playfully. Noah scooted closer and didn't stop, even once on the next cushion. He kept going, because the other hand was reaching for his cheek and he was pretty sure—

They kissed. It started soft, but he responded hungrily, his free hand moving to touch that perfect face and to slide away the hood. When he pulled back, he saw the golden locks he'd been dreaming of, the blue eyes sparkling in amusement.

Noah laughed happily, then he asked, "What's your name?"

The man considered him, his gaze half-lidded. "My name's Ryan, and I'm your new boyfriend."

Noah slowed as the car entered the city limits of Gatesville. No doubt the local police were eager to hand out traffic tickets and earn some cash. Reducing speed was made harder by the way his pulse raced. So many memories came flooding back—how they had stayed up all night talking, Ryan proving himself just as witty as he was handsome. When the twins were ready to return to San Antonio, Noah refused, claiming he was too tired to drive. Ryan had a solution. They pooled their cash and stayed in a cheap motel. Ryan was old enough to rent rooms and buy them booze, which led to a party of their own the next night.

Noah hadn't cared about any of that. His focus narrowed until he could see only one person. He and Ryan took a shower together and had sex for the first time. Afterwards, still standing beneath a hot stream of water, Noah had declared his love. He felt stupid and naïve in retrospect, but the fledgling feelings really did turn into love eventually. For them both.

Their stories were similar. Ryan's parents had also cast him out, refusing to accept that their son was gay. Ryan had been dealing with the fallout for years, whereas Noah had just begun that struggle. Being with someone who knew the ropes, who could guide him and stop him from making mistakes, was comforting. At first. Later it had been Noah who did all the caretaking. Getting money for drugs, watching over Ryan when he was high and unresponsive, and then toward the end, when it got really crazy... He didn't like thinking about that part, but today it was impossible to ignore.

The prison was in view. Noah pulled over to the side of the road and stared. Did he really want to go? This was only the second time he'd been there. He studied the soulless complex, which was surrounded by watchtowers and barbwire fences, and tried to imagine what it would mean to call that place home. Three square meals every day, a bed, and a roof, but Noah would still rather be out on the streets. At least there he could enjoy the sun, sit by a river, window shop, or splurge on an ice cream. His life wasn't joyless. Prisoners probably managed to find happiness too, but it must be in shorter supply.

Noah put the car back in drive. The least he could do was brighten one of Ryan's days, even if it darkened his own.

Previous experience prepared him for the procedure of prison visits. His car was searched, Noah worrying briefly that Harold had weed stashed away somewhere. Then he parked, leaving everything behind except for his ID and a Ziploc bag full of quarters. He was patted down, had to fill out a form, and then waited. Eventually he and some other visitors were herded into a room that resembled a cafeteria. Only little details, such as the bolted-down tables and chairs, and the walkways full of guards, gave away that this environment didn't belong to a school or hospital.

Noah went to the assigned table, then waited, feeling nothing but apprehension until he saw Ryan's smile. The expression summoned tender memories of intimate moments. More than he could count. Noah stood, seeing only the guy he had fallen in love with—sassy and sexy, too good to be true. Then he noticed the guard escorting him, and noticed how skinny Ryan had become, the dark half-moons beneath his eyes suggesting he wasn't getting enough sleep. When they hugged, Noah attempted to find the familiar scent he had once known, but it was drowned out beneath generic body soap and cheap laundry detergent. God he felt boney!

"I'm so glad you're here," Ryan said, wiping tears from his eyes. "I thought I'd never see you again."

"I know." They sat at the table, Noah choosing a chair across from him until Ryan insisted he move closer. "I got your letter. I don't like what you wrote. Suicide?"

Ryan rolled his eyes. "Hey, that got me into the psych ward for a week. I know that sounds bad, but trust me, it's better than..."

He didn't finish the sentence. Noah was scared to ask him to, not wanting to know what atrocities Ryan was subjected to while stuck here.

"So you were just pretending to be suicidal?"

Ryan pursed his lips. "I didn't say that."

"Don't," Noah pleaded with him. "I know things are bad—"

"You don't know! And you don't care. It took me wanting to kill myself for you to visit!"

Were they doing this already? "I do care! Making the trip out here isn't easy! If you'll remember, I sold the car to pay for your lawyer. Last time I visited, I hitchhiked halfway and had to walk—"

"But you made it."

"Barely. I'd come visit all the time if I could, but—"

"You could live in Waco."

"I'm homeless!" Noah snapped. "I tried staying there and the cops were jerks. It's not like Austin."

Ryan sighed. "Then how'd you get here this time?"

"A friend loaned me his car."

Ryan studied him. "A guy friend?"

He thought of easy-going Harold, who seemed a million miles away from this sort of world. "Yeah."

"You're seeing someone else? Are you here to break up?"

"No!" He only addressed the first question. The second was too loaded. "He's just a friend."

"Good." Ryan's hand was on the table. It moved closer to him, but it looked different than the one that had slid across the couch all those years ago. The skin was paler, and four of the fingers had horrible prison tattoos, shaky letters that spelled out *love*. They had argued over that during the previous visit, Noah feeling that it marked Ryan forever. His boyfriend—if that was even the right term anymore—had defended his choice. The hand that now declared love was the same one that had held the gun. Ryan had sworn to never again raise it in anger, thus the tattoos.

Noah tried to ignore this history as their fingers intertwined. "I'm worried about you," he said. "You don't look so good."

"Gee, thanks!" Ryan said, attempting to pull away.

Noah didn't let him. "I don't mean it like that. You're still gorgeous, but are you getting enough to eat?"

Ryan grimaced. "The food here is terrible."

"Maybe I can help with that." Noah pulled the baggie full of quarters from his pocket. Twenty bucks' worth, which was the maximum amount allowed.

Ryan's eyes lit up like he'd been presented with gold pieces instead. "For real?"

"Yeah!" Noah said with a chuckle.

"You probably need it more than I do," Ryan said, but the hopeful expression remained.

"I'm doing okay. Don't worry."

"In that case..." Ryan grabbed the quarters. "Let's go shopping!"

The only option was a row of vending machines, but Ryan was like a little kid, rushing from one to the other, unable to make up his mind. He got a little of everything—candy bars, chips, cola, and even a pack of gum.

"You'll still love me when I'm fat," Ryan said when they were seated again and he was opening his third candy bar, "right?"

"It'll take more than that to make you fat," Noah laughed.

"I wish I could get huge," Ryan said wistfully. "Maybe then my cellmate would stop—" He seemed to choke on the words or the candy before he continued. "—stop making eyes at me."

Noah feared there was more to it than that. Ryan didn't glow as he once had, but he was still good-looking. If half the stories about prison were true, Ryan would need to be on guard, or maybe do what was necessary to survive. Noah couldn't judge, but he still felt sorry for him. "I want you to eat more. I'll put money in your account too."

Noah knew it was a mistake the moment he said it. He should have done so anonymously. Maybe Ryan would have assumed it was from his parents. Instead his chewing slowed. Then he swallowed.

"Where's all this money coming from?" Ryan asked.

"I got a job. I'm still at the shelter, but I've managed to save a little."

Ryan relaxed somewhat. "A job? Where?"

Noah looked away. He wasn't against stretching the truth, but it wasn't elastic enough for this situation.

"You're tricking," Ryan said, reading him like a book.

"Don't be mad!" Noah pleaded. "You know what it's like out there. This is the only way I can get back on my feet."

"You'll find yourself knocked on your ass! You might have been lucky so far, but remember the time that guy almost broke my nose? I blew the ugly fucker and then he elbowed me in the face and pushed me out of his car! Is that really what you want?"

"No!"

"You're worried about me having a death wish? You're the one putting your life on the line!"

"It's not like that. I'm safe."

Ryan glared. "Really? Is that what you think?"

"It's the truth! I'm working for a service. They screen out the bad guys." Another slip. When would Noah learn to keep his mouth shut?

"An escort service?" Ryan asked, voice quiet. "Which one?"

"Does it matter? I don't want to think about any of that. Let's just enjoy the time we have left."

"Which one?"

Noah crossed his arms over his chest. "I'm done talking about this."

"You're working for Marcello."

Noah remained perfectly still. It didn't work.

"The Gentlemen's Agreement Club? Isn't that the name of it?"

Noah's arms went loose and he sighed. "Just drop it, okay?"

Anger would have sucked. Hurt tears would have been difficult to deal with, but Ryan looked excited, which was worst of all. "Have you seen him?"

"Who?" Noah said, knowing damn well who he meant. "Marcello? We talked for five minutes when I applied. That was it."

"Not him," Ryan said. "Tim."

"Why would I see him?" Noah snapped. "He isn't a client, as far as I know. I don't think he even works for Marcello, so no, I haven't seen Tim and doubt I ever will."

"You could give him a letter," Ryan continued unabashed. "Marcello, I mean. You could give him a letter, and he could give it to Tim. It would have to be from you. If they saw it was from me..." He reached out and took Noah's hand. "You'll do it, right? Please! I need to clear my conscience."

Noah sighed. "You're not supposed to have any contact with him."

"I need this," Ryan said, gripping his hand tighter. "If I'm going to move on, there are things I need to say to him."

Like what? *Sorry I shot you and held your boyfriend hostage.* How would that help anyone? Then again, those blue eyes were pleading, and Noah didn't see anything malicious in them. Instead they were sad and on the verge of tears.

He exhaled. "Fine."

Ryan perked up. "You'll do it?"

Noah clenched his jaw, hesitating again. Then he nodded. "Yeah."

Ryan leapt to his feet. "I need paper. And a pen."

"You can mail it to me," Noah said, but it was no use. Ryan had already rushed over to one of the prison guards, engaging in a conversation that became increasingly heated. Eventually Ryan spun around, face twisted with anger, and headed back toward him. That didn't bring back good memories either. Ryan had always gotten agitated when the subject of Tim Wyman came up. At first this hadn't seemed so unusual. Most people felt emotional when discussing previous relationships, especially those that hadn't ended well. Ryan took it to an entirely new level. He became obsessed, eventually disappearing for two weeks. Worried about an overdose or worse, Noah called the police and discovered that Ryan had been arrested for shooting Tim.

Noah never doubted his guilt. As much as he loved Ryan and wanted to believe in him, Noah had all too often glimpsed a shadow-side to his personality. At the time he had almost felt relief, thinking Ryan might spend a few months behind bars, sober up, and come to his senses. Tim hadn't died. It wasn't murder. Noah sold the car, hired an attorney to make sure that he was given a fair trial, and then it all went to hell. According to Ryan, Marcello had hired an even better lawyer and manipulated events to make sure he received the severest sentence.

"That stupid asshole won't let me go back to my cell for one minute, and god forbid he ask Officer Dipshit over there to—"

"Stop," Noah said softly.

"—grab some paper, because I guess they don't pay him enough and—"

"Please!" Noah said, already noticing multiple guards tensing at Ryan's behavior. "I came all this way to see you. Don't let them take that away from us."

Ryan glared, but he sat again. "I have *got* to get out of here."

"I wish you could," Noah said honestly. "Just focus on me. Have some more chips."

Ryan didn't seem to hear him, still fixated. "I'll mail you the letter, like you said. And then you can— Marcello is nosy. Even if the letter is from you, he'll probably still read it. No, you better give it directly to Tim."

"That's not what I agreed to!"

"Please!" Ryan said. "You're my only chance."

He sighed. "How am I supposed to find Tim?"

Ryan shook his head. "He works at a gallery. I was high out of my mind, so I can't remember which one, but if you search online, you should find it."

"That was years ago," Noah said. "He might not be there anymore. He might not even live in Austin! Can't you just let it go?"

"No," Ryan said firmly. "If I could, I would. This is the only way."

"Fine." Noah focused disinterestedly on the vending machines instead of the person across from him. What was the point in making conversation when Ryan was only interested in one subject? At first this protest didn't seem to register, but eventually Ryan spoke again.

"Hey, remember the time we hopped the fence of that country club?"

Noah smiled, unwillingly at first. "You mean the buffet?"

"Yes!" Ryan grinned. "They were set up for a party of some sort but nobody was there yet. We never found out what the occasion was, did we? I wish we could have seen the caterers' faces when they saw we had eaten a little of everything. The best part was swimming with you."

"Swimming?"

Ryan nodded. "Remember the pool?"

He had the details wrong. Ryan had already started shooting up at that point, but only occasionally. The pool had been at night, not during the day, and it wasn't at the country club. It was a public pool in a quiet neighborhood. It must have been three in the morning on a hot night, and what they had done together was even hotter. They had skinny-dipped, neither owning a swimsuit, Noah certain that the police would arrive at any moment. Ryan hadn't been concerned. He pinned Noah in a corner of the pool and kissed him. Hungrily. Then they had traded places, Ryan in the corner, facing away from him. Noah hadn't been gentle. That's not how Ryan preferred it, but as violent as their lovemaking could be, the aftermath was always tender and sweet. What Noah liked most about that night wasn't the sex. The best part was when they had gotten dressed and spooned against each other in one of the deck chairs. The world around them had been still, the stars above twinkling for their pleasure alone.

"You know I love you," Ryan said. "Right?"

"I love you too," Noah responded truthfully.

"Good. Find yourself a different job. I don't like the idea of you getting hurt."

"I don't want you to get hurt either," he replied, and he meant it in many ways. He didn't want other prisoners or guards hurting Ryan; didn't want Tim's inevitable lack of a response to reopen old wounds. He especially didn't want Ryan to get hurt when he realized that Noah needed to be set free. What they'd had together belonged in the past. Noah wasn't sure what the future held, but if allowed to make a few wishes, he wouldn't choose Ryan, even if unburdened by so much addiction and rage. Their relationship had ended long ago. Noah just needed to find the courage to tell him so.

Noah felt like he was the one escaping from prison by the time he left. He eagerly got into Harold's car, a maroon Chrysler Sebring Limited, he noted for the first time. It was a nice little ride, and he had fun putting the top down on the short trip to the highway. Just being inside the vehicle felt like a reassuring hug from Harold, prompting Noah to speed a little on his way back to Austin. He wanted to see Harold again. Enough that he was already regretting his decision to work tonight, especially when he returned the vehicle to its owner.

"How'd it go?" Harold asked. "Did you have fun visiting your friend?"

"Fun?" Noah repeated, already deciding not to lie. They were standing in Harold's driveway, and he was hoping for an invitation inside. "It was more of a social obligation. One of those people you have to see, even if you don't really want to. Still, thanks for loaning me your car! It really helped. What do I owe you?"

"Nothing," Harold said. "Maybe a tank of gas?"

"I filled her up just a few minutes ago."

"Then we're even!" Harold declared.

"Great." Noah realized with some discomfort that he would rather be indebted to Harold, since it might result in more excuses to interact.

"You working tonight?"

"Yeah!" The text message had come during his visit with Ryan, Noah strategically ignoring it. He showed the name and address to Harold, who scowled.

"No fucking way!" he snarled.

"Whatever it is this time," Noah said, "I'm sure I can handle it."

"Okay, tough guy," Harold replied. "Do you like fisting? Wait, let me rephrase that. Do you like *getting* fisted?"

"No!" Noah exclaimed. "Are you serious? Do I really have to—"

Harold was already shaking his head. "Come on. I'll fix this."

Yay!

Noah did his best not to act thrilled as they went inside. "I'm a top," he said. "Guess I should have mentioned that sooner. Do I really have to do things like this?"

"You should be a little versatile," Harold said, leading him to the kitchen. "That's just realistic. Some guys will want to get fucked by you, others will want to fuck you, but things like fisting… That's different! A specialty. We already have escorts who are into that. Is there any reason Marcello would think you're one of them?"

"Nope," Noah said. "He's probably out to get me."

"Huh? Why?"

Noah exhaled. "The whole secret past thing, which no, I'm still not going to tell you about."

Harold laughed. "Grab a drink and have a seat. I gotta make some calls."

Noah helped himself to a glass of tap water, and while sitting at the kitchen table, watched Harold use the phone. He didn't just start barking orders or leap right to the reason he was making each call. He first asked how each person was doing, personalized chitchat coming before business. This only made Noah adore him more. Hot *and* nice! Or nice and hot. Either way, what a guy!

"Okay!" Harold said, joining him at the table and setting down the phone. "I rearranged stuff. You've got Chester tonight. He's a sweetheart. That's who I wanted your first date to be with."

"You're not getting fisted for me," Noah said. "Are you?"

Harold scoffed. "I like you, but not that much! No, a different guy will take care of that client."

"Do you think Marcello will be mad about this?"

Harold shrugged. "Maybe. If so, tell him to take it up with me."

"You're the best!" Noah said, and he meant it. He couldn't imagine doing better than Harold.

"I'm just doing what I'd want you to if our roles were reversed. Speaking of which, we better get ready. We've got dates to impress!"

"Any tips about Chester?" Noah asked as he stood.

"Nah. He's easy. Just don't be there in the morning."

"Why not?"

Harold grinned. "Because he turns into a pumpkin."

Chapter Six

Noah showed up at a restaurant the same evening and confirmed his reservation with the hostess, all of which felt reassuringly normal. No blindfolds or mind games this time. His only complaint was that the place was kind of fancy, and Noah was wearing a goofy checkered shirt like he'd just fallen off the turnip truck. He had no doubt that other people could make such clothing appear sexy or even sophisticated, but Noah needed something dressier to make himself feel confident. Another time perhaps, because the hostess had led him to his table, an old man already seated there.

"Chester!" Noah declared, like they were old friends. "I'm so glad to see you!"

Chester smiled and got to his feet, a little shaky while doing so. He was eighty—maybe even ninety—his back slightly hunched. His white hair was wispy, part of it sticking upright. His ears were large, his nose bulbous, and the tweed suit a few decades out of style. Kind eyes helped chase away any apprehension Noah felt.

Chester's smile was generous as he opened his arms for a hug. "Less than ten words and you've charmed me already," he said.

Noah braced himself for old-man stink, like his grandfather always had, but Chester smelled like aftershave and shoe polish.

"Thanks for the dinner invitation," Noah said, shaking his head when the hostess asked if he wanted anything to drink.

Chester wouldn't allow it. "I'll have that bottle of wine now," he said. "Two glasses, if that's okay with you?"

"Yeah!" Noah answered eagerly. It had been a long day with many ups and downs, and the idea of a drink sounded appealing. He knew he should be on guard, but he also trusted Harold's assurance that this wouldn't be a tricky assignment.

"Tell me a little about yourself," Chester said.

Easy enough. Noah gave him the Disney version of events—a small-town boy who had traveled to the big city to find love. Or at least to find others like himself. He included enough details to carry them through the first glass of wine, and after their food arrived, he answered Chester's follow-up questions while they ate.

"Unbelievable!" the old man declared. "So much has changed since my time. When I was your age, I had just married my wife. Only then did I lose my virginity, but I suppose that was unusual for a man, even back then. My parents were very religious. They had me terrified of going to Hell."

"My parents are religious too," Noah said, feeling bad for misrepresenting events. "They aren't too thrilled, to be honest but… I need to live my own life. I have to do what's best for me."

"That's a very modern attitude," Chester replied. "I was raised to obey my parents, serve my community, better my country…"

"The good old days," Noah said, thinking again of his own grandfather, who seemed to talk solely about the past and how much better it had been. That's what made Chester's answer so surprising.

"More like the bad old days! We were taught to fear Communism and anything slightly different than ourselves, and let me tell you, that concept of 'us' was one big lie. We were all deceiving each other just to get by, or drinking ourselves to death, because no one was having any fun. Thank god for the sixties, or I would have given up the ghost a long time ago."

Noah laughed. "Really?"

Chester nodded. "My life was one torment after another until I met—" He smiled so broadly that it interrupted him. "Until I met Raymond."

"You're making me jealous," Noah said. "Who's this Raymond person? I thought you only had eyes for me."

Chester clearly appreciated the flirtation, but he didn't give in so easily. "You have serious competition, I'm afraid. Raymond was the love of my life. We were together for fifty-two years."

Noah gasped, not having to feign his awe. "Fifty-two?"

"That's right," Chester said with a nod. "More than half a century of that fool keeping me on my toes and making me slowly lose my sanity. And my hair! I'd have more if it wasn't for him."

Noah laughed. "Tell me everything!"

No easy feat considering how long their relationship had lasted, but Chester tried his best as they ate. "Raymond was a bus driver," he said, "the sort who knew all his regulars by name and loved talking with them. They were like an extended family to him. When he came home for dinner, he'd have so many stories to tell, little updates on people I had never met. I worked in publishing. Most of my time was spent with manuscripts, not other human beings. I didn't realize how lonely my job was until I met Raymond. The entire world was his friend."

Noah thought warmly of Harold again, how he too was easygoing. "So what happened? Did you switch jobs to be less lonely?"

"Goodness no! One of us had to earn a decent living! Raymond was always loaning money to folks, a sucker for any sob story he heard. Drove me crazy. Eventually I started my own publishing company, and that helped me become less isolated. I was dealing with employees more than actual books, and I found I needed Raymond's advice on how to get them motivated. He had a great understanding of people, although I didn't think so at first. I confronted him once about being taken advantage of, since few people ever bothered to pay back those loans. Raymond just shrugged and said 'I know, but I figure they need it more than me. Otherwise they wouldn't be asking.'" Chester shook his head. "I could never decide if I wanted to strangle him or hug him."

"I bet I can guess which you did more of," Noah teased.

"Don't be so sure," Chester said. "When Raymond started giving away *my* money…"

"No! Really?"

"I'm afraid so! This only made me work harder. I was scared if I didn't that we'd both go broke! Speaking of which, would you mind if we settle the tab? I'd like to continue our evening somewhere else."

"Sounds nice!" Noah said, experiencing a pang of doubt. He had figured that sleeping with old guys would be part of this job, but he was nervous about how much he would enjoy it, or how the logistics would work. He couldn't get too crazy. Chester seemed frail. He was slow to rise from the table, and he didn't walk much faster. Noah was moving at about half his usual speed, and as it turned out, they would remain at that pace.

"Do you have a car?" Chester asked. "No? A fellow walker then. How wonderful!"

"You like to walk everywhere?" Noah asked.

"Always have," Chester said, already heading for the sidewalk. "That's the secret to my longevity, although I might be pushing my luck. These days I walk until I get tired, then I call a cab. Is that okay with you?"

"Totally," Noah said. The night was warm, the humidity low, the sort of weather that would make it easy to sleep outdoors, if he was still forced to. "Where exactly are we going?"

"You'll see," Chester said. "I assume you also take the bus sometimes?"

This topic led to more stories about Raymond. Noah didn't mind. It felt too easy, like getting paid to hang out with a much more chill version of his grandfather, one who was gay and had an inspiring relationship behind him. All Noah had to do was listen and ask the occasional question.

"Here we are," Chester said.

They stopped on a street corner downtown, only ten blocks from Jerusalem. Around them were trendy shops selling second-hand clothes or vinyl records. Most were closed due to the hour. A few bars and restaurants were still open, pedestrians hustling in or stumbling out.

"Where is this exactly?" Noah asked.

"We're at the beginning," Chester said. He pointed across the street. "That nail studio used to be a bar. I was twenty-five and had just been told by my wife that she wanted a divorce. Dorothy was terribly unhappy with me. Understandably so. I wasn't a good husband to her, being so uninterested in our relationship. I don't just mean sex. We had little in common, so conversation was just as forced as what took place in the bedroom. After learning that our marriage was ending, I went out walking to make sense of it all and ducked inside that very bar without thinking."

"Was it a gay bar?" Noah asked.

"Back then? No. It was full of blue-collar workers, all of them having a better time than me. I was already drunk when Raymond showed up. I had never met him before, but he had one of those faces. He made you *want* to be his friend and feel like you could trust him with anything. So I did. First we talked sports and work. Then I started in on my problems. By the time the bar closed, I had said more about my feelings to Raymond than just about anyone in my life. Except for one thing, but as we stood on this street corner, I couldn't stop blubbering. I told him what I'd scarcely admitted to myself. I didn't want my wife back or any other woman. I wanted to be with a man. Raymond asked me if

I was absolutely sure about that. The only thing I was certain of is that he was about to punch me and storm off. With the last of my courage, I nodded, and then..." Chester pressed his hand to his cheek briefly, as if still in disbelief. "Then he kissed me. Thank god the streets were empty or we both would have been locked up or worse, but it was one of the happiest moments of my life."

Chester had tears on his cheeks. He looked up at Noah, expression both hurt and longing. "That's why I like to come here. To remember. To relive that moment." He closed his eyes.

Noah stared, comforting words poised on his lips, but if he understood the situation right, his mouth was needed for other purposes. He was here to play a role, so he moved closer, putting a hand on Chester's shoulder. This caused the man to raise his chin expectantly. Noah kissed him, but first he tried to put himself in Raymond's shoes, attempting to guess what he had been thinking at the time. He had just watched a drunk guy get emotional and cry, which had to be way less common back then. Had Raymond found that attractive? Endearing? Maybe as they talked he had fantasized about comforting Chester and replacing the wife who had just left. Then, at the very end of the night, he discovered those fantasies could come true and had acted. Probably a little drunk himself, Raymond had gone for broke.

Noah kissed Chester, but it wasn't a gentle peck. He filled it with passion, hurried and desperate. When he stepped back, he saw that the tears in Chester's eyes were now of the happy variety.

"My goodness!" the old man breathed. "That was almost like traveling back through time!"

"I tried my best," Noah said, "but you've already convinced me that there's no competing with Raymond."

"If anyone could," Chester said, taking his arm, "I think it would be you. Let's keep walking."

They didn't need a taxi, as it turned out. Progress was slow on the way to Chester's apartment. Along the way, more stories from his relationship with Raymond helped pass the time. A brief reprieve came when Chester politely asked about Noah's personal life.

"Do you have anyone special?"

"No," he admitted. "but there is someone I really like."

"And does he like you?"

"I'm not sure," Noah admitted.

"You haven't told him how you feel?"

"What?" Noah was aghast. Then he laughed nervously. "No way! I couldn't!"

"You could," Chester said, patting his hand. "I can't stand people who insist that life is only worth living if you have a spouse, or children, or whatever motivates them to get out of bed in the morning. Still, it does seem that everyone needs *something*. That might be a career or hobby for some. For many it's a family. I tried a little of everything, to be honest. I had children, but wasn't much of a father. I threw myself into my work for many decades and found that more fulfilling. I don't have many regrets. Looking back, the only thing I still want more of is love. If that's also what you want, you should pursue it."

Easier said than done! He felt relieved when the subject changed and wasn't brought up again during the remainder of the walk. Chester's home provided further distraction. The apartment wasn't in a complex, like where Doug lived or Noah had pretended to. Instead it was a tall building downtown with a polished lobby. An elevator took them to a private floor, the rooms spacious and tastefully decorated. Chester's tweed suit might be outdated, but his furnishings were contemporary and well-maintained.

"A man's home is his kingdom," he said when noticing Noah's awed expression. "Would you care for more wine?"

"Please," Noah said.

The kitchen and living room, while both large, blended into each other. He decided to wait by the twin sofas rather than get in the way, eventually wandering over to one of the bookshelves. On it was a framed photo of two guys with their arms around each other. He barely recognized Chester. If not for the same blue eyes, he might have been unrecognizable. He was young! And handsome! The guy next to him must have been Raymond, but he wasn't anything near what Noah was expecting. Chester had put the man on such a high pedestal that he had envisioned Clark Gable or some other sex icon from decades ago. Instead he looked more like the chubby guy from the Honeymooners. Raymond was average-looking and a little overweight, but his smile was endearing, and he really did seem like the sort of person you could confide in.

"I don't know who the people in that photo are," Chester said, returning with two glasses, "but they ran off with my body a long time ago and left me with this old one."

"This is really you?" Noah asked. "You look so—"

"Ugly? I know. Thank goodness I aged well." Chester laughed, handing him a drink and clinking glasses. "Don't worry too much about your own future. Your best years are still ahead, you'll see. Eventually you'll turn into an old mummy like me, but not for a while yet."

Noah took a sip. "It's nice to put a face to the legend."

"You mean Raymond? I have more photos, if you'd like to see."

"Sure!"

They sat side by side on the couch, working their way through another glass of wine as Chester flipped through the pages of a photo album. Noah supposed that some people might find the fixation on a previous relationship tedious, but he was fascinated. Scarcely had he allowed himself to dream of finding something similar. He had experienced some romance with Ryan, but so many other concerns had demanded their attention. Finding money for gas or food, or entertaining themselves, which at first meant sneaking into movies but later turned into finding more drugs. Mostly for Ryan. Sometimes for Noah too, but not the heavy stuff. He'd held back the first time it was offered, and after seeing what it did to Ryan, had wanted no part of it.

"We had our troubles too," Chester said, as if reading his mind. "I don't want to give the impression that everything was perfection, because that's never the case. We argued, I had doubts, and there were plenty of hurt feelings and shed tears. That's just part of love. I knew in my heart that I wanted to stay. A night away from him was all it would take to remind me." Chester shut the photo album. "If there's one thing I haven't grown accustomed to over the years, it's how cold an empty bed still feels. I hate it. I don't use that word lightly, but I do."

"I'm sorry," Noah said. "Um. How did…"

"I know. I've told you the beginning and much that followed, but not the end. Raymond died quite some time ago. One heart attack is all it took. I always found that unjust. If Raymond had one strength, it was his heart. How could it give out so easily? Did he use it too often? Did he love me and everyone else a little too much?" Chester looked away.

Noah took his hand. "I'm sorry. I can't even imagine. I think I would—" A flash of memories. The first time Ryan had been so high that he became unresponsive. Noah had thought Ryan overdosed and was about to die. Just the idea of losing the man he loved, of being powerless to stop it—

"Don't cry," Chester said. "Oh, look what I've done! I've been rambling on about my losses without thinking of your own feelings."

"I'm fine," Noah said quickly. "Really! It's just so beautiful what you had together. I wish I could give him back to you!"

Chester patted his hand. "You really are a sweet boy. Some pretend to be, but you're genuine. Hold on to that. You don't realize how precious it is."

Noah wiped at his eyes, then took a swig of his wine, emptying the glass. "Sorry," he said. "I'll calm down. Just give me a second."

"I'd like to give you all night!" Chester said. "That is, if you're willing to stay with me."

It seemed an odd transition. They had just finished crying over old photos and lost loves, and now Chester was suggesting they move to the bedroom?

"You can voice your concerns," Chester said. "Half of you do. The others treat this as a job and don't really care."

Noah wasn't one of them, but it did seem a rude question to ask, especially after such a vulnerable moment. Still, he had to know. Was this all a game to win over guys like him? He chose a more tactful way of broaching the subject. "Do you ever worry about what Raymond would think?"

Chester smiled, as if pleased with the question. "Not often. I know I've painted a portrait of a saint, but as it turned out, I wasn't the first man that Raymond had kissed and I certainly wasn't the last. He had a healthy appetite! Always in the mood, always wanting more, and not just from me. The first time he brought someone home, I was upset. Raymond led me to another room, took my hand, and said, 'If we do this, it's together or not at all.' That wasn't him threatening to leave me. He simply meant that he wouldn't sneak around behind my back. He was too honest for that. But he had needs, and the man he invited to dinner *was* very handsome. I soon got over my reservations and discovered another activity for us to share. I don't know if you believe in ghosts, but if you do stay the night, just be aware that we're probably being watched. In a way, I'm the one bringing men home for Raymond now."

Noah laughed. "Is this all an act? I bet it is! You've had all these years—all these *decades*—to come up with the perfect pickup line. How many guys have fallen for it before me? Actually, I don't want to know."

Chester chuckled in response. "I wish I was so devious. But I'm not. I've told you nothing but the truth. So what do you say? Would you care to stay the night? Spare me from facing that empty bed alone. Please."

Noah nearly nodded. The only thing that stopped him was Harold's advice about not being there in the morning, but why? Chester seemed sweet enough, and Noah hadn't done what he was there to do. Sure, an escort could be hired just for companionship, but Chester had already implied he wanted more. Could Noah really leave without performing his duties?

He took one look at those tired blue eyes and tried to imagine being so old. Noah designed an entire future for himself in an instant. He and Harold fell in love, got married, built new lives for themselves, and enjoyed decades of shared happiness. Then Harold died. The world grew dark, Noah's bed grew cold, and occasionally—when he couldn't take it anymore—he sought comfort. Companionship.

Noah stood and offered his hand. "The night isn't getting any younger, and neither are you."

Chester chuckled in appreciation. Then he slid his hand into Noah's, the skin soft and slightly loose. That would probably describe the rest of his body too. Noah would need all of his imagination to get through this one. He helped Chester to his feet. Together they walked down a hall to the bedroom. There they parted, Chester wanting to freshen up. Noah sat on the bed. He returned to the recently created fantasy and wound back the clock. Harold hadn't died yet. He was old. They both were, but it wasn't important because their attraction to each other had ceased relying on the physical. They loved each other so deeply that it didn't matter if their bodies were fading. Besides, the way Harold looked at him made Noah feel young again.

He raised his head, a figure appearing in the doorway. Harold. At the moment he was wearing an elegant silk robe, his wispy white hair freshly combed. A hint of cologne accompanied him as he came near. He might not resemble the handsome boy he had fallen for, but the easy smile was the same, as were the eyes which crinkled with joy.

Noah shot to his feet, the breath catching in his throat. "Are you wearing anything beneath that robe?" he asked.

"Nothing at all," Chester replied.

"Then you have me at a disadvantage." Noah gestured to the bed so that Chester—no, *Harold*, would sit. "Let me catch up with you."

Once his audience was seated, Noah slowly unbuttoned his shirt, shooting a shy smile toward the bed a few times as if still bashful after all their years together. His cock betrayed just how untrue this was, already straining to be set free as Noah undid his jeans.

"My goodness!" Harold breathed.

"Don't act like you haven't seen it before," Noah said. "Sometimes I think you love this thing more than me."

In the back of his mind, he worried that he might be losing his client, but Chester probably assumed he was trying to be Raymond. Noah abandoned his self-delusion just long enough to be sure everything was okay, and it was. They would comfort each other tonight, adding a physical component to the fantasies that accompanied their daily existence.

"I've missed it," Harold said. "Come, let me give it a kiss."

Noah was all too eager to comply, padding nude across the carpeted bedroom and sucking in air when saliva helped cool searing hot flesh. He allowed himself to be selfish, enjoying the pleasure and letting it inch him closer. Not too close. He wanted to enjoy their time together. Noah got on his knees, spreading Harold's legs until the robe fabric pulled away enough to reveal his prize.

Harold was already responding, his cock half-hard and stiffening. Noah caressed the low hanging testicles, a lifetime of gravity making them pendulous. That was hot enough to spur him forward. He opened his mouth and used his lips to massage Harold's dick, coaxing it into a full salute. Then he looked up hungrily, hoping they shared the same desire.

"Let's take this further," Harold said.

Noah nodded. He didn't complain when Chester turned off the lamp next to the bed, casting them in darkness. No doubt this would make it easier for them both to fantasize. Condoms and lube were on the side table. Noah made use of them and listened for any protest when putting one on himself. None came. Good.

Harold got on his back, the robe fluttering open. Noah was gentle as he started raising one of the legs.

"I'm not quite so spry anymore," Harold said. "Here, let me roll over."

No problem. Noah reached down to stroke himself, then he took aim. They started slow. This wasn't Ryan. He didn't want to hurt Harold, no matter how passionately they felt for each other. In the dark it was difficult to see his expression, so Noah listened instead for little gasps that turned into sighs. Then he let himself move his hips like a gentle wave, one that increased along with the pleasure, building into a crescendo. "I love you," Noah said, lost in his vision. It felt so good to say it out loud! "God damn, I love you!"

Harold laughed, voice warm when he responded. "I love you too. I always will. Help me up."

Noah leaned forward to kiss his neck and helped Harold to his hands and knees. One of his favorite positions.

"Wanna try teaching an old dog some new tricks?" Harold joked.

"Definitely!" Noah said, moving his hips again. Then held his breath, because he was getting close. How could he not? The person before him was the love of his life. They weren't old anymore. They were young, entire decades still ahead of them. Countless days spent at the grocery store, or having dinner at a friend's house, or visiting museums, and yes, plenty of sex too.

Noah grunted and tensed. "Just tell me—"

"I'm ready," Harold responded.

Noah kept pumping, trying to make it last even though the pleasure was maddening. Then he growled, eyes clenched shut as he slowed, only stopping when he heard Harold hissing his satisfaction. No. Not Harold.

The fantasy had been beautiful, but as he pulled out and rolled over to his side, he forced himself to accept that it had only been an illusion.

"The sheets," Chester said. "Get beneath them with me. I'm always so chilly!"

Noah did as he was told, the real Harold's warning echoing in his thoughts again. He wouldn't stay the night. He would sneak out in the middle of it, when Chester was sound asleep. Let him go to bed this night feeling like Raymond was there to hold him. Their fantasies were different in that way. Noah could dream of the future and all its potential. Chester could only look back and try to recapture the best days of his life.

Noah nestled near, wanting to provide whatever comfort he could. The mattress contoured to the shape of his body, the sheets cool and soft. Finding comfort for himself wasn't difficult. The wine in his belly, combined with the increasingly warm form next to him, made drifting off all too easy.

Noah woke with a start, blinking against the beam of sunlight that warmed his face. He slowly got his bearings, then swore under his breath. He hadn't meant to fall asleep. He thought again of Harold's warning, wondering how bad it could be, and spotted a folded pile on the side table. Fluffy white cotton. He reached for this, discovering a robe, towel, and wash cloth. His clothes were draped on a nearby chair. So far, so good.

Noah rose, poking his head into the nearest doors and finding a huge closet in one and a bathroom in the other. He made use of the latter and was clean and dressed half an hour later. All he needed was to brush his teeth, but that could wait. If he wasn't mistaken, he smelled breakfast!

He followed his nose to the kitchen. Chester stood at the stove, jiggling a frying pan. The older man was dressed more casually today in white pants and a light sweater. Maybe he intended to go golfing later.

"Good morning!" Noah said.

Chester stiffened, not turning around immediately. Then he shut off the burner and offered him a tentative smile. "Did you sleep well?"

"Very," Noah said. "Looks like we both worked up an appetite last night."

Chester's expression remained guarded. "You're hungry?"

"Starving!"

Chester was the first to look at the table. Noah followed his gaze and saw two settings. Plates, glasses, forks and knives. He walked closer, wondering which seat was intended for him. They seemed identical, except for one that had a framed photo before it. He moved toward this without thinking, catching a glimpse of the photo's subject. Raymond. That seat was intended for him, and Noah didn't think he was supposed to stare at the photo while pretending to be the man. Maybe Chester wanted to sit there instead and have the photo handy to help him pretend. Or maybe Noah's services were no longer needed. He looked to Chester in confusion.

"I'm sorry," the old man said. "It's usually just Raymond and me for breakfast. I suppose I could set another place."

"I don't want to be any trouble," Noah said uneasily.

"No! None at all. It's just that… I can't let you take his place. I know what you must think, but I still love him, and I'm still loyal. In my heart. Maybe I'm being foolish and you should stay. I just… I just don't know. Excuse me."

Chester turned around, but not before Noah noticed the tears in his eyes. He looked back at the table, wondering how many breakfasts Chester had eaten with only a framed photo for company. Did he talk to Raymond? Did he ever hear a response? The old man wasn't senile. Their evening together had convinced him of that. Chester had simply found a way of coping with Raymond's death, and this was part of it. Breakfasts alone, and who knew what else, aside from the occasional body to help warm the bed. Noah had fulfilled his purpose. Now it was time to leave.

"Holy smokes!" he said theatrically. "Is that the time? You shouldn't have let me sleep in!" It was only half past eight, but Chester played along.

"There's somewhere you need to be?"

"Dentist appointment." Noah patted his pockets to make sure he had everything. "I wish I could stay but…"

"I understand," Chester said, looking relieved. "Here. I already wrote you a check."

Noah took it without reading the sum. Then he gave Chester a big hug. "Thank you for letting me be a part of your life for one night," he said. "It was an honor."

"You're too sweet," Chester said, seeming genuinely happy now. "I hope we see each other again soon."

"You've got my number!" Noah said. "Goodbye. Take care of yourself."

"You too," Chester said, walking him to the door.

Noah breathed out once he was in the elevator. Nothing too serious. Chester found the mornings a little confusing, that's all. Noah did too. His self-induced fantasies were starting to mess with his head. Part of him still felt giddy, like he and Harold really had hit it off and declared their love for each other. It wasn't difficult to understand how Chester took satisfaction in willful delusion, and hey, at least he'd had the real thing. A life spent with someone special. As Noah left the building and started walking toward the shelter, he tried to imagine how happy he would be if his own dreams became reality.

Something was wrong. Noah wasn't receiving any assignments. Five days had gone by, each more grueling than the last. He kept texting Marcello every afternoon, the responses all variations of: *Sorry, nothing for you today.* Noah had gone back into penny-pinching mode, eating breakfast and dinner at the shelter and making sandwiches when hungry in between.

More upsetting than the lack of work was Harold. He was gone. After leaving Chester's apartment, Noah had decided to play it cool and let Harold chase after him. An entire day passed with no contact, so he had given in and texted. The reply didn't make him happy.

Traveling with a client. Not sure how long it'll be. I'll text you when I'm back. Or you can call if you have any questions or problems.

That was nice, but Noah lacked an excuse to contact him because he wasn't going on any assignments. He missed working. Having an occupation—no matter how dubious—gave him a sense of purpose. Without regular work, he was back in the library, reading books to pass the time, or walking the streets for exercise and sunshine. His life felt empty again. No Harold, no challenges, no money, and no fun.

He was so desperate for human contact that upon arriving at Jerusalem in the evening, he was ecstatic when Edith told him he had a letter.

"It just came in the morning," she said. "Right after you left. I told the mailman to chase you down the street. He didn't think that was funny, which is fine, because I wasn't kidding."

Noah accepted the letter gratefully, even nodding at the glowering bouncer—Pete—and not feeling bothered when the gesture wasn't returned. "Thanks," he told Edith.

"Who is Tim Wyman? A friend of yours?"

"Huh?" Noah glanced down at the letter. That it had come from Ryan was no surprise. Seeing who it was addressed to gave him pause.

To: Tim Wyman

c/o Noah Westwood

Real subtle. Feeling less enthusiastic about the contents, he shoved it into his back pocket. "Friend of a friend," he answered.

"Ah," Edith said. "Well, if your friend needs a place to stay, he's welcome here too. You can't share a room though. Speaking of which, your rent is due tomorrow. Don't forget!"

Noah swallowed. "I'm not sure I'll be staying."

"Why not?" Edith said, already sounding upset.

"Money is tight." As in, he wasn't sure when he'd be seeing more, if ever. He still had well over a thousand dollars in the bank. Chester had been generous, and Noah had been careful. He intended to remain so.

"You let me know," Edith said. "Not everyone can pay on time. That is okay."

He nodded his thanks, then went upstairs, attempting to enjoy the room while he still could. The privacy was appreciated, but he didn't have much to do there except charge his phone and wait for someone to contact him. Speaking of which…

He pulled out the letter, shaking his head at the way it was addressed before opening it. Three pages long. Front and back. He glanced at the top of each page, searching for his own name. When he didn't find it, he double-checked the envelope. Nothing. Ryan had written a long letter to Tim, but hadn't bothered to say anything directly to Noah. He was so irritated by this that he stuffed the letter back in the envelope without reading it. Noah wouldn't be able to deliver it anyway. Not when so cut off from Marcello's world.

Feeling frustrated, he sent the man in question another text. *Anything?*

Afraid not, Marcello responded. *Patience is a virtue!*

So is hope, he shot back, but he might as well have been talking to himself. Noah flopped back in bed and stared at the ceiling. He was pretty sure Marcello was cutting him off on purpose. He hadn't gone on the fisting date, and that had no doubt pissed Marcello off. As gruesome as the prospect sounded, now he wished he had at least tried. Then again, maybe not. There were some things he wasn't willing to do for money. Noah considered searching for another job but felt just as trapped as before. Without an education, job history, or a reference, he wasn't likely to get much. Still, he had a phone. Marcello would probably take that away too, but he hadn't yet. Applying for a fast food job would be easier now. Tomorrow he would start looking.

The light outside began to fade. It was nearing dinner time, but he didn't have an appetite. Not for food. Grabbing his phone again, Noah sent another text, this time to Harold. He thought long and hard before he sent it, deciding that he didn't have anything to lose.

I miss you. Can't wait until you're back.

To his delight, the response was almost immediate.

I'm at the airport! Just landed. Got a dinner invite, but tomorrow?

As in them seeing each other? Absolutely! *Cool,* Noah texted back. *I'll see you in the afternoon.*

This improved Noah's mood considerably. He wished he could be careless with his money because he wanted to buy a new outfit so he could look his best tomorrow. When the day came, Noah made sure he was just as polished as when going on a date. Freshly shaved, showered, and wearing clothes warm from the dryer, he showed up at Harold's house feeling great, naturally high from their impending reunion.

When Harold threw open the door, hair mussed like he'd just woken from a nap... There had been a time when Ryan wasn't able to get his drugs. Five miserable days for them both. Ryan suffered all sorts of withdrawal symptoms, both emotional and physical. Noah suffered the brunt of his ever-shifting moods. When Ryan finally got more heroin, he had cried tears of joy, even before the needle slid into his arm. Noah hadn't understood that at the time, and didn't want to, but this was close. Seeing Harold again felt good. Too good!

"Check you out!" Harold said, looking him over. "Got a date soon?"

"Not unless you're taking me to dinner."

Harold laughed at this, then gestured for him to enter. "I am *pooped*!" he said once they were in the kitchen. "Coffee?"

"Sure." Noah didn't like coffee breath, but if they both had it, and they just happened to kiss, neither would notice. The idea was almost too exciting to contemplate.

"You look happy," Harold said. "How have things been? Marcello still throwing you curve balls? I kept waiting for you to call."

Noah now wished he had, even without a good excuse. "Actually, I haven't had an assignment since Chester."

Harold paused before filling two mugs. "Did something go wrong?"

"It was fine," he said quickly. "Chester is really nice."

"Yeah, he is. So you just wanted the time off or what?"

"Nope." Noah accepted a mug, then followed Harold's lead and sat at the kitchen table. "I keep asking Marcello for work, and he keeps saying there isn't any."

"That happens. I didn't work once for two weeks. A lot of our guys must have started dating, or had more important things, like business or traveling. They don't always take you with them."

"That's right! Where did you go?"

"Puerto Rico."

"Really? Wow! What was that like?"

"It's a tiny little island," Harold said with a grin. "I love it there, but the guy I was with is a total bully. He's always telling people off, or shoving his way to the front of a line. You wouldn't believe the amount of clothes I had to take with me. He made me change three times in one day."

"You had to change your outfit?"

Harold shrugged. "Dude's a control freak. He's got family down there, and they really get it bad. I'd never want to hang out with him for free, but at least he's handsome."

Noah felt a stirring of jealousy. Were looks so important to Harold? Noah couldn't say they didn't matter, but personality counted for more. He had learned that from dating Ryan. As pretty as he was, and as amazing as the sex had been, Ryan's sour moods tended to overshadow any of his good traits. What use is a handsome face if you can't stand to be around it?

"Coffee too strong?" Harold asked, misinterpreting his expression.

"No. I just, uh... I'm just overwhelmingly jealous. I've never been out of the country. I've never even left Texas."

"No! Really?"

"For real," Noah said. "Am I missing much?"

"Wow," Harold said, chuckling and shaking his head. "Um... Yeah, it's a big world out there, but if you ask me, nothing beats home. Know what I mean?"

Noah nodded eagerly, even though ages had passed since he'd been there. Despite his parents kicking him out, the farm in Fort Stockton was still home, and he did sometimes long to return. "Did you take any photos? Show me what I'm missing."

Harold rose to get his phone, then moved one of the kitchen chairs closer to Noah to show him everything. They were sitting near enough for their arms to touch occasionally. He found this distracting, so most of the photos were lost on him, especially those consisting of scenery. Some were of Harold and his client, who as it turned out, was just okay-looking. The best photo was on the beach, Harold bare-chested and brown. His body wasn't exceptional. His muscles were small and not overly toned, but it didn't matter, because he was so damn beautiful. That smile managed to outshine the sun!

"Don't look too envious," Harold said, noticing him gawping. "There must have been something in the water, because I spent most of the next day on the pot."

"Gross!" Noah cried. "Tell me your client isn't into that sort of thing."

"I wouldn't put it past him," Harold said, shoulders shaking with laughter. "I felt cruddy, but I was glad for the night off."

"A little downtime can be good." Noah fought down a smile. "Like tonight. Got any plans?"

"None!" Harold said. "What were you thinking?"

He was about to suggest they go out to dinner, and afterwards find somewhere to dance off the calories. Then he remembered who he was dealing with. "How about a nice night at home? We could smoke up, watch something on Netflix, and have food delivered."

Harold grinned. "You're speaking my language! That's exactly what I'm in the mood for. Why wait? We can start now. Be right back."

He guessed that meant getting stoned right away. Noah didn't really need to get high. He was already buzzing, but he wanted to stay on the same wavelength. With the entire evening clear, who knew where it could lead. Tonight might be the night!

The phone on the table rumbled. The one belonging to

Harold. He frowned at it, having a bad feeling. He was even tempted to pick it up, read the message or whatever, and clear it if need be, not wanting anything to interfere with the evening they had planned.

"I should have drained this before I left town," Harold said, returning with his bong. "The water stinks! Just let me get it rinsed out and we can start."

Noah nodded, debating if he should mention the notification. Maybe it wasn't even a message. It could be spam, or a retweet, or something else. Like an emergency. What if Harold's mom was in the hospital and she needed her son?

"Your phone vibrated," Noah said before he could stop himself.

Harold looked over while standing at the sink. "Oh. Okay." He didn't stop his work. Only when the bong had been washed out with dish soap and was rinsed did he set it on the counter and return to the table. He picked up the phone, looked at it, and grunted. "The hell? I'm supposed to have today off!"

"What's up?" Noah asked, already feeling disappointment.

"I've got a date tonight," Harold said, rolling his eyes in exasperation. "Damn… I just got back into town!"

"Do you have to accept?"

"It would be lame to cancel with such short notice. Sorry, man."

In other words, the evening was ruined. Or maybe not. They couldn't hang out, but Noah could still earn some brownie points. "I wouldn't mind the money. What if I take your place?"

Harold looked up from the phone with a hopeful expression. "Really? I don't want to ruin your night."

"I've had enough time off lately. Seriously. I don't mind."

"Wow! Okay. Uh…" Harold chewed his bottom lip. "I better ask Marcello."

"You didn't last time."

"And I got told off."

Noah's mouth dropped open. "Really? You didn't tell me that!"

"It's fine. I just have to run stuff like this by him." Harold's thumbs moved as he texted. Then he let the phone hang limp as he waited for a reply. When it came, he didn't like what he saw because he sent another, glaring at the screen while anticipating the answer. Then he sighed as if exasperated. "Sorry. Marcello wants me on this assignment. He says it's an important client. I don't really see why, but whatever. Apparently the other guys are all booked up. I told him if we're that busy, he needs to give you work too."

"Thanks," Noah said. "I didn't mean to get you in trouble."

"No big deal," Harold said, sitting at the table again. "We can still hang out, but I can't get high. Not before work."

"That's fine. Are you hungry, because—"

Now it was Noah's phone that rumbled. He didn't have to guess who it was. Marcello had texted his next assignment… with Marcello. "Check this out," Noah said, sliding the phone across the table.

Harold's face lit up. "Cool! That's a good sign. I bet Marcello just wants to get a feel for you—no pun intended—before he sends you out into the field again."

"I'm going on a date with him?"

"Yeah! Don't worry, it's usually a lot of fun. Last time we flew to Vegas. He gave me a literal bucket full of chips. You know, like the kind used in poker games? We blew through them all in a casino. I lost every single one, but Marcello didn't blink an eye. He thought it was funny. The next day he tells me to watch him play instead. He started out with a hundred bucks' worth and made the money back I lost. It took all night, but he did it!"

"Cool," Noah said, but he wasn't able to fake his enthusiasm. He was too worried that this date wouldn't be quite what it seemed. Somehow, he didn't think a carefree trip to Las Vegas or anywhere else was in his future.

Chapter Seven

Noah went shopping. His impending date with Marcello had him nervous, and he needed every scrap of confidence he could muster, even if that meant paying for it. No way was he going to feel like a country yokel in farmer clothes while mentally sparring with the man. Instead he bought a cranberry dress shirt and brown pants from H&M. He knew the clothes would have been much more expensive at other stores—and probably higher quality—but the seventy-five-dollar total already made him blanch. He told himself that the outfit could be repurposed for job interviews, if need be. Next he bought shoes, choosing a pair that were stylish and yet practical for walking. His footwear always took a pounding, so he felt less guilty about this purchase, but it drained another ninety bucks from his resources.

The expenses continued. Marcello wanted Noah to meet him at the studio, which wasn't convenient for walking. He could leave early and sweat in the heat, using a bus to get him as near as possible like last time. Or he could splurge on a taxi and show up in pristine condition. Noah debated this while in his private room at Jerusalem. He had paid the next week's rent, figuring he had enough to handle without losing his one semblance of a home. This made it even harder to justify spending more money.

He nibbled on a thumbnail while deliberating. Then he noticed a letter on the small table, the one Ryan had sent. Tim might be at the studio. Noah wasn't sure how likely that would be, but it was possible. He grabbed the letter and shoved it into his back pocket. Then he used his phone to go online and request a taxi. If this was his last hurrah, then he might as well go out in style. If it really was just a date, then he would probably make his money back by the end of the evening.

Half an hour later he was standing outside Studio Maltese. Back to where it had all begun. So much had changed since then. Noah had been half-starved and possibly delirious from too much sun when he had run through the building in a desperate bid for help. And he had gotten it, but not while being completely honest. Still, he had worked hard without complaint. Wasn't that worth anything? He went inside to find out.

Dave the security guard met him in the hallway. The man

took one look at him and tensed. "You aren't going to give me any trouble today, are you?"

Noah laughed. "Nope. I'm here to see Marcello, and this time he's actually expecting me."

He leaned against a wall while Dave made a call. When told to wait there, Noah did. Sort of. Dave went back into his office, leaving him free to poke his head inside the nearest room. Noah discovered a photo studio, the men standing near camera equipment briefly turning to consider him, but none of them had the legendary good looks of Tim Wyman. Ryan had showed him a photo once, and while Noah was sketchy on the details, he did remember feeling envious and insecure. None of the guys here made him feel that way. Maybe one of the other rooms? He crossed the hall to another door which led to a breakroom. Empty.

"Are you searching for me?" a voice trilled. "How flattering. I do love an open display of enthusiasm."

Noah spun around. Marcello filled the doorway, blocking any potential exit. He tried to remind himself that this was his date, not an adversary. Forcing himself to relax, he smiled. "When the famous Marcello Maltese asks you on a date, you don't want to leave anything to chance."

"Meaning?"

"You could have realized that I'm beneath you and found someone better-looking to take you out."

Marcello didn't seem bowled over by this attempt at flattery. "You're not beneath me," he said. "Not yet, anyway. Shall we go?"

"Okay."

Noah followed his boss outside to where a car was waiting. He was too jittery to notice what kind, but the back was spacious. The front included its own driver. That was something. He slid into the back seat next to Marcello, wishing he could enjoy this luxury, but dread still tainted everything. As the vehicle pulled out of the parking lot, he braced himself for difficult questions. Marcello remained silent. Noah had only met the man once before, but during the encounter, Marcello had kept a firm grip on the conversation, steering it where he wanted it to go.

Maybe this was a test. Noah had worried that this date was an opportunity for Marcello to confront him about his past, but maybe this was more like an employee evaluation. Noah had been on a few dates, and then Marcello had cut him off until he could assess if Noah was a good fit for the job or not. Time to make small talk and prove himself!

"Where are we going?" seemed too simple and boring, so instead he asked "What's a guy like you do for fun?"

"If you're asking what I'm into," Marcello said, "the answer is yes."

Noah grinned. "I didn't mean sexually."

"Nor did I. You'll find there is very little in this world that doesn't interest me." Marcello's smile was warm, but something about his tone was hard. Unforgiving.

"Where are we going?" Noah asked, deciding that simple and boring was fine after all.

"It's a surprise," Marcello said. "Even I'm not sure where we'll end up. We might be there already." He looked out the window at an intersection dominated by fast food chains and pharmacies. "No. No, this won't do at all. Drive on!"

Was he being funny? Should Noah laugh? Ugh! He needed to get into the zone. If this was a test, he was failing fast. "I'm flattered that you want to spend time with me. The big boss man! I mean… wow."

"You needed work," Marcello said with a shrug. "Enough that you complained to poor Harold, apparently."

"I didn't!" Noah said. Then he reconsidered. "Okay, I did, but not because I thought he would talk to you about it. I swear."

"I don't mind. I've always taken great pleasure in stimulating the economy."

"But I didn't—" Noah was getting worked up, while Marcello sat there in his perfectly tailored gray suit—vest and all—without so much as a bead of sweat on his forehead. Noah decided to abandon any pretense of being charming or debonair and just be himself. "I don't need a pity date, if that's what this is."

"I assure you it isn't," Marcello said. "In fact, I am devoid of pity. I find it rarely serves me well, either elevating me to arrogance or making me a victim of my own assumptions."

Was that a reference to him giving Noah a chance? Did he regret it? "I appreciate the work you've given me," he said. "I'm still trying to find my feet, but it's already been very helpful. I hope Chester and the others are satisfied with my performance.

If you're trying to find out how good I am on a date, just know that you make me nervous as hell, but that I'm usually better than this. I feel confident that I make my clients happy. I just don't know if I can do the same for you."

Marcello was quiet for a few blocks. When they drove down a ramp and merged onto the highway, he sighed. "Nothing quite so disarming as the truth. Let's make that a theme of the night, shall we?"

Noah didn't answer. Some truths were too dangerous. Marcello was aware of that. He had promised to find out Noah's secret. If only Noah had invented a story in the interim, a fake secret to replace the real one—a reason why he had known about Marcello, his business, and his friends. Who wouldn't find that threatening? It was a miracle that Noah had made it this far, but perhaps it wasn't too late. There had to be another feasible explanation. Anything besides a psychotic boyfriend who had put a bullet in one of Marcello's closest companions.

"Ah! Here we are!"

Noah looked up, so lost in thought that he didn't realize how far they had traveled. They were at an airport. Not Bergstrom International, which he had visited once out of sheer boredom, but one much smaller. *Austin Executive Airport*, a sign declared. Noah noticed the hangar, a two-story building next to it, and a large free-standing roof that was designed to provide protection against the elements. Not just for people, but vehicles as well, including planes. A private jet was currently parked beneath the roof, the car making a beeline for it.

"We're flying somewhere?" he asked in disbelief.

"It would seem we are," Marcello responded.

Noah grinned, his worries forgotten. "Really? I've never been on a plane!"

"Never?"

"Nope!" He pressed himself against the window, leaping out of the car the second it stopped. Then he walked around the jet while laughing. This was too cool! He finished making a loop and found Marcello waiting next to the open stairs. He seemed taken aback.

"You have no concerns?"

"About flying? No way. I can't wait!"

Marcello smiled gently. "Then let us depart immediately."

Noah shook his head. "This isn't like TV at all! Where are the other passengers? Don't we need tickets? What about the TSA? We're not allowed to wear shoes when we go through security, right?"

Marcello waved a hand to silence his concerns. "You'll find this is nothing like television. It's a shame you haven't flown economy before. I'm afraid you won't fully appreciate what you're about to experience. Still, I do enjoy a B.J., and I'm sure you will too."

Noah laughed. "Is that what this is about? The mile-high club?"

"The abbreviation stands for Business Jet," Marcello explained. "I'm not sure what you're referring to, but that smile of yours has become rather unsavory."

Noah didn't buy the innocent act for a second. He went to the stairs and looked up them. Marcello put a hand on his back encouragingly. After seeking permission, Noah took the stairs two at a time, only stopping when he was close enough to touch the plane's rounded exterior. Then he walked inside. He counted seven seats, large and cushioned in ivory-colored leather. Toward the back was a door, the small room beyond sporting a kitchenette and another seat, possibly for a flight attendant. Noah took in every detail, murmuring words of amazement to himself.

When he looked toward the front of the plane, he saw Marcello standing there, his dark eyes shining. "How unfortunate that you're so secretive about your past," he said. "I'd like to know more about where you come from."

"I can tell you," Noah said. As a peace offering. He understood that Marcello wanted answers that Noah wasn't willing to give, but he could at least be open about the rest of his life. First they met the captain, then they were seated and the aircraft began taxiing to the runway. Every ding and blinking light attracted his full attention, and when the plane accelerated and took off, he felt the same mixture of fear and amazement that he associated with roller coasters. The view was spectacular. Austin fell away beneath them, the buildings and cars soon resembling the model village on Harold's dining room table. As they rose higher, the tiny city was hidden beneath a soft ocean of clouds.

Eventually he turned toward Marcello, a grin plastered on his face. "We're flying!"

"Indeed! I had nearly forgotten what a wonder this is. I've taken it for granted in recent years."

"Do you fly like this every day? Is this your plane?"

"No and no," Marcello said. "You see this button here? One push and it will allow your chair to swivel. I know the view isn't as impressive, but I believe you promised me an enlightening conversation." He demonstrated, turning his chair toward the narrow aisle.

Noah did the same so they were facing each other and resisted the urge to see if he could spin in a circle. "What do you want to know?"

"I could be wrong, but it's unusual for someone your age to have never flown before. Where exactly are you from?"

"I'm surprised you haven't found out on your own," Noah teased.

"Fort Stockton," Marcello answered instantly, "but that is an unrevealing fact. I want a story, not statistics."

"Oh." Noah considered giving him the romanticized version, like Harold had coached him to do, but he didn't think that's what Marcello wanted. Instead he began by talking about his parents, the versions of them that he knew as a kid. Supportive and loving, firm but fair. Then he spoke of his shift in awareness.

"You're familiar with Genesis, right? The Bible chapter, not the band. My life was a lot like that. My parents provided for me in the same way that God did for Adam and Eve. They loved and protected me. I never thought that would change, but all it took was something small."

"Like an apple?" Marcello suggested.

"Exactly, and I was definitely tempted by a snake." He meant this to be a joke, but he said it in tones too somber. "The apple symbolizes knowledge. Adam and Eve became self-aware, and somehow that's supposed to be a sin. For a while, I actually agreed. Figuring out I was gay felt like a curse, and I wished I could go back to the way I was before. Ignorance is bliss."

"I've always found the opposite to be true."

Noah thought about it and nodded. "I agree with you. I didn't back then, but I do now. I'm better off this way. I just wish it hadn't come at a cost. I always thought it was messed up that God cast Adam and Eve out of the Garden. What sort of parent does that?"

"The kind who turn their back on a child for any reason,"

Marcello said grimly. "I take it your family was less than sympathetic?"

"Yeah. As soon as I accepted myself, they rejected me."

"I'm sorry to hear that." Marcello unbuckled his seatbelt and rose. "A drink will help ease the pain. What do you prefer?"

"Coke."

"I'll be back in two shakes of a lamb's tail."

Marcello returned a few minutes later with two glasses of champagne. "They were out of Coke," he said unapologetically. He handed a flute to Noah, then raised his own. "Here's to eating apples and charming snakes."

Noah grinned and clinked glasses. Then he drank, enjoying the taste. His first glass of champagne, but he wasn't about to admit that. He had already made a fool of himself over the plane.

"How do things stand between you and your parents now?" Marcello asked. "An uneasy truce?"

Noah shook his head. "We never see each other and barely speak. I've called home a few times. My mother will still talk to me. My father won't. I'm not sure which is worse, because all Mom has to say is that God will forgive me if I ask him."

Marcello sniffed. "He won't. I tried once while deeply intoxicated. I'm afraid God is the sort to hold a grudge. How old were you when tensions boiled over?"

"Sixteen," Noah said. "I've been on my own ever since."

"And you're twenty-two now. Has nothing changed over the previous six years? I don't have much experience in family matters, but from what I understand, most conflicts resolve themselves given enough time."

"Not my parents," Noah muttered. "I think it would take a new version of the Bible that says gay people are holier than angels. Even that might not change their minds."

"Well," Marcello said, swirling his near-empty glass, "I'm sure you've told that story to many people over the years, and I'm equally certain you've heard tiresome advice about how your parents will come around eventually and welcome you back with open arms. I happen to think you're better off without them. Free of their small-minded bigotry, you have a much better chance of attaining personal happiness."

"I'd feel better if I hadn't made a mess of my life since then."

"Oh? What happened? Tell me the rest."

Noah opened his mouth to do so. Maybe it was the champagne, or how Marcello seemed to care, because he was tempted to keep talking. That would quickly lead to Ryan, a subject he intended to avoid. Maybe he could tell the rest without mentioning him. Some of it Marcello probably knew already.

"I've been homeless ever since. For a while I stayed with friends, or slept in my car. These days I'm kind of on my own, but like I said, I'm really grateful for the opportunity you've given me. It's helped. A lot."

Marcello's expression remained neutral. He seemed to be waiting. For what, Noah wasn't sure, so it became a staring contest. Eventually Marcello set down his glass and rested his head on one fist. "Six years is a long time. Somehow you managed to sum it up with three—maybe four sentences? There must be more to the story than that."

"I know what you're really asking," Noah said.

"Good. Then you must also know the most appropriate answer. Tell me the truth. How did our lives become intertwined? I don't believe you were aware of me when you fled Fort Stockton. What happened between then and now?"

Noah shook his head. "I get that you've been trying to punish me by choosing the trickiest clients, but I don't care. I'm willing to do the work. Isn't that all that matters? If you're worried I'm going to tell people about the Gentlemen's Agreement Club, or try to blackmail anyone, I won't. I just want to work and finally get my life together. Please."

Marcello's eyes searched his, moving repeatedly from one to the other. Then he nodded. "Very well." He pulled a cell phone from his jacket pocket, appeared to send a quick text, and turned his chair forward again. Were they done talking?

"You can trust me," Noah tried.

"I've done so already," Marcello said. "I'm not sure I appreciate the results."

"Why? What have I done?" Noah leaned forward, attempting to capture Marcello's attention again and failing. "Talk to me!"

His pleas were ignored. Noah sighed, flopped back in his chair, and tried to think of anything he had done wrong. The first two clients had been a learning experience, but he had performed well enough. The third... "I didn't ask Harold to change my assignment. That last one with Chester, he just offered. I didn't know it would get either of us in trouble!"

"Harold has a good heart," Marcello replied.

Meaning what? That Noah didn't? Or that Harold was too trusting and could easily be hurt? "You've been keeping us apart on purpose, haven't you? That's why you sent him out of town, and why he ended up working on his day off. You're trying to keep him away from me."

"You have the order reversed," Marcello said, attention on his phone again.

"You want to keep me away from him? Why? Just because I—" Marcello was extremely well informed. Noah wasn't sure how he knew half the things he did, but even he couldn't see into another man's heart.

"I'm very interested in the remainder of that sentence," Marcello replied.

"I'm sure you are," Noah mumbled. Then he turned his own chair forward. The plane had dipped and was descending. He was pretty sure they hadn't flown long enough to really get anywhere. Most likely they would land at the same airport in Austin where Noah would officially be fired.

If this was a tactic, it was working. He didn't want to lose anything. Not the job and definitely not Harold. His one comfort was that Marcello couldn't stop them from seeing each other. Not unless he poisoned Harold's mind with lies. Or threatened his job as well. It wasn't hard to imagine what Harold would choose. The job he loved so much, or the guy he barely knew. Noah frowned, realizing just how true that was. Harold didn't know that Noah was homeless, or that his life had been a struggle for the past few years. Marcello might be right to keep them apart. Noah hadn't been dishonest exactly, but he wasn't very truthful either. He had been skating a thin line somewhere in between.

They passed through a bank of clouds, the ground reappearing below. Noah considered it glumly. Austin's skyline wasn't visible from this side of the plane. All he saw below was brown land and green trees. The private airport didn't appear nearly as magical from up here. Or as nice. Where was the building the jet had been parked beside? All he could see were two elongated aluminum hangars, which he definitely didn't remember. The airport they had left had been state-of-the-art, but now it seemed rundown.

They were landing elsewhere.

"Where are we?" he asked, feeling a jolt of panic as the wheels touched down.

"I haven't the foggiest," Marcello said. "Shall we go find out?"

Noah could refuse. Maybe this is how Marcello dealt with his problems, by flying troublemakers out to the middle of nowhere and leaving them to rot. Or by making sure they couldn't return. How much would it cost to clean this private jet if his blood splattered the seats? Was he any safer inside?

"Come along!" Marcello said, already up and moving toward the exit. "I never could stand suspense."

Noah followed, reassuring himself that if Ryan hadn't been killed, then he wasn't likely to be either.

Marcello wasn't in the best position to lecture him about transparency because he definitely knew where they were. A car met them on the runway. The second they were inside, it whisked them past dinky buildings, Noah straining to see a sign that might reveal their location, but the driver was in a hurry. They cruised along a mostly abandoned road that failed to offer any helpful clues, but when they merged onto I-84, Noah knew. He had driven down that same road the week before.

They had landed in Gatesville. They were here to see Ryan.

Noah's mind raced in an attempt to do damage control. He could admit to having known Ryan once. That was unsavory, but it would explain why he knew the things he did. After casually checking the dashboard clock, he saw that visiting hours were over. Marcello might bluff and say they would ask Ryan how he and Noah knew each other, but it wasn't going to happen. Not today. Noah could claim that they had parted ways a long time ago and were no longer in touch. Not exactly true, but it might be enough to allow him to keep his job. And remain friends—if not more—with Harold.

The car slowed and pulled over. It was damn near the same spot where Noah had stopped previously. The prison had just come into view, a bleak concrete fortress that had everything in common with despair.

"Still feeling tight-lipped?" Marcello asked. "Fine. I'll tell you my version of events."

"Wait," Noah said.

"Why should I?" Marcello snapped. "I've given you ample opportunity to explain yourself. I told you we would meet again at the finish line." He jabbed a finger toward the prison. "*That* is the finish line, and we are about to cross it, whether you are willing or not!"

"Okay," Noah said weakly. No sense in lying now, or trying to pass off half-truths. If any chance of salvation remained, it would only come through honesty. "Ryan was the first guy I ever fell in love with."

"Which shows exceedingly bad taste."

"Which shows how young I was!" Noah shot back. "After my parents kicked me out and I finally found someone willing to love me again—" His voice faltered, but he forced himself to continue. "I had friends. I wasn't alone, but that's not the same. I was pretty sure my parents didn't actually love me anymore, so yes, I fell for Ryan quicker than I should have, and I couldn't bring myself to let him go, even when it got really bad, because he's all I had left."

"A depth of poverty beyond comprehension," Marcello said, still glaring. "Parting ways with that brat would have made you vastly richer."

Noah stared at him. Then he shook his head and reached for the door. "You obviously don't know what love is. Goodbye." He yanked at the handle, but the stupid thing was locked. He looked at the driver, who steadfastly ignored him, even when Noah yelled that he wanted out. Then he felt a hand on his shoulder. This only made him more eager to escape.

"Please," Marcello said. "Calm down. I do know what love is. If anything, love is what has me so angry. Imagine the tables were turned and it was my friend who had shot Ryan instead. How would you then feel about me?"

Noah stopped trying to escape. "I wouldn't blame you for what someone else did."

"I'm not blaming you," Marcello said, "but you must admit that it's highly suspicious. Had you shown up at my office that day and been open about your history—"

"You would've been so impressed with my honesty that you would have trusted me completely? Really?"

Marcello seemed to consider the scenario. "I suppose I still might have wondered if there was some greater scheme at play."

"Exactly," Noah said. "If it was up to me, you never would have found out, because none of it has anything to do with you. My history with Ryan—hell, even my present with him—is none of your business."

"Ah, and we were doing so well," Marcello said, his tone cold again.

"Meaning?"

"Tim Wyman's welfare *is* my business. Are you telling me that Ryan hasn't asked you to speak with Tim on his behalf? Or perhaps he wanted you to—oh, I don't know—deliver a letter?"

Noah's mouth dropped open. How did he know these things? Was he psychic or— None of that mattered. The situation was spiraling out of control. The last thing Noah wanted was for Marcello to think he had some ulterior motive. He imagined that impression getting back to Harold, like Noah had just gotten friendly with him as part of a ruse. He needed to prove beyond a shadow of a doubt that he could be trusted.

Noah leaned forward, reached into his back pocket, and pulled the letter free. Then he thrust it out. "Here. I haven't read it yet. Do whatever you want. Burn the stupid thing, I don't care."

Marcello took it tentatively, examining the address. "You haven't read it?" He sounded more curious than angry.

"Nope."

"Why not?"

Noah took a deep breath. "Because he didn't bother to write me at the same time, and because it'll be the same stupid things Ryan always said when Tim's name came up."

"Enlighten me."

Noah crossed his arms over his chest. "He'll say they had a good start, but Ryan was still upset over the way his family treated him, so he turned to drugs, which made him cheat, which made Tim cheat, and it was all a big misunderstanding, but if they could only try one more time…" He shook his head in disgust.

"Ryan would say such things while you two were dating?"

"Yeah," Noah said. "I don't think he meant to hurt me. He was just really messed up over the whole situation. Tortured, like he couldn't get past it. I learned to change the subject whenever Tim was mentioned, or at least not feed into it, because he'd get really upset."

"Upset enough to attempt a triple homicide."

Noah exhaled. "I don't think that was his intention."

"Have you read the police report?"

"No."

Marcello pulled out his phone, tapping the screen for the better part of a minute. Then he handed the device to Noah. "I have my own reading to do," he said, opening the letter. "Please. Feel free."

Noah couldn't concentrate at first. He knew many of the details. He had often been there in court but always struggled to focus, not only because of the conflicted emotions raging inside of him, but also due to the confusing legal proceedings. Back in the present, he noticed that Marcello hadn't left the screen at the top of the police report. Instead it showed an account of events according to the victim, Benjamin Bentley. Noah knew next to nothing about him, just that he was the guy Tim had cheated on Ryan with, and that he had still been around when Ryan showed up at their house with a gun.

The victim, Benjamin Bentley, describes the suspect, Ryan Hamilton, as being shaky and irrational. After entering through the backyard entrance without permission or announcement, the suspect proceeded to the kitchen where he pointed a firearm at both residents present, demanding that one, Jason Grant, identify himself. The suspect became increasingly agitated during this, stating "Tell me or I'll put a bullet in his head." Suspect made various accusations toward Bentley (see witness statement Attmt. A), before Bentley stepped in front of Grant in an effort to shield him. Another resident, Tim Wyman, arrived on the scene and entered the home. In the course of trying to reason with the suspect, Hamilton turned the gun on Wyman. The conversation quickly escalated (see witness statement Attmt. C) before the suspect discharged the firearm, striking Wyman in the upper left shoulder and—

Noah clenched his jaw and looked away. He could barely listen as events were described in court, skipping the most crucial dates, because the bare-bone facts were difficult enough to accept. Ryan, the guy who had on more than one occasion cried in his arms, who was so hurt over the people who had abandoned him, and who had often kissed Noah on the nose and whispered, "Thank you for loving me" before they drifted off to sleep—how could he be this same monster?

"The line about putting a bullet in young Jason's head haunts me most." Marcello's attention was still on the letter. "I don't believe you've met him. Jason is humble and unassuming. Friendly as well. Perhaps it would help you to imagine Harold instead. Think of him being on the other end of a gun, and having to stand there and watch his father not only get shot, but slowly bleed out on the kitchen floor."

"Jason is Tim's son?"

"Yes, and if it wasn't for his quick thinking, Tim would have died that day, and your friend Ryan would be facing the death penalty. In that way you owe Jason a debt of gratitude. Excuse me a moment."

Marcello finished reading, Noah not having the courage to do the same. He didn't need to know every detail. The crime Ryan had committed was horrendous. Noah had never disputed that.

"Interesting," Marcello said, looking away from the letter. "I take it you and Ryan are no longer involved?"

God how he wished he could deny it! "Technically we never broke up, but in my mind, the relationship is over."

"It would seem you are in agreement, unless I am misinterpreting this part here." Marcello tapped a paragraph, then handed the letter to Noah so he could read it.

There's a reason you found me outside the bar that night. There's also a reason our stories are so similar. We both came from the same place. Our parents were cold. We grew up without love. The only difference is that I didn't have an Eric. Or maybe I did. You were my Eric, but I was too young and stupid to let you help me. I'm not now. I need you. Not just your forgiveness or your love but your testimony, because if that doesn't happen, then I don't think we can be together. I'm willing to take whatever I can get. This time I won't mess up. I won't hurt you. You're my guardian angel, Tim. I just need one more chance. I'm all alone. Please.

Noah clenched his jaw. Part of him felt betrayed, which was dumb because he didn't want to be with Ryan anymore. Noah had moved on too, both physically and emotionally. What did he care if Ryan would rather be with Tim? This wasn't a revelation. He had reached the same conclusion long ago, knowing that someone like Ryan wouldn't want him normally. Only because Ryan had been so hurt over the guy he couldn't have did he settle for Noah.

Betrayal was one emotion competing for his attention. Anger was another. *I'm all alone.* What the hell? Noah had made the effort to visit Ryan. He hadn't managed often, but he had written more letters than he could count, and just the other day, sent extra money to Ryan despite the uncertainty of his employment.

He scowled as he scanned the paragraph again. "Who's Eric?"

"That's none of your concern. Were you aware of Ryan's intent?"

Noah shook his head, not understanding. Then he saw the line about testimony again. "Why would he want Tim to testify? The trial ended years ago."

Marcello scrutinized him. "You truly weren't aware? Ryan didn't confide in you about his plans?"

Noah started flipping through the letter, searching for keywords. "He didn't say anything to me last week when I visited."

"He intends to file an appeal."

Noah looked up. "Will that work?"

"That depends on his goal. A reduced sentence? Perhaps. His immediate release? I sincerely doubt it. Not while blood still pumps through these veins."

"What are you going to do?"

Marcello considered him. "I'm still deciding if I should trust you or not."

Noah didn't know how to prove himself. Trust usually came with time and experience, and they had very little of either together. He supposed the one thing he could do was finally answer Marcello's initial question. "After my parents kicked me out, I stayed with friends I had been chatting with online. By stay, I mean I would park in front of their house and sleep in my car. Part of me liked the freedom, the rest was still hurting. That changed when I met Ryan. He made me feel loved. I don't think that was a lie, and I definitely loved him back. The drugs changed him. Me too, I guess, because I started questioning our relationship. We were together for almost two years at this point. We got into a really bad argument just before he disappeared. That's when Ryan shot Tim. You'll probably hate me for what I say next, but I knew nobody else would be there for him. Not his family, that's for sure, and Ryan didn't have many friends. Love is supposed to be unconditional. As far as I was concerned, all was forgiven. Tim hadn't died. I thought jail would force Ryan to get clean so we could start over. I sold my car to pay for his lawyer, not that it helped. Ryan was locked up anyway, and I was left with even less than before. It sucked to lose the car, but what I really missed was him. The streets are a lot scarier on your own. I survived though. Not that I didn't run into trouble."

He looked over to see if Marcello was even interested in his story anymore. He had the older man's full attention. Marcello even nodded encouragingly. "Go on."

Noah hesitated, eyes darting to the driver. "This is where it gets personal. For both of us."

"I understand. Charles, would you mind?"

The driver nodded and stepped out of the car. The keys remained in the ignition, the air conditioner still running.

Noah swallowed. "I stay at a homeless shelter downtown called Jerusalem."

"I'm familiar with it," Marcello said.

"Oh. Well, one night about a month ago, I had missed dinner because I dozed off in a park. I was hungry. Starving. Another homeless guy sitting next to me on a bench heard my stomach growling and offered me food. Kind of. He showed me the food, but then he asked me to—" Noah hesitated before remembering who he was talking to. "He wanted to suck my dick. I didn't let him. I barely slept that night I was so hungry, but I kept telling myself I was worth more. Then I started asking myself how much. I knew I had a price. More than a couple slices of bologna and some stale bread, that's for sure. Ryan had told me about your escort service. More like ranted, especially once he was locked up. He blames you for a lot of things."

Marcello sniffed. "My conscience is clear. I did nothing to him save inform Tim when Ryan started having unprotected sex with virtual strangers. Once you settled on your plan, did you inform Ryan of your intent to seek me out?"

"No. He just found out last week. I didn't want him to know at all. I'm guessing you think I wanted to infiltrate your business, maybe so we could blackmail you. I swear there's nothing going on like that."

"Maybe not, but the heart is a fickle thing. You might decide that you want Ryan back after all. If I let things continue the way they have, I would be putting myself in an increasingly vulnerable position."

"That won't happen!"

Marcello patted his hand as if he were being naïve. "It might. You can't guarantee that it won't."

"I can," Noah said, pulling his hand away. He knew what he needed to say, his throat tight with anticipation. "It won't happen because all my heart cares about is someone else."

Marcello locked eyes with him. "Who?"

Noah looked toward the front. He could see the driver leaning against the hood, head bobbing to whatever was streaming through his earbuds. He supposed it didn't matter if he did overhear, or if the whole world found out, because Marcello would probably make sure they never saw each other again.

"Harold," he croaked. "I like him. A lot. It might be love."

"You barely know each other," Marcello said dismissively.

"So? What difference does that make?"

Marcello paused. Then he chuckled. "Very little, come to think of it." He was quiet a moment, leaning back against the cushioned seats as if wanting to get comfortable. "I asked myself this morning if there was anything you could possibly say to win me over. Had you been more forthcoming… Experience has taught me that some people will lie and continue to lie until you have them cornered and they're left with no other choice."

"I didn't lie," Noah said. "I just didn't want you to find out about my past because I knew it would damn me."

"It's your future that concerns me more, and you *did* tell a lie that first day in my office."

He thought about it and winced. "Okay, I did. I was desperate."

"And we both know what desperation can drive a person to do." Marcello nodded toward the prison.

"I'm not him."

"No," Marcello said. "You aren't. For one, you're not averse to hard work, and you do seem grateful for the help you receive."

"Just give me another chance," Noah said. "I'll do anything. Two clients a day? No problem."

"Your work ethic hasn't been called into question, but you do face a difficult decision. We stand at a crossroad." Marcello glanced out the window. "Hm. I should have instructed Charles to stop at an intersection. How poetic that would have been!"

Noah grinned, but the words that came next made him somber again.

"It's time to determine the nature of our relationship," Marcello continued. "I can either be your enemy, or I can be your friend. Whichever you choose has a direct consequence in regard to your relationship with Ryan. As my friend, you must sever all ties with him. As my enemy, you will be in my line of fire should you choose to stand by his side. I don't make idle threats. Decide now."

Noah swallowed and looked at the prison. He put himself behind those chilly stone walls and tried to imagine being surrounded by people who had committed worse crimes. Murderers. Rapists. Child molesters. No loving parents would be there to provide hugs and reassurance on visitation day. Not even an ex-boyfriend. Just unhappy memories of the past and a future without hope. He didn't hate Ryan. Noah loved him. That didn't mean he wanted to continue their relationship, but he did intend to be there for him as a friend. And yet, doing so would mean losing a good job, a potential relationship, and a future that wasn't on the streets.

Noah tore his eyes away from the prison. Ryan was trapped there because of mistakes he had chosen to make. Noah hadn't stood idly by and let him. He had cried and shouted to try to get him off the drugs, pleaded with him to forget about Tim both before and after the shooting, and sold his only means of transport to see that Ryan received a fair trial. Hadn't he done enough? And what had Noah gotten in return? Guilt trips, a bruised self-esteem, and a whole lot of misery by association.

"Take your time," Marcello said, sounding just as patient as the words themselves.

"I've already decided." Noah locked eyes with the large man. "I'll do what you want."

"Oh?"

"On one condition."

"Naturally. Let's hear it."

Noah steeled himself. "If I agree to not see Ryan anymore, I want it to be like I never knew him at all. As far as you're concerned, I'm just some guy who overheard a rumor about the Gentlemen's Agreement Club and decided he wanted a piece of the action. No more punishing me for what I didn't do."

"In other words," Marcello said, "a clean slate."

"Yeah. I know you can't make yourself forget—"

"I've certainly done my best to try. Speaking of which, let's wrap this up. I'm getting thirsty."

Noah gritted his teeth. "This isn't an easy decision for me!"

"I understand, but your willingness to bargain reveals that you have already made up your mind."

"Don't think I can't change it again!"

"I have no doubt, but you've already demonstrated many times over that, when you decide on a course of action, you see it through to the bitter end, and we both know just how bitter your relationship with Ryan has become. What you really desire is a sweet new beginning. Am I wrong?"

"No." His voice sounded hoarse to his own ears. Noah was tempted to look back at the prison again, but if he was going to do this, he might as well start now. He offered his hand. "No more Ryan."

Marcello studied him, then gripped his palm and shook it. "Music to my ears. Now then, you've given me what I want. It would be remiss of me not to extend the same courtesy. What can I do for you?"

Noah's mouth moved, but no sound came out. Most people probably had a burning desire or two that they could easily name, but needs and wishes were all he had left. How could he possibly choose from among them?

"I'll make it easy on you," Marcello said. "Let's begin with our surroundings. Surely there is somewhere you would rather be. The jet is still fueled and waiting at the airport. Pick a place."

"Uhhh."

"Come now! The deserts of New Mexico, the mountains of Colorado. Or perhaps you would rather travel east instead. How do you feel about Cajun?"

"The food?"

"The boys! They have a certain charm: laidback and patient at times, simmering and spicy at others. Now that you mention it, I suppose they aren't so different from gumbo."

Noah made a face. "The green guy?"

"You're thinking of Gumby. This won't do at all! How can we enjoy each other's company when you don't understand my jokes? You clearly need your horizons broadened. We'll start slow, don't worry."

"Just a finger or two?"

"Ha!" Marcello seemed pleased as he gestured for his phone. Once Noah returned it to him, he used it to send more texts. One must have been to Charles, who returned and got behind the wheel. Marcello nodded once, setting them in motion, expression still jovial as he tucked Ryan's letter in the inner pocket of his suit jacket. Only when the car made a U-turn did his expression grow serious, Marcello glancing in the direction of the prison with a disdainful sniff. Another enemy defeated, Noah supposed. He felt a chill, wondering what would have happened had he chosen to side with Ryan, but that fear was fleeting compared to the guilt settling into his stomach. Noah attempted to drown this with another glass of champagne, once they had boarded the business jet, but to little avail.

"Have you given any more thought to that wish?" Marcello asked as they soared above the clouds. They were seated, their chairs facing each other across the aisle again.

Noah decided to keep his wish simple. "I'd like to go on a date."

"I thought we were in the midst of one," Marcello said, winking to show he was only kidding. "If you're still trying to prove your work ethic, there's no need. You handled the challenges I set before you with immaculate grace. I'll put you back to work, never fear."

"So you really were out to get me!"

Marcello chuckled. "I was only trying to scare you away, and not entirely because of your history. I must admit there are aspects of this arrangement that have me ill at ease."

"Like what?"

"Statistics, particularly those relevant to homeless gay youth, who are much more likely to turn to sex work in an attempt to survive. I find myself somewhat torn on the issue. I've always been a proponent of consenting adults being allowed to reach their own agreements. If both you and a client find a beneficial arrangement, then who am I to judge? And yet, I didn't offer you all the options that I should have. I needed to learn more about you first, and when I discovered your connection to Ryan… My apologies. That issue is firmly in the past now. My point is that you've impressed me enough that I'm willing to offer you another position instead. The pay might not be as lucrative, but there are opportunities for advancement, and of course you would have an easier time explaining your work history to any future employers."

"What kind of job would it be?" Noah asked.

"We're a small studio. We don't have a mail room as such, but there are always correspondences to be weeded through and either discarded or answered. At times you might run errands for a photographer, or see to the needs of our more demanding models. In essence, you would be at the beck and call of anyone who requires your assistance."

"Not so different from my current job," Noah joked. "How much would it pay?"

Marcello told him, and while it was a respectable sum for an entry-level position, it didn't come close to the hundreds of dollars a night that he could earn as an escort. Noah had catching up to do. Most people his age had their own place to live, a car to get around with, and maybe even a savings account or retirement fund. Reaching the same status would be a lot easier if he kept tricking. Besides the money, he actually enjoyed the work. Meeting new people was fun, and he liked the challenge of figuring out how to make each client happy. Whether fulfilling needs emotional or physical, Noah ended each assignment feeling good about himself, like he had something special to offer. He had never felt that way before. Now that Marcello was on his side, he would probably get easier clients like Chester, but he felt capable of dealing with the thornier ones too.

"I appreciate the offer," he said, "but I'd like to keep the job I've got."

"It's yours," Marcello said, "although I don't feel it constitutes a satisfactory wish."

"That's because you misunderstood me," Noah said. "Even before you tried keeping Harold and me apart, he was usually busy at night. I was too. That's why I'm asking for a date. As a client."

"You want to employ Harold's services? Why not simply request a night off for you both?"

"Because I don't think he would agree," Noah said. "I, uh… This is embarrassing, so promise you won't laugh."

"You have my word," Marcello said solemnly.

"Harold asked me out already. That's what I thought, anyway. We had dinner, but it was just a training exercise, and worst of all, he figured out that I thought we were on a real date."

"Oh dear."

"Yeah." Noah covered his eyes briefly, as if this could erase the humiliating memory. "He let me down easy. Harold is generous like that, but he also said something about how this job requires him to stay single."

"Nonsense."

"I figured. I think I know what he means though. Most people would probably have mixed feelings about dating an escort, but I'm one too, so who better to understand where he's coming from?"

"Indeed," Marcello said with a nod. "I take it you're not the jealous type."

Noah shrugged. "I'd feel lucky if a guy like Harold noticed me, even for a little bit."

"How sweet," Marcello said. "You really do care for him, don't you?"

"Yes. It's not just that he's handsome. He seems like a nice guy, and he makes me laugh and—You know how adorable it is when a guy has a dog? Harold is like that with his house. He values it more than anything, even though he could have the world. Don't you think? If Harold wanted to marry some rich guy or backpack across the country or get an impressive job, he could. I figure Harold could have whatever and whoever he wants, but he chooses to stay at home, building models and getting high."

"And you find this endearing?"

"Not many people understand how precious a home is. When you don't have one, sometimes it's all you can think about."

Marcello nodded thoughtfully. "I often wonder if attraction is based on us recognizing what we ourselves lack."

"Everyone wants to feel complete," Noah said.

"I suppose so." Marcello clapped his hands together. "Very well! You shall have your date. At another time. I'm tired of competing with these other boys, both past and present. You're supposed to be my date!"

Noah pantomimed clocking in. "I'm all yours."

"All but one part," Marcello said. "It sounds as though your heart is already spoken for."

True enough. Noah wasn't sure if what he felt could be called love, but adoration, affection, infatuation, and so much more kept pulling him toward one destination. He only wished he knew how Harold would react once he got there.

Chapter Eight

Noah shifted to the right where sunlight made the sheets glow. He let this warm his face, entertaining all the memories he had made. Marcello had flown him to New Orleans, as promised, and after an amazing meal, walked with him through the streets of the French Quarter, pointing out significant architecture and telling the most scandalous stories of local history.

Not wanting to leave, they checked into a hotel (a suite!) and spent the next day shopping, eating, and playing tourist. They had arrived back in Austin late last night. Noah felt recharged. More than that, he felt cleansed. His past was finally behind him, the future full of promise. Especially the coming evening. With that in mind, he rose from bed and considered his little room in Jerusalem. He needed to put away the new clothes Marcello had bought him and find a place for the goofy souvenirs. What was he going to do with a costume mask or a jester's hat? It had been a long time since Noah owned anything frivolous.

First he decided to shower and eat, and see if the shelter needed help. They did. New beds had arrived, meaning many of the old frames had to be taken apart and the more tattered mattresses thrown away. Noah was glad to be of use. He hadn't worked for more than a week. As fun as his trip to New Orleans had been, he didn't leave the city feeling fulfilled.

By late afternoon when the work was finally done, Noah was ready for a little recreation. He had worked up enough of a sweat to justify another shower. Once back in his room, he felt his phone vibrate. Noah picked it up, grinning automatically when he saw the text message was from Harold. Had he heard the news? Did he know what tonight was going to bring?

Hey! I heard you're back in town. Are you at home?

Yup, Noah texted back. He sat on the bed. *Did you miss me?*

Yeah. I really did. What are you doing? Busy?

Just hanging out, Noah texted, eyes darting up a line to reread it. Harold had missed him! *What about you?*

I'm parked outside your place. I was in the area. Wanna hang out?

No! Well, yes, but this was bad! Harold wasn't waiting outside the shelter. No doubt he was at the nearby apartment complex and wondering which door belonged to Noah. The answer, of course, was none of them.

Bad time? Harold texted.

Not really, Noah responded. *I'll be right out. Just give me a few minutes.* He'd need more than that. Currently he was wearing nothing but his underwear. He stood and grabbed a shirt, but before he could put it on, another text distracted him.

No invite? I wanna see your place.

His fingers flew to respond. *It's too messy.*

You've seen where I live. It can't be much worse than that.

Next time? I'll be out in a minute. Noah tossed the phone on the bed, ignored it as he finished getting dressed, and hesitated despite the time crunch. He wanted to look nice, not just grab an outfit haphazardly. He ended up changing shirts twice. Then he struggled to locate his wallet and keys. Once he finally found them, he felt himself sweating again. What a disaster! He should be reveling in the fact that Harold had sought him out this time, had *missed him,* instead of scrabbling to maintain another lie. Did the apartment complex have any vacancies? If so, maybe after another week or two of work, he could get a place there and bring some truth to this ridiculous deception.

Noah rushed from his room and the shelter, rounding the corner of the busy street and aiming for a quieter neighborhood. How much time had gone by? Twenty minutes? More? He checked his phone again, seeing a text from a few minutes ago.

Should I go? We can meet later.

"Don't go!" Noah said out loud, breaking into a run. He forced himself to stop when the apartment complex came into view. He couldn't show up panting. When he saw the maroon convertible, his heart sank. The top was down. Harold stood outside the car while leaning against the door, his head occasionally turning toward the nearest apartments. Harold's back was to him, so if Noah could creep around the front of the car without him seeing and come at him from the side…

He nearly made it. Noah had just reached the back of the car when Harold spun around. His face lit up, but then his eyebrows shot back down in confusion.

Harold looked toward the building, then back again, jerking his thumb over his shoulder. "I thought you lived on this side?"

"I do," Noah said. "I just had to take out the trash." He glanced behind himself, praying for a dumpster to be near. Instead all he saw was a clubhouse and more parking spaces.

The confusion remained on Harold's features until he shrugged and flashed his easy smile. "How'd it go with Marcello?"

"Great!" Noah said, walking around the car to join him. "We finally set aside our differences."

"I bet!" Harold said with a knowing expression.

"Not like that! We didn't sleep together."

"You didn't— Oh, I get it. You had sex though."

"Nope. He didn't even try."

Harold shook his head as if this didn't make sense. "Why not?"

Probably because Noah couldn't stop talking about the guy in front of him. Even though he had promised to focus on Marcello, it felt too good having someone he could confide in, someone who actually knew Harold better than he did. Marcello seemed amused by this fixation, occasionally throwing Noah a tidbit of information, like how Harold had a weakness for waffles. Not the frozen kind. They had to be freshly made. If Noah actually lived here, he would have bought a waffle iron already and invited Harold in for a treat. Or maybe he would have saved that surprise for the morning after. "I guess I'm not Marcello's type," Noah said.

"You're male and you're alive," Harold said. "Maybe his age is finally catching up with him."

Or maybe Marcello was the kind of guy who wanted to feel like a star, which took more than a very distracted escort who couldn't go two seconds without thinking of— Hey! Was that the Sesame Street logo on Harold's T-shirt? Could he get any cuter? Oh right, the conversation. Back to that. "I'm kind of relieved, to be honest. Marcello isn't my type either."

Harold smirked, shrugged, and looked away.

"Is he your type?" Noah asked, worried he would have to put on weight and figure out a way to age prematurely.

"He might not be traditionally handsome," Harold said, making eye contact again, "but man, does he know what he's doing! Marcello has made me feel things with my clothes on that other guys couldn't manage with me naked and in their bed all night."

"Wow," Noah said, his mind traveling in two different directions. Now he was wishing he and Marcello *had* hooked up, if only to steal some of his moves. The rest of him was picturing what it would be like to have Harold in his bed for an entire night. Such as this very evening. "Have any plans tonight?"

"Why do you ask?" Harold said, looking amused. "Actually, I don't. So far I haven't gotten an assignment. You?"

"Nada."

"Cool. I just went grocery shopping and need to get home before anything melts. You wanna come with and hang out?"

"Sounds good," Noah said.

Harold nodded but didn't move. "Do you need to grab something from the apartment? Wallet? Phone?"

"I've got it all with me," Noah said, moving toward the passenger side. "Let's get your ice cream home. Or knowing you, it's probably frozen yogurt."

"I love froyo!" Harold said with a chuckle. "It's even worse than you think. No ice cream, just frozen fruit for my smoothies."

Noah groaned. "Someday I'm going to invite you out for real food."

"Like what?"

"Doesn't matter as long as it's deep-fried. That reminds me! Marcello took me to the most amazing restaurant!"

As they drove, Noah talked excitedly about his trip to New Orleans. Harold hadn't been there yet, but he shared details of trips he had taken with clients, the conversation continuing as they carried groceries inside and got them unpacked. Comparing notes was nice, not because Noah still needed guidance, but because this reinforced a growing certainty that they were compatible. They both were passionate about their work, valued downtime at home, had the same sense of humor… Maybe that wasn't a lot, but it was enough for a start.

"—so if anyone wants you to sunbathe nude on their yacht," Harold was saying as he loaded up the pantry, "just make sure there isn't a boatload of tourists nearby. I don't want to know how many vacation photos I ended up in."

"I do," Noah said before he could stop himself.

Luckily this went unheard. Harold was pulling the phone from his pocket to read the screen. "Typical. Just when we're having fun, I get another— Huh."

"What's up?" Noah asked, despite already knowing.

"New assignment, but now I'm sure that Marcello is getting

senile, because he put your name instead of the client's." Harold looked up. "I guess he still has you on his mind!"

"He doesn't seem the type to make mistakes," Noah said casually.

"No." Harold consulted the phone again. "I don't recognize the address. New client maybe? Hold up."

He watched as Harold sent a text, no doubt asking Marcello for corrected information. Noah could stop him, put a hand over his and reveal that *he* was the client tonight. A pang of doubt hit him then. Harold might find this scheme insulting instead of charming. Noah didn't want to pay for sex. He just wanted—

"Marcello says it's not a mistake." Harold's head whipped up. "I don't get it."

Noah tried a smile. "Like you said, we keep getting interrupted. I figured this was the best way to make sure we have the night off."

"By hiring me?"

Noah swallowed. "Well… Yeah."

Harold eyed him a second longer. Then he leaned against the kitchen counter. "You're crazy!"

"Just a little. So what do you want to do tonight?"

Harold guffawed. "You're the client! That's for you to decide."

"This client wants to make you happy. I can't fly you anywhere in a private jet, or take you shopping, unless you like the dollar store."

"Love it," Harold admitted. "Although if you want to know what I really *really* want…"

"Yeah?" Noah said, chest feeling tight.

"More of this. I love my job, but sometimes I just want to go out with a guy wearing an old T-shirt and jeans. No more fancy restaurants. I'm always worried about staying in shape, but that fried food you mentioned earlier sounds good. I want to burp and yawn without worrying about offending the other guy, and I want to get ridiculously high and act goofy."

"So basically you want to be a slob." Noah said. "Sounds perfect!"

Harold grinned. "Are you sure? Now I know why you dressed so nicely. We can do fancy."

Noah was happy that Harold not only noticed the new outfit but also approved of the style. He was wearing a short-sleeved shirt, and while it wasn't a button-up, it did have a collar. No farm-boy pattern on the fabric, just a solid emerald green that made his eyes pop and went nicely with the dark blue jeans. The weather was a little warm to be wearing long pants instead of shorts, but he knew Harold kept the air conditioner cranked up, and he hoped a lot of their night would be spent here. "I just want us to relax. Like we always do."

Harold eyed him curiously. "It's always so easy with you. I'm glad we met."

"Me too," Noah said, trying not to blush. "Don't forget how much you like me when I drag you to Culver's tonight."

"Culver's?"

"It's really healthy, you'll love it. They have frozen custard instead of ice cream, which goes great with their bacon deluxe butter burger—

"*Butter* burger?"

"Yeah! Of course you've got to try their fried cheese curds too."

"You're killing me," Harold groaned.

"I'm not, but the food might."

"In that case," Harold said, "if we're actually going to do this, I want beer too."

"Really?"

"Yeah. Take me out for a drink. That way we're forced to walk off some of those calories."

"Physical exertion," Noah said, feeling daring. "I'm sure we can squeeze that in somewhere."

Harold shook his head ruefully. "You've been spending too much time with Marcello." He looked back at his phone. "I'm still confused about this address. Are you sure he didn't make reservations for us somewhere? I'll map it and see."

"It's fine," Noah said hurriedly. "Really. We've got plans already."

"Yeah, but what if someone doesn't get a table because... Oh."

Noah's mouth was almost too dry to speak. "What does it point to?"

"A homeless shelter. I don't think we're meant to eat there!"

"Yeah," Noah said, managing a smirk. "Who would want to do that?"

Harold didn't laugh. "You better give Marcello the right

address. He'll need to mail your tax forms or whatever. I wouldn't mind having it either. Just in case I want to send a birthday card or prank you with some pizzas. Here, I'll put it in my phone and then text it to him."

Noah clenched his jaw. He grabbed a can of black beans, shoving it into a kitchen cabinet even though he wasn't sure if it was the right one. Picturing how the conversation would play out was all too easy. Once Harold learned the truth, he would be too kind to judge Noah, but that didn't mean he wouldn't feel pity. No longer would they be on the same level. In his eyes, Noah would be some poor wretch living on the street and digging through dumpsters for food or half-empty beer bottles. That's what people thought of the homeless. Harold would just assume that Noah hid these things well or— Screw it! No matter what happened, this was the truth, and if Harold was ever going to love him he needed to know it.

"I'm not homeless," Noah said, turning to face him, "but I live at the homeless shelter." That sounded ridiculous, so he tried again. "I live at the shelter because I don't have a home of my own. I don't know what that makes me."

Harold shook his head. "But the apartment—"

"Wishful thinking," Noah said, pinching the bridge of his nose. He sighed and let his hand drop "I was ashamed of my situation, and I didn't want you to think less of me, so when you were taking me home that night and... You know what? Could we start over?"

Harold nodded uncertainly. "Okay."

"Great." He waved, trying to inject humor into the situation. "Hi there! My name is Noah, and I'm homeless, even though I'm sometimes in denial about that, but I'm doing better now and I—"

"You can live here."

Noah's jaw was still open from his interrupted speech, but it was just as well, since it would have fallen open anyway. "I can what?"

"You can live here," Harold said, his brow knotting up. "You should have told me! Do you really think I would have let you sleep on the street or at a shelter if I'd known?"

"I don't need charity," Noah said, conflicting emotions making him feel both hot and cold. On one hand, he was moved by the generous offer. On the other, it was exactly as he feared.

Noah wasn't an equal worthy of falling in love with. He had already been reduced to a good cause.

"It's not charity," Harold said, gesturing toward the dining room. "I only have a couch for you to sleep on, but I figure that's got to be better than… Are the shelters nice? I mean, because if they are, then I get why you wouldn't want to stay here."

Noah's shoulders slumped. "I don't want you to feel sorry for me. I'm okay on my own."

"Okay," Harold said, holding up his hands. "Just keep it in mind as an option. I could clear out the spare room." He hugged his arms to his chest and glanced around. "Sometimes it gets lonely here all by myself, so I wouldn't mind. That's all I'm saying."

Noah felt like kicking himself. The guy he had a crush on was asking him to move in, and instead of thanking him and reaping the benefits, he had managed to make them both feel awkward. At times he hated pride. At others it was the only thing that kept him going. "I'm getting a place of my own. I just need to make sure I have three or four months' rent saved up and a landlord who's forgiving about my lack of employment history."

"Sounds good," Harold said, nodding curtly. "Sorry for butting in. I should mind my own business."

Distance was the opposite of what he desired. Noah wanted them to be able to confide in each other, not just about the simple facts but their darkest secrets and brightest dreams as well. "It's a nice offer. You just took me by surprise. I've been on my own for a while, and I'm not used to letting people help me. Can I think about it?"

"Yeah!" Harold said, nodding eagerly. "It's an open invitation!"

"Thanks." Noah licked his lips. "I know you probably have a lot of questions, but can we just go have fun? I was really looking forward to it."

The easy smile reappeared. "Totally! It's on me though, okay?"

Noah looked skyward and groaned. "I don't need—"

"Never turn down a free meal," Harold said, a mischievous glint in his eye. "Let me show you how it's done. Offer to pay for everything tonight."

"I'm paying for everything tonight," Noah said firmly.

Harold shrugged. "Cool. Ready to go?" Without waiting for an answer, he turned and walked toward the front door.

Noah stared after him, wondering if he had just been tricked, and decided that he didn't care either way. He was going on a date with Harold! For real this time.

As a child, one of Noah's favorite board games had been Hungry Hungry Hippos. The entire goal of the game was to make a plastic hippo eat as many marbles as possible. On the way to Culver's, he couldn't help envisioning a different version of this game. Hunky Hunky Harold! He didn't find this idea quite as amusing after they had consumed a ridiculous number of fat-saturated calories. Noah had no regrets, but his date didn't seem to be doing so well.

"I'm not going to barf," Harold said, stumbling along the sidewalk, "but I kind of wish I would."

Noah sucked shamelessly on the frozen custard shake he had gotten to go. "I'm thinking about doubling back for another of these."

"Seriously?" Harold sounded repulsed, but then he gave himself away by looking over his shoulder. "What was the flavor of the day again?"

"Cherry berry cheesecake," Noah said, laughing around the words. "You know, you don't have to be so perfect all the time. Live a little."

"Me?" Harold said, sounding genuinely surprised. "I'm not perfect! Not even close."

"Prove it."

"I will!" He seemed to think about it for a few paces. "Okay. Got it!"

They came to a stop on the sidewalk, Harold poking at his phone. Noah glanced around. The street they were on was familiar to him. Many in Austin were, and yet now they seemed transformed. Before, the endless city blocks had been exhausting and sometimes scary. Tonight they were inviting. The patio bar with thumping music, the secondhand shop promising today's treasures at yesterday's prices, or even the coffee shop and bookstore combo—all of these were potential places for him and Harold to explore, to have fun, to grow closer. The world was built for two. Noah had experienced a hint of that with Ryan, but the guy currently at his side was so much more upbeat, and despite his claims, perfect in every way. Or maybe not.

"There ya go," Harold said, holding up his phone to reveal a photo.

At first Noah thought he was being shown a little brother. The family resemblance was there. The kid had Harold's smile, but his face was excessively chubby, implying he was overweight. Acne speckled his cheeks. The smiling eyes were the same too, making Noah wonder if it wasn't a sibling after all.

"That's you?" he asked, still uncertain.

"Yup." Harold turned the phone to inspect it. "I'm twelve, maybe thirteen. Pretty hot, huh?"

"You've definitely changed a lot," Noah said diplomatically.

"Because I stopped eating food like that!" Harold nodded at the cup in Noah's hand. "I also forced myself out of the house more often. Just for walks, but it helped make a difference. Later I started playing tennis and—"

"You've been perfect ever since," Noah teased.

"I'm really not."

"Uh huh. I'm guessing you were one of the popular kids."

Harold shook his head adamantly. "I wasn't."

"You sure about that?"

"For real!" Harold hesitated. "Although I was prom king junior year."

Noah snorted. "I knew it."

"I get along with most people," Harold said as they continued walking. "I hung out with the geeks and nerds. I played D&D! That's not something popular kids do. But yeah, I also got invited to parties, and I went through a phase where I thought sports were cool, mostly because I love how guys look in uniforms, so I'd find excuses to talk to them—to everyone, really. It's weird, because my instinct is to stay at home alone, but I really do love people." He shrugged. "Like I said, I get along with most folks."

"And they like you in return?"

"Sure."

Noah smirked "Define popular for me."

Harold opened his mouth. Then it snapped shut again.

"You were popular," Noah said, grinning victoriously. "Give me something better than that! Your biggest regret, or something you hope nobody will ever discover."

"I'm a freaking prostitute! That's not enough for you?"

"It's a perfectly respectable occupation," Noah said, doing his best to imitate Marcello. "Why, surely it must be one of the world's oldest professions, and what an honor it is for us to uphold that tradition."

Harold laughed. "Not bad! I'd like to see you do that voice the next time Marcello is around."

"Stop changing the subject."

"Fine," Harold said. "I'll think of something. Over a beer. Sound good?"

Noah nodded his agreement. They entered the next bar they saw, which turned out to be a little place on the corner filled by locals, most of them older and wearing permanent sneers. He and Harold chose a booth in the most distant corner, both of them making faces after discovering how sticky the table was. When no one came to take their order, Noah rose and went to buy their drinks.

Harold seemed excited upon his return. "I think I've got it!"

"Confession time?" Noah asked, setting the beers on the table and sitting. "Want me to call a priest before you get started? Or maybe a lawyer?"

Harold laughed. "It does involve theft."

Noah leaned forward. "Seriously?"

"Yeah. But first…" He held up his glass. After clinking it against Noah's, Harold drank deeply, as if needing to work up his courage. Then he began. "I was eight years old."

Noah rolled his eyes. "I was hoping for a serious crime. What's the worst a kid could do?"

"The goal is to prove that I'm imperfect, not that I belong behind bars."

Noah thought uncomfortably of Ryan and tried to shove away the mental image. This took a lot of pushing and a few hearty swigs of beer. "Go on."

"Okay. There was this kid, Donny. He and I were friends at school. Not best friends. Donny ran with a different crowd, but we'd meet on the playground occasionally and have a good time. We were into the same shows, and especially the same toys. The thing was, he had way more than I did. I couldn't believe the stuff he claimed to own. I thought he was lying, especially because I could never get an invite to his house. Then, out of the blue, he said I should sleep over. I was flipping out with excitement. My parents dropped me off, and I got my first glimpse of Donny's room."

"And?"

"He was telling the truth. Donny had everything, but none of it could compare to what I saw in the basement. His dad had this massive train set, but it was the buildings that really— Well, you've seen my place. This was the first time I'd been around models like that. I just wanted to stand there and stare, but Donny thought it was boring and insisted we go outside. I figured I'd have a chance to see it again later."

"Pretty scandalous so far," Noah teased. "Let me guess, you ended up stealing one of the little figurines, or maybe an entire building."

"You're way off," Harold said, shaking his head. "Donny and I went for a walk to a nearby park. That was pretty fun, but the longer we were out there, the more I needed to answer a call of nature. We were having a good time, so I tried to ignore it. Eventually I had no choice and told Donny that I really needed to go. No problem. He leads me where the park has a restroom, and I'm near tears with relief until we see the sign on the door. Closed for the winter."

No surprise to Noah. He knew that officials did this to prevent pipes from bursting if the weather dipped below freezing. He had been inconvenienced by the policy more than once. Not that it ever stopped him. "So you whipped it out and spelled your name on the wall?"

"You misunderstand," Harold said sheepishly. "I didn't have to pee. Or maybe I did, but the more pressing concern—literally—was that I needed to sit down for a nice long think."

"You had to poop?"

"Like never before or since," Harold said, grimacing at the memory. "And before you ask, this park wasn't private. There were houses all around, it was the middle of the day, and if there were any convenient bushes, I don't remember seeing them. I told Donny I wanted to go back to his place, which took some convincing, but eventually he agreed. My stomach hurt at this point and uh... We didn't make it very far. I pooped. In my pants."

Noah laughed, but mostly in confusion. "Why didn't you just

drop your pants and squat? I know it would be embarrassing but it had to be better than—"

"I was a stupid kid! I thought I could make it to his house. I don't remember deciding to crap myself. At a certain point, it just happened."

"Okay," Noah said. "That's a bad thing to live through, but most kids have had an accident before."

"I'm not done," Harold said. "I promised you a crime. I didn't let on that I had just crapped my pants. We went back to Donny's place, and I used the restroom and did my best to uh... empty the contents into the toilet. Things were still pretty crusty though."

"Dude!"

"There's no turning back now! I know this will sound crazy, but try to remember your priorities when you were a kid. All I could think about was the model train set in the basement. Donny was more interested in showing off his toys instead, which seemed to go on forever. His parents ordered us pizza, we ate it in his room, and I kept begging him to go downstairs. Meanwhile, my butt was getting itchier by the second, and I bet I didn't smell so good. I knew I had to do something, so I suggested we take a bath."

"This is beyond weird," Noah said. "You're messing with me."

"I'm not! Donny had all these plastic boats. Pirates and stuff, so that was my angle. I acted like I was really eager to play with them in water. His mom ran a bath for us and loaned me a pair of his swim trunks. We weren't naked together. It sounded like a fun idea, when really, I just wanted to get my butt clean. Part of me knew I should call my parents and go home, but those models... I had to see them again! So anyway, we get changed on opposite sides of the room, have our fun-filled bath time, and when it's all over, I was the first back to his room. Donny had to pee, so I went there on my own and noticed that he wore the same kind of underwear that I did. I'm guessing there's not a lot of variety for kids. Anyway, I grabbed his undies, put them on, and then hurried to grab my crusty pair and put them with his pile of clothes on the floor. When Donny came back in the room and noticed, he flipped. He screamed and shouted, but I played innocent, even when his mom came to see what the fuss was about. Turns out that Donny used to have accidents himself, so she instantly thought he had—I don't know—a relapse or something. He got in trouble, I was sent home, and the absolute worst part is that I never got to see those models again because he never invited me back."

Noah let the story sink in. "So basically, your favorite hobby is a tribute to the time you crapped your pants and stole some poor kid's underwear."

Harold thought about it. Then he nodded. "I guess so, which makes me pretty fucked up, right? Or in other words…"

"You're not perfect," Noah said. "Back then at least. You are now though."

Harold scowled while slowly shaking his head. Then his expression changed, and he seemed to be concentrating. Or pushing.

"You wouldn't!" Noah cried.

"You leave me no choice," Harold said. "That butter burger is about to make an early departure." Then he grinned. "You know what? I'd rather you think I'm perfect than go through that again."

"It's not like it's a bad thing," Noah said. "Most people would take being perfect as a compliment."

"I know. I guess I get tired of the pressure sometimes. These dates we go on, we're kind of forced to never reveal our bad sides. We have to be flawless for our clients, because even though they would probably disagree, they aren't looking for a real connection."

"You don't think so?"

"Most people don't want to hear my poop story. It's too real. Kind of like what I told you about your parents kicking you out of the house, but now I feel like a dick, because that's when it started, isn't it? That's when you lost your home."

Noah nodded. He didn't hold back like he had with Marcello. He didn't wait until he was backed into a corner before the truth came out. Not this time. Through the first round of beers and during another, Noah told Harold everything. Maybe not the minute details, but the truth about how he had slowly found himself on the streets with a guy who seemed decent at first, but had too many demons to be reliable.

Harold listened intently, not interrupting or trying to give him pep talks. He didn't even express his sympathy. Instead he reached across the table, took Noah's hand, and said, "I get it now."

"Get what?" Noah asked, loving the feel of the fingers clutching his.

"Why you're so strong. You've been through all that stuff. No wonder those clients weren't a challenge for you. Forget them! You faced off against Marcello and came out on top!"

"I don't know about that," Noah said, thinking of Ryan again. He had told Harold about the deal, but not how it made him feel. He didn't even like to admit that to himself. "We'll see what sort of clients Marcello sends me next. Then we'll decide how well I've done."

"You'll be fine," Harold said, sounding confident. "You've already gotten past all the basic hurdles. You do okay with older guys, which is important, and you can obviously handle a weird fetish or two."

"Yeah," Noah said, "but there are other things I'm not sure I can handle. Certain activities."

"Fisting?" Harold's voice was a little too loud. "Like I said, we've got people who cater to those clients."

"It's not just that," Noah said. "It's not really a fetish but more like basic things I've never done, and I—"

"Are you about finished here?" The bartender had marched over and was glaring at their touching hands with disdain. "We have a large crowd coming in soon and we'll need the table."

Noah glanced around. Plenty of tables and stools at the bar remained empty. He doubted they were ever full, but the glares from other patrons made him feel unwelcome.

"We were about to leave," Harold said. "We want to go, but we're stuck to the table." He feigned difficulty in lifting the hand that held Noah's, like it was glued to the table's surface and he had only been trying to pry them both free. "So sticky!" he gasped. "Ever heard of soap and water?"

Noah caught on and fought against him, keeping his hand pressed against the table. The bartender didn't find this amusing. After hissing something under his breath, he stomped away.

Harold shot Noah a wink, like none of it mattered. "Let's get out of here."

Noah let go of his rising anger, deciding he would rather focus on what the rest of the evening could bring. His body was humming with a nice buzz when they walked outside. Better yet,

Harold still held onto his hand. "Where to next?"

"There's a nice park ahead," Noah said. Deciding to test the waters, he added, "It's one of my favorite spots to sleep."

"Really?" Harold asked. "Show me why."

God he was awesome! Noah squeezed his hand in appreciation and led the way.

"We kind of got interrupted in there," Harold said.

Noah mentally backtracked, trying to find where the conversation had left off. When he did, his cheeks grew red. "Oh. It's not important."

"It is to me," Harold said. "If there's anything that makes you uncomfortable about this job, I want to know."

"Fine," Noah said. "It's the bottoming thing."

"Oh. Right. You said you prefer to top. So you don't like to bottom at all?"

"I've never done it before. Maybe that's a good thing? The GAC can advertise me as a virgin. That's gotta be worth money."

Harold seemed surprised. "You've never done it before?"

"Not unless a finger counts."

"Did that feel good?"

He had been tied up and thought he was being molested by a police officer, but the pleasure had been there. "It did, but most guys are bigger than a finger."

"Yeah," Harold said. "It's trickier, but if you know some basic techniques… I can give you pointers. Still, I get why it would make you nervous. Especially with a client. Ideally your first time should be with someone you trust."

Noah glanced over at him. "Was it that way with you?"

Harold's response seemed a little pensive. "With a guy I was dating, so yeah."

"Oh." This was the first mention of any prior relationship. "Tell me about him."

"Nah," Harold said, letting go of his hand to scratch his nose and not reaching for him again. "There's nothing interesting to tell. Just the usual rushing in and slowly growing apart. We've all been there."

True enough, but Noah still felt hungry for details. What did this former boyfriend look like? Would Noah be able to compete? What had this guy done wrong? At least then he could avoid making the same mistakes.

"Is this the park?"

Noah took in their surroundings. They had arrived. Past a cast-iron fence that only went up to his waist was a park that didn't appear any different from most. The usual signs lectured about picking up after dogs and listed what hours the park was open to the public. A concrete path wound past trash cans, benches, and a small playground. Noah led Harold beyond this to a small manmade pond surrounded by dense foliage. The idea, according to a nearby sign, was to support wildlife in the middle of the city. The pond was for frogs to live in and smaller critters to drink from. Flowers supported bees and other insects, and the tall reeds on the far side created cover for anything that needed it. Including himself.

"This is it," Noah said when they reached the reeds. "I usually push my way through to the middle, where the ground is higher and dry. Once you're in there, it's pretty cozy and you can't really be seen. My sleeping bag is padded. That helps. Oh, and over there is the angel."

He pointed to a small statue rising from the water, its base a cylinder of submerged concrete. In truth the sculpture was of a fairy with butterfly wings, but to him it had always felt protective, like it kept watch over him while he slept. That's why he tended to think of her as an angel. He turned to Harold, knowing he would need to explain, but the other man was still staring at the reeds, a frown on his face.

"We can go," Noah said. "If you want. I guess it's kind of boring here."

Harold's attention shifted to him. He took Noah's hand again, expression determined. "You're sleeping in a real bed tonight," he said, "in a real house. Not just tonight, but for as long as you want. I'll take the couch. I don't care. You're not sleeping out here ever again."

Noah already had a real bed, and a roof over his head, but not someone to share either with. He still needed to give the offer thought, but the evening was a definite yes. There was only one little detail he took issue with. "I don't want either of us to sleep on the couch. Not tonight. Is that okay?"

Harold's hand tightened over his own. Then he nodded. "Let's go home."

* * * * *

Noah was intoxicated. The two beers made his head feel light, but the shortness of breath, the pounding pulse, and the urge to giggle—these side effects weren't caused by alcohol but rather the guy he was trailing behind. If each person had their own energy signature, then Harold's was something special. Just being near him felt good. His vibe was positive, his smile contagious. Ridiculous as it sounded, Noah felt more alive around him. They had just walked up the driveway and were standing at the front door. Harold was digging through his pockets when the keys fell out and hit the concrete with a metallic crash.

"This is why I never lock it," Harold grumbled, "but you made me paranoid."

Before they left, Noah had told him a story of how he and Ryan had once gone door to door, pretending to be Jehovah's Witnesses, when really they were checking to see if anybody was home. If no one answered, Ryan would try the knob, but they never had any luck, to Noah's relief. The scheme had made him uncomfortable, but so did a lot of things at the tail end of their relationship.

He swiftly stooped to pick up the fallen keys, and when Harold extended a hand for them, Noah decided he couldn't take it anymore. Those perfectly sculpted lips, the flawless white teeth, and the soft brown eyes that always seemed to glisten with sympathy…

Noah's hands were on Harold's chest, the keys balled into one fist as their lips touched. Harold pulled back ever so slightly, surprised and then amused before he reciprocated. When he did, Noah's knees nearly buckled. The kiss was fine. Harold didn't possess some secret technique that Noah hadn't experienced previously. Instead it just felt right, like this was the guy he had been waiting for his entire life, and the kiss somehow confirmed that. Even though they still had so much to learn about each other, the potential was just beneath the surface, and if a simple kiss helped reveal it, then Noah couldn't wait to see what further physical contact would do. He pulled back, curious to know if he was alone in these revelations.

Harold seemed pleased, but not life-changingly so. Instead he made a joke. "What will the neighbors think?"

"That depends on how long it takes you to get the door open," Noah said, handing him the keys. He sounded confident, but inside he was holding his breath for a reaction.

Harold's eyes moved to the street, then back to Noah and over his body. His gaze stopped at one place. "I guess when you've got one that big, it's not easy to hide."

Noah was hard. That was no surprise. What took him aback was when Harold reached to rub a palm against his crotch, coming close for another kiss. By the time he finished, Noah was ready and willing to do just about anything.

"Wanna take it out?" he asked.

"Here?" Harold laughed. "Why do all my clients have weird fetishes?"

"Inside is fine too," Noah said. "Just hurry up or I'll break down the door."

"Got a crowbar handy?" Harold said with half-lidded eyes.

"Sure do." Noah put his hand on his jeans, like he was about to undo them. This prompted Harold to get the door unlocked. Noah thought they would stumble into the house and start groping at each other, but Harold swiftly turned on the living room lamps and made a beeline for the kitchen.

"Thirsty," he said when he noticed Noah's confused expression. "Want something?"

Noah shook his head and watched as Harold filled a glass with tap water and leaned against the counter to drink it. He didn't make eye contact while doing so. Not until he had set down the glass.

"I've slept with friends before. It can get complicated."

Noah's stomach sank, not just because of his careful tone, but that word. *Friends*. "Complicated how?"

"Feelings."

"Oh." No sense denying it. "I like you."

"I like you too, but—"

"Then we're good. It doesn't have to be any more complicated than that."

Harold seemed uncertain, then shook his head as if he was being foolish. "Right. Of course. So, uh... What do you want to do?"

"Got any pineapple juice? I was planning on drinking as much as possible. Then, in half an hour or so, we'll need to go somewhere waterproof."

Harold gawped. Then he started laughing. "I mean it!"

"I don't have as much experience as you," Noah said, "but

as far as I remember, these things don't have to be planned. You start with a kiss..."

"We did that already," Harold said playfully.

"And then another."

"We did that too."

"Three for good measure," Noah said, walking forward. Interesting that he was forced to take the lead. He had imagined Harold being more aggressive, certain of his own needs while detecting Noah's. Instead he seemed nervous and shy, which only made him more endearing. Noah pressed against him, inhaling through his nose as they kissed once more, the musky scent of cologne driving him wild. He shifted his hips, his package rubbing against Harold's, which was definitely hard now. That was all the confirmation he needed. They were both into this!

Noah grabbed the hem of Harold's T-shirt and pulled it up and off. Then he kissed the flawless skin of his shoulder, tasting a hint of salt from their walk. He didn't resist when Harold did the same to him, except when he felt his belt being tugged.

"No way," Noah said, taking a step back. "You've already seen everything I've got to offer, and that was a whole ten minutes after we'd met. It's your turn!"

"Fair enough," Harold said, gesturing at one of the kitchen chairs. "Let's see if I can pass this job interview."

Noah eagerly took a seat. Harold's demeanor was self-assured now. He held his body in a way that made the most of his build, rolling back his shoulders to make his chest appear larger, and when he reached up with one arm to scratch behind his head, flexing casually while his other hand yanked the jeans lower on his waist...

"How often have you practiced that pose?" Noah asked.

Harold let his arms flop to his sides and laughed. "Way too often. Stop calling me out. I'm trying to put on a show here!"

"No sense in trying so hard when you're already perfect," Noah said affectionately.

Harold grinned at the compliment, lifting a foot to take off a shoe. "So you're the type that likes to keep it simple."

"I'm hopelessly vanilla," Noah confirmed. "I just want to see you naked. Isn't that enough?"

"I sure hope you think so!" Harold continued grinning as he got his shoes off, then his socks. He wiggled his toes, winked, and started working on his jeans. Both of them were laughing now. Harold wore designer boxer briefs that cupped his bulge, enhancing it, when in truth they were already too full. He hooked his thumbs into the waistband, teasingly moving it side to side and a little lower, flashing skin and carefully trimmed pubes. Then, just as he pulled them down, he turned around. His butt was breathtakingly beautiful—a nice firm bubble that Noah wanted to squeeze, lick, and slide inside of. He nearly drooled as it was shaken back and forth, and almost cried out in protest when Harold starting turning again, because he wasn't done looking. Of course doing so would deny him the privilege of seeing another part he was desperately curious about.

Harold faced him, a shit-eating grin on his face, hands on his hips. His cock was fine. While it was just as flawless in shape and tone as the rest of him—straight and hard enough to stand upright—his length and girth were average at best. Actually, the longer he stared, Noah decided it was on the lower end of the spectrum. Borderline average.

"Okay," he said. "So you're not perfect after all."

Harold's grin faded. Then he sulked. "What are you, a size queen?"

"Maybe," Noah teased.

"We can't all be monsters!" Harold's arms dropped to his sides. "I'd like to know what they fed you back on the farm."

"Lots of meat," Noah said, standing and stroking himself through his jeans. "Lots and lots of big hard meat."

Harold bit his bottom lip. "Can I see it again?"

"Now who's the size queen?"

"Call me whatever you want," Harold said. "Just get that bad boy out."

Noah walked closer so that Harold could do the work for him, gasping with relief when his cock was free. In truth, size didn't matter that much to him. At all really. He wasn't sure he could handle anything as large as himself anyway. What mattered most was Harold's kind spirit. When it came to the physical, his handsomeness was enough to make most guys envious, but even that couldn't compensate for a cruel personality. He liked to think that the magnetism between them didn't rely on anything so superficial as appearance, although the carnal was quickly taking precedence. Harold was stroking him now, but what Noah really couldn't wait for was to drop to his knees and start sucking, so that's what he did.

Harold responded with whispered encouragement, occasionally pulling his dick free to slap Noah in the face with it, as if to chastise him for making a size joke, or to prove his masculinity. As he worked, Noah let his hands wander to that magnificent backside, squeezing its firmness and sliding a finger between the cheeks. This reminded him of a client who had recently done the same to him. That had felt good, and Noah hadn't even liked the guy.

Noah stood, accepting a few kisses before speaking. "There's something I want. Not a fetish, but a special request."

"Shoot," Harold said. Then he snorted. "But not yet, because I'm still way into this."

"Me too," Noah said, matching his gleeful expression. "Do you think you could… I don't want my first time to be with some random guy who's paying me money."

Harold searched his eyes. "You want me to top?"

"I think so." Noah was horny enough that anything sounded good, but when he searched himself emotionally, that's when he felt certain. He wanted to offer something to Harold that nobody could ever have again. Noah wanted him to become a permanent part of his history. His present too, but this way Harold would always be the guy who took his virginity. "Yeah, I'm totally sure."

"Okay," Harold said. "It can be a little complicated at first. There's some prepping."

"Lube and condoms. I've got them if you don't."

"More than that," Harold said. "Follow me."

They didn't stop in the living room, or proceed to the bedroom. Instead they ended up in the bathroom. For a shower? As it turned out, Harold really did want to make sure he was clean, but in a different way. "When's the last time you uh… One thing to learn, is that bottoming isn't always convenient. Timing. Get what I mean?"

In other words, if Noah hadn't sat instead of stood recently, there might be a nasty surprise. Luckily he was pretty regular. Same time twice a day, and both had already happened. He should be good until morning. "No need to worry about that," he said.

"Yeah, but some movements are more solid than others, or

there's a little bit of a mess left behind. I don't want to get graphic, but trust me when I say it's a good idea to use one of these."

He pulled a small instrument from a drawer. One end was a thin plastic tube, the other a rubber bulb, like an old bike horn used. The sort that clowns were always honking. "What do you expect me to do with that?"

"You fill it with water," Harold said, pointing the tube's tip upward. "Then you insert and wash things out."

"Like a douche?"

"Not like. That's what it is. Listen, I know all this can be a mood-killer, but it's better than making a mess when you're in the heat of the moment. We're talking about butts here, so of course poop is a factor, but this minimizes the risks and lets you have fun."

Noah let his uncertainty show. "Maybe I don't want to bottom after all."

"Really?" Harold asked. "That's okay, but I won't lie; I was really looking forward to doing this with you. For whatever reason, most guys want to fuck me."

Probably because of that amazing bubble butt!

"It's been awhile since I've topped," Harold continued longingly, "but I also want you to feel comfortable. I'm cool with whatever you choose."

He was right. All this prep work was a mood-killer. Noah wasn't even hard, and a second ago, Harold hadn't been either, but he was getting there again. That he wanted to do this made Noah want to also. "Let's try. I'll need privacy."

Harold nodded, a smile tugging at his lips. "Awesome. Here, I have one that's still in the package. The lube is right here. Fresh towels in the cabinet. Anything else you need?"

"Vodka?" Noah suggested. "And some weed?"

"We can do that if you want," Harold said. "It's been ages since I got stoned."

"A whole week?"

"That's practically forever." Harold looked him over, as if struggling to decide what he wanted more.

Noah knew what he wanted, but the weird bulb and complicated preparations had him nervous. "Maybe just a bowl."

"No problem." Harold took a robe from the back of the bathroom door, the skimpy one he'd been wearing when they first met. "I have some flannel PJs my mom gave me last Christmas. They're too long. She always acts like I'm bigger than I am—no jokes!—but they might fit you.

Noah agreed. While it nearly broke his heart for them to get dressed again, he felt this was the best idea. They would chill out together and give his courage time to recover.

Chapter Nine

Noah felt groggy when he awoke the next morning. He still wore flannel pajamas. The mattress beneath him was too soft to belong to the shelter. Where the hell was he? Noah lifted his head and found himself in Harold's bedroom, the owner of the house stirring from next to him. He too blinked and looked a little surprised.

"Good morning!"

"Good morning," Noah said with less enthusiasm. He was trying to put together the events of the previous night, but most of them were a blur. "Did we…"

Harold laughed. "All we did was get way too high and pass out. Eventually. But no, we didn't have sex."

"Why can't I remember anything?"

"Because you insisted on doing shots."

"I did?"

Harold rubbed his eyes and sat up. He was shirtless, maybe even naked, but the sheets obscured the rest. "Yup. Mixing booze and weed isn't the best idea, unless you're a pro."

Noah felt disappointed. Then again, it would have been worse if they'd had sex and he couldn't remember their first time together.

"So," Harold said, his expression naughty. "Are you a morning person or night?"

"Both," Noah said. "Usually. I feel grody."

"Take a shower. I'll make breakfast. We'll have you in shape again in no time."

Harold slid out of bed. Yes, he was definitely naked! Noah stared longingly at his butt as it sashayed out of the room. Then he forced himself to rise and shower. He wasn't thrilled about changing into his clothes from the previous day, but he had no other option. When he made his way to the kitchen, he began salivating. Breakfast smelled delicious!

"You're frying things," Noah observed as he entered the room. "I knew Culver's would change your life."

"Don't be so sure," Harold said, still facing the oven. "Have a seat."

Noah did as requested, having already decided he would

enjoy anything put on the table. He was starving! When a plate was set before him, emotion hit him unexpectedly.

"Is that all right?" Harold asked, sitting across from him with his own plate. "After yesterday, I know you're not vegan."

"It's fine," Noah said, recovering quickly. The two slices of bread had circles cut out of them. These missing pieces were toasted and on the side of the plate. In their place, trapped in the middle of each bread slice, was a fried egg—a sight straight out of his childhood. With a few differences. "Where are the yolks?"

"Egg whites only," Harold said. "The yolks have too much cholesterol."

"Uh-huh," Noah said, poking at the food with his fork. "And what sort of bread is this? It's full of bird food."

Harold laughed. "It's flax-seed bread. Now stop dissecting it and start eating."

He watched as Harold dashed Sriracha over his eggs. When offered the bottle, Noah looked longingly toward the fridge.

"I don't suppose you've got ketchup in there."

"Sure do," Harold replied. "Sugar-free, low sodium, and certified organic." A groan prompted him to add, "It's just normal ketchup, you brat. I'm not that bad!"

Noah leapt up to fetch the bottle. He used it to drown the eggs, ignoring the face Harold made. "Errrph grrrd!" Noah said during his third bite.

"Promise me you don't eat that way around the clients," Harold said while grinning.

Noah swallowed. "Nope! This is all for you."

"What do you think?" Harold said, nodding toward the plate. "Ever had UFOs before?"

"UFOs?" Noah asked. "My mom always called them a toad in the hole. No idea why."

"So you've had these before?"

"Yeah," Noah said, frowning at his plate. "I used to love them. Still do!" He attacked the plate with renewed gusto, but it was too late. Harold had noticed his true reaction.

"When's the last time you heard from them?"

Noah chewed, when he really felt like crawling back into bed and sleeping until the topic had passed. "My parents? They never call me. I call them, but only when I'm feeling self-destructive."

Harold made a face. "Huh?"

"I usually end up regretting it, that's all. My dad has never been the sort to talk on the phone, and my mom quotes a lot of scripture."

"You mean the Bible?"

That he even had to ask made Noah envious. "Yeah."

Harold polished off one of his eggs-in-toast, and it almost seemed the topic was over, but no. "Is it any better when you see them in person?"

"In person?"

Harold shrugged. "Visits and stuff."

"Never happens." He looked up when this was met with silence and saw a shocked expression.

"Never?" Harold pressed. "What about the holidays?"

"Same as any other day."

"Not even Christmas? Or your birthday?"

Noah set down his fork and sighed. "They told me I wasn't welcome in their home. Not if I wasn't willing to get better."

"The gay thing," Harold said, as if it was easy to forget.

Maybe it was forgettable for him. If everyone had accepted Noah for who he was, he'd have spent a lot less time thinking about his sexuality and all it had cost him. No. That wasn't right. His sexuality hadn't cost him a thing. His parents' small-mindedness had cast him out on the street. That, and their religion.

"Sorry," Harold said. "Maybe it's a little early to talk about this."

Noah resumed eating, but he remained tense, knowing it wasn't over. Sure enough…

"I'm sure if you saw them again—" Harold began.

"—that they'll welcome me back with open arms?" Noah spat. "You have no idea what they're like."

"Then maybe you should show me."

"What?"

"Things have changed in recent years. A lot of churches accept gay people now. Maybe theirs does too."

"Then why didn't they call me to say so?"

Harold leaned back. "Do they have your number? You didn't have a phone until you started working for the GAC. Or does the shelter have one?"

"Yeah," Noah replied. "I've called them from there, but

they've never asked for my number when I call. Not once."

"Why would they when it shows up automatically on the screen?"

"I don't think they have cell phones. When I lived there, they didn't even have Caller ID."

Harold stared. Then he snorted. "Come on, man. They've got cell phones. Everyone does! When's the last time you visited?"

"Not since I left."

That sobered Harold up. "When you were sixteen?"

Noah was impressed, and a little flattered, that he remembered. "Yeah. It's been awhile."

"Six years!" Harold said.

That gave him pause. Six years? Could that be right? The math was simple. He didn't need to think long to verify it. "Maybe they do have cell phones. I don't know."

Harold laughed, but not cruelly. "Forget any sort of phone. You need to go home again!"

"No thanks."

"Don't you want to see them?"

"Yes, but…" He hesitated, wanting to avoid the subject, but he knew that this was too important. If he and Harold were going to be anything to each other, Noah would have to be more open. "I'll just end up getting hurt again. I know it."

"It's worth a try," Harold said gently. "These are your parents. Your family! It's normal that you don't agree with them. Past the philosophical differences… man, your mom will be thrilled to see you! I promise."

"Forget about it," Noah said. "I'm fine."

"You looked like you were about to cry when you saw those eggs." Harold moved aside his plate. "Listen, I don't know everything about your family, but I think it's worth a shot. If it helps, I'd go with you."

"To Fort Stockton? It's a five-hour drive!"

Harold shrugged. "I'm always up for a good road trip. Moms love me. Wait and see. I'll have her eating out of my hand. Literally. It's going to be disgusting. You'll love it."

The image made Noah laugh, and even though Harold's eyes were twinkling, he remained serious.

"I mean it. Let's do this!"

The idea of being shut in a car with him for ten hours,

roundtrip, had its own appeal. "Maybe someday," Noah conceded.

"Not someday. Today."

Noah was very glad he had stopped eating or Harold's face would be covered in egg and toast right now. "Today?" he spluttered.

Harold's shoulders rose and fell again. "Why not?"

"We have clients." Although no assignment had come yet. Marcello had probably assumed they would be too lost in the afterglow.

"I can get us another two days off. If money's tight for you, don't worry about it. I'll pay for everything, and I'll make sure Marcello gives you a generous tipper for your next date. At the very least, it would be cool to see where you come from."

How could he resist that? Noah considered the quickly cooling eggs on his plate. Then he lifted his fork to finish them off, but before doing so, he gave his answer.

"Okay."

Heaven couldn't be a very large place, because somehow they had managed to squeeze it all into a maroon Chrysler Sebring. The route wasn't scenic. In fact, the landscape seemed to grow more desolate the farther west they traveled, but it didn't matter because they were together. Even the radio stayed off for most of the trip. Instead they talked, telling stories from their respective pasts, such as the time Harold had lost all but one of his front teeth, just in time for school photos. The other kids had called him Fang for months and months, and when his teeth finally grew back and the nickname was all but forgotten, the yearbook came out and reminded everyone.

"I *still* run into people who call me Fang," Harold said. "This was grade school! Ages ago. I wouldn't mind if it was a sexier nickname like Muscles or Pound Cake."

Noah snorted. "Pound Cake?"

"Sure! It's sort of like Cherry Pie but manlier."

"Meaning your cake gets pounded a lot."

"No, more like I have a reputation for doing the pounding!"

Noah shook his head ruefully. "Yeah, I can't imagine why a bunch of first graders hadn't thought of that. I guess they didn't realize what a stud you were."

"Must be it," Harold said approvingly. Then he smiled, which he did a lot, not that Noah ever got sick of it. He still reacted like it was the first time. In fact, he decided his goal was to make Harold smile as often as possible, so he told the story of when he had tried to keep a wild animal as a pet.

"I was bored out of my mind one day," he said, "walking around the farm when I found a horny toad."

"Horny toad?" Harold snorted. "Is this going to be a Marcello-style story?"

Noah rolled his eyes. "You know what I mean."

"I really don't."

"A horny toad? Oh fine. I get it. You want the proper name. I found a horned lizard." Noah scoffed when Harold still looked blank. "City boy. Horny toads aren't toads at all. They look like little dinosaurs. Here." He did a search on his phone and held up a photo for him to see.

"Wow! It's like a prehistoric iguana!"

"Exactly. I named mine Mr. Snickers. He lived in our barn."

"Is that how you lured him there?" Harold asked. "With a pile of Snickers?"

"No. I simply picked him up and carried him. They aren't very big. I did have to feed him though, so I transplanted a colony of fire ants to the barn. Obviously! I called him Mr. Snickers because I used to practice my standup routine with him and, in my imagination at least, he was always laughing at my jokes."

"I didn't realize that you're into comedy. I mean, you're funny but, uh—"

"It was a phase. A very brief phase. Anyway, Mr. Snickers and I didn't make it very long. Not only was I getting sick of being bit by fire ants—"

"Those suckers are mean! Horny toads really eat them?"

"Yes, and the original colony didn't appreciate being uprooted and moved. They left. To keep Mr. Snickers fed, I had to dig up more for him, which was always a painful experience. As it turns out, I wasn't the only one into digging."

Harold tore his eyes from the road to glance over. "Mr. Snickers made a break for it?"

Noah "Yup. Showed up at the barn one morning and found a hole. It matched the one in my heart."

"Awww!"

"This is the part when people usually start crying," Noah informed him helpfully, "but I suppose you can be forgiven since you're driving. In a way, I guess you could say that Mr. Snickers was my first relationship. I swept him off his feet, got burnt in the process, and I was never quite the same again."

"Can't stand horny toads now?"

"No, they still fascinate me, but I never had another pet. Not since Mr. Snickers. I'm too heartbroken. Of course I found out later that horny toads only eat normal ants, and that they need sunshine every day. I'm lucky I didn't kill the poor thing. So in retrospect, I wasn't a very good boyfriend. Er… Pet owner."

Harold laughed, which was great. Not quite as nice as him reaching over to take Noah's hand, or him leaning over to sneak a quick kiss. Neither of these things happened. In fact, since last night, it seemed they were back to being friends. Or maybe not. Harold didn't talk about his romantic history very much, but after some prying, he mentioned a guy named Calvin. Another escort, and when Noah asked if that had made it easier or harder to be together, Harold's response revealed one crucial detail.

"I never had to explain things to him," he said. "Some guys I've been with get upset when the relationship isn't very physical. They think it means I don't like them, when really it feels too much like work. We give so much to these guys that it doesn't—Sex is still special when it's with someone you love, but you find other ways of expressing how you feel. Like how I used to hand-feed him. Usually just some fries or whatever, but nobody else did that, so in a weird way it felt special. You know?"

Noah could imagine. When they did stop for fast food, he was tempted to try doing the same, just to show Harold how he felt, but he knew it wouldn't be a good idea. They would have to invent some other affectionate gesture of their own, but for now, he was okay with Harold's lack of physical contact. It didn't mean that these steadily growing feelings belonged to Noah alone. They could be falling for each other simultaneously, but mere kisses and touches wouldn't be what revealed it. What form their feelings would take remained a mystery, but Noah was looking forward to finding out.

His optimism was shaken just outside of Fort Stockton. The landscape here was bleak and brown. No mountains filled the horizon with symbolic zeniths. The ground here was flat, the soil unyielding. Grass grew during the wetter seasons but rarely stuck around, and the trees that managed to take root were spindly and short. Noah had once heard the town described as a living museum to the frontier lifestyle. He could understand why someone would take an interest in history, but few longed to suffer the harshness of those frontier days.

"You said it was small," Harold remarked, "but I didn't realize how small."

"Well, you grew up in Austin," Noah said. "I'm still baffled by how big it is there, how you can keep walking for hours and not reach the edge of the city. That's not how it is here. I bet you could walk up and down every street in a day and still be home in time for supper."

"Maybe it's grown since then. I keep seeing hotels."

The hotels were almost the only businesses that appeared modern and maintained. "People stay here on their way back from Big Bend. Or on the way to somewhere more interesting. I used to think it was fun to walk the parking lot and see how many out-of-state license plates I could find. I even kept track. Never found Alaska or Hawaii though."

Harold brought the car to a halt at a stoplight and looked over at him. "Are you sure you aren't a comedian?"

"I'm dead serious. I'm sure my parents still have the journal, assuming they haven't burnt all my things in a bonfire."

"Speaking of which, where exactly are we going?"

Noah gave directions, feeling a mix of nostalgia and dread as they neared the house where he grew up. Despite the dreary surroundings, part of him was excited to be back. Maybe they could check into one of the hotels instead of visiting his parents. They could even slowly drive by the farm. No need to stop and talk to anyone. And yet, Noah had to admit that he missed his family. They weren't so bad. At least, not before the issue of his sexuality came to light. Before then they were strict, sure, but they had taken care of him and tried to guide him toward a good life. Look where he had gotten without them: years spent on the street and a job that most people would turn up their noses at.

"Maybe this isn't a good idea."

"Maybe you're just nervous," Harold said. "This way still?"

Noah nodded. After they turned south, the town came to an abrupt end. Before long, all they could see was dirt and empty sky, like they had been dropped into some dystopian setting where humanity was only hanging on by a thread.

"Slow down," Noah said, even though they weren't going fast. Then he noticed the road that lead to the farm. "Turn here. This is it."

If Harold was expecting lush green fields full of crops, or idyllic barns full of happy pigs and sheep, he was in for disappointment. The land his parents owned was dominated by massive tanks that spawned fish. The rest was fenced off for cattle to graze on, although the land only supported a few. That he couldn't see any now implied that his father had finally made the switch to mule deer, or had implemented some other scheme. If his parents still lived here. They could have moved sometime in the past six years. As they pulled down the drive and the ranch-style house came into view, he knew that his family was still right where he had left them.

"Nice place!" Harold said optimistically.

The house, like so many in Fort Stockton, was worn down from too much wind, dust, and sun. He knew the interior would be fine. His mother always took care of the house. His father's domain was the surrounding land. Good ol' fashioned roles and values. Yuck. "That was fun," Noah said. "Now turn the car around."

Harold braked and looked over. "You don't really want to leave. Do you?"

"No," Noah admitted. He wanted to see his family too much. "Park over there by the shed."

The front door to the house was open before Noah stepped out of the car. His mother was standing there, drying her hands with a dishrag as she peered in their direction. Noah's stomach sunk at the same time his heart leapt, making him feel torn in two. Then his feet carried him forward.

His mother, Arlene, had changed. She was a little older, the chestnut hair more frazzled and gray, but she was still his mom. He remembered the calloused hands pressing half an onion to a bee sting, her sagging arms spreading loving warmth when hugging him, and her eyes crinkling up with joy whenever he acted goofy.

"Noah?"

She dropped the dishrag to the ground and ran to him. Noah,

too overcome with emotion to do the same, stopped in his tracks, choking back tears as he discovered that not everything had changed. Her hugs felt just as good as he remembered.

Noah had been very silly for the past six years. Sure, he'd gotten in an argument with his parents and they had kicked him out. Such things happened. Parents were human too, just as subject as anyone to the whims of emotion. They could make mistakes and feel regret. Maybe they had too much pride to ask him to come home, but clearly he was still loved.

Currently he was sitting at the kitchen table, a glass of cold lemonade in his hand. Harold was at his side, grinning broadly at having done a good thing. And he had! This was awesome! Noah regretted not visiting sooner. Mostly.

"This is a lovely house," Harold enthused.

"Thank you," Arlene said, but Noah noticed the way his mother grimaced slightly. Probably because of the poor word choice. "Lovely" wasn't a word that boys used. He remembered her teaching him such things. "Tell me everything," she said, keeping her attention on Noah. "Are you working?"

"Yes," he answered. "I've been saving up, trying to get a place of my own."

"Is this your roommate?" she asked, shooting an uneasy glance toward Harold.

"Coworker and buddy," Harold said easily.

Arlene relaxed visibly. "What sort of work?"

"I, uh—" Noah coughed and took a sip of lemonade.

"Customer service," Harold answered for him. "We work for a big production studio. Do you read any fashion magazines? Esquire? Vogue? GQ?"

"I certainly do not!" Arlene said. "I have better things to do with my time."

"I'm right there with you," Harold continued unabashed. "I only ask because the studio we work for does a lot of photo shoots for big brands and even bigger clients."

"It's good honest work," Noah added quickly. His parents had never been impressed by frivolous things like fashion. "I get paid to make people happy."

"You always were my little ray of sunshine," his mother said, a hand pressed against her cheek. "I still can't believe how big you've gotten. You should have come home sooner!"

Noah agreed and would have been here years ago, had he known what a warm welcome awaited him.

"I should call your father. He'll be thrilled to see you."

Noah watched with amusement as his mother rose and went to a phone on the wall. The old-fashioned kind with cords. It even had a rotary dial! He was tempted to ask Harold if he had ever seen such a thing, but another question took precedence. "Dad has a cell phone now?"

"I bought him one," Arlene said, jutting out her chin. "I'm getting too old to go chasing around the farm just to tell him that lunch is ready. Oh! Clarence? You'll never guess who's here!"

Noah took the opportunity to check on Harold, whose pleased expression gave way to one that was hopeful. "Everything okay?" he murmured, giving a thumbs-up.

God, he was a dork! A wonderful, sweet, considerate dork. Noah returned the thumbs-up and felt his eyes getting misty. It was good to be back. Fort Stockton might not be perfect, but it was home.

"He'll be right here!" Arlene said. "We should celebrate. A big dinner! What do you say? You both need some meat on your bones."

"Meatloaf?" Noah said hopefully.

"I'll get right on it."

"I'll help," Noah said. He stood, but before he could do much of anything, the front door opened and he heard heavy boots approaching the kitchen.

He turned around and saw his father, who paused in the doorway. Noah's red hair came from Clarence, as did his height and build, except his father had spent a lifetime working on farms. His skin was bronze and his arms were covered in lean muscle. His father's strength was practical, his hands gnarled from so much use. As always, he wore overalls and a blue button-up shirt. A cowboy hat too, which he took off and set on the nearest counter. Then he nodded and thrust out a hand.

"Son," he said by way of greeting.

"Dad," Noah answered, unable to be so stoic. He grinned while shaking his father's hand, fighting hard against tears. He was wanted here. If not, they never would have made it this far. "How's things?"

"Good," his father said, nodding some more. "Cattle are gone. Mule deer are a right pain in the ass. No wonder people are so eager to shoot them."

Noah laughed, even though the joke made him uneasy. "How do you keep them from jumping the fence?"

"They don't jump unless spooked," Clarence answered. "Still had to build the fence up higher. Want to see?"

"Sure," Noah said, looking back to see if it was okay with Harold. That's when he remembered that he hadn't done the introductions. "Dad, this is my friend, Harold."

"Nice to meet you," his father said with a nod. Then he reached for his hat, put it on, and turned around. Harold signaled that he was okay with staying behind, so Noah rushed to keep up with his father's long strides. "The Kincaids down the road, they got in a dozen mule deer, but old Andy didn't walk the fence after the Mexicans built it. One of the support poles had fallen over, and they all got out. Now don't tell him I said this, but last time I did a headcount, I had two extra. I think they got in somehow."

Noah laughed out of politeness. His dad's intense masculinity always put him on edge. Noah didn't normally feel insecure in that regard, but six years in the city had made him weak. He even shoved his hands in his pockets so his father wouldn't see how soft they had become.

"Fish still doing well?" he asked.

"Got a contract," his father grunted. "One of the hotels. Some nonsense about locally sourced food. You ever heard of that?"

"No," Noah lied. "Sounds good for business."

"Yup. Next time I go in I'll try selling them on venison. It's fine meat. Lots of flavor. I like it better than beef."

Noah thought about his request for meatloaf and regretted it. He supposed it was hypocritical to not eat deer when he had already consumed so many steaks. They were so cute though! Cows were too, in their own way.

"Did you ever get that new tractor?" Noah asked, opting for a change of subject.

His father also had other topics he wanted to broach. "Who's that boy?"

"Harold," Noah said. "I introduced you, remember?"

"I know his name." Clarence spit out of the side of his mouth. "I want to know who he is."

"He's my—" Noah hesitated, which was a terrible mistake, but the word friend didn't feel right. "We work together."

"Is he queer?"

Noah resisted an exasperated sigh. "Yeah. He is."

His father nodded. Noah almost interpreted this as acceptance, until Clarence said, "Why bring him here?"

"He drove me," Noah said. "And he was the one who insisted I should see my family again. Do you wish he hadn't?"

Clarence was quiet for a long time as they walked. Then he said, "It's good to see you." For his father, this was the equivalent of an emotional outpouring. Noah was so encouraged that he barely grimaced when Clarence added, "You got a girlfriend?"

"No."

"You should try finding one."

"Okay." Noah wasn't agreeing. He was simply acknowledging the request because he was starting to think he could do this. He wasn't the only one with homophobic parents. Lots of people had headaches after holiday visits, but at least they had a family. Surely that was better than nothing.

"Neighbors on the south side are moving," his father said. "The Walkers. Never could stand them, but I'm considerin' buying their land. Expanding."

"More mule deer?" Noah asked.

"Your mother thinks we should try goats. Says we can sell the milk, maybe make cheese. Of course we don't need all that land for goats. I was thinkin' of…"

And so the conversation went. This was compromise, both of them tacitly agreeing to avoid hotter issues. Then again, Noah's mother had always been the more religious of the two. She had the most fear in her heart, always concerned that they would all burn in hell unless they lived right. His father was more practical. Noah had tried talking current events with him once and his father had said, "Politics are for people with too much time on their hands. I've got enough to worry about here." Noah could appreciate that, even if he didn't agree. Had his parents chosen to ignore his sexuality instead of combating it, Noah would probably be helping his father build a goat pen right now.

He entertained this fantasy as they continued to walk the land. His father showed him much that had changed. When a call interrupted them, his father took it, grunted a few times, and returned the phone to his pocket.

"You mother wants me to get cleaned up for supper. I think she just wants to see you again."

Noah wanted that too. When they returned to the house, succulent aromas were drifting in from the kitchen. Harold was on the couch, flipping through a religious book, judging from the cover. He seemed bored out of his mind, but he smiled and stood.

"Everything okay down on the ranch?" he said.

Clarence ignored him and went to wash up.

"Sorry," Noah said. "He's a little gruff sometimes."

"It's fine," Harold said. "I think your mom is warming up to me. I helped her cook. Did you know that we're eating venison tonight?"

"Sorry," Noah said again. "I was surprised about that too."

"Venison has even less cholesterol than chicken. I like it!"

Noah snorted. "I should have known. Hey, want a tour?"

"Sure!" Harold sounded like he'd been offered a trip to Disneyland. He was definitely bored!

There wasn't a lot to see. Noah wasn't about to take Harold into his parents' room. That just left one for sewing, a minimal office space, and his old bedroom. To his surprise, little had changed in his absence. He had mixed feelings about this. Unlike many sixteen-year-olds, he didn't have posters of bands he liked or films he enjoyed or anything relating to pop culture. His parents disapproved of such things, so the decorations were fairly neutral. A poster of a growling panther, the high school mascot. Another of a cowboy and horse with Big Bend National Park in the background. Noah didn't have many possessions to feel nostalgic about, other than books and a catcher's mitt and ball.

"They made it a guest room?" Harold asked.

"No, this one's mine."

"Oh." Harold glanced around, his expression strained. "Did they make you keep everything personal under the bed?"

"Huh?"

"Never mind." Harold put on a grin and flopped onto the mattress, back first. "Cozy! Think we have time for a nap before dinner?"

Noah looked to the hallway, then back again. "Maybe you shouldn't. My parents might think we're..."

"I get it," Harold said, laidback as ever. He rolled to his feet again. "Let's hang out in the living room instead."

Noah shot him a grateful expression. Soon they were seated

on the couch, an empty seat cushion between them. Clarence returned with fresh clothes and damp hair to take a seat in his favorite chair. He steadfastly ignored Harold and asked Noah about his life in Austin. Most of what he wanted to know centered on work, which was difficult to tap dance around. That wouldn't be an issue when Noah found a different occupation. He wanted his parents to be proud of him, and the escort thing had always been a temporary solution. This could work! The occasional visit to Fort Stockton, an unsuppressed life in Austin, and best of all, a family again. Like normal people.

The doorbell rang. Noah looked at his father, who shrugged like he didn't know either, but his expression was guarded.

"Go ahead," Clarence said.

That was his cue. Noah rose and tried to think of other relatives his parents might have called to surprise him, but those were distant both figuratively and literally. A childhood friend, perhaps? Noah opened the door and saw a slender girl in her late teens with straight brown hair and enough skillfully applied makeup to imply that she was attending something important. She looked him over, raised an eyebrow and smiled, the gap between her two front teeth cute rather than off-putting.

"Hey," she said casually. "Noah, right? Remember me?"

He did not, but he didn't need to look far for the answer. Stepping onto the patio behind her was a man just as thin as his daughter except much older. His hair was a mess, curling upward behind his ears like wings and much grayer than Noah remembered. He felt like slamming the door shut, grabbing Harold, and bolting out the back.

"Noah!" Pastor Stevens said, opening his arms wide as if they would hug. "What a handsome young man you've become, wouldn't you agree, Bethany?"

"C'mon Dad," Bethany replied. "Stop being so weird."

Pastor Stevens tsked and shook his head, but his eyes were smiling as he held out his hand. As for his teeth, to Noah they seemed to be brandished like a snarling animal.

Noah opened his mouth but no sound came out.

"Don't be rude," Clarence said from inside. "Invite them in!"

Noah would rather die! Pastor Stevens, always called that even when on duty as a family physician, was the monster who convinced Noah's parents that he had the cure for the gay:

regular doses of testosterone, which was supposed to make him a man and chase away any homosexual thoughts. Prayer circles with Noah on a chair in the middle, his face burning with embarrassment and shame. Or the deprivation that had come later. Noah's books, any male friends, even foods like salad that were deemed too feminine.

"Somethin' sure smells good," Bethany said gently. She looked a little concerned herself. Noah didn't have many memories of her. Those he retained weren't bad. "Better than my dad's cookin', that's for sure!"

"Come on in," Noah said, stepping aside, but only for Bethany. He turned away and returned to the couch rather than wait for Pastor Stevens to enter. Before he could sit, Noah's mother entered the room.

"Oh how wonderful!" Arlene said, eyes shining with delight. "It's always a pleasure to have you here, Pastor. It's been too long."

"My stomach agrees," Pastor Stevens said. "You know all those potlucks we have at church are just so I can sample your scrumptious meals."

How charming! How quaint! Noah clenched his jaw and turned to Harold, just in time to see him rise and introduce himself.

"Nice to meet you," the pastor said without warmth. He even wiped his hand on his pants afterwards.

Noah wanted to deck him. "Harold and I need to check into a hotel," he said, grasping for an excuse. "We'll be back a little later."

"I thought you were staying here," Arlene said, sounding hurt. "Supper's almost ready! I made meatloaf, like you wanted."

"You can check in later," Clarence said firmly. "They won't be running out of rooms. Don't upset your mother."

"I wasn't trying to—" Noah took a deep breath, noticing the way that Pastor Stevens was sizing him up—diagnosing him—just like he used to. "Fine."

"You'll be glad you stayed," Arlene said. "I just know you will. Let me set the table and we'll get started."

"I'll help," Noah said, eager to escape the room.

"No no no," his mother replied. "Let me. You relax and catch up with your friends."

Friends? He barely knew Bethany, and if Pastor Stevens was drowning, Noah wouldn't even throw him a twig. He did have one friend. Noah sat next to Harold, trying to shoot him a look that explained what a devil this person was, even if he appeared to work for the other guy instead.

"Those are some mighty fine looking deer you've got out there," Pastor Stevens said, addressing Clarence. "Saw a pair racing along the fence as we pulled up. Bethany has a natural touch when it comes to animals. Quite a few FFA ribbons. Just like you, Noah, she won first place for rearing a pig. Isn't that right?"

"Sure is," Bethany said, cheeks a little red as she turned to him. "How heavy did yours get?"

"I don't remember," Noah lied. He knew. He just didn't like revisiting that memory because he had grown attached to the pig. It had become like the dog his parents never let him have. This "dog" was butchered and eaten, his father threatening to beat him if he wasted food, so he had complied, crying through each bite.

"Time to become a man," his father had said. "This is the way of the world."

Maybe that was true, but he didn't have to like it. Or eat pork ever again, which to this day, he still didn't.

"What about you?" Bethany asked, nodding at Harold. "Were you in the FFA?"

Harold smiled, causing her cheeks to grow even redder. "That's the farmer thing, right? I never took that elective."

Clarence scoffed.

Pastor Stevens raised an eyebrow. "No, I suspect you took theater classes instead. Or maybe dance."

"Nope," Harold said, sounding genuinely confused. "What makes you think that?"

Before the inevitably shitty answer came, Arlene returned to the room, nearly bursting with joy. "Would y'all care to join me in the dining room?"

Noah's treacherous stomach grumbled. The scent filling the house really did smell great. He didn't understand why the pastor was here, and his suspicions weren't fun to entertain, but... Food. Meatloaf. Harold. Getting to see his parents again. Noah would focus on the good things and ignore the bad.

This became a lot harder when they were seated. The dining

room table was long enough to seat three on each side. The pastor was given a place of honor at one end, Clarence at the other. Noah, to his dismay, was seated to the pastor's right, sandwiched between him and his daughter. Noah's mother sat across from him, meaning Harold was about as far away from him as possible. He soon realized how intentional this was.

"What a beautiful pair you make," Arlene said as she sat. She was looking from Noah to Bethany and back again. "You played together as children, and well... Who knows what the future might bring!"

Noah could confidently make one guess. Whatever the future held, in no scenario were he and Bethany a couple! Not only was he not interested, but her eyes kept drifting to Harold. So far it seemed the only thing they had in common was their taste in men.

"This smells amazing!" Harold said, picking up a fork. "Thank you so much, Mrs. Westwood!" He had a bite almost to his mouth when he noticed the disapproving stares.

"I'm not sure how things are done where you come from," Pastor Stevens said, "but here we don't just thank the host. We thank the Lord as well."

"Right!" Harold said, his face flushing. He set down the fork. "Sorry. My parents aren't very, uh... They aren't too formal about eating. A lot of the time we ate in the backyard. Like, on the patio. Not on the grass or anything. We aren't *that* bad." He laughed.

Everyone else continued to stare. All but Noah, who smiled encouragingly. "I really need to meet them," he said. "They sound great."

"To each their own," the pastor murmured. His voice grew louder when he spoke again, matching the one he used when giving sermons. Probably because that's what he seemed intent on delivering. "Nothing warms my heart more than seeing a family reunited. With that in mind, let's all link hands."

Arlene very gladly took the pastor's hand. Noah wasn't so willing, but if he could just get through this to the food... Unclenching his fists, he brought them out from under the table, offering one to Bethany first. She took it without any creepy squeezing. Touching the pastor wasn't so easy, but Noah managed in the name of peace. The table was united now. Almost. Arlene didn't seem to mind accepting Harold's hand, probably because she always did the pastor's bidding. Clarence clearly struggled with touching Harold. In the end, Noah's father opted to grab his wrist instead.

"Thank you so much, Lord," the pastor began, "for proving in your infinite wisdom that love always wins."

Seriously? He was stealing lines from a movement that he absolutely did *not* represent.

Pastor Stevens wasn't finished. "We are all faulted sinners, no matter how we might strive to make ourselves worthy of basking in your presence. All men stumble and fall in this life, and it's by your grace that we not only stand again, but we do so taller than before. Please continue to guide us with your infinite wisdom, your just punishments, and the endless compassion that you showed us through your son. We thank you too for this bounty in which we are about to partake. Amen."

"Amen," most people around the table murmured.

Noah didn't. He practically shook free from the pastor's hand so he could eat, even though he was barraged with questions about his life. These he answered as curtly as possible. When the pastor asked what he'd been up to, Noah simply said, "Working." Likewise when asked about the nature of his career, he used the same answer as before but without elaboration. "Customer service."

Harold tried to keep things lively, but no matter what he said, it was met with silence. This made Noah angry. As did the constant efforts to force a connection between him and the pastor's daughter.

"Bethany is a hopeless bookworm," Arlene said cheerfully. "What did the librarian say about you again?"

Bethany squirmed a little with so many eyes on her. "That nobody my age uses their library card as much. They can tell with the new system. I helped set it up, actually. They were still running Windows 98! No kiddin', so I whipped up a dummy database using Linux and—"

"Don't bore everyone with computer talk," Pastor Stevens said. Then he addressed Noah. "Out of everyone twenty-one and under, she reads the most. Isn't that something?"

"I guess she's allowed to because she's a girl," Noah snapped.

"Sorry?" Pastor Stevens said. Then it clicked. "We were trying to help you. Now that you're an adult, I'm sure you understand."

"I really don't," Noah said, ignoring the unhappy faces his parents made.

"We all make mistakes," Pastor Stevens said.

For one very foolish second, Noah interpreted this as an apology, or at the very least, an admission of guilt. But no.

"I've made a few myself," the pastor continued. "I'm guilty of theft. I know that might shock you, but it's true. When I was a boy, my family was too poor for anything frivolous like candy. We didn't have large grocery stores back then, nothing like the supercenters that keep popping up these days. Back then a store owner knew his customers and trusted them. There was no need for hidden cameras or security guards."

"Sounds like there was," Noah retorted, still focused on his plate.

"Noah!" Arlene chastised.

"No, he's right," Pastor Stevens said. "I was shopping with my mother one day, and when her back was turned, I shoved some pieces from the pick-a-mix into my pocket. You're correct, Noah. I broke the store owner's trust."

This was enough to get Noah to look up, but he still wasn't sympathetic. "You mean the little Brach's candies, right? Aren't they like three for a dime? Most people have stolen those."

"I have not!" his mother said disapprovingly. "If I'd known you had, your father would have given you a whooping!"

Pastor Stevens kept his attention on Noah. "You say most people, and once again, you're right. Perhaps it wasn't candy or theft, but we've all sinned. The important thing to remember is that we can be absolved of those sins. We can be forgiven!"

"I've heard all of this before," Noah said wearily.

"But you haven't accepted it into your heart. If a thief can become a pastor and dedicate himself to God, then it's possible for a homosexual to change his ways too."

Harold cleared his throat uncomfortably. "The mashed potatoes are amazing!" he tried.

Pastor Stevens held up a hand to ward him off, eyes never leaving Noah's. "It feels good to be home again, to be surrounded by the love of your parents. Doesn't it? Were you happy in Austin? You can't tell me it was better. You belong here with us."

"And then what?" Noah snapped. "I'm supposed to marry your daughter? Start passing out hymn books on Sunday and spend the rest of my days collecting deer shit while denying who I really am?"

"There's nothing wrong with good hard work," Clarence growled.

"I didn't mean it that way," Noah said, already feeling terrible. The sensation was familiar. For years it had accompanied him through every single day, a pervasive shame that colored every minute and made his life miserable.

"Don't you want to give your parents grandchildren?" Pastor Stevens pressed. "Don't you want to live as God intended?"

"No!" Noah snarled. "Not if that's how he really feels, which I don't think it can be, or he wouldn't have made me this way. And frankly, it strikes me as really freaking arrogant that you think you know what God wants. Did he tell you all this personally?"

"God left his intentions to us—"

"In the Bible, which definitely hasn't lost anything in translation or been altered by those in power who, guess what, want to keep people scared and doing what they are told. Just like you!"

"Noah!" his mother said again.

He didn't ignore her this time. Instead he turned a pleading expression on her. "I love men. That's it! I'm still me. Nothing has changed. I'm just going to marry a man instead of—"

"That sacrament is between a man and a woman only."

Noah ignored the pastor, looking between his parents. "It's not a big deal. It's not a sin. I'm still your son. Please let me be that! Don't listen to him instead of me. I'm your family. He's not!"

His mother was tearing up now, but it wasn't a breakthrough. She looked at her husband and said, "Clarence. Please."

"You need to apologize," his father said instantly. "To your mother *and* the pastor."

"Do apologize to your mother," Pastor Stevens said, "but if you need to work this out, I'm more than willing to talk it through. You're confused, Noah. You might well have feelings for a male friend, but that's not the same as love. Such a thing—love in the romantic sense—is only possible between a man and a woman."

"You don't know what you're talking about," Noah said, his temper rising, and as much as he tried, he couldn't keep it under control. He stood, his hand shaking as he pointed across the table at Harold. "You really have no clue, because I love him! I feel it deeper in my heart than I ever have with anyone else, so you're wrong!" His voice cracked, his anger giving way and making his chin tremble. "I love him."

Harold was wide-eyed. Clarence crossed his arms over his chest and turned his head. Noah's mother was shaking hers, as if desperate to deny what she'd just heard.

As for Pastor Stevens, he remained infuriatingly calm. "You're confused, Noah," he said. "Let me help."

"Fuck you," Noah snarled. "You don't know what love is! You're a monster!"

"That's enough!" a voice shouted. It wasn't the pastor or even Noah's father. It was his mother. She was on her feet now, pointing at him and shaking just as much. They were so much alike. Couldn't she see that? Noah was her son, so they should be closer than anyone else, and yet he knew what was coming.

"If that's how you feel," she said, "if that's how you're going to *behave*, then you aren't welcome here."

Noah looked to his father. The man's head remained turned away from him. Nobody else at the table mattered. Only one person, and he had gone pale. Harold shouldn't be here. Noah never should have let this happen. What a terrible place to confess his feelings! Everything was ruined now. Fort Stockton was a cursed place, so devoid of love that it had the power to destroy it.

"Thank you for a wonderful meal," Harold said, taking the napkin off his lap and setting it aside. Then he stood. He seemed to have composed himself, maybe drawing on years' worth of occupational practice. "It's a long drive back to Austin, so I'm afraid we have to get going, but thank you so much for your hospitality, Mr. and Mrs. Westwood. I'm not surprised by it though. You have a wonderful son. I hear that from all the people who get to know him. Noah is a good person. Only a fool would think otherwise." He nodded to the pastor as if saying goodbye, a glint of disdain in his eyes. Then he looked to Noah and smiled. "Ready?"

"Yes," Noah said gratefully. He thought about trying to say goodbye, or making sure they knew where to reach him, but it was pointless. Instead he stood and left the room, fighting back tears, because he had done enough crying over his family. At least now he knew. He no longer had to wonder if he had overreacted six years ago or been too hot-headed. All that anger felt justified. And it had helped keep him going.

He was out the front door and waiting by the car when Harold finally caught up. He didn't ask for an explanation or try to make him see the situation from a more enlightened angle. He simply unlocked the car doors so they both could get inside. The engine had just revved to life when someone ran from the house.

Bethany. She went to the passenger-side window. Noah rolled it down, certain she would have a message from the pastor. Another offer to save his immortal soul, perhaps. He was wrong.

"I'm sorry about my dad," she said, casting a worried glance behind her. When she saw the coast was clear, she added, "Is it really better? In Austin, I mean. It's not as bad as here?"

"It's a million times better," Noah said.

Bethany nodded, as if her suspicions were confirmed. "If I ever escape, I'm never coming back. Not ever!"

"Do it," Noah said firmly. "You won't regret it."

That's all he could manage. He rolled up the window and nodded to Harold. They backed out and pulled away from the house. Noah stared at it as it slowly shrank into the distance. He was eager for it to disappear completely. Bethany watched them go, waving just before the car turned and drove away.

Chapter Ten

The best thing about a small town is how quickly one can reach the borders to leave it. Maybe some small towns were actually nice to live in. Little communities where people really did care about each other instead of judging and gossiping. Fort Stockton wasn't that place. Harold suggested they get a hotel room since they were facing a five-hour drive, but Noah couldn't stand the idea of staying there one more night.

Only when they were two hours away and Harold couldn't stop yawning did Noah offer to drive. That didn't last long. His thoughts were too jumbled and demanding for him to focus. More than once the rumble strip on the side of the road jarred him back to reality and toward the center of the lane again.

"I don't think either of us can handle this for three more hours," Harold said. "Let's find a hotel."

"Okay," Noah conceded. "Sorry I've been so quiet. Everything's just so…"

"I get it," Harold said. "Actually, I don't, but I keep trying to imagine what it must be like and, uh… I'm sorry, man. I really am."

"Thanks," Noah said glumly. He wasn't ready to talk about it yet, so he changed the subject. "Did you find anything?"

"Oh. Let me see." Harold messed with his phone until he had a viable option. Another half hour, and they had parked in front of a no-name motel.

"I'll take care of it all," Harold said, hopping out of the car.

Noah watched him hurry to the reception office, which was small enough to resemble a toll booth, and felt a surge of gratitude. He got out of the car to stretch his legs and gathered up what little they had brought with them.

"Room number eight," Harold said when he returned. "Super nice guy. Name sounded familiar though. Norman Bates. That ring a bell?"

Noah laughed. "I'm sure we'll be fine as long as we avoid the shower." But when they got into the room, that's what he wanted most. Once the bathroom was free, Noah closed the door behind him and stripped. He stood for a long time under the hot stream, washing every particle of dust from Fort Stockton down the drain.

He felt alone. More so than ever, because at least before this trip, he could wonder if things had changed, if he was the one not open to reconciliation. The conclusion he had reached as a sixteen-year-old remained the same. He wasn't the problem. Nothing was wrong with him. He could find plenty of targets to assign blame to, starting with Pastor Stevens, but he wanted to leave those people behind. Let them also be washed from him.

Once he had dried off, Noah returned to the bedroom with a towel wrapped around his waist. He expected to see the television on, but it wasn't. Nor were the lights except for a bedside lamp. Harold sat on the mattress, knees pulled up to his chest. When he looked at Noah, his expression was miserable.

"I'm sorry."

"I'll be okay," Noah said. "Don't worry. I've been through this before. Seeing them again just—"

"It's my fault," Harold said. "You didn't want to go and I forced you, thinking that it couldn't be that bad, but it was way worse than I ever imagined."

The pain Noah felt was drowned out by the love that flooded him. His feet took him to the bed, his knees moving across the mattress so he could be closer to Harold. He settled down next to him, their shoulders touching.

"This trip was a good thing," Noah said. "Now I know for sure. I really can move on this time."

Harold sighed. "I want you to have a family again."

"You want me to feel loved," Noah said.

Harold met his gaze, eyes pained. "I do, but—"

"I feel that way with you. I don't feel alone when we're together."

Harold clenched his jaw, still not willing to forgive himself. "Noah—"

"I need you," Noah said, leaning forward to show the sincerity in his eyes. "That's all. You're enough for me."

Harold just stared.

Noah leaned back. "I get it. Never mind."

Harold grabbed his hand. "I'm here. If you need me, I'm here."

That's all the encouragement he required. Noah reached over, placed a palm on the side of Harold's neck, and brought their lips together. He sensed hesitation, but before he could worry, it was replaced by hunger. Harold kissed him back like he'd been longing to for ages. Noah felt the same way. He didn't worry about the towel as it started to slip, more concerned with getting Harold's clothes off.

Warm night air blew in from the window. They wouldn't need to hide beneath blankets tonight. That was good. Noah wanted to explore every inch of him. The glowing motel sign from outside cast a red light on his tanned skin. Noah found it erotic, so after nibbling his neck and licking a nipple, he sat up and reached over to turn off the bedside lamp. Now the unusual light had Harold's skin glowing crimson, making him resemble the sexiest devil imaginable. When he held out his arms, Noah would have gladly signed over his soul if that was the required price. He tumbled into that embrace, Harold rolling over on top of him as they kissed. Noah was on the verge of crying. This is what he needed. Not a small town populated by judgmental minds, but someone who loved him for who he was.

Strange how emotions could manifest physically. Sorrow became tears, happiness a grin, and love… A racing heart, flushed skin, dilated pupils, and yeah, his body reacted in other ways too. The right sort of love could transform into lust. Noah wanted nothing more than to go down on Harold, to help the emotional merge with the physical, but when he tried to rise, Harold pressed down gently on his chest.

"Nuh-uh. I've been waiting way too long for this." He sidled down, taking hold of Noah's dick and gazing at it with wonder. "And speaking of long…"

Noah was no stranger to cock worship. Most guys acted impressed, but that didn't mean they knew what to do with it. In fact, some were especially incompetent about handling the extra inches. It remained to be seen if Harold could— Whoa! Wow wow wow! Ten minutes later Noah was still gasping for breath and pounding the mattress. Harold definitely knew what he was doing; changing techniques, lolling his tongue around the head, nibbling his inside thigh playfully, and making Noah feel like he had never experienced a real blow job until tonight.

"Hold up," Noah gasped. "I just need to run a quick errand. Think they sell engagement rings around here somewhere?"

Harold freed his mouth so he could laugh. "I can do this all night. How much sleep were you hoping to get?"

"None, but I need a break or I'll go crazy."

"No problem." Harold flopped over, on the same level now, and put his hands behind his head. "How should we pass the time?"

Noah didn't need to be a mind reader. He eagerly went down on Harold, breathing in his scent and reveling in the taste, but still it wasn't enough. Maybe because Noah had done those things with other guys recently. What he felt needed to be expressed with a grander gesture. One that had begun the other night until Noah chickened out. Now he was fearless. He moved up and swung a leg over, bringing his butt down to sit on Harold's crotch.

Harold looked concerned. "Are you sure it's—"

"Yes," Noah said. He was as clean and ready as could be reasonably expected. Physically, at least. Mentally he was still a little scared, but he would do this—do *anything*—to make Harold understand. Noah was giving up more than his virginity. He was giving away his heart.

"There's a little bottle in my overnight bag," Harold breathed. "A condom too."

Noah rushed to get both before he could second-guess himself. He handed the lube to Harold, unsure of what to do with it. He understood the basics, of course, but the finer details remained a mystery.

"Just relax," Harold said. "I won't hurt you. I promise. Kiss me."

That he could do! Noah leaned over, barely flinching when Harold rubbed a lubricated finger between his cheeks before sliding it inside.

The second finger and third finger were more of a challenge, but Harold's other hand reached down to stroke him, keeping the pleasure going until the fingers started to enhance instead of distracting from it. Then they pulled out.

"You're getting close," Harold said, squeezing the head of his cock to bring him back from the brink. "I'm not done with you yet. Are you ready?"

"For you," Noah said, rolling over onto his back.

Harold chuckled. "It's easier if you roll over and—"

"I know, and I don't care. I want you on top of me."

Harold shook his head. "I know what I'm doing. We should start in a different position."

"It's my religious upbringing," Noah joked. "Anything but the missionary position is a sin." In truth, if he was going to do this, he wanted to give himself over completely and not be in control. Besides, he had enough experience with Ryan to know just how much roughness a guy could take. He could handle this.

"I'll go slow," Harold said, still unsure.

"Only at first, I hope," Noah replied. Once Harold was suited up, between his legs, and pressing against him, he didn't feel as confident. When the head slid inside, Noah felt grateful that Harold wasn't hung like a porn star. "Wait!" he hissed. "Don't move."

"Keep talking to me," Harold said. "That's important. Let me know when you're ready for more, or if you want me to back off."

The pain was receding, so Noah went in for a kiss until it disappeared. Then he nodded, and Harold moved slowly. The motion felt good, although each time he went deeper became another test of his determination. Each time Noah focused on the love he felt. It would see him through this. Harold took his time, always easing off when asked to, until he was finally inside completely. The pain had gone. Noah moaned, clutching at Harold and pulling him closer.

"What do you think?" Harold whispered in his ear.

That I love you! The words came out as a shapeless sigh instead, Noah straining to kiss Harold's shoulder. "More."

"That's all I've got!" Harold said with good humor, but he understood and started moving in a shallow rocking motion that steadily built in tempo. "Some like it soft and gentle…"

Noah was already convulsing with pleasure, but he was willing to see if he could feel even more. "I won't know until we try."

Harold took that as his cue and stopped holding back. The pain returned for a brief second before it was blown away by wave after wave of euphoric gratification. Noah hadn't known a sensation like this before, and as he raced toward the point of no return, he tried to speak a warning but could only keep moaning. When he finally found words, they came unbidden.

"I love you," he moaned.

Harold pulled back, and Noah could see he was assessing the truth of these words. People said crazy things during sex, but this wasn't one of them.

Noah had meant what he had said over the dinner table and

he meant it now. "I love you. I really do. I love you so much."

Harold stared a second longer. Then his mouth was on Noah's, his hips continuing to pump. Noah could feel him—truly feel all of Harold, like their bodies had become one. This was the opposite of loneliness. Noah knew that sex wasn't always like this. It had made him feel empty before, but not this time. They were connected on a spiritual level and would never be separated.

Noah couldn't take it anymore. He sought permission with his eyes, Harold nodding in agreement as they grunted and growled together, Noah exploding like never before. Harold was right there with him, keeping perfect pace, chest tensing and heaving. Noah stared up at a face cast in red light, which only served to accentuate how handsome it was. He wanted it to be the first and last thing he saw every day, starting now.

After a satisfied sigh, Harold collapsed into his arms. "Are you okay?"

"Better than ever," Noah said truthfully.

Harold chuckled and nuzzled his nose against Noah's ear. "What'd you think?"

"I think I might be a bottom," Noah said.

Harold pushed himself up to look him in the eye. "That better be a joke."

"Why?"

"Because next time, I want you to return the favor."

That sounded good. The sex, sure, but more than that, the promise of a next time. Noah wrapped his arms around Harold, willing his body to stop trembling and praying that his heart would never stop beating. Not for this man. They were meant to be together. The long dismal path of the last few years had been worth it because every unexpected twist and turn had led him here, to this room, to this person. To his soulmate.

Noah awoke in an empty bed. The bathroom door was open, the space beyond unoccupied, and looking through the window to the parking lot, he could see that the maroon convertible was gone. Noah didn't panic. No need to with a guy like Harold, who had been nothing but generous with him, even offering to share his home. Noah was still astounded by the offer, and now with his true feelings revealed and accepted, was starting to think of it as a real possibility. He wanted to spend every free minute together. The empty parking spot filled with a car again, like a ship pulling into harbor. He watched Harold get out of the convertible and struggle with a greasy white bag and a drink carrier with two coffees.

Noah rose to open the door, intent on starting the day with a good morning kiss. Before this could happen, he grimaced.

"You all right?" Harold asked, noticing his expression.

"Ugh. Maybe I'm not a bottom after all!"

"Sore?" Harold asked, closing the door behind him with his foot.

"A little."

"Sorry." Harold set the drink tray on the nightstand, then plopped down on the mattress. "Think you can handle some food?"

"That depends how much granola is involved." Noah sat next to him. "Are those donuts? Someone is living dangerously!"

"Hey, this was the only place around and it was still a ten-minute drive." Harold opened the bag and looked inside with concern. "I asked if they had a sugar-free jelly donut, and I swear the guy started reaching for a gun beneath the counter."

Noah laughed. "Are *any* donuts sugar-free?"

"I just meant the filling. You should have seen his face when I asked if the coffee was fair trade. It's like I was speaking a foreign language."

"I know how he feels," Noah teased, leaning closer to see. "Dibs on the rainbow sprinkle."

He took the donut and checked Harold out while nibbling on it. He was already showered, shaved, and dressed in shorts and a brown hoodie. No shirt underneath, if he wasn't mistaken. Noah already felt like pulling down the zipper to expose more skin.

"Good?" Harold asked, taking a half-hearted bite of a plain donut.

"Delicious," Noah responded. "A guy could get used to this."

Harold's smile was a little tight. "No rush, but when you're finished, we should head back. I've got some things to take care of."

"You're the boss," Noah said with a sigh. "At least last night you were. Tonight will be different."

"We've gotta work sometime," Harold said.

"True, true. Stop ruining my fantasies!"

Harold laughed and seemed to relax. "No rush."

After eating breakfast, Noah shut himself in the bathroom until he was presentable again. Then they checked out and began the drive home. Noah was in high spirits. He talked about everything but his messed-up family, although Harold's responses seemed a little short.

"Did you sleep okay?" Noah asked.

"Like a baby," Harold replied, not expounding or offering another subject.

Maybe he was sick of talking. Noah felt that way sometimes too, so he surfed the radio, finding different tracks he liked and asking Harold for a simple thumbs-up or thumbs-down after each. When this game wore thin, he turned off the radio and tried to settle into a comfortable silence. That wasn't easy, because he wanted them to keep interacting and having fun.

Harold seemed to have other things on his mind. When they had pulled into town and their phones vibrated with new assignments, he almost seemed relieved. "Who have you got?"

"Stanley Burnett," Noah said. "Who's he?"

"Another easy one. He mostly just wants company. The most you'll have to do is whack it in front of him."

Noah laughed. "What about yours?"

"Mine is into go-go dancers. Has a pole and everything in his basement. I'm looking forward to the exercise."

"You're gorgeous!" Noah said, poking his stomach. "Stop being so down on your body."

"I just mean that I'm restless from so much sitting the last two days."

Maybe that's why he was getting tense. Some guys needed to move, to blow off steam to feel happy. No big deal. Noah tried not to bug him for the remainder of the trip. When they reached Harold's house, he was invited inside.

"I should probably check in with the shelter," Noah said as they stood on the patio. "I've got a friend there, Edith, and she worries about me."

Harold chewed his bottom lip before speaking. "I meant what I said the other day. You can stay here from now on."

And yet, unless Noah was mistaken, Harold seemed to want his space. "It's cool," he said. "I've got my own room now, and the idea of working my way to the top is motivating. Besides, I don't want to suffocate anything."

"Huh?"

"What's just starting. You know. Don't make me say it."

Harold licked his lips. Then he angled his head toward the house. "Come inside real quick. Okay?"

For a kiss? Or more? Noah grinned and followed him in.

Harold led him to the living room and turned around. He didn't suggest they sit. "Remember how we talked about the downsides of this job?"

Noah shook his head. "No."

"About how relationships don't work. Maybe I'm way off, but that's what you're after, right?"

Noah rolled his eyes and smiled. "I know, I know. We're not boyfriends or committed. But I like you, and I know what I felt last night. Let's see where that leads."

"Nowhere!" Harold said, brow knotting up. He shook his head, paced away, and turned to hold up a hand. "Sorry, I didn't mean for that to sound— We're friends. That's all we can be. It doesn't matter how I feel about you, or vice versa. In this line of work... We've talked about this! I know we have."

"Yeah," Noah said. "I remember now. Calm down, okay? I'm not asking for a commitment. I just think we should be honest with each other about how we feel."

Harold's eyes grew wide with concern. "I am being honest! I don't do relationships."

Noah swallowed. His throat felt raw. "I get why we can't be in a monogamous relationship, but in case you haven't noticed, I'm not the jealous type. I've got to earn money too, and right now this is the best way, so—"

"It doesn't work," Harold sat on the coffee table.

Noah didn't plan on going anywhere until they had this figured out, so he sat on the couch in front of him. "Talk to me. Tell me what you're so worried about. If we're honest with each other, we can get through anything. Okay?"

"Okay." Harold started to reach for Noah's hand but thought better of it, his expression pleading. "I've tried this before. I know you won't listen, or think that I'm right, but I've done this a few times now. With other escorts, with people who had no idea about what I do for a living, and once I even made it so far that—" He sighed. "It doesn't last. Not being home most nights, not being able to have sex spontaneously, STD scares, stalkers, or sometimes even the really nice clients, all those things get in the way. I'm flattered and if I had any other job, then maybe." Harold shook his head. "We can be friends. Nothing more."

"Then what was last night all about?" Noah asked, trying to prove a point, when as it turned out, it was the question he should have been asking all along. "Oh."

"Don't be angry," Harold said. "Please."

"Why would I?" Noah spat. "I hired you for a job. You did what we always do. You made the client feel loved."

"Noah..."

"Am I wrong? You either have feelings for me or were pretending to. Which is it?" He gripped the couch cushions on either side of his legs. "I know what I felt! Or am I just deluded? We agreed to be honest so tell me. Am I crazy?"

He waited to be corrected, to be reassured that he wasn't wrong and that they did indeed have a connection, even if their careers made it impossible. Harold's expression was strained, but he didn't say anything to the contrary.

"This is humiliating," Noah muttered under his breath. He stood, mostly wanting to leave, but a tiny part of him still hung on to hope.

"I want to be your friend," Harold said, standing too. "That hasn't changed."

"Of course," Noah said tersely before heading for the door. "Why would we be anything more?"

"Because—"

Noah stopped and turned around. "Because what?"

Harold's eyelids fluttered and then closed. He rubbed at them before his hand dropped and he met Noah's gaze. "Anyone would be crazy not to fall in love with you, all right? I'm the problem, not you. Let's be friends."

"Better than being a pity fuck just because I have crappy parents," Noah said. "I'd rather be your client than that. What do I owe you?"

"Don't," Harold said. "Last night wasn't about pity. And it sure as hell wasn't about money!"

"Of course it was," Noah said, grabbing his wallet and fishing out a couple of twenties. "Sorry I don't have more. I'll send you a check, I promise." He held out the bills.

"I don't want your fucking money!" Harold snarled.

"Then what was last night?" Noah asked, his voice cracking. His feelings were hurt, his pride injured. "If last night wasn't a job, and if you weren't just trying to make me feel better, then what the hell was it?"

"A mistake," Harold said.

"A mistake," Noah repeated, trying on the word for size. He supposed it was a good fit. He had given his virginity to someone without bothering to discuss the very basics: What were they to each other and where were they going? He knew the answers now. They were a mistake and going nowhere.

He tossed the twenties away and turned. He was almost at the door when Harold intercepted him, the money in hand. "Take this back. I don't want it. I don't want a check from you either. Please. Let's be friends."

Noah ignored the bills. Instead he stared into Harold's eyes and tried to understand the feelings behind them, and why they were so red. Was he holding back tears? If so, who were they for? Noah? Or himself? Despite how hurt he felt, Noah still wanted them to be together. He wished he could wind back the clock and not be stupid enough to broach the subject at all. "I won't talk about my feelings anymore," he said. "I promise. Can't we go back to the way things were?"

"Yes," Harold said. "But only as friends." He shifted from one foot to the other. "Last night… We shouldn't do that again."

"The sex, or all the stuff before it too?"

"Just friends," Harold repeated.

Noah shook his head. "You might be able to do that, but I can't." He walked to the door and left, each step more difficult than the last. He kept waiting for words to stop him, or for Harold to spin him around for a kiss. He was halfway down the driveway when he looked back and saw that he wasn't being followed. Harold wasn't even at the door. The fucker! Noah's pride might be injured, but it wasn't dead. He stomped back toward the house and threw open the door. Harold was just a few steps away.

"I love you!" Noah said, his voice quivering. "Is that so wrong? Why am I being punished?"

"You're not being—" Harold exhaled and shook his head. Then he opened his arms. "Come here."

Noah would have liked to resist, but every ounce of him

wanted that hug, so he gave in. He moved forward, confused how the feel of Harold's body pressing against his could both comfort and wound at the same time.

"You're going to be okay," Harold said, pulling back to look him in the eye. "You'll find some awesome guy, and he won't be as stupid as me, and before you know it, you'll be glad that we didn't end up together. I still want to be in your life. Invite me to the wedding. Hell, I'll be your best man! Just promise me we can be friends."

Noah didn't want that. He shook his head and a few sobs racked his body before he regained control. Then he nodded, feeling that he was betraying himself. Harold too, because the promise seemed impossible to keep. Already it hurt too much, the idea that he and Harold would never be more than this. Spending time around him—as *friends*—would be a constant reminder and cause endless heartache. What choice did he have? To burn another bridge, just as he'd done with his parents and then Ryan? Even his messed up ex-boyfriend sounded appealing right now. For all his faults, at least Ryan had been willing to accept Noah's feelings, and had managed to reciprocate them, in his own flawed way.

Thank you for loving me.

Noah clenched his jaw against the memory. "Friends," he managed to say. "That and nothing more." He pulled away, hating how Harold's hands slid off him and how badly he wanted to put them back where they belonged. At least, where he had felt they belonged.

Noah couldn't take it anymore. He whimpered a goodbye and left the house. By the time he reached the sidewalk, he had already decided to never return there.

Part Two
Austin, 2016

Chapter Eleven

Everything changes. People grow together and others fall apart. Age causes some to slow while youth is bestowed on a new generation. Buildings are torn down and new bricks are laid in their place, all while the globe keeps spinning, unwinding some plans and tightening others. That nothing remains the same can be of comfort to those who are struggling. For the people who are content with their lives, change can manifest as sorrow and fear, because how does anyone say goodbye to what or who they love without losing a crucial part of themselves?

Noah pulled up to Studio Maltese in his truck, a nineteen fifty-three Chevrolet 3100. The make and model hadn't meant anything to him when he began searching for a vehicle. He only knew that he wanted an old truck, one that matched the country-boy image cultivated by— Well, the image that someone had first established for him, and that Noah continued to maintain. The truck was a murky green color and rusty enough to give the impression that he had found it on some abandoned field of his father's farm, done just enough work to get it running again, and had driven to Austin to start his new life. That's exactly the story he sometimes told. His clients loved it. Perhaps a little too much. One had asked him to chew tobacco during a trip together, Noah barely able to keep the sweet and spicy substance trapped in one cheek. As habit-forming as such things were purported to be, he had no trouble quitting.

After parking, Noah let himself in the studio, unconcerned when Dave poked his head into the hallway. Noah nodded at the security guard, and without saying hello, moved to the elevator. A second later the doors opened of their own accord. He didn't need to push any buttons once inside, but this no longer wowed him. Once he arrived at the top floor, he had a harder time being dismissive of Marcello's office since it was designed to make an impression. To establish hierarchy. No need. He and Marcello already knew their roles and, over the past year, had firmly settled into them.

"To what do I owe the pleasure?" Marcello asked, rising from his desk and smiling as if this visit was spontaneous, when in truth, they had an appointment.

"My test results," Noah said, holding out the folder.

"Nothing unexpected I hope," Marcello said, ignoring the documents and instead gesturing to the chair. "Please, get comfortable."

"Clean bill of health." Noah sat and placed the folder on the desk's surface. "The doctor said he's seen guys fresh out of boot camp in worse shape than me."

"To imagine that he gets paid to inspect men," Marcello replied. "I don't suppose he mentioned which branch of the military?"

"No. Why?"

"I've always been partial to the Navy myself. Something about the uniform. Who doesn't like digging around in a box of Cracker Jacks for the prize?"

Noah wasn't entirely sure how the conversation had gotten there, or where it was headed, although the gutter seemed most likely. With Marcello, he had learned to press on with whatever he needed to say rather than get sidetracked by his boss's whims. "I think the GAC needs an overhaul." Noah slid a USB stick across the desk. "This is something I've been working on."

"An overhaul," Marcello repeated. "Are conditions so dire out in the field?"

"Not really, but they could be better." Noah nodded at the stick. "Take a look. This is just a rough concept. You would need to hire an actual programmer."

Marcello took the stick and inserted it into his laptop. Noah didn't move to check the screen, having worked on the file long enough to have it memorized. Right now his boss was viewing a mockup of a database. The client's name, image, and contact information was in the upper left corner. Below this and to the right was a dossier describing crucial information about the client including birthday, line of work, and known fetishes. The bulk of the text in the center provided a simplified biography, ending with a bulleted list of tips. Things like *Recovering alcoholic, avoid the topic and don't drink*, or *Likes it rough in bed and pretends to be out of lube. Bring your own.*

"This is more than a concept," Marcello said. "You've used an actual client. Did he volunteer?"

"No. He has no idea. None of the clients will. These files will only be for us. No more surprises or embarrassing mistakes, like what I went through. Every escort would have access to the same information, whether they've worked here for three days or three years."

Marcello smiled as if impressed. "How clever of you. And yet…"

"What?"

"I remember when you first started out. Quite a few clients contacted me to sing your praises. Not just due to your appearance or performance in bed. No, most of them kept mentioning your heart."

Noah snorted. "My heart?"

"Genuine was the most common descriptor. They spoke highly of your authenticity. The mistakes you found embarrassing were part of what endeared you to them."

Noah started to roll his eyes but remembered he was in front of his employer and ended up looking away. "There's only one part of me they should be interested in. Anything else and they're deluding themselves."

"So it's your belief that this job is purely physical?"

Noah met his gaze. "That's how it's supposed to be. I'm not there because I love them. I'm there because they're paying me."

Marcello was quiet long enough that it seemed he might not respond at all. Then he blinked and leaned back in his chair. "Chester called me the other day. He's a kind man, always willing to write a check for a good cause. Imagine my surprise when he told me—"

Noah raised a hand to stop him. "I can explain. Chester got too attached. He started talking about love, and not just when we were roleplaying. So the last time we met, I told him how it had to be."

"That you were no longer willing to see him."

"Yes."

"Hm. I understand. Chester falling in love with someone other than his departed husband might cause him emotional turmoil. That's why you were so concerned."

Noah laughed, thinking it was a joke, and was surprised when his boss remained somber. "I called it off because that's not my job! I'm not there to start a relationship with people, or to pretend that I love them back. In the bedroom, sure, but the rest is just shadow puppets."

"Make believe?"

"Exactly. Besides the physical part, the rest is just an act."

"I see." Marcello continued to study him. "You've been with us for how long now? A year?"

Noah nodded. "Almost exactly."

Marcello sat upright suddenly and clapped his hands together. "Let's go to lunch. We'll celebrate!"

"I have other errands I need to run."

"Yes, but you'll have to stop and eat regardless. You're also due for your employee evaluation. We can either proceed here while I'm increasingly emaciated and therefore irritable, or we can seek out a more conducive environment."

"Thanks," Noah said, "but I'd rather not. I'm dieting."

Marcello appeared crestfallen. "How strange."

"What?"

"It strikes me that, not too long ago, a disheveled young man showed up in this office willing to do just about anything for a bite to eat. Now he's sitting before me and intentionally starving himself. Where exactly did we go wrong?"

"Nothing's wrong," Noah said, unable to meet his gaze again. His old self never would have turned down a free meal. That he could do so now was a sign of progress. Or that he was already taking his new life for granted. "A quick meal."

"Excellent!" Marcello said. "Shall I drive? Or perhaps a limo, just in case we have one too many, or preferably, five too many."

"However you want to get there is fine. I can even give you a ride, but you'll have to find your own way back. I have things I need to do in town."

"I'll make my own arrangements then," Marcello said. "I'll text you the address." Then he stood and gestured to the door, like Noah should leave. He didn't look pleased.

"I offered you a ride there," Noah said, feeling the need to defend himself.

Marcello nodded curtly. "Your generosity has been noted. I look forward to dining with you."

Noah rose, still feeling uneasy. "Have you seen my truck? I'm not sure it's up to your standards. You know what? Never mind. I can give you a ride both ways, no problem."

"There he is," Marcello said with a warmer expression. "I was afraid we had lost you. No, let's meet at the restaurant. I don't want to keep you from your errands."

Noah excused himself, unsure what to make of the conversation. *There he is*? Like he had been missing? Whatever concerns Marcello had, they would no doubt be brought up during his employee evaluation, if that's even what the meal was about. Marcello's true intent rarely revealed itself. Not before it was too late.

Noah arrived at the address Marcello provided, feeling like he was on the clock. His evenings were full of such dates, the kind where he would be attentive and interested before he switched gears to seductive and willing. He almost had it down to a science. Make the other person feel important. Build up the client until he was confident enough to think he could have any guy, Noah included. He wasn't vain. Noah simply understood that if his clients could get what they desired without resorting to paying for it, they would. For a few of them, hiring an escort was more about convenience, but ultimately, a nice healthy injection of self-esteem was just as essential as the inevitable sex.

He decided to treat this meal as if he were on a date. What better way to prove his capabilities to his employer than by demonstrating just how well he could perform? The location surprised him—a seafood place, a national chain that could be found in any middle-class suburb in the United States. The prices were cheap considering the portion sizes, the food of acceptable quality. He just couldn't imagine Marcello dining anywhere so common. Noah entered the restaurant, almost expecting to see his boss on the waiting area bench, smooshed between two hungry families.

He wasn't. Nobody was waiting, the lunch rush already over. Noah looked to the bar, which should have been his first port of call. Sure enough, Marcello was perched atop a stool and chatting happily with the bartender.

"Dining by yourself today?" asked a greeter standing at a podium.

"Actually, I'm supposed to—"

"There he is!" Marcello declared loudly as he approached. "What a delight!"

The tone was welcoming, as was his expression, but the words weren't lost on Noah. *There he is. I was afraid we had lost you.*

"Will you both be at the bar?" the greeter asked.

"Of course not," Marcello said, clapping a hand on Noah's shoulder. "I never drink before midnight. Anytime after is acceptable, which come to think of it, includes now, but today I believe a nice cozy booth would be preferable."

The greeter grabbed two menus. "Right this way!"

Noah didn't feel quite so chipper as he followed the pair, still trying to get himself into the mindset of a date, but the environment had thrown him off. As did those three words that sounded harmless, but kept nagging at him. *There he is.* Where else would he be?

"Is this okay?" the greeter asked, pausing by a booth.

"Fine, thank you," Marcello said. Then something caught his eye. "Actually, by the window over there. If it's no trouble."

"No problem!" the greeter said, leading them in that direction.

Noah remained silent until they were seated. He tried flashing Marcello a confident smile, but it came out more like a grimace.

"Not feeling well?" his boss asked.

"I'm great," Noah said. "Just taken aback by your choice."

"You mean the restaurant? We're here for the cheese biscuits. The main courses are passable, but those cheesy biscuits are exquisite. I can't imagine anything more delicious right now."

"Hi there! My name is Felix and I'll be taking care of you today. Can I get you something to drink?"

Marcello cleared his throat. "I stand corrected."

Noah tore his eyes from the menu, not understanding Marcello's response. Then he saw the waiter standing next to their table. He was young, eighteen or nineteen at most. His skin was just a few degrees shy of Caucasian, hinting at a Mexican or Native American heritage. Black hair swept across his forehead to mostly conceal it, but what really stood out—literally—were the ears. Perfectly round, they sat on each side of his head in a way that reminded Noah of when, as a child, he would imitate a mouse. He had always pulled on each ear or pressed a finger to the back of them before tilting his head from side to side and squeaking, a stunt that never failed to make his mother laugh. Their waiter was in permanent mouse mode, not that he seemed to mind. His smile was wide and genuine in a way that Noah's clients had probably once appreciated. Not a calculated gesture, but an honest emotional reaction that transformed the face into something truly stunning.

"Sir?" the waiter said, still beaming at him. "Something to drink?"

"Coke," Noah managed to croak out.

"Lemon lime?"

Noah shook his head. "Huh?"

"Oh!" The waiter blinked and laughed at himself. "Sorry. I'm used to my regulars. I like to serve Coke with a slice of lemon and a slice of lime. It's my own invention. Most people seem to enjoy it."

"That sounds magnificent," Marcello enthused. "We'll each have one. Please hurry. I can hardly wait!"

The waiter's wide smile reappeared. "Okay! I'll be right back."

Marcello matched his expression. "Thank you, Felix."

Noah waited until the waiter was gone before he snorted. "Poor kid. He looks like a mouse and his parents named him after a cat."

"He doesn't resemble a rodent at all," Marcello replied. "The ears, yes, but the rest of him is cute as a button. I find him quite endearing. Evenings would surely be richer with someone like him around."

"I get it," Noah said. "I know why you brought me here and made sure we were sitting in this section."

"Do you?"

"Yes." He took a deep breath and exhaled again. "I've let the job become too routine. When I first started out, I was constantly nervous and desperate to please, but trust me, I'm still giving my all every night. I'm just not as naïve anymore. I'd rather be authentic than pretend to be innocent. If those early clients can't accept that I've changed, then maybe you should send someone else to them instead."

"I don't think it's your innocence they miss," Marcello said. "They are aware of your occupation, and the level of experience that comes with it. Rather I suspect it's the emotion they find absent."

"That's not my job! I'm there to—"

His argument was cut short by the waiter returning. Felix had their drinks, and sure enough, of pair of yellow and green citrus slices floated in each. That wasn't all. A small paper umbrella stuck out of the top of each glass. Noah's was pink.

"How extraordinary!" Marcello raved, looking from his drink

to the waiter. "You're an artist! I don't mean that figuratively. You must paint in your time off. Or do you sculpt? Please, allow me to inspect your hands."

Felix laughed bashfully and held out his palms. "I'm not an artist."

"Your inspiration must come from somewhere," Marcello continued. "Is it divine? Are you very religious?"

"No," Felix said, wiping his hands on his apron.

"Love? That must be it. Who's the lucky fellow?"

Felix laughed again. "Oh my god."

"See! I knew you were religious!"

Noah shook his head, fighting down a smile of his own. "You don't have to answer his questions."

"I don't mind," Felix said, eyes darting to him and away again.

"You'll regret it the longer it goes on," Noah warned.

"Pay him no heed," Marcello purred. "We're just getting to know each other, that's all. Now then, if it isn't spirituality or romance that inspires you, what is the source?"

Felix looked like a deer in headlights. Or a mouse. "I just like to have fun."

"Ah," Marcello said, as if this made perfect sense. "Then you are certain to have a happy life. Finding joy in what others might consider superficial is a skill that should be taught in schools. How fortunate that you've mastered this already."

"Um," Felix said, starting to squirm. "Have you decided what you'd like to order?"

"Surprise us." Marcello paused to take a sip of his soda. "Anyone capable of concocting such a refreshing draught will have no trouble selecting two of this establishment's finest dishes for us. Off you go now! Don't come back without those delectable cheese biscuits I adore so much."

Felix wisely took this opportunity to flee.

"I would have preferred to order for myself," Noah said. "I hate shrimp. Lobster too. Anything with shells, actually."

"I'm sure he picked up on that. He seems an astute young man." Marcello reached inside his suit jacket and pulled out a flask, spiking his drink without trying to conceal his actions. When Noah declined the same treatment, the flask disappeared again. "Isn't youth invigorating? Just being in the presence of someone so unhindered by roles and routine makes me question my own. As adults, we slowly adopt the most efficient and effective habits to traverse through life, not realizing how this also restricts us, that instead of choosing either lemon or lime in our soda, we can have both."

"Message received," Noah said, looking around to make sure they wouldn't be interrupted this time. "You want me to be more like him."

Marcello tilted his head to one side. "What we cannot find deep within ourselves, we should seek out in others."

"You want me to recruit him? Seems like he's happy enough being a waiter."

"You're being exceptionally dense today."

Noah stared. "You want me to *date him*? Like for real? He's a teenager! Not to mention that he—"

—had returned with cheesy biscuits and two side salads. Noah held his tongue, which was a mistake because it gave Marcello free rein to wag his own.

"Older or younger?" Marcello said, offering the waiter a serene smile.

"Sorry?" Felix said, concentrating on setting down their dishes.

"When you date, do you prefer someone younger or older?"

"Oh." Felix stood up, his face red again. "I don't have a lot of experience."

"None at all?"

Felix tittered nervously. "Just a little. I had a boyfriend for three weeks, but we were the same age. Actually, he was a few months older than me so—"

"Then you do have a preference!" Marcello said, looking ready to pounce. "Older, although from the panic in your eyes, not excessively so. Perhaps someone the same age as my hopelessly single friend here?"

Felix's eyes darted to Noah once more but didn't remain there. Then he laughed like he was the victim of a prank. "Yeah right. If only! Um. Your food will be right out." Then he turned and hurried away.

If only? That would have been flattering if the situation wasn't so embarrassing. "What are you doing?"

"Enjoying myself," Marcello said shamelessly. "You should try it sometime."

"I'm perfectly happy the way things are."

"Are you?"

"Why wouldn't I be?"

Marcello's full attention was on the biscuits as he pinched off bite after bite. He snacked in silence, the topic forgotten. Noah had relaxed just enough to start on his salad when his boss spoke again.

"It's a little miracle, really."

"What is?"

"This." Marcello wiped his fingers on a cloth napkin, then used them to fish out a cube of ice from his drink. He set it on the table between them. "What is this?"

"Ice," Noah said. "You know, the stuff they put around champagne bottles to make them cold."

"Wrong," Marcello replied. "It's water that was placed in a particular climate, one that made it hard and unyielding. But look at what is happening, even now. The ice is melting."

Sure enough, a small puddle was beginning to form around the cube.

"They didn't teach you about this in school?" Noah asked.

Marcello ignored the question. "This little cube could have remained in the freezer for years, and no matter how hopeless the situation might have seemed, it was never too late. This heatless condition isn't permanent. If given the right opportunity—if circumstances are generous enough—the ice can return to water again, free to flow and change shape or perhaps even evaporate into the air. I've always felt that water was the most passionate of the elements. Some may equate desire with flames, but it's liquid that courses through our hearts with each beat, not fire. Water cleanses. It sustains! And it constitutes the majority of our being. Rather like certain emotions, wouldn't you agree?"

Noah's throat felt tight. "I think you've had too much to drink."

"Perhaps you're right." Marcello helped himself to another pinch of biscuit. After swallowing, he said, "Harold visited me the other day."

"Oh." Noah waited for him to say more. The last thing he wanted was to express interest, but he couldn't help himself. "How's he doing?"

"Good. Harold is turning into quite the little gym bunny. He claims that too many late-night orgies have made him chubby."

"Orgies don't make people fat."

"They do when they're with Mary Jane and her friends Ben & Jerry. His joke, not mine. I adore how silly he can be."

Noah did too, or once had. He tried not to think of a model village without a train, or a body that had been perfect enough without visits to the gym. He failed to avoid these mental images, memories of touch and scent chasing along after them.

"He always asks after you."

Noah speared a tomato with his fork. "Are you trying to fix me up with the waiter or with Harold? Make up your mind."

"I'd be fine with either," Marcello replied.

"Why?"

"Because it's painfully obvious that something is missing from your life, and I've always believed in starting with the simplest of solutions."

"You're one to talk! If love is the answer, then where's your boyfriend, huh? I see guys come and go, but none of them last. If love makes people happy, then why didn't you get married years ago?" His anger ebbed somewhat, making room for regret. "Sorry. I shouldn't have said that. I've been a little on edge lately."

Marcello seemed unfazed. He nibbled a couple more pinches of biscuit, then took a sip of his spiked soda. "Would you like to know what makes me happy? This. Conversing with other people. Spending time with them and seeing little glimpses of their lives. I also enjoy being the best in my industry, savoring even the smallest victory over the competition. I like to explore my mind, whether through alcohol, drugs, art, or simply a compelling book. And at times, I choose to invite others into my life for more intimate experiences, but I learned ages ago that long-term relationships don't make me happy. I daresay many people share that sentiment, even if they are too scared to admit the truth. A successful life isn't about how much money is earned, or how chastely a marriage is conducted. Discovering what makes you happy—that is key! I pride myself on being able to assess what brings people joy, and if you'll excuse me for saying so, you were most at peace when Harold was still part of your life."

Noah clenched his jaw. "He was barely in my life. We weren't even together!"

"That may be, but I don't believe Harold is the only person

capable of making your heart sing. Some in this world are most fulfilled by love, and if I'm correct, you are one of them. In that case I recommend frequent practice, because relationships are a complicated enterprise, especially as they go on. If you start honing your craft now, there's a greater chance you'll eventually find success."

What he really needed was a change of topic. "I thought we were here to talk about work? I still think my database is a good idea. The more prepared we are, the happier clients will be. If each escort knows what he's getting into beforehand—"

Marcello's jowls shook. "They aren't hiring actors. The members of the Gentlemen's Agreement Club are seeking legitimate experiences, albeit on terms they are comfortable with. Any relationship begins with a gradual dance of getting to know the other person. Robbing them of that natural progression seems callous to me."

"I'm trying to spare their feelings," Noah shot back. "You haven't been there in the morning when Chester is overcome with guilt, and maybe you haven't heard George talk about the time someone told him he was disgusting just because he's into—" He glanced warily at the nearest table. "Pineapple juice. Maybe I went a little overboard in the mockup database I gave you. We don't need every detail of their lives. Just enough to make sure they don't have any bad experiences."

Marcello considered him. "I'm very pleased that you forced your way into my office last year."

"You are?"

"Indeed. You have a good heart, and perhaps I was too quick to dismiss your idea. It may have merit."

Felix returned with their two mystery dishes. He set Noah's down first. Fried catfish. One of his favorites. He looked up to see that Marcello's plate held an entire lobster. The kid really did have good instincts.

"Let me know if there's anything else I can get you," Felix said. He looked at each of them, but his attention lingered longest on Noah.

"Your phone number would be helpful," Marcello said. "That way we can call if any urgent need springs to mind."

Felix took this as humor, laughing before he spun away to visit a nearby table. Noah forced himself to look away and focus on the food instead. Much to his relief, the rest of the meal was less about his personal life, or cute waiters with big ears, and instead focused on his database idea and how they could tweak it to maintain surprise while also avoiding pitfalls. By the end of the meal, he felt certain that his boss was pleased with him.

"I've got this," Noah said when it came time to pay, slipping the waiter his credit card before Marcello could protest. He felt good that money was no longer an issue—or at least only as much of a limited resource as it was for most people. He also paid because he worried Marcello might try stuffing a fifty-dollar bill down poor Felix's pants. With that in mind, Noah left the waiter a ridiculous tip for putting up with so much.

"Save the receipt," Marcello said as he rose. "Business expense. The company will reimburse you."

"I want to pay. It's my treat."

"Then save it as a tax deduction."

Noah grabbed the customer copy of the receipt and noticed scrawled handwriting.

I hope you enjoyed your lunch! Next to this was a crude drawing of a cat with a fish in its mouth. Cat plus fish. Catfish. Felix had written his name below, along with seven digits. His phone number.

"Anything of interest?" Marcello inquired.

"Just making sure he got everything right," Noah said, shoving the receipt in his pocket. He couldn't help searching for the waiter as they left. Another table occupied his attention, but Felix looked over his shoulder and flashed a bashful smile. Noah was too surprised to do the same. Funny how that worked. Almost every night was taken up by a guy who was interested in him, but out here in the real world—with no money involved—the attention felt more flattering.

He and Marcello parted ways with an amiable hug and a promise to discuss the database idea further at another time. Noah then ran what errands he still could before he returned home, got ready for his date, and went out again. Tonight's client was only interested in one thing. No dinners or semblance of a date. As always, he just wanted to blow someone and take his time while doing so. That was fine by Noah. He didn't think of Harold while this took place. He didn't think about much of anything when working these days. Whenever he had sex with a client, Noah's mind went somewhere dark and silent, allowing his body to take over.

Once his work was finished, Noah collected his check and returned home. He had once fantasized about renting an apartment from the complex where he had pretended to live. Noah had even toured those apartments with a leasing agent, not completely satisfied with their quality. Sure, they were cheap, but he had more money now. Ultimately he chose a place away from the downtown area where he had so often wandered the streets—away from Jerusalem and away from Harold's neighborhood too. Noah's apartment complex was gated and offered a number of perks, such as the indoor pool and gym, a drop-off laundry service, and underground parking to keep the rows and rows of shiny cars pristine. He could only guess what the other residents thought of his rust bucket, but he didn't know, because this wasn't the sort of place where neighbors stopped to chat. Instead the apartments seemed to be populated with people who wished to remain anonymous—like he did.

He had chosen a two-bedroom unit for himself, despite not needing the extra room. He had plans to use it as an office, but at the moment, the second bedroom remained empty. Noah let himself into the apartment. A cool gust caressed his face. He always left the air conditioner running at this time of year. The large kitchen was filled with supplies to cook, despite Noah rarely doing so, and the lush couch in front of the widescreen television could seat four, even though he never had anyone over. The few exceptions were all trusted clients.

Noah liked his home, and his truck, and the bank account that didn't dip below five figures anymore. He was never hungry or woke up cold and wet. His life was finally stable. Then why wasn't he happy? He had to admit that Marcello was right. Something was missing from his life, but it seemed like a joke that it could be a guy. All Noah had were guys, so many that he occasionally forgot a name. His job forced him to socialize daily, and physical contact always accompanied that. What else was there?

Emotion. Marcello had made a comment about that being absent. From his job or his personal life? Noah couldn't remember what his boss had been referring to so he began to pace, finding himself drawn to the extra bedroom. He shut the door behind him and was surrounded by white walls and beige carpet. Neutral. Blank. Empty. The perfect place to meditate and figure it all out. His hands were in his pockets, one touching a phone, the other fingering a receipt that included a drawing of a bad pun. And a phone number.

Maybe he just needed a roommate. Or a pet, or a friend, or anyone who didn't treat him like a vending machine for love. Feed the money in and push the button for the corresponding craving. He wasn't complaining. It really was a lot of cash. Noah was compensated too well to feel used, but that didn't mean he couldn't feel used up.

Sometimes he wished he could turn back the clock, never come out to his parents and experience the normal life of a teenager instead. No living on the streets or working as an escort. Just school followed by graduation and maybe a job waiting tables while he tried to figure out what to do with his life. Is that what Felix had? Is that why he could be so enthusiastic about lemons and limes?

Only one way to find out. Noah didn't hesitate. If his profession had taught him one thing, it was how to talk to complete strangers and keep conversations going. He pulled out his phone and the restaurant receipt, then sat cross-legged on the carpet. He tapped in the number and hit the green phone icon, already grinning because he was doing something different. His life had become a routine of going on one date and prepping himself for the next. Now he was finally breaking that routine… even if it was just for another sort of date. He was chuckling to himself when the ringing stopped and was replaced by a nerve-racked voice.

"Um. Hey! I mean… Hello?"

"Do you always answer the phone like that?" Noah asked. He could picture Felix holding the phone in his hands like a hot potato before answering, wondering if the unknown caller was the guy he had left his number for.

"Oh god," Felix said. "I didn't expect you to actually— I mean, I'm not insecure or anything. Okay, maybe I *am*, it's just…" A sharp inhalation of breath. "Hi there!"

"Hello," Noah said coolly. "Could I talk to your older brother, please? I'm getting the impression that you're even younger than I originally thought."

"How old did you think I was?" Felix asked, sounding hurt.

"Twenty-five," he replied despite the number being way higher than his actual estimate. Noah still remembered what a compliment it once was to be mistaken as older.

"Oh! That's close. I'm twenty. Two."

"Okay," Noah said. "I'm not saying I don't believe you, but I'll need to see some ID before we go on our date."

Felix gasped audibly. "Our date?"

"Yeah. I'm not much of a phone guy. In fact, I'm about to hang up, so let's make plans before it's too late. Are you free tomorrow night?"

"I have class."

"High school?"

"College!" Felix shot back. Then he laughed. "You're messing with me, aren't you? There's no high school at night. Except for adults, I guess."

"You're not an adult?"

"I am! Ugh. This is a disaster. Do over!"

The phone beeped in his ear, then went silent. Felix had hung up on him! Noah stared at it in puzzlement before he finally understood. He called the number again, the voice that answered sounding sultry this time.

"Why, hello. I knew you would call. I'm *very* confident."

"Too bad," Noah murmured. "I have a thing for nervous wrecks."

"I'm that too!" Felix said hurriedly. "So where are you taking me? We're going on a date, you know."

"I didn't," Noah said, playing along, "but I like the idea. What should we do?"

"Oh. Dinner? And maybe a movie?"

The movie sounded okay, even though they would both be staring at a screen and not talking. Dinner sounded tedious. Too much like work. They probably had that in common, come to think of it.

"Tell you what," Noah said, "if you could do anything tomorrow night, what would it be? Aside from winning the lottery or flying to some exotic country. There must be something in Austin you've always wanted to try but haven't yet."

"Bottoms one up."

The words sounded like nonsense and yet were strangely

familiar. Noah was briefly confused until he remembered a local bar. Bottoms 1UP was the name of the place, but he was sketchy on the details. "We can do that. What time should I pick you up? Or would you rather meet there?"

"Ummm."

"It'll be a public place," Noah said helpfully. "You'll be safe. How come you've never been there before?"

"Just never got around to it," Felix replied.

Noah was pretty sure it had more to do with his actual age and decided to tease him more. "So your idea of a dream date is to get wasted together?"

"No! I just want to play."

"Sorry?"

"Video games. It's a barcade. They have a ton of cabinets there I've never seen. And the new *Game of Thrones* pinball!"

The words "new" and "pinball" didn't seem compatible, but maybe this was a retro trend, like vinyl records making a comeback. In fact, he remembered a bleary conversation on that very subject. What was his name? Albert? Yeah, definitely a client of his. Albert was crazy about doing shots, and not just ones filled with alcohol. "I think I know the owner."

"Really?"

"Yeah. I'm sure he'll give us a tour of the place."

"That would be amazing! My class gets out at eight. Do you think you can pick me up? I share a car with my… roommate."

Noah sighed. "I'm not into dishonest guys. Try again."

"I share a car with my little sister. So humiliating."

"Nothing wrong with that," Noah said. "Where should I pick you up?"

"ACC. The Eastview campus."

Austin Community College. Noah used to wander the grounds when he was homeless, since his age made it easy to blend in. That, and they had a decent library. "Okay. Enjoy the rest of your night."

"You're hanging up?"

"Yeah."

"Are you really going to be there?" Felix asked.

"You have my word," Noah said. "Good night."

"Oh. Good night."

Noah made sure the call was disconnected. Then he laughed.

Felix was cute. He couldn't remember the last time he had been charmed by someone, probably because that was normally his obligation. Regardless, tomorrow would be a welcome diversion from the usual. Sweet instead of sexy. Cute instead of carnal.

Chapter Twelve

Noah arrived back at his apartment in the late afternoon, drenched in sweat but satisfied. The time spent with his clients often involved drinking, and considering how many nights he worked, the calories really added up. Noah didn't enjoy jogging, and he wasn't interested in lifting weights. To stay lean he walked. Maybe it was a habit left over from being on the streets for so long. If he didn't move, his body would grow restless. Often he would drive to Balcones Canyonlands, a wildlife refuge outside of Austin. There he would walk for hours on end. He supposed most people would consider it hiking, but he didn't load himself up with gear. He simply set out with nothing more than a bottle of water and his driver's license in a pocket. His wallet stayed home, as did his phone. No distractions. Just him and limited resources. Like how it used to be.

Noah didn't miss those days. He was always eager to get back to his refrigerator for a cool drink and a snack. But being outside helped center him and acted as a reminder of how lucky he was. Not happy exactly, but no longer starving or fearful for his own future. He wasn't nearly as alone, either.

Noah picked up his phone before going to the kitchen and noticed more notifications than usual. Three missed calls. At first he thought maybe Felix needed to change plans or cancel. Then he recognized the number because he had once considered it his own. Jerusalem. Why would the shelter be calling him after all this time?

Edith was the most likely answer. Noah felt a pang of guilt. The social worker had always worried about him, and done her best to help when he was still at the shelter. They had stayed in touch after he moved out but with decreasing frequency. He told himself that she had more pressing concerns, other people she needed to help, when really he wanted to distance himself from his own past. Now he questioned that decision. Noah checked his voicemail, and sure enough, Edith's lightly accented English politely asked him to stop by the shelter at his earliest convenience.

He made a note to do so, then went to take a shower. When getting dressed, he decided on a casual T-shirt and jeans, again not wanting to feel like he was working that night. He put on some music, made a salad, and ate it while catching up with TV shows he liked. He still had time to spare, so he searched Netflix for documentaries on gaming, figuring it would at least give him and Felix something to discuss if their date got awkward.

He found one, but struggled to maintain his focus while watching it because he felt… Nervous? About going on a date? He grinned and decided to embrace the sensation. Noah hopped up, went to check his hair, floss, brush his teeth, and put on cologne. He kept the casual clothes and watched the clock, deciding to leave early in case of unexpected traffic. He reached the community college with time to spare. His heart was actually thudding as he circled the campus, trying to guess which door Felix would exit from.

This wasn't love, or even a crush, because he knew too little about this person. Still, it was kind of exciting. Anything could happen. Felix might not even show up! But he did. After what might have been his tenth loop, Noah spotted him standing next to the curb, wearing a black dress shirt while biting his bottom lip and looking slightly panicked. Noah parked the truck next to him and hopped out, intending to open the passenger door.

"Wow," Felix said, eyes sparkling, but for the vehicle instead of Noah. "This is just like… I bet you're a big shot movie producer. You're just trying to impress me, aren't you?"

Noah looked to the rusty truck, then back to his date. "Are you making fun of me?"

"No! It's like the video for *Material Girl*. You know how in it Madonna doesn't like guys who try to impress her with money, so the movie producer pretends he's poor just to get her in bed. Her fault for having such weird standards." Felix grimaced. "You don't know what I'm talking about, do you?"

Noah decided to spare him further embarrassment by ignoring the question. "Are you a big Madonna fan?"

"Yes! Although I like Britney more, and Lady Gaga is the absolute best! Lately I've been listening to a lot of Beyoncé. Have you heard her latest single?"

"Sure," Noah said, mostly so the topic wouldn't be drawn out further. "Hop in."

Felix climbed into the truck. Noah shut the door, grinned at him to make him blush, and went around to the driver's side.

"Ready?" he asked once behind the wheel.

"Actually, I have one question."

Noah's hand was on the ignition, but he let it drop. "Okay."

Felix's brow knotted up. "What's your name?"

Noah laughed in surprise. "You don't know my name and you agreed to go on a date with me?"

"I should have looked closer at your credit card," Felix said. "I usually try to remember my regulars' names, but it was your first time, and I—"

Was nervous about leaving his phone number, but Noah decided to spare his feelings again. "You were busy drawing that awesome cat, which I *loved* by the way."

Felix perked up. "Really?"

"Yeah." He extended a hand. "I'm Noah Westwood."

"Felix Ramos," came the reply.

The hand that touched his was warm and a little sweaty. The fingers were dainty and the grip gentle. Most of all, it felt strangely intimate. Despite all the things Noah did on a regular basis, somehow this simple gesture felt more significant. He let go, despite not wanting to, and moved his hand back to the ignition. "Ready?"

"Are we going to Bottoms 1UP?"

"Yeah! You still want to, right?"

Felix winced. "There's something I need to tell you. I'm not twenty-two."

"No!" Noah said, pretending to be shocked.

"I'm so sorry! I'm only twenty. Almost. My birthday is next month, so it's really close."

Noah made a gimmie motion with his fingers. "ID. Let's see it."

Felix complied, shifting to pull a nylon wallet from his back pocket. From it he took his driver's license and handed it over.

Noah looked first at the photo, which showed an even younger Felix with a squinty-eyed smile so wide that most of his teeth were on display. Adorable! And those ears… Noah looked to the current Felix, who had only gotten better with age. Then he checked the birthdate before he allowed himself to get any more interested than he already was. Felix had told the truth. He was nineteen on the verge of turning twenty.

"Don't lie to anyone," Noah said, handing back the license.

"Especially to impress them. If someone doesn't like you for who you are, they aren't worth your time."

Felix seemed taken aback by this, but he nodded. Noah started the truck and pulled out into traffic, worried he was being too bossy. He didn't want to be the older guy who thought he knew better, or worse, come across like a teacher lecturing his student. Their age difference wasn't that big. Noah was only three years and a few months older, but he supposed he'd been forced to grow up sooner than most people.

"I don't usually lie," Felix blurted out. "It just sucks being under twenty-one. You get excluded from so much, and people who *are* old enough leave you behind. Not that I can blame them."

"I remember," Noah said.

"We don't have to go to that bar. Anything is fine. I'm easy. Going! Easy going."

Noah did his best not to laugh. "Let's try the bar. Maybe I can pull some strings. So, your last name is Ramos. That's Mexican, right?"

"Nope! Try again."

"Spanish? As in Spain?"

"Almost. Keep going."

Noah glanced over at him. He dug the black hair and dark eyes. "Greek?"

Felix laughed. "Don't worry, nobody gets it right. The name is Spanish, but I'm Filipino."

"Like from the Philippines?" Noah asked. Then he shook his head. "Pretend I didn't ask such an obvious question. Did one of your ancestors marry a hot Spaniard?"

"No, it was the Claveria Decree in eighteen forty-nine. Most people in the Philippines didn't have a last name, which I guess the Spaniards didn't like—we were part of their empire back then—so the governor of the Philippines sent out a list of names for people to choose from. The rest is history. Literally."

Noah glanced over at him again. "If you're trying to impress me, it worked." He returned his attention to the road, but not before noticing how Felix blushed at the compliment. "Is that what you're studying? History?"

Felix breathed out. "I don't know what I'm doing. My mom says I need to take my basic college courses while I figure it out. I'm working fulltime to save up for whatever university I end up choosing, which is dumb because I know she needs the money. I'd rather just work and help her out, at least until my sister graduates high school. She's a dancer and wants to do it professionally. Between you and me, I'm really just saving up to help put her through school."

"Aw!" Noah said, genuinely moved. "That's so sweet! You must be a really good brother."

Felix shrugged. "I try. What about you? Are you still studying or..."

"Never went to college," Noah admitted. "I work fulltime."

"Doing what?"

"Customer service." Wasn't that the truth!

"Like what exactly?"

"I work for a studio—"

"I knew it! You *are* a movie producer!"

Noah laughed. "Not that kind of studio. I guess they do dabble in movies, but it's mostly about photography. They have a bunch of high-profile clients. My job is to make sure a particular group of them are happy and stay that way." All true, even if he was intentionally being misleading. The high-profile clients had little to do with the group of clients Noah tended to. Occasionally an overlap existed, but rarely. He didn't feel bad about being obtuse. Even if Noah wanted to be more forthcoming, he was sworn to secrecy. Only if things became serious between Felix and him would he reconsider.

The bar was just a handful of blocks away when Noah found a parking spot. The rare kind that wasn't even metered. He took it, hoping that Felix didn't mind walking.

"So you're into video games?" Noah asked when they were strolling down the sidewalk.

"Yeah." Felix shot him a demure smile. "Especially the retro stuff. It just feels more exciting when you consider how groundbreaking each game must have been. Genres didn't exist back then. Not like now. Someone had to create the first shoot 'em up—*Space Invaders*—or the first platformer."

"*Mario Brothers*?" Noah guessed, wishing he had paid more attention to the documentary.

"Close! *Donkey Kong* was the first true platformer, which is also Mario's first appearance. Even that's exciting to me. Whoever invented that game—"

"You don't know?"

Felix chuckled nervously. "I was trying to tone down my geekiness. Anyway, I doubt Shigeru Miyamoto had any idea how famous his character would become, or knew that he was creating an entire genre of gaming. Video game designers back then were true pioneers. It must have been an amazing time. I wish I could go back and live through it all."

"It's better this way," Noah said. "You have access to all of those games now. I'm sure you can get most of them as an app on your phone."

"Not the same," Felix said, shaking his head. "I want to play them how they were originally intended. They have a *Donkey Kong* cabinet at this bar. Did you know that? I've only ever seen it once before, at a bowling alley, and the screen was too messed up to play." They rounded a corner, the sign for Bottoms 1UP visible ahead. "I hope I can get in!"

He sounded like someone approaching a trendy New York nightclub, not a person about to enter a murky bar with overpriced drinks and worn-down furnishings. As for Noah, he wasn't worried about getting in because he had already talked to the owner earlier in the day. Still, as they approached the bouncer, he made sure to put on a show.

"Better stay back here," Noah said, holding an arm out to stop Felix. "Wait by the curb. I'll see what I can do."

He strolled up to the bouncer, making sure to stand where Felix wouldn't be able to see the other man's face. After showing his ID, Noah nodded toward the interior.

"Is Albert still here? He's expecting me."

"You're Noah?" the bouncer asked, standing up from his stool and looking more attentive. "You can go on in or—"

"Just a sec. I need you to act like I'm causing trouble. There's a kid waiting by the curb. Don't look yet. When you do, be sure to glare and shake your head."

The bouncer seemed confused. "Why?"

"Just having some fun with a friend of mine."

The bouncer shrugged, then put on an impressive show, scowling past Noah and frowning as he slowly shook his head. Maybe it was a little overkill, but it worked, because an audible groan came from behind.

"Okay," Noah said with a low chuckle. "I'm going to act like I'm telling you off. Then we'll get Albert out here." He started gesticulating broadly and even pounded his chest once, like some deranged alpha male. He tried to keep a straight face, but the bouncer was laughing, which made him want to also. He just hoped that Felix couldn't see their expressions from where he stood. "I think that's enough. Let's see what the boss man has to say."

The bouncer took out his phone to contact Albert. Noah turned around and shrugged at Felix, whose sagged shoulders and downtrodden appearance made him want to rush over and give the guy a hug.

"Noah!" a voice said.

Albert appeared dressed in a T-shirt too small to cover the bottom of his gut and jeans that were stained with oil and at least one burn. He was into electronics and nerdy as hell, but also a super nice guy. Albert preferred variety, so Noah had been with him only once, but he had tried to make it memorable. Judging from the warm reception to his call, he had.

Albert beamed at him, then caught sight of Felix. "And that must be who you're trying to impress."

"It is," Noah said while giving the man a hug. "What do you think?"

"Precious," Albert said. "Those ears are the cutest things I've ever seen!"

"Aren't they?" Noah grinned proudly. It felt good that someone so sweet wanted to be around him at all. "He's really into retro-gaming. Like I said on the phone, he's not old enough to drink, but that's not why we're here."

"It's fine, it's fine," Albert said, waving away any concerns. "Just promise that I'll get to hear details if you two hit it off. And if you don't, I wouldn't mind his phone number!"

Noah laughed and offered a handshake. "I owe you one. That's all I can promise."

"Sounds good. Here. On the house." Albert reached into a pocket and scooped out a handful of tokens. He placed them in Noah's hand, took another look at Felix, and then addressed the bouncer. "Friends of mine."

The bouncer nodded in understanding. Albert went back inside. As for Noah, he turned around wearing a grim expression. He maintained this while approaching Felix, then said, "Bad news. They won't let you in to drink, no matter how much I argued. They're okay with you playing video games though, but only if you stay away from the bar."

"Really?" Felix said, eyes lighting up. "You're the best!" He moved forward and started to open his arms, like a hug was imminent, but then got himself under control. "Um. Thanks. Can we go in now?"

Noah chuckled. "Sure. Let's go play some *Donkey Kong*."

Once they were inside, Felix ran from machine to machine, babbling incoherently. "Oh my gosh! *Skulls & Crossbones*. Terrible game. Can't wait to—Oh! *Joust*! The cocktail version. So perfect! I'm gonna get me some eggs! Ha ha! Hey! *Turkey Shoot*? I've never even heard of that one. Do you like pinball?"

Noah didn't answer because Felix was already racing off in a new direction. Instead of trying to keep up, he went to the bar to get them both Cokes. While waiting for the drinks, he looked around. The place seemed okay. Games lined every wall, and some stood in clusters in the center of the room. A decent number of people were playing, some with determined expressions, like video games were serious business. Once Noah had the drinks, he found his date next to a token machine, feeding in dollar bills.

"I have a bunch already," Noah said, jerking his head toward the nearest bank of cabinets. "Let's go play."

"I don't even know what to start with," Felix said, clearly overwhelmed.

"How about that one?" He nodded at a random machine.

"*Street Fighter II*?" Felix didn't sound impressed but he peered thoughtfully. "It *is* two-player. Okay!"

Most of the machines had cup holders installed on the sides, which was convenient. Once their hands were free, Noah fed in two tokens and focused on the screen. Felix chose the only female character available; Noah went with some weird green guy. Then they were pitted against each other, hammering buttons as their characters punched, kicked, and yelled words in Japanese. Noah had played the game before, but Felix obviously had more experience, winning the first round before a minute was up. Round two went a little better after Noah remembered how to make the green guy radiate with electricity. That's the one move he stuck with, which annoyed Felix to no end.

"That's so lame!" he laughed. "Come on. Fight with honor!"

"Not my style," Noah said, jabbing the buttons faster.

Felix redoubled his efforts too. The arcade cabinets weren't very wide. In fact, he and Felix were pressed together so they could both get at the controls, their arms touching. This distracted Noah enough that his attention left the screen. Felix swooped in to mercilessly end the fight.

"Again?" Noah asked, mostly because he wanted to stay close.

"Let's play something else," Felix said, looking around. Then he sighed happily. "There she is!"

Donkey Kong, of course.

"Is it two-player?" Noah asked.

"Not co-op, but yeah! Let's go while it's still free!"

Noah followed along, carrying their drinks because Felix would have forgotten them otherwise. He was disappointed by the next game. Sure, it was two-player, but only as separate turns. That meant they weren't nestled against each other. Eventually he suggested they play something co-op, hoping he had the term right. They moved to *Teenage Mutant Ninja Turtles*, which was cool but also much wider since it allowed up to four players. In other words, no physical contact. Noah decided to make peace with that, helping Felix beat the entire game, even though that meant dashing for more tokens. More games followed, Felix never tiring. They talked a lot while playing, mostly about Felix's happy memories of gaming while growing up.

"Let's take a break," Noah suggested after a round of *Tapper*. "They have food here. Buffalo wings, nachos, and some other stuff."

"Nachos sound good," Felix said, reaching for his wallet.

"I've got this," Noah said. "You're not allowed near the bar, remember? Grab us some seats."

"Okay. Thanks!"

Felix smiled at him. Probably. He had been grinning nonstop since they walked in the door. Once food had been fetched and they were sitting together at a table, Noah found he was more interested in focusing on his date than eating.

"What else do you do for fun?"

"Sorry," Felix said, shaking his head while staring at the table. "I didn't mean to dominate the evening with my obsession."

"Why are you sorry? I'm having a good time!"

Felix looked up in surprise. "Really? You don't think it's boring?"

Noah popped a tortilla chip in his mouth, considered Felix while he chewed, and swallowed. "You weren't kidding when you said you're insecure. Where does that come from?"

"Oh." Felix looked away again. "I'm not very good at dating."

"Says who?"

"My first boyfriend. I don't think he liked me much. I've been on a few other dates, and the guys are never interested in talking to me."

"Let me guess, they were only interested in getting into your pants."

Felix's eyes darted to meet his. Then he nodded. "Yeah."

"That's just guys being tactless and horny. All it says about you is that you're attractive."

"I'm not."

"You are! Do me a favor. No more talking down about yourself for the rest of the night, okay? Be more confident!"

Felix smiled sheepishly and nodded once.

"That's not enough," Noah said. "Let me hear you say something positive about yourself. Anything good. Go on."

Felix looked around the room for inspiration. "I guess I have a good memory. Not just for gaming history. I never need to study much. When I want to learn something, most of it sticks on the first try."

"Which means you're smart."

"I wasn't trying to—"

"Say it."

Felix laughed. "Fine. I'm smart."

"I agree. Confidence is sexy. Remember that. So what's up with this guy who didn't appreciate you?"

"Marcus," Felix said with an exasperated sigh. "My first... my *only* boyfriend. That was senior year. I had just come out. Kind of. My mom and sister have known since I was twelve—"

"*Twelve*?" Noah said disbelievingly.

"Yup! Not because I was brave. I was so naïve. I figured I needed more vitamins or something because I was more interested in boy bands while most of my friends had become obsessed with girls. So I asked my mom what was going on and she told me."

"I kind of did the same thing," Noah admitted. "I knew something was going on and asked my parents for help after they caught me with another guy. I was only fourteen. We weren't having sex, but like you, I wasn't into girls at all. I thought my parents could fix me. They thought so too."

"Uh oh," Felix said, his expression sympathetic. "That's never good. Being gay isn't a choice."

"That's right, it's not. I figured that out. They didn't. We don't talk much these days." Or at all.

"How terrible!" Felix's hand moved across the table toward him.

"It's fine," Noah said, playfully putting a tortilla chip on top of Felix's hand instead of taking it. "The upside is that my sad story gets me lots of sympathy from cute boys."

The compliment wasn't lost on Felix, whose cheeks flushed as he absentmindedly played with the chip. "Have you had a lot of boyfriends?"

"Just one," Noah answered honestly. "And I'm not sure he liked me either. So how did your mom take it?"

"She was incredible! We talked about sexual orientation, but she didn't know a lot about it either, so we did research together to figure out the rest."

"And your dad? You haven't mentioned him yet."

Felix's expression became more somber, but he didn't seem upset. "He's around. My parents are divorced, and my dad lives outside of Austin. I still see him. We just never really clicked. My sister has a better relationship with him. She was my biggest defender. My dad wasn't thrilled about the news, but he got over it. I didn't come out at school until close to graduation. I already got picked on enough as it was."

"And that's when you met your first boyfriend."

"Yeah." Felix made a face. "That whole thing was weird. Marcus always seemed irritated by me, like I couldn't do anything right. He told me once that if I wasn't the only other openly gay guy at school, that he wouldn't even have been with me. Was your first boyfriend that bad?"

A pit opened in his stomach. "Ryan? Not really. The problem was that he had already fallen in love with someone before he met me. I couldn't compete."

"That can't be right." Felix broke the chip in half while doing his best to appear stern. "Now *you're* talking down about yourself. There's no way he wasn't into you!"

"Stop."

"I mean it! You're handsome, you're nice, and you're a good person."

"You don't even know me."

Felix wouldn't be discouraged. "So what? I'm already sure you would be a great boyfriend."

Noah thought of his past, and the less comfortable details of his present. "I really wouldn't."

"Prove it."

He shook his head, not sure he understood. "What's that supposed to mean?"

Felix jutted out his chin. "You told me to be more confident. That's what I'm doing. I want you to be my boyfriend." Then the mask slipped and he covered his face with his hands. "I didn't just say that!"

"No takebacks," Noah joked.

He couldn't help considering the question seriously. He enjoyed Felix's company. Sure it had only been a handful of hours, but in some ways, Noah was seeing how his life could have been: understanding parents, a sheltered upbringing, and the normal post high-school void of not knowing what to do. No checkered history of life on the streets or a boyfriend with a needle in his arm. Noah had experienced a lot for his age, more than he probably should have. At times he felt wise about the world. At others he felt embittered. He didn't want to be jaded. He wanted to leap around a bar full of old video games and feel the same unbridled joy that Felix did. Marcello was right. Something was missing from his life, and whatever it was, Felix had it.

"No takebacks," Felix said. His hands were flat on the table now, his face determined, if not a little terrified. "I know you would be a good boyfriend. I'm smart, remember? I notice these things."

But he didn't know all the facts. Most relationships began that way, he supposed. Noah could tell him the full truth right then, but he wanted to be more than just an escort and was tired of that job defining him. He missed having a life outside of his work. His only concern was, instead of Felix lifting him up, that Noah might drag him down.

Not if they were careful though. "You shouldn't rush into

things," Noah said, smiling enough to reassure Felix that he wasn't getting the brush-off.

"Why?"

Now he laughed. "What do you mean *why*? Don't you wish you had taken things slower with Marcus? If you had, you could have avoided a bad relationship."

Felix thought about it. "No. I'm glad we rushed in. At least now I can say I've had a boyfriend. And I got to do other things for the first time."

"I'm sure you did. It's still the wrong answer. Try again. Don't you wish you had taken things slower with Marcus?"

"Boy, do I!" Felix said, hamming it up. "I should have saved myself for marriage."

"You don't have to take it that far. There's this new-fangled thing called dating, you know."

"Dating?" Felix paused to bite his bottom lip. "What's the difference?"

"Only that we take it one date at a time. If one of us decides it's not working, then we call it quits."

"Sounds just like being in a relationship."

"It is a relationship of sorts," Noah said carefully.

Felix cocked his head. "So let's see, if someone asks if I'm single, I get to say that I'm dating someone. Not bad. What if they ask if I have a boyfriend?"

"Tell them that you're dating someone."

"Mm-hm. And what if they ask *me* on a date."

"I don't like the sound of that," Noah said. "Who is this guy, anyway? Is he bugging you? Want me to talk to him?"

Felix laughed happily. "Okay, dating sounds fine."

"You sure?"

"Yeah! I get to brag about you, we still get to do all the relationship stuff, and you'll act jealous if anyone hits on me. What more could a guy want?"

Noah's smile froze in place. "What if someone wants to date me?"

"Just don't tell me about it," Felix said. "I cry easily."

"Seriously?"

Felix nodded. "Yeah."

Okay. This could work. Noah wouldn't be cheating on him by doing his job, and if he didn't have to report what he did every night, then they had potential. For what exactly, he wasn't sure, but he was looking forward to finding out.

He considered their surroundings. Bleeps, bloops, and digital riffs came from each arcade cabinet. The deluge of sound was mixed in with music playing on the bar's sound system and the drunk patrons who were shouting at each other to be heard. "Do you want to get out of here?"

Felix also surveyed the room, reaching a different conclusion. "But I love it so much!"

Noah laughed. "We can come back some other time. I want to be alone with you."

That got Felix's attention. "Okay. Where should we go?"

Noah hadn't thought that far ahead. He was about to suggest a stroll through one of his favorite parks when Felix came up with a different idea.

"Do you want to go home with me?" After seeing Noah's smirk he added, "Not like that!"

"I'm not sure I'm ready to meet your mother."

"She's not home. She works nights at the hospital. My sister might be there, but she'll leave us alone."

Homes held a special appeal for Noah, maybe because he had gone so long without one of his own. His current place didn't feel much like a home, most of the time. Yes, the apartment was his and provided comfort and shelter, but some crucial element was missing. "Sounds good," Noah said. "Let's go." When he noticed Felix's hesitation, he added. "We don't have to."

"No! I want to. It's just... *Baby Pac-Man*. I've never played it before."

"One game!" Noah said, shaking his finger sternly. "Then we're out of here."

One game turned into five, not that he really minded. The game didn't interest him much, but standing next to it and getting to witness Felix's gleeful expression, face lit by blinking lights, was worth the delay. When they were in the truck and on the road again, Felix raved about what they had seen and done, like they had gone on a grand adventure. Noah didn't mind that either. Better a boyfriend who was obsessed with leveling up than one who was desperate to shoot up.

They drove to a neighborhood on the eastern edge of Austin. The apartment complex where Felix lived was set in the middle of a commercial zone filled with block after block of fast food restaurants, grocery or liquor stores, and pawn shops. If the landlord switched off all the street lamps on the property to save money, Noah wagered there would still be enough residual fluorescent light to illuminate the parking lot.

Any concerns he had about the area evaporated when they entered directly into the living room. Once the door was shut behind them, the outside world was sealed away, leaving them in a small space that felt cozy. He sized up the furnishings, such as the worn leather couch, the widescreen television several years out of date, and numerous school photos on top of the entertainment center. An attached dining room contained a table partially filled with mail, school books, and other clutter. This bled into a minimal kitchen. Felix offered him a drink, Noah following along and noticing that the refrigerator was covered with old drawings, more family photos, and tests with impressive scores.

"I love it here," Noah said, cracking open the can of generic soda he was handed.

Felix looked at him like he was crazy. "Really? Then your place must be really small. Do you live on your own?"

"Yeah," Noah said. "Size isn't everything, you know."

"Oh-kay!" said a female voice.

He looked over in time to see a slender form turn and head back down the hallway.

"Darli!" Felix said, pushing past him. "We were *not* talking about… You know."

"I don't know," Darli said, spinning around again, this time with mischief on her face. "Is this him? The one you couldn't stop talking about?"

"Would you knock it off!"

Noah sauntered forward and introduced himself, Darli giggling as she shook his hand.

"My sister," Felix said without much enthusiasm. "She can't stick around because she has lots of studying to do. Right?"

"With my headphones on," she added, "so I can't hear anything *untoward*."

This last word she said with a stuffy British accent. Then she stuck out her tongue at Felix, who pushed her further down the hall where they had a hushed conversation. Noah loved every second of this. He felt like a bad boy with a questionable reputation, and now the sweetest, most innocent boy at school had brought him home.

"Sorry," Felix said as he returned. "She's terrible."

Except it was clear that they loved each other. "I like her," Noah said generously. "Good first impression."

"Really?"

"Yeah! Great sense of humor."

This seemed to please Felix, who gestured to the nearest door. "My room," he explained.

"After you."

Noah wasn't sure what he was expecting, but it wasn't the visual assault that greeted him. Felix's room was busy. To say the absolute least. The walls were covered in posters, most for video games, anime series, pop stars, and television shows. The theme continued. A number of shelves were squeezed into the room, loaded with graphic novels, CDs, DVDs, and even VHS cassettes. Books were there too, as well as small figures, various knickknacks, and yet more books. An old square television was at one end of the room, an impossible number of cords snaking from it to a variety of game consoles and media players. In the center of everything was a neatly made full-sized bed. Noah moved toward it instinctually, as it was the only free space in the room.

"I need my own place," Felix admitted, noticing his reaction. "Imagine all this spread out over an entire apartment and not just this room. That makes it less nutty, right?"

Noah shook his head and laughed. "Is there anything you're *not* into?"

"*World of Warcraft*, gangsta rap, and those shows about people wanting to buy a house."

Noah wasn't sure if he was kidding or if that was the complete list. "How much do you make in tips? You're secretly rich, aren't you?"

Felix considered the clutter around them. "I'll let you in on a little secret. One reason I'm so into retro stuff is because it's all I can afford. I'm always hitting charity shops and garage sales. I'm the ultimate bargain hunter. Give me twenty bucks and I can fill the back of your truck with stuff."

"If you had told me that earlier," Noah said, "I wouldn't have believed you." He tried taking it all in but was overwhelmed.

Instead he focused on small details, nodding to one of the posters. In it, two silhouettes stood on a cliff, staring dramatically at a distant beam of light. "Who are they? Your sister and you?"

"No!" Felix said. "Very funny. That's Avatar Korra and Aang. You've seen *The Last Airbender*, right? Wait, are you making fun of my height or hers?"

"I noticed that she's taller than you, that's all. And no, I've never seen that show." He nodded to another piece, an amateur drawing of one guy pressing another up against a wall. "What's up with that?"

"Sterek," Felix said, as if this was explanation enough. When he noticed Noah's lack of a reaction, he tried again. "Stiles and Derek? *Teen Wolf*? Do you even watch TV?"

"Not enough, apparently. Did you draw that?"

"My friend did. What are you into?"

The question from any other lips would have been much less innocent. "I like to read."

"Harry Potter?" Felix asked, rising to consult his shelf.

"Loved it."

"Hunger Games?"

"The first two were good."

"Divergent trilogy?"

"Just started it last week. If you spoil anything, I will break up with you!"

Felix grinned, either because of the reference to their relationship, or because they were speaking the same language. The kid was crazy about pop culture. Noah might have been too, if raised in a less religious household.

"You're still into cartoons," he noted, looking to the posters again. "I might need to double-check that ID."

"Some of the best stories are animated," Felix replied. "You really should watch the two Avatar series. They have nothing to do with the James Cameron movie. My sister gave me that poster, by the way. It's an SDCC exclusive. That's another money-saving tip: Use those birthday wishes wisely!"

"SDCC?" Noah repeated. "That's some sort of convention, isn't it?"

Felix was so stunned by this lack of knowledge that he was forced to sit. "San Diego Comic Con is the place I most want to go. That's my biggest dream right now. That, or maybe E3."

Noah shook his head. "We're going to need a translator."

"We won't," Felix said, shrugging the topic away. "It's all dumb."

"Not if it's your dream, it isn't," Noah said. "I like that you're so passionate about your interests."

"Really?" Felix leaned forward, like this might be the moment of their big kiss. "What's your dream?"

Noah took an interest in the soda can he was holding, not wanting to feed into the idea of them being here to get it on. He had enough sprinting to home base with his clients. "That's a big question. My dream… I've been thinking about it lately. I'm finally stable. Financially, anyway. I have a lot of free time when I'm not working. What am I supposed to do with it?"

"Time is easy to spend," Felix replied. "It's money I can't imagine having."

"You should try. That reminds me of a mental exercise I always used to play. If some mysterious benefactor put three thousand bucks into your bank account every month, what would you do? That's enough to live on, if you're careful, but not enough to do anything crazy like buy a yacht."

"Why not imagine more money?"

"Because it's more realistic this way. If you didn't have to work, what would you do?"

"Keep working so I could really help support my family."

"That's a good answer."

"Thanks," Felix said. "Kind of depressing too. Even if I had the money for SDCC, I wouldn't feel right wasting it on that. I feel bad enough about all this stuff."

"You shouldn't," Noah said. "Especially when you spend as little on it as you can. You've got to have something to keep you going. Otherwise life is all work and nothing else." He had the uneasy realization that his own life was on the verge of becoming just that.

"So you don't know what your dream is?" Felix pressed.

Noah thought of all he had seen tonight—a sweet guy with a big heart, and a family who didn't have a lot, but were probably happier than he had been in years. "This is long-term, so I don't mean right now, but I think I want kids."

"For real?"

"Yeah. I'd also like someone with me. To help raise them."

He was about to ask if Felix wanted the same, but his expression said it all. Noah inquired anyway, wanting to hear the sound of his voice, which never seemed devoid of enthusiasm. They kept talking, the hours whizzing by. Noah explained what had happened with his family in more detail and listened to the problems Felix had with his father. They talked about the posters on the wall, played a video game so old that it was literally just giant pixels moving around on the screen, and laughed as they took turns doing terrible impressions of the two presidential candidates. He was surprised when checking his phone to see that it was nearly five in the morning.

"You don't have a window in this room?" Noah complained.

"It's behind one of the shelves," Felix said sheepishly. "I needed the display space. Is it seriously that early?" He checked his own phone and groaned. "I'm supposed to be at work in five hours. I guess I should get some sleep."

"That's my cue," Noah said, standing and stretching.

"You're not too tired to drive?"

He could guess what that meant, but he played innocent, just to discover if he was right. "I don't have much choice."

"You could stay the night. Or the morning, I guess."

Noah smiled. The offer was nice, it's just that… "I mean it about not rushing into things. It's better this way."

"Just sleep," Felix said. "I promise."

Noah really was tired, and despite the chaos of the room, he felt comfortable here. "Okay."

"Awesome!" Felix leapt to his feet. "I have pajamas, but I don't think they'll fit you."

"I'll be fine. I just need to use the restroom."

"Oh." Felix nibbled his bottom lip. "We need to be quiet. My mom sleeps on the couch."

"How come?"

"So my sister and I can each have our own bedroom. Another reason I need to move out as soon as possible. Don't worry, she's cool. If she does wake up—"

"I'll make sure she doesn't."

"You can use my toothbrush if you want," Felix said, following him to the door. "It's the blue one."

He knew married couples who refused to share but wasn't surprised at this point. Felix didn't have a lot of boundaries. Or maybe he was just really generous. Noah went to the restroom for the usual business and ended up using the toothbrush. When he returned to the room, the sheets were turned down and Felix was standing there in pajamas themed with some other show Noah hadn't heard of. All he knew was that Felix looked cute.

"I'm beat," he said, yawning as he casually stripped off his shirt. He pretended not to notice Felix staring and waited until he was alone in the room before he undressed down to his boxer briefs. Then he slid beneath the sheets.

Noah was used to sleeping in unfamiliar surroundings and had almost dozed off by the time Felix returned from the restroom. The lights were switched off and a body joined his.

"Good night," Noah murmured.

"Good night," Felix replied.

Noah closed his eyes. A few minutes later, he opened them again, just in time to see another pair quickly shut. A nightlight made of three glowing triangles had been switched on. The golden light revealed that Felix was facing him, his eyelashes fluttering gently, implying he was either peeking or trying not to. Noah felt amused, endeared, enchanted…

"Come here," he said, pulling on Felix's hip. "Roll over."

"Bark bark," Felix answered, complying and scooting closer. "I'm a cat, not a dog."

"I don't mean it like that. And we're just spooning. Don't be getting any ideas."

"Too late."

"I bet," Noah said, lips brushing against the back of his neck. "Get some sleep."

"Sweet dreams," Felix said, a sigh in his voice.

"You too," Noah replied, and while it took some time to settle down, he enjoyed every restless minute spent holding on to the warm body next to his.

Chapter Thirteen

Noah woke three hours later, annoyed that his internal alarm lacked a snooze button he could hit. He disentangled himself from Felix as carefully as possible. Sometime in the middle of the night—or morning—he had rolled over onto his back. Felix had an arm and a leg draped over him, a boner pressing against Noah's hip. It felt good to be loved, he supposed. Resisting the urge to wake Felix by grabbing hold of it, he slipped out of bed, got dressed, and opened the bedroom door a crack. The apartment was silent.

He looked back, wanting to leave a note or something, but he didn't see pen and paper handy. He did, however, spot a stuffed animal—a white cat with a crescent moon on its forehead. Noah took this and carefully placed it in the crook of Felix's arm. That way he wouldn't wake up alone. Cats liked sleeping together, didn't they? He took a photo with his phone, wanting something he could look at during the day. Then he slipped outside the room and down the hall.

The couch was occupied. Noah couldn't see much of the person beneath the quilt. Just the outline of a body and the back of long hair. Meeting the mother sounded charmingly quaint, but not like this. Noah held his breath, praying to get outside undetected because he could already imagine an awkward conversation with a half-awake stranger. Luck was on his side for once because he closed the apartment door behind him without waking anyone.

Noah drove home, took a shower, and got dressed. He could try to get more sleep, but he was used to long nights. Some clients liked to take their time. Especially the edgers. If he gave in to sleep now, most of his day would be ruined, not that he had plans. What he wanted was to see Felix again. Having a normal connection with another human being, and not just an exchange of services, had felt good. He checked his phone in case Felix had risen and texted. Nothing. Then he browsed the other recent messages. A bunch from Marcello that were work related, and a series of polite but increasingly worried texts from Edith. Why not?

Noah checked the clock. The shelter wasn't too busy at this

time of day, so he drove over, wanting to see her. Not just to assure her that he was okay, but also to spend time with someone who had looked out for him when he'd had nothing.

After finding a parking spot and walking the rest of the way to Jerusalem, he discovered the front desk was occupied, just like he imagined. Except it wasn't the right person. Pete the bouncer was still glowering after all this time.

"How's it going, Pete?" Noah said cheerfully. "Remember me?"

Pete nodded. Talkative as always!

"Hey, is Edith around? She's been calling a lot lately."

Pete studied him, remaining eerily still. Then he leaned forward, grabbed something from the desk, and set it on the counter. A bundle of envelopes held together by a rubber band. "These are for you."

Noah ignored them. "He speaks!"

"When I feel like it," Pete said, nodding at the envelopes. "There you go."

"Thanks," Noah said, taking a step forward. He examined the first in the stack, stomach sinking at the return address. The prison in Gatesville. Of course. Ryan had been busy writing him. He flipped through the corners of the envelopes to make sure all came from the same sender. They did.

"Mail forwarding," Pete grunted. "Go to the post office and give them your new address."

"But then I wouldn't have the pleasure of seeing your cheerful face," Noah said, not surprised when the joke fell flat. "Listen, did I do something to offend you? Or does everyone get the five-star treatment?"

Pete took his time answering. "You remind me of bad times."

"Because you used to be on the street too?" Noah snorted. "You're in the wrong line of work then, because this entire place must be one big reminder."

"Not because of that," Pete grumbled. "Because of the Gentlemen's Agreement Club."

Noah stared. First he thought that Pete must have been a client. Not a current one, or chances were that Noah would have at least heard of him. Then he reappraised the man, the muscles of the large arms soft now, but they had probably once been hardened through training. Pete was attractive, in a hulking macho sort of way. The hair covering his knuckles or escaping the neck of his T-shirt, along with the bald head, indicated a ton of testosterone. Noah could think of more than one client who preferred that type. Undeniably manly. "You used to work for Marcello."

"I still do."

The letters Noah held in one hand felt heavier somehow. "That's how he knew about Ryan, isn't it? Because of you!" He clenched his jaw. "You haven't done me any favors!"

"I was thinking of Tim Wyman. Not you. I like him."

"You and everyone else," Noah said, turning to leave.

"You should quit."

The change of tone halted Noah. Pete's voice was no longer laced with disdain. Instead he sounded concerned. Noah shook his head at himself for not leaving, then spun around. "Quit the GAC?"

"It's not good for people."

"You might have had a bad experience," Noah said, "but this job saved me. Would you rather I go back to sleeping on the streets? Or here?"

"Marcello will give you another job. That's what he did for me. Ask him."

"And I bet you're making just as much money now, right?"

Pete resumed glowering. "I help people."

"So do I."

"People who actually *need* help. Never mind. I knew you wouldn't understand."

Noah was torn between irritation and curiosity, but ultimately, he was looking forward to having a good day, and an argument about his lifestyle wasn't part of the plan. He wasn't even here to get his mail. "Is Edith working today?"

"This afternoon. She'll be here then."

"As much as I'd love to stick around…" Noah pushed away from the counter.

"You could at least return her calls," Pete said.

"I'll add that to the list of things I've done wrong," Noah retorted. "Let me know if you think of anything else."

Once he was outside, he took a deep breath and exhaled. Pete was right. Maybe not about everything, but Noah did feel guilty for ignoring Edith for so long. Before he could overthink it, he trapped the letters beneath one arm, pulled out his phone, and called her.

"Hello?"

"Hi," he said. "It's Noah. Um. Noah Westwood."

"I know who you are!" Edith said. "Is everything okay? Where are you?"

"At the shelter. I stopped by to see you."

"But you're okay?"

"Yes!" Noah said with a chuckle. "I'm fine. I just thought it would be nice to catch up."

"My shift doesn't begin until three, but I can come in early."

"Don't do that! It's sweet of you but… Do you have any plans for lunch?" He figured he at least owed her that much. Another idea occurred to him, one that could potentially double his happiness. "I know a great seafood place. Actually, the food is average at best, but the staff… It's worth visiting for them alone!"

Edith was seated across from him. She looked much the same. Still tall, ramrod thin, and marked by perpetual worry. Her hair was dark and pulled back except for wiry gray hairs that had broken loose. The creases on her forehead might be a little deeper than he remembered. He hoped that wasn't his fault. Noah was glad they were having lunch. As much as he had wanted to distance himself from the shelter, he only had positive memories of her because any night that he stumbled into Jerusalem and saw Edith at the front desk had greatly increased his chances of being fed and sheltered.

"I want to thank you," he managed to say.

Then the waiter appeared.

"Hi! My name is Felix and I'll— Oh my gosh!"

Noah laughed at the flushed cheeks. All he had to do was say one word for the color to deepen. "Hey."

"Hey! Um… Okay." Felix tried to get himself under control. "Who needs a drink? Besides me? Ha ha."

Noah turned to Edith. "They have these amazing lemon lime Cokes here. You really should try it."

Edith shook her head. "Too much sugar."

"I can do diet!" Felix said. "Works just as well!"

"They're his own invention," Noah said across the table. "If you say no, it might break his heart."

"Very well." Edith was holding back a smile that came out in full force once Felix had left again. "What's this? A love connection?"

Noah laughed warmly. He had almost forgotten how weird her English could be. "We just met recently. Last night was our first date."

"That's wonderful," Edith said, but with some reservation. "He isn't— Are you still working the same job?"

"He's not a client," Noah said. "Are you kidding? Just look at him! Felix is so adorable that he could have anyone he wants. He hasn't figured that out yet, so please don't tell him."

"I will keep your secret." Edith smiled. "You look well. Are you still living in the same apartment?"

"In other words, you want to make sure I'm not on the streets."

"I've been worried about you!" Edith said, fussing with the cloth napkin and cutlery. "I'm used to faces disappearing. That's how this job is, but you were so young when you first came to us. You seemed so lost."

He had been on his own for the first time. No more friends to lean on, and no Ryan to guide him. "That's what I wanted to talk to you about. I'm thankful for everything you've done. You aren't the only social worker at the shelter, but you're the only one who really cared about me."

"They all care," Edith said, clearly flattered, "but we each have our special cases who go straight to our hearts."

"I'm sorry I worried you, and that I wasn't in touch. Once I got away from the shelter, I didn't want to go back again."

"Two lemon limes," Felix said, setting them on the table.

"What is this?" Edith cried happily. "A little umbrella!"

"I take it you don't drink many cocktails," Noah teased.

"Wine never gets such decorations. What a pity!"

"I can get you a daiquiri," Felix offered.

"Ignore him," Noah said. "He's full of temptation."

Felix tittered and blushed again. They placed their food orders, Noah letting Felix decide for him. Then they returned to their conversation.

"I wouldn't worry so much," Edith said, "if you had a different occupation."

"I know." He didn't expect anyone to accept what he did.

Noah had once shared the common judgmental view of sex workers. It was a different world from the inside, and not one that many people would ever see. "I'm safe. Trust me."

"I'm concerned with more than just physical safety or STDs," Edith said. "I have a friend who shared your line of work. He doesn't talk openly about it, but if I asked, maybe he would be willing to tell you his experiences."

"Pete?"

Edith looked surprised. "How did you know?"

"He started bossing me around about it earlier today."

"That's very unusual. He doesn't talk much at all!"

"I noticed," Noah said, wondering if he had been too hasty earlier. He didn't realize that Pete was so guarded about his past. Still, he didn't need a lecture from him or anyone else, no matter how well-meaning. "I'm fine. I'm not the same kid who showed up at the shelter that night. I've made some dumb decisions, but I'd like to think that I'm still smart. Have a little faith."

Edith nodded. "I worry too much. I know. Blame my brother for that."

"What do you mean?"

She shook her head like it was inconsequential, but at Noah's encouragement, she spoke more. "My little brother, he was always restless. We grew up in a small town, but it wasn't as it is here in the States. A small town isn't so oppressive where I come from."

"Where's that?"

"France. You are familiar with Alsace? Or maybe Strasbourg?"

"Uhhh..." He jogged his memory and came up barefoot and blistered. "Are those cities? I don't know. Sorry."

"I am used to it."

"I always thought you were German."

"Close! We were not far from the border. I liked it there, but... My brother was the artist of the family. Painting, writing, singing, acting—he wanted to do it all. He felt that New York was his best chance. Me? I thought of Paris, but I could never say no to Hugo. So I made sure to get accepted into a New York university, and he followed. I knew he would never go to school. I was his only hope. As he made sure to tell me over and over."

Noah laughed. "I'm an only child, but from what I understand, most siblings don't help each other out like that."

"We were very close," Edith said. "The first year was good. We explored the city together. New York became Hugo's muse. He did impressive work there. He sold pieces and was accepted by a gallery. Everything seemed fine. Then I fell in love, and maybe I got distracted. Or maybe the art world is to blame, but I should have noticed sooner."

"Drugs?" Noah guessed.

Edith nodded. "Heroin. I didn't go to school to become a social worker. I wanted to be an accountant! Not very similar, I admit, but when Hugo disappeared and I started going to the shelters, I was upset by what I saw. The staff were overworked. I would show them Hugo's photo, they would look for one second, maybe two, then shake their heads and run off to do more work. I never forgot that."

"What about your brother?"

"That is a long story. I found him eventually, and I moved us as far away from New York as possible. I don't blame the city. Many people go there, even artists, and they don't succumb to addiction. Hugo always drank too much, even in France. He never knew when to stop."

"So what happened?"

"I met a man while in New York," Edith said. "Tom, a fellow student. He was from here, and when we both graduated, he said I should come home with him and get married. I said I couldn't go without my brother, and Tom said to bring him along. He and Hugo became friends, and I was certain that everything was going to be okay. An addiction can be difficult to outrun. As it turned out, Texas wasn't far enough."

"My ex was a junkie," Noah said. "The guy who keeps sending letters to the shelter."

"So you've witnessed what it can do. You understand."

He nodded. "Yeah."

Edith sat up straight. "Well, that's enough cheerful conversation for today, don't you think? Let's talk about sad things instead!"

He laughed at her joke, but quickly grew somber again. "I understand if you don't want to talk about it, but I'm curious to know what happened with your brother."

"I don't know. He was using drugs, and one day he didn't come home, so I searched the shelters. This time I did not find him, but I again saw how hard the people there worked and decided that was my best chance. I started volunteering and eventually it became my career. I'm not only there for Hugo. I believe in the work, but I'm still hoping to find him. Maybe someday."

Noah swallowed. "I'm really sorry."

"That's life," Edith said, putting on a brave face. "It's full of good and bad that is impossible to avoid, but at least it gives us something to talk about."

"If there's anything I can do…" Noah said.

"Take care of yourself. That is what I ask. You remind me of him."

"Was he a redhead too?"

"No. Like you, he could seem quiet and shy, but when the mask was taken away—" Edith had a twinkle in her eye. "I think you are trouble. Am I correct?"

"I plead the fifth."

Their food arrived. They talked more about each other's pasts while eating. Noah regretted not doing this sooner. He liked Edith. She had a complicated history of her own, but it only seemed to empower her instead of dragging her down. He wished he could say the same.

"How long do you think you'll do this work?" Edith asked when they were finished eating.

"As long as I can. The money is really good."

"Risky jobs always pay well. You are happy, at least?"

He hesitated. "I'm working on that. Are you?"

"Oh yes! I never have trouble sleeping at night."

"No wonder! You work hard. I've seen you busting your butt at the shelter."

"Hard work isn't enough for me to sleep. I have to feel good about what I do."

She didn't sound judgmental. He didn't even think the comment was directed at him. It was the simple truth. She received her sense of fulfillment from the work she did. He could use a little more of that himself.

"I miss being at the shelter," he said. "I don't want to sleep there again, but I wouldn't mind stopping by more often. I used to help out where I could. What if I volunteered? Is that possible?"

"We *always* need more help," Edith said. "Yes! I'm holding you to that. What time will you show up tomorrow?"

He grinned. "I'll check my schedule."

They ordered coffee and shared a dessert. Noah insisted on paying. He walked Edith to the parking lot and said goodbye, then went back inside the restaurant. He found Felix clearing their table.

"People are such slobs," Noah said, shaking his head in disdain.

"Tell me about it," Felix moaned in mock exasperation. "The guy who sat here is really weird too. He keeps showing up and leaving me ridiculously huge tips."

"I know the type," Noah said. "He probably wants something in return."

Felix smiled. "Like what?"

"A goodnight kiss. I have to work tonight, and I need to get some sleep, but what if I stopped by your place? Just for a couple minutes."

Felix looked like he was about to faint, so Noah took the tray from him. Then he helped clear the table, only able to walk to the kitchen door before he was stopped.

"My boss would flip," Felix explained.

"I'll get out of here before I get you in trouble," Noah said, handing him the tray. "Tonight?"

"I'll text you when I'm home."

"Good," Noah said, shooting him a wink. "See you then."

He waited until he was in his car before checking his next assignment. The text had come while he was eating with Edith, but he hadn't wanted to read it in front of her. Once he did, he couldn't stop staring at the client's name.

Nathaniel Courtney.

Noah arrived at Studio Maltese that night dressed to impress and smelling fantastic. He felt a little uneasy when Dave the security guard asked him what he was doing there. Noah wondered the same. Nathaniel hadn't seemed the type to hire an escort. He'd been preachy about that aspect of Marcello's business, but then some clients were like that. Publicly they were all Bible quotes and baptisms, but behind closed doors…

"Appointment with Nathaniel," he said, keeping it simple.

Dave checked his list and nodded. Noah wouldn't have been upset if the man had turned him away instead, saying the appointment was canceled. Nathaniel was a married man! Normally that was none of his business. Not everyone was monogamous, but more often than not, the married guys wanted to meet him somewhere neutral, like a hotel room. Or, like now, a private office.

On the ride up to the second floor and during the walk down the hall, he tried to shake these feelings and get himself into a professional mindset. Charming. Seductive. But why him? Nathaniel hadn't seemed to like Noah much. That could be it. People got off on all sorts of crazy things. He found the right door and knocked.

"Come in," barked a gruff voice.

"Hey," he said when entering, still not in the correct headspace. "We have an... appointment?"

Nathaniel looked up from his laptop and nodded. "That's right."

"Cool." Noah shut the door behind him and stood there awkwardly. "Are we staying here?"

"Yeah," Nathaniel said as he typed. "I just need to finish this and we'll get started right away. Make yourself comfortable."

So he was one of those guys! Noah came closer, unbuttoning his shirt and shrugging it off. He let it drop to the floor, but Nathaniel didn't even look up. Maybe he was hard to please. Size impressed most people, so Noah started on his belt, the metal buckle clanking and clattering. Nathaniel tore his eyes away from his computer, shooting him an irritated glare. Then he did a double-take.

"What are you doing?"

"My job," Noah blurted out.

"Hold it right there." Nathaniel said. He grabbed his phone, tapped it a few times and held it to his ear, looking him over as he waited for an answer. "It's me. Yeah, still at the office. There's a guy here, just took off his shirt and looks like he's about to whip it out. Seriously. No, I didn't ask him to. Mm-hm. I think you could take him in a fight. No, no knives please. What? Do we even have a rolling pin? Wait, now he's putting his shirt back on. Looks like you can stay home. Say hi to Zero. Okay. Bye."

"Very funny," Noah said, fumbling with his buttons and

getting angry. "You're the one who sent for me! Call your husband back and tell him that!"

"Just because we asked you to come here doesn't mean—" He stopped because a phone had been thrust in his face. Nathaniel read the screen. Then he leaned back in his chair. "Sorry. Not your fault. Marcello is messing with me. Here." He loosened his tie and took it off. "Put this on the doorknob outside."

"Why?"

"Because it's our turn to mess with him."

Noah did what he was told, face still burning when he returned to the desk. "I hate him. Should I go?"

"No. We really do need you here. Just not for that."

"Fine by me," he said, flopping down in a chair. Then, having regained some of his sense of humor, he added. "Your loss. Believe me."

"I can only imagine," Nathaniel said. Then he held a finger to his lips.

"Oh!" said a voice in the hall. "My my." Then louder, it added, "What's this tie doing on the floor?"

Nathaniel rolled his eyes, Noah not needing to explain that he had put the tie firmly on the knob.

"I should probably return it to its rightful owner," Marcello continued. "I'll just see if anyone's home. No, I mustn't! Mustn't I? I'm so torn! Still, it would be a shame if some thief ran off with such a nice tie. I'll just slip it inside. Pun intended."

The door creaked open a crack, a beady eye appearing and taking in the scene. Then the door flew open.

"Hollow out a mountain," Marcello said, "and there still wouldn't be enough room to contain my disappointment. Where's your sense of adventure, Nathaniel? And you, Noah, where's your sense of duty?"

"I already called Kelly," Nathaniel said. "There's a price on your head. You brought this upon yourself."

"I shall face my fate in the same way I came into this world," Marcello said. "Naked. We'll see what your hitman thinks of that!"

"That's one way of scaring him off. Now if you don't mind, we have a ton of work to get through."

"Understood," Marcello said, strolling the rest of the way into the room. He placed the tie on the desk, nodded cordially at Noah, and took a seat next to him. "Let's get started, shall we? We asked you here tonight, Noah, because I sense you are ready to make a difference in the world."

How could he know about that already? Was Noah bugged? Or was Felix a spy? Then it hit him. "Pete told you."

Marcello's expression remained neutral. "Told me what?"

"That I'm going to volunteer at the shelter again."

"How wonderful! And what a coincidence. Helping the homeless is exactly what I had in mind. We're holding a benefit on Saturday evening. A charity ball. All proceeds will go toward renovating a local shelter, and we were hoping you would see fit to participate."

"Sure!" he said.

Nathaniel grunted. "You might want to read the fine print before making a deal with the devil."

"Or not," Marcello said. "It's really quite simple. I find myself in a predicament. The catering service I normally use has switched ownership, and my preference for an all-male staff sits uneasy with him."

"Marcello wants shirtless waiters," Nathaniel explained.

"Which wasn't a problem previously, but now I'm told I need an even mix of men and women, and while I personally have no issues with nudity, no matter the gender—"

Nathaniel interrupted. "Picture a room of rich gay guys faced with the first boobs they've seen up close since they stopped nursing."

"Can't you have them all wear shirts?" Noah suggested.

"That's precisely what the new owner suggested," Marcello said, looking baffled. "Some ideological differences are too vast to overcome. I'm left in a pickle, because tomorrow is the only day we have left for preparations."

Noah looked to Nathaniel. "Maybe it was instinct that drove me to take off my shirt."

"Meaning?" Marcello asked. "Did I miss something?"

"He knows what you want from him," Nathaniel answered. "Some of it, anyway."

"I see. Do you have experience waiting tables?"

Noah shook his head. "Nope."

Marcello sniffed. "No matter. If you have a sense of balance, you can perform this task."

"Just me?" Noah asked, still confused.

"Heavens, no!" Marcello declared. "We have quite the guest list. While it would already be helpful if you agreed to wait on them that night, the biggest hurdle we face is convincing your fellows."

Now he got it. They wanted him to call the other escorts of the GAC, but he didn't know most of them, just Harold and two guys he had been in threesomes with at the behest of the respective clients. That was it. "I'm not a secretary."

"No," Marcello said unabashed, "but these are unusual circumstances. You'll be compensated, both for that night and this one. There's another favor I would ask of you. For this particular fundraiser, I thought it would be amusing to host a date auction. Are you familiar with the concept?"

"I've seen that episode of *Saved by the Bell*, yes."

"Oh!" Marcello said, leaning toward him. "Tell me, are you Team Zack or Team Slater?"

"Gentlemen," Nathaniel said impatiently. "The clock is ticking."

"Very well," Marcello said. "All proceeds from the date auction will go to charity, and since this one is on the books, it means you shan't be allowed to sleep with the winner. Officially, anyway."

His entire job was based on what he did unofficially, so that didn't bother him. Noah just needed to decide if this was something he really wanted to do. He thought back to earlier in the day, when Edith had bemoaned how Jerusalem was always filled to capacity and was often forced to turn people away.

"Which shelter would this benefit?" he asked. "Have you chosen one already?"

"I'm open to suggestions," Marcello replied easily. "Is there one you happen to be partial to?"

Noah opened his mouth to answer. Then he shut it again. Marcello already knew which shelter he cared most about because the man knew way too much about everything. It probably wasn't a coincidence that Pete had ended up at Jerusalem. Marcello had given him that job. Isn't that more or less what Pete had said? Noah wouldn't be surprised to learn that Marcello owned the shelter. "Gospel Ministries," Noah answered at last.

"Pardon me?" Marcello started blinking rapidly. "What did you say?"

"The Gospel Ministries shelter," Noah clarified. "I stayed there a few times. They make you take turns reading aloud from the Bible and you have to pray before getting into bed. Very wholesome. You'd love it."

"And you can't think of another shelter that you are—oh, I don't know—more indebted to?"

"Nope," Noah said. "It's that one or I'm not interested."

They stared each other down, a low chuckle breaking the silence. Nathaniel. For once he seemed amused instead of irritated. "I think he's got you figured out, boss."

"Is that so?" Marcello challenged, attention still on Noah.

"I've only connected two pieces of a very complicated puzzle," Noah said dismissively. He didn't want to be considered a threat. Marcello still intimidated him too much. Noah had seen first-hand what happened to people who got on his bad side. "I figure you either own Jerusalem, or you are friends with the owner."

"I shall neither confirm nor deny your theory," Marcello said. "And yes, proceeds will go toward its further renovation. To be truly successful, we would need to raise enough to establish a satellite location. That would relieve the burden most effectively, although if this city's homeless population increases further, I'll be tempted to leave them on the streets so that people and politicians alike are forced to address the underlying issues."

"I'm in," Noah said, loving how passionate Marcello was on the subject. "I'll do whatever I can to help."

"Thank you," Marcello said warmly, standing and patting him on the shoulder. "I'll leave you gentlemen to your work. I have my own tasks to complete."

Noah waited until Marcello had left the office before he turned to Nathaniel. "He owns Jerusalem, doesn't he?"

"Absolutely," Nathaniel said. "He enjoys being enigmatic though, so next time, if you want to make him happy, pretend you don't see right through him."

Noah sighed in exasperation. "That won't be a problem. I still don't understand him most of the time."

A smile tried to wrest control of Nathaniel's lips and failed. "You and me both. Let's get started. We have a lot of people to call."

The work wasn't as hard as it was tedious. For each call he had to explain who he was, cover the background details, and describe what each person's job would be. Some were marked, like himself, to potentially participate in the charity auction. Most were agreeable to the suggestion; some couldn't make it that night. Noah was two hours into this task and had just ended a call when he saw the next name on his list:

Harold Franklin.

His stomach sank. Noah always felt a variety of emotions on the rare occasions he let himself think of Harold. Longing, because he wished they could have been more to each other. Regret, because had he allowed things to develop naturally, maybe they would still be together. Instead he had made his move too soon, Harold had rejected him, and Noah ran, just like he had done with his parents. What was the alternative? Stay and fight? Maybe that was the key. Not for battles that were already lost though, so he copied the name and number to a scrap of paper and walked across the office to Nathaniel's desk. He waited until the other man was finished with his most recent call, then slid the scrap of paper toward him.

"Do you mind taking this one for me?" he asked.

Nathaniel barely glanced at it. "I've got my own list to finish calling."

"I know, but—"

"You have a history together. I get it, but this is business, and that means setting aside personal feelings. You can angst over it later when you're home. Now get back to work."

Geez, he was such a jerk! Noah returned to the table and chairs in one corner of the room. After he sat, he allowed himself to sulk, but not for very long because he could tell Nathaniel was still watching him while pretending not to. Why couldn't they have traded numbers? Their workload would have remained the same.

He was tempted to skip over Harold, but now that Nathaniel had seen whose name it was, he would notice if Noah said a different one. Maybe he could get through this anonymously. Harold wasn't going to recognize his voice after all this time! Feeling foolish for even worrying about it, Noah dialed the number.

"Hello?"

"Hi there!" Noah said, trying to make himself sound upbeat and professional. "I'm calling on behalf of Marcello Maltese regarding an upcoming fundraiser. The benefits will go to help Austin's homeless, and all you have to do—"

"Who is this?" Harold sounded more confused than angry.

Noah swallowed, wishing that voice didn't make him want to fall to his knees and beg for another chance. "As I said, I'm calling from Studio Maltese. Do you happen to have Saturday night free? Any obligations you have with the GAC will be rescheduled and you'll be paid time and a half at the usual hourly rate."

The line was silent except for a barely audible hum. "Noah?"

Hearing that voice again had been hard enough, but when it spoke his name… "Yeah," he croaked. "It's me."

"Why didn't you say so from the beginning?" Harold laughed, sounding happy. "Man! How have you been?"

"Great," he replied. "I uh… I have a lot of calls to get through, so do you think you can be there? It's one of Marcello's—"

"Fundraisers, I know. I've helped out with them before. Is he short on waiters again?"

"Basically. There's also this date auction thing to raise extra money. Think you'd be up for it?"

"Sure!" Harold replied. "Are you going to be there that night? It would be fun to catch up."

He wanted to say that, no, in fact he would not be there and they would never see each other again, thank you very much. But that wasn't true, in regard to either future events or current desires. "I'll be there."

"Cool! So I'll see you then?"

"I've got you down on the list," Noah said. "Sorry. I need to contact the next person now."

"No problem. I'm really glad you called."

"Thank you for helping out," he said quickly. Then he disconnected the call before Harold could say anything else. He looked up and got an approving nod from Nathaniel, so at least there was that, but the brief conversation had left him shaken. As did the idea that they might see each other again. He redoubled his efforts to get through the list. Afterwards, his help was required for other small tasks, but this was a welcome distraction. When he was finally free and had left the studio, he knew the perfect cure for his uneasy heart.

Where are you? he texted.

Home, came the response, along with a blushing emoji.

Noah grinned and got in his truck. Fifteen minutes later, he was parked in front of Felix's apartment complex.

Come outside, he texted.

Mom's not home. Come inside!

I wouldn't get any sleep. Again. And neither would you.

LOL True.

He waited next to his truck, watching as Felix left the apartment and looked around uncertainly. Then he spotted Noah and shyly smiled while walking over to him. He was wearing an outfit too pressed to be the one he had worn to class, and his dark hair was freshly styled. He might have even showered recently, because Noah could smell body wash or cologne.

"So," Felix said when close enough. "Do we talk first, or do we just… Um."

"Get over here," Noah said, pulling on him. "You're adorable, you know that?"

"No," Felix answered seriously. "Are you sure?"

Noah laughed. "I'll prove it."

First he stared into those dark eyes, watching them widen as their faces neared. They closed at the same time their lips touched, Noah keeping it short and simple. More than just a peck, but a kiss that was innocent despite being intimate. When he pulled back, Felix nearly fell forward, clearly not wanting it to end. He was shorter than Noah, which meant those big vulnerable eyes were trained upward, like a pet who knew the most effective way to beg.

"You really are my cute little cat," Noah said, brushing the smooth cheek with the back of his hand. "Except without any whiskers."

"I can try growing some," Felix offered.

"I like you just the way you are."

"Oh. Because I was thinking of dyeing my hair. Sometimes I like to add a little color, but if you don't want that, then—"

Noah smooched him again to stop him short. Then he pulled back. "Some relationship advice: If a guy wants you to change, especially this early on, don't waste your time on him. He's not worth it."

"Okay." Felix thought about it. "Are you saying I *shouldn't* change? It would just be a couple of streaks."

Noah laughed. "Do whatever makes you happy, and if you're

with the right person, he'll be happy that you're happy."

"Got it," Felix said. "Are you sure you don't want to come inside? That would make me happy."

"I bet it would! Get some sleep. We'll have time for happy things another night."

He stayed longer anyway, asking about Felix's day and able to describe most of his own, for once. Noah was tempted to invite him to the fundraiser, knowing it would be fun to have him around, but he didn't want Felix getting mixed up in that world. Instead he kissed him goodbye and returned home, thoughts of Harold now distant enough that Noah fell asleep without thinking of him. Much.

Chapter Fourteen

Noah kept a careful eye on everyone in the ballroom, and not just because it was part of his job. He had already unloaded two trays' worth of champagne and was working on a third, stopping along the way to flirt or catch up with familiar faces. Now he was especially glad he hadn't brought Felix along. Many of the people here were clients of his. Not all, or even most, but enough that an awkward conversation might have ensued. He had already lost track of how many times people found excuses to touch him. Probably more often than he realized, because his attention was often elsewhere, checking each face in the vicinity just to avoid one person.

So far he'd had three close encounters with Harold, near misses where he still managed to escape into the crowd. He checked again, since he was currently pinned down by a guy who loved to talk politics, but thankfully, the area was clear. Then he did a double take. The person he had spotted wasn't Harold, but he was equally as handsome. Maybe even more so. Familiar too, since Noah had seen photos, but they didn't do him justice. Tim Wyman was striking, especially his eyes, which were a gray pale enough to appear silver. The dark hair only helped further this illusion. As for his body, Tim filled out his tuxedo so nicely that Noah could imagine the outfit was enjoying itself.

Most people would probably look at Tim with lust, but deep down, Noah still considered him the competition. All too often he had listened to Ryan rave about how amazing Tim had been, placing him on an impossibly high pedestal, although such conversations usually ended with Ryan knocking him back down again.

"I hope *you* registered to vote," said his conversation partner.

"Of course," Noah said, giving his best smile and hoping it was suggestive enough to change the subject. It didn't.

"Good. When you go to the polling place, remember that more than one position is at stake here. Choose your president, but also make sure the local seats are filled by reputable candidates."

Fine, great, but right now he was busy avoiding one person while trying to figure out what to do with the other. He had read the most recent batch of Ryan's letters. Desperate was the best way of describing them. Ryan had guessed at the reason why Noah no longer visited.

I swear I won't mention Tim again. I was being self-centered. As usual. I know I need to work on that, and while I still don't think I'll be able to move on until I've had a chance to talk to him, I recognize that isn't your burden to bear. Just come see me. We'll talk about us instead.

That final plea was repeated in later letters too.

Since I saw you last, I've only had one visitor. My little sister, Felicia. My parents were with her, but they waited in the car. I wasn't surprised. It stung anyway. Felicia was writing a paper for school about prisons and thought I could help. Later she admitted that she just wanted to visit because she doesn't have many memories of me. Do you remember how much younger she is? I don't know what she was expecting, but she was terrified. Felicia was trembling when we first sat down together. That's when I realized how she must see me. To her I'm just a junkie and an attempted murderer. You know there's more to me than that, right? I hope so because I need someone who has seen my good side and who knows I'm capable of love. I hate to put that burden on you, but there's no one else. Please visit me again. When all people do is treat you like a criminal, you start to see yourself that way. Please. Just one more visit.

Noah wasn't heartless. He felt plenty guilty about turning his back on Ryan, and if not for his promise to Marcello, he would have gone. That would have meant a tedious drive and a trying conversation with his ex, but at least he still had his freedom. Noah could comfort himself with cookies or alcohol. He could go to a movie, see a comedy, and cheer himself up. Ryan could only sit in his cell and regret the past.

He was wrong too. Noah wasn't his only hope. Another person knew that Ryan was capable of love. Tim had also dated him, and like most romantic relationships, it must have begun well. Ryan had certainly described it that way on many occasions.

He searched the crowds to find Tim again. A shorter guy with brown hair was standing directly in front of him and reaching for his face. Tim recoiled, but when the other man put on a patient expression—one that said he might soon *lose* patience—Tim uncrossed his arms and gave in. The other guy touched his face, wiping away food or scratching at a flake of skin, Noah didn't know, but the display was cute. As was the way Tim ruffled the other guy's hair, laughing when this got him in trouble. He seemed nice. Nice enough to forgive the person who had shot him? Noah wasn't sure anyone was that kind.

"Ladies and gentlemen," boomed Marcello's voice from the front of the ballroom. "Seeing as how we're about to begin our charity auction, I'd like to ask my volunteers to please join me here on stage."

"I'm afraid that's me," Noah said, eager to excuse himself. He didn't have anything against politics, but his arm was killing him. He noticed a waiter slacking off, handed him the tray, and went to the front of the room. Noah was climbing the steps to the stage when he noticed who was in front of him. Harold. Of course! They were both in this auction, but at least they wouldn't be able to speak. Once on the stage, Noah held back anyway, letting two other guys go ahead of him. Only then did he join the line, standing shoulder to shoulder while facing the audience.

"Now then," Marcello was saying. He stood behind a podium, auctioneer's gavel in hand. "Do keep in mind that this is for a good cause. Forget for a moment your age, gender, or even your marital status. Neither rank nor profession matter here. Any of these beautiful men are yours for the taking. Why stop at one? Have two or three! The highest bidder is guaranteed an evening of exquisite company, but first, a few ground rules for the bidding process. If you plan on participating, please step forward so—"

"Hey."

The person to his left moved, trading places with someone else. He could already tell from the cologne who it was because maybe, just maybe, Noah had gone shopping for it after they had parted ways, spraying it on his pillow for a few weeks before he decided to stop torturing himself. He had thrown away the cologne, but the scent and the memories associated with it had never faded from his mind.

"Hey yourself," he replied, trying to sound casual and cool. He kept his attention forward, which was difficult because he knew Harold was only wearing a bowtie from the waist up. Exactly like himself. He felt bare skin touch his, a shoulder pressing against his own, whether by accident or design.

"How have you been?" Harold asked.

"Great," he replied stiffly.

"I was hoping to run into you tonight. We should talk. I don't like the way things ended between us."

Noah didn't respond. He tried to focus on what Marcello was saying. The first guy was up for grabs. And gropes and fondles, more likely than not.

Harold didn't seem to notice. "You're still mad. I get it. Can we talk anyway? At least let me explain."

"You already did," Noah said, "and I understood. There's nothing left to discuss."

"There is, because—"

The audience erupted in cheers. "Eight hundred dollars!" Marcello declared. "A princely sum for some handsome prince."

The audience laughed, then the next guy swaggered to the front.

"When you and I first met—" Harold began.

"Not now," Noah hissed. "Seriously. People are starting to stare."

The truth was, plenty of guys were looking in their direction, even when they stopped talking, sizing them up as potential prizes. That was fine. Noah started smiling at them, winking or checking them out in return. Harold might be hotter, but maybe Noah could still bring in a higher price. A petty revenge, but it *was* for a good cause.

"Another generous donation, and from the same esteemed bidder. You, sir, are in for an interesting night! Now then, who do we— Ah! Harold! Let's see if we can't find your Maude."

There were a few boos and hisses from the audience.

"What?" Marcello said, spreading his palms wide. "I see, you thought I was making an age joke, when in truth, I was complimenting you on your vivacious energy and passion for life. Why not prove how young at heart you are with an opening bid of say, one thousand dollars?"

Harold got his bid right away. No wonder, because when Noah leaned forward to get a better view, he saw that Harold's body was more toned than before. The face was just as alluring. He could only see the profile, but the white teeth that were flashing and bringing in more bids got his pulse pounding. Noah didn't need all of that though. He sure liked it, but he would rather hand Harold a shirt to put on, go home with him, and just hang out in the living room again like they used to. Maybe they would get high and watch TV. Or maybe they would just sit there and talk the night away.

"Three thousand, six hundred dollars. Going once. Going twice! Sold!"

Noah knew he wouldn't be able to beat that amount. He could only try to come close. He watched Harold hop off the stage and hug the winner. Then it was his turn, and to his surprise, he was actually nervous.

"Ladies and gentlemen," Marcello said in hushed tones. "Please don't make any sudden movements or loud noises, because here we have an exceptionally rare treat for you. The elusive ginger! I'm told his spirit is just as fiery as his hair, and speaking of heat, I'd like to remind you that we cannot be held responsible for anyone who burns their fingers while out with this young man. Look to your heart's content, but touch at your own risk!"

Noah appreciated the sales pitch. He felt less nervous now. The homeless shelter was all that mattered, so he put troubling thoughts out of mind and focused on working the audience. "I'm also good with a mop and a bucket," he said, "so if you've got floors that need cleaning, I'm your man. No job is too dirty!"

This earned him laughs.

"Any good at fixing cars?" someone called.

"No, but I can pose next to them like models at an automotive show." He demonstrated, pretending Marcello was a car. Noah walked from one side of him to the other, gesturing up and down his boss.

Marcello banged the gavel again. "Let's start the bidding before he attempts to drape himself over my hood. Shall we cut to the chase and begin with two thousand dollars?"

That was way too high! Noah felt his face turn bright red, but he got his bid. He looked into the audience and saw a familiar old man with his hand raised. Chester! That was sweet of him, especially considering that Noah refused to see him these days. He felt bad about that, but if Chester won, he would make sure to—

"Two and a quarter," Marcello said, acknowledging another bid. "Do I hear two and a half?"

Chester again. The old man kept bidding against other people, driving the price up to thirty-five hundred dollars. He was close to breaking Harold's record!

"Going once," Marcello said.

Please please please! Noah met pair after pair of eyes, using a pleading expression on each.

"Going twice!"

Okay, desperate times. He started flexing, knowing he didn't have enough muscle to truly impress, so he played it up, acting silly. He got more laughs, but no more—

"Four thousand."

He sought out the bidder. So did much of the audience. Harold moved to the front, hand still raised. He even managed to surprise Marcello!

"This is highly unusual," their boss said.

"Neither rank nor profession," Harold replied, lowering his hand. "That's what you said."

"Indeed I did! Well, let's continue then. Do I hear higher? Four thousand five hundred?"

He looked at Chester, who seemed to be waiting for guidance from him. Noah didn't want Harold to win, so he shook his head. Chester nodded his understanding, except he had gotten it wrong, because he didn't place any more bids. He thought that Noah didn't want him to bid more! Noah was about to gesture that he should continue when the gavel swung down.

"Sold!" Marcello cried. Then he pointed the gavel at Harold. "This little stunt is coming out of your paycheck, young man! Who do we have next? Colby! If you're looking for a one-man talent show… Excuse me, Noah, but I'm afraid your fifteen minutes of fame are over."

He felt his cheeks flush. Noah was still standing center stage like an idiot. Everyone before him had left the stage to thank whoever placed the winning bid. He wasn't sure he could handle that, but luckily he had a few options. He saw Tim off to one side, ignoring the proceedings and looking as though he was about to leave. Noah also wanted to have a word with Chester to clear the air between them. Then there was Harold, who probably shared the same desire. Noah kept his eyes lowered as he walked down the stage steps, still unsure what to do. Fate decided for him.

"Hey."

The greeting was casual and accompanied by an equally relaxed smile. Noah soon averted his gaze, because Harold was too damn handsome. "Hi. Sorry, but there's someone I really need to talk to."

"I know the feeling," Harold replied.

Noah chuckled like it was a joke, his attention on Tim again, who was definitely heading for the door. "Sorry. This really can't wait."

Couldn't it though? As he rushed away from Harold, he realized he didn't know what he would say to Tim. *Remember that guy who shot you? He's awfully sad these days! Why don't you cheer him up again?* Tim would probably tell him where to stick it, and rightfully so, but that was better than facing the alternative. He glanced back over his shoulder. Harold was still standing there wearing a dejected expression. Noah forced himself to turn forward again, and when he noticed Tim disappear through one of the doors, he broke into a sprint.

"Wait!" he called out when close enough. "Mr. uh.... Mr. Wyman?"

That did the trick. They were at the far end of the kitchen, the room abuzz with activity. As silver eyes locked onto his own, he realized with some irony that he was running away from one gorgeous guy to get the attention of another, and if given the choice, he would gladly replace them both with two average joes. That would make getting over Harold a little easier, and facing Tim… Noah's stomach burbled with nervousness. He could see why Ryan was still clinging to the memory of this person, and how he himself had failed to measure up. On a purely superficial level, Tim was in a different league.

Those silver eyes moved over his body, no doubt taking in the skimpy outfit. "Sorry. I'm off duty tonight. If you need anything, just ask Nathaniel."

"Huh?" Noah replied. Ten points for being a smooth talker!

"You're either a waiter or you're *way* underdressed," Tim joked. "I'm guessing we worked together before. I'm not volunteering tonight, but like I said, Nathaniel can—"

"I used to date Ryan," Noah blurted out. "Ryan Hamilton."

Tim's friendly expression faded. His attention even darted to Noah's hands, as if seeking a weapon there. Then he started to move away. "I gotta check on my dog. She needs to…" He shook his head, went toward another door, and pushed through it.

"Wait!" Noah cried, giving chase. "I just want to talk." Now he knew how Harold must feel. "Please."

They were in a dim hallway, Tim already halfway down it,

but his steps slowed and he stopped. Then he spun around. "If this is about an STD, I've already been tested. For everything. Multiple times. Seemed like a good idea after being with someone like Ryan."

"It's not about that," Noah said. He reached for a nearby switch and flicked it on, wincing against the light before forcing himself to meet Tim's stare. "I'm worried about him."

Tim's laugh was humorless. "Me too. I keep worrying they'll let him go and he'll show up at my house again with a gun."

"What he did was seriously wrong," Noah said quickly, "but that wasn't Ryan. He was never perfect, but he also wasn't that bad. You know he wasn't."

"He stole from me. He cheated!" Tim clenched his jaw. Then he exhaled. "But I never saw him get violent. Not back then."

"Because he wasn't," Noah stressed, "I was with him after you guys were together, and he was good. Messed up, yeah, but still okay. The drugs changed him. He was just starting out when we met. I know it sounds lame, but I blame the heroin. The real Ryan was a loving person."

"He could be." Tim said grudgingly. He leaned to one side to see down the hall toward the kitchen. "Does Marcello know you're here?"

"Yes. Not *right here* right here. He asked me to be a waiter tonight. That's not the usual sort of work I do for him, but he knows who I am. He knows my history."

"Huh. I'm guessing he doesn't know that Ryan asked you to talk to me. That's what's going on here, isn't it?"

"Kind of."

Tim digested these words. Then he pulled out his phone.

"What are you doing?" Noah asked.

"Calling my husband, because my crazy ex asked an escort to get me alone, and that has me worried."

Noah glared. "All I said is that I work for Marcello! How do you know I'm not a photographer? Or an accountant?"

Tim lowered the cell phone long enough to give him a look that said, *You really want me to answer that?* Then he raised the phone to his ear again.

"Please," Noah said. "Just give me ten minutes. I only want to talk!"

"Hey," Tim said, but not to him. "Are you all right?"

"Five minutes!" Noah pleaded.

"Nobody weird is bugging you?" Tim said, still speaking to the phone. "If you see Marcello or Nathaniel, maybe you should—"

"He's suicidal," Noah said. "I'm worried he's going to kill himself."

Tim's face went slack as he gauged the gravity of his tone. Then he spoke to the phone again. "I'm still letting Chinchilla out to go potty. A guy named Noah is with me. He's one of the waiters. Could you tell Marcello? Just in case he worries."

Or in case Marcello had never heard of him. Even though Noah had a legitimate reason for being there tonight, it wouldn't take long for his boss to put the pieces together. He had a few minutes at most, and once those had passed, he would probably find himself unemployed. With that in mind, he decided to make this conversation count. First he wanted to put more distance between himself and the ballroom.

"We can talk while you let your dog out," Noah said, gesturing away from the kitchen. Attempting a humorous tone, he added, "We shouldn't keep him waiting."

"Her," Tim said, proceeding down the hall. "So you used to date Ryan, huh?"

"After you two had broken up, yeah. All he did was talk about you."

"I bet," Tim spat.

"Good things!" Noah said, happy when the hall led to the middle of another and offered two options. They turned right. With luck, anyone in pursuit would choose the other direction. "Ryan regretted a lot of what he did. He never got a chance to tell you, but he realized that he let—" Noah's throat went raw, matching the rising emotion. "He let the love of his life get away."

Tim looked over at him. "He told you this while you were still together?"

"I know it sounds bad," Noah said. "Maybe it was, but he and I were both messed up. The reasons weren't the same, but we were both lost. Talking about that was part of what brought us together. He loved you. Probably more than he's loved anyone."

"He's got a funny way of showing it," Tim said, his tone softer. They turned down another hall, this one leading to a living room. As exposed as Noah now was to extravagant lifestyles, he still stopped to stare at the large space. The ceilings were vaulted, the television mounted on one wall was bigger than his bed, and the furnishings were all expensive and well outside his price range. He was soon distracted by another detail. A head rose from the large U-shaped couch, the dog's brown fur nearly matching the soft pale leather. A gleeful grumble and a wagging stub came next as Tim approached the dog and kissed her head. Noah was temporarily forgotten as Tim showered his pet with baby talk.

"Chinchilla! Who's feeling lonely all by herself? I've got some daddy love for you. Yes I do! And some snuggles!"

Tim might not live here, but Noah could imagine Ryan showing up to interrupt the happy scene, a gun held in one trembling hand. Maybe Tim was having similar thoughts, because when he stood upright again, he appeared grim.

"It sucks that Ryan is having trouble or whatever, but I need to think of my family."

"I get that," Noah said. "I really do. I wouldn't have asked if there was any alternative. Ryan's parents aren't there for him. Mine aren't either. We all have that in common, right?"

Tim eyed him for a moment. Then he patted his leg so Chinchilla would hop down and follow him to a glass door. This opened onto a wide patio. A lit swimming pool and deck took up most of the space. Beyond, twinkling on the horizon, was Austin's skyline. Tim ignored all of this, leading them to one shadowy side and the nearest patch of grass where the yard began.

"He doesn't have anyone," Noah pressed. "I wouldn't have troubled you with this if he did."

"Sounds like he's still got you," Tim said, keeping his focus on the dog. Even in the limited light, a scowl was visible. "I'm done with him."

"He doesn't have me," Noah said, voice strained. "I cut him off too. Even if I hadn't, I don't have what he needs."

"And what's that?"

"Closure. He wants a chance to explain himself and apologize. I have these letters he wrote you, or at least I used to, and they… Listen, I don't expect you to start visiting him every week, or be his shrink or whatever, but I figure it's worth a shot. He's been needing this since he was locked up. All I'm asking is that you see him again, just once."

"No."

Tim's answer came without hesitation, and even though it sounded final, Noah didn't give up.

"Why not?"

Tim turned to face him. "Like I said, I need to think of my family. Ryan might have his good side, but he's still a manipulative little shit. If I show up at that prison and spend time with him alone, he'll probably say—" Tim shook his head in exasperation. "—*something*. I don't know what. That I threatened to kill him or anything to get me in trouble and pull his ass from the fire. I won't give him that chance."

"Even if it means he ends up killing himself?"

Tim swallowed. "I know it sounds cold, but he broke into my house! He held my husband and son at gunpoint! In that kind of situation, you have to make ugly decisions. If I have to choose between the people I love and Ryan—"

"Except he's not standing in your house with a gun," Noah interjected. "He's safely behind bars and trying to find any reason why he should go on living."

"I can't be that reason!"

"No, but you can help absolve him of guilt!"

"Why should I?"

They were both shouting now, Noah glancing behind him and expecting to see more lights on than before. "All you need to do is show up, just once, and listen. That's all I'm asking. Give him a chance to say what he needs to. After that, you've done your part. You'll have gone above and beyond what anyone could reasonably expect, which will be your only consolation when he does kill himself."

Tim frowned. "You really think he will?"

Noah exhaled. "I sure hope not. I'm scared though. I really am."

Tim thought about it. Then he shook his head. "I can't. I don't trust him. Like I said, he'll get me alone and afterwards he'll claim—"

"I'll go with you." Noah nearly grimaced after the words slipped free, but then he realized it made sense. He was probably fired anyway. Once Marcello found out that he had begged Tim to see Ryan again, it was as good as over. Breaking his promise to stay away from the prison wouldn't matter anymore. "I get that you don't know who I am or if you can trust me, but you can. I'll sit there with you both and be a witness. Or you can take your husband along instead."

"No fucking way," Tim said, shaking his head adamantly. "I wouldn't do that to him. Jason either. I shouldn't even do this to myself."

"But you will?" Noah asked, detecting a glimmer of hope.

"Everything all right out here?" a voice boomed.

Noah turned to see Nathaniel marching toward them.

Tim greeted him with a handshake and a smile. "You should have brought Zero tonight! Chinchilla misses him. She thought there was going to be a party."

"He's at home with Kelly," Nathaniel said, gripping Tim's shoulder before releasing his hand. "If you want, I could have him come get Chinchilla too."

"Or your husband could join us. Shouldn't he be taking photos for—I don't know—some sort of promotional thing?"

"He's got a nasty sinus infection," Nathaniel replied, casually sizing up Noah from the corner of his eye.

They kept talking about people and places that Noah wasn't familiar with. He stood back helplessly, unsure what else to say. Pleading with Tim in front of Nathaniel didn't seem wise anyway.

"Time to get back to work," Nathaniel said eventually, jerking his head toward the house.

"Okay," Noah replied. Ready to admit defeat, he trudged along behind Nathaniel.

"Wait up," Tim said as they reached the door. He held out a business card. "The bottom one is my personal number."

Noah glanced at the card, seeing something about an art gallery. Then he looked up and flashed a smile. "Thanks!"

"Don't thank me yet," Tim said. "I haven't made up my mind." He turned and walked back to his dog, shaking his head along the way.

Nathaniel was glowering, so Noah didn't loiter any longer. He pocketed the card and followed him back through the house. They stopped at the door to the kitchen where Nathaniel spun around, his large frame blocking the way.

"What do you think you're doing?" he demanded.

Here it comes! Noah was about to get fired, which made it easier to be defiant. "I'm trying to help a friend."

"In that case, you need better friends," Nathaniel growled.

"Or you need to start recognizing the ones you've got while you still have them."

"Like who?" Noah shot back. "You?"

Nathaniel didn't address this question. Instead he mentioned the person who had no doubt sent him. "Marcello sees potential in you."

"But only if I play along," he shot back. "If I do whatever he wants and agree with everything he says, he'll be my best friend. That's how it works, right?"

Nathaniel snorted. "You know what I can't stand? The work you do. The entire escort service is a risk, and not even a profitable one, but to Marcello it's a conviction. He thinks he's trailblazing future standards while fighting against the infringement of personal liberty. I'm sick to death of hearing about it, but do you know what I do?"

"Suck it up and stay on his good side?" Noah answered, already seeing where this lecture was going. Or so he thought.

"Hell no! I argue with him every time it comes up, and he respects that. But if I started sneaking around his back and trying to undermine that part of his business…"

"That's not what I was doing!" Noah said. "This was all spontaneous, I swear. I saw Tim was here tonight, and the Ryan stuff has been hanging over my head lately, so I thought talking to him might help. And I thought that *he* could help."

Nathaniel studied him before speaking again. "Marcello's not the only one who thinks you have potential. Like I said the other day, you need to prove that you can be professional. When you're at work, your personal life should be set aside."

"I'm not at work! I'm volunteering."

"You're being paid, and you're representing the GAC. Even when you're not interacting with the clients, you're still being watched."

"By you?"

"By people who care. It's up to you what that can turn into."

He wasn't sure what that meant, and he didn't have time to ask. Nathaniel pushed his way into the kitchen and walked to a group of waiters who were standing around and talking, berating them for not doing their jobs. Maybe that was his hobby. Noah realized he hadn't been fired yet and decided to increase his chances of staying employed. He grabbed a tray of *hors d'oeuvres* and returned to the ballroom, stopping to make pleasant conversation with anyone who seemed to be alone, although he was unable to find Chester. He did manage to get two of his clients talking about a subject they both enjoyed. Maybe they would become friends or more. His tray was nearly empty when he was approached by Harold again.

"Five minutes!" Harold said before he could retreat. "That's all I'm asking!"

Noah nearly laughed, having so recently been on the opposite side of the situation. "At the end of the night when we're off duty. Okay?"

Harold flashed another heart-melting smile and nodded. Noah waited until he had walked away before sighing. Why couldn't the past remain where it belonged? That would be easier for him. For Tim as well, he supposed, and probably a slew of other people too.

As the evening wound down, he found himself longing for the new future he had started to build. As soon as Nathaniel had unlocked the cabinet where their cell phones were kept and Noah had his own back, he sent a text to Felix.

Confession time, he wrote. *My life is full of crazy people. You're the only one who makes any sense. Is it okay if I never introduce you to anyone else I know?*

He didn't have to wait long for the response.

Does that mean I don't have to share you?

Noah grinned. *Exactly.*

Sounds good to me. Are you off work yet? When do I get to see you again?

Tomorrow, Noah texted. He had a client, but he knew from experience that it would be a quick one. *After school? I can pick you up.*

And then?

Noah thought about all the places they could go. *You've shown me your apartment. Ready to see mine?*

The response was a series of exclamation points and a blushing emoji. He hadn't meant it quite like that, but he wouldn't shoot down the possibility. Noah looked up and saw Harold making a beeline for him.

Duty calls, he sent quickly before pocketing the phone. Then he looked Harold over as he approached, trying to find any detail flawed enough to take him down a notch. When this failed, he took a deep breath and went to where his backpack sat among the piled belongings of the other volunteers.

"You're not running away from me again, are you?" Harold asked, moving to join him.

"Nope," Noah said easily. "Just putting on my shirt. You should do the same."

"Why?" Harold asked, flexing an arm. "I've been making some serious gains!"

"I didn't notice," Noah lied, and since he had abandoned the truth… "I also don't care. Here. This is your backpack, right?"

He knew exactly which one belonged to Harold. The faded red one with brown straps that matched the convertible. Noah had teased him about it once. He handed over the backpack and focused on buttoning his own shirt. By the time he had finished, he was relieved to see that Harold had put on a worn T-shirt, not that it diminished his sex appeal much.

"You look good," Harold said, "like you've been taking care of yourself. Marcello says you have your own place now."

"I'm not living on the streets anymore, if that's what you mean."

"I'm glad," Harold said. "Seriously. I've worried about you. A lot."

Noah forced himself to relax. "How have you been? Are you doing okay?"

"Yeah," Harold replied. "Days get a little lonely. Know what I mean? Speaking of which, let's talk about our date!"

Noah laughed. "Don't worry, I won't make you go through with it. I get that you just wanted us to talk, and we can, but you don't need to pay four thousand dollars for the honor. I'll cover half the amount. It's for a good cause, right?"

Harold frowned. "I don't want you to pay half. I want my date!"

Wait, he was serious? Jesus, that was flattering, but… "I'm sort of seeing someone right now."

"Oh." Harold shook his head. "Yeah, of course! I uh… It would still be fun to hang out and catch up, you know? As friends."

"Sure!" Noah said. Was he really letting him down easy? Had the entire world turned upside down? Because guys like Harold were the ones who had to find gentle ways of explaining why it would never happen.

"Have you ever been to the Austin Country Flea Market?" Harold asked. "Even if you're not into buying old stuff, it's still fun to go and look around. They have live music and terrible food. The Frito pie is my favorite."

Noah laughed. "I've never been, but it sounds perfect." No candlelit dinner or romantic boat ride down the Colorado River. Just two estranged friends browsing a bunch of junk.

"They're only open on the weekend," Harold said, sounding upbeat. "I was thinking Sunday because—"

"Mr. Westwood, a word if you please."

Noah knew that voice. Marcello was standing a few paces away. His presence had changed the activity in the kitchen. The waiters were joking less, and everyone seemed to have found tasks to do.

Even Harold, who shouldered his pack, "I'll text you with the details," he said before heading for the exit.

"I want my four thousand dollars, Mr. Franklin!" Marcello called after him, but he was smiling. At least until he turned back to Noah, the shadows on his face seeming to deepen. "I understand you took a break from your duties to explore my home and associate with my friends."

Oh boy. "I wanted to talk to Tim, that's all."

Marcello's eyebrows shot up. "That's all?"

He could either let Marcello rip the truth from him, bone by bone, or he could tear open his own chest to expose his heart. "The letters I got from Ryan recently are more desperate than usual. I'm worried he might kill himself. I honestly believe that Tim can help. The only way he would agree to see Ryan is if someone else was there, so I volunteered. I realize that I've broken my promise, and if that costs me my job, then so be it. At least I can live with myself this way. If Ryan does take his own life—and no matter what you think, I hope he doesn't—then at least I'll know that I did all I could instead of ignoring him for a paycheck."

He was practically panting at the end of this speech, but it didn't cause Marcello to burst into applause. Regardless of Nathaniel's advice, his boss didn't grab his hand to start shaking it. Instead, he appeared even more displeased than before.

"It's a shame that our relationship is strained by our contrasting feelings toward one solitary individual," Marcello said. "Otherwise you would find me a very reasonable person. Not when it comes to Ryan. No. I find it very hard to think rationally when it comes to him, or anyone else who would harm Tim."

"Why?" Noah challenged.

"Common decency."

"Fine, but why Tim in particular? Why not Nathaniel instead?"

Marcello examined his nails. "Make no mistake. I would defend Nathaniel just as ferociously, but he is capable of taking care of himself. Mr. Wyman is too, I suppose. He did well considering the circumstances. The only difference is that I promised one of my dearest friends to look out for his best interests, and unlike you, I am not the sort of man who abandons his word."

"I'm sorry," Noah said. Then he clenched his jaw. "But not for talking to Tim. I'm sorry for making that promise in the first place! I should have come to you first before breaking it, but it all just sort of happened. I wasn't trying to go behind your back or hide anything. I didn't know I would see Tim tonight, or that we would talk. It wasn't a plan. I was only trying to help someone that I once loved. Even if it costs me my job."

"Oh, you're still gainfully employed," Marcello hissed. "A new job requirement has been added, that is all. When you and Tim visit Ryan—and yes, he will agree to accompany you—then it's *your* job to see that Tim doesn't get hurt."

Noah shook his head. "How am I supposed to do that?"

"I don't know," Marcello said, jabbing a finger at him. "But you had better figure it out!"

"Great," Noah breathed while watching his boss storm out of the room. "Not only am I an escort, but now I get to be Tim's babysitter too."

Chapter Fifteen

Noah kept looking at the phone on the seat next to him. He would touch the screen to activate it, see the time, and cuss under his breath. For once he was glad the truck didn't have a modern stereo with a digital display. Otherwise he would have stared at the minutes slipping away until he drove straight off the road.

He was late. Just fifteen minutes so far. Noah had already sent an apologetic text saying he was on his way, but he worried that Felix would think he wasn't important. Or needed or desired. The kid was a sweetheart, but he wasn't very confident. As for Noah's stupid client, why had he chosen this night? The guy had always invited him in, blown Noah, and shown him to the door. Every single time! Except tonight, when he had asked if they could cuddle afterwards. Then his client had moaned about how he was scared to find love and always sabotaged himself. Noah had heard that story plenty of times before, and ever since Harold's version of it, he struggled to muster any sympathy. He pictured someone standing at a window, faced with a street filled with drive-thrus, restaurants, and even food trucks. The person at the window? They stood there moaning about how hungry they were. Well, get out there and fucking eat! Either that or stop complaining about having an empty belly.

Noah noticed white knuckles on the steering wheel and forced his hand to unclench. He took a deep breath while waiting at an intersection, not even honking when the driver ahead of him needed extra time to look up from their phone and notice that the light had changed. Almost there. He just didn't want to let Felix down. Noah wished he had time to go home and shower. Worried that he smelled like another man, he stopped by a gas station restroom to brush his teeth and wash his face. A kit of essential toiletries was kept in the truck's glovebox, since he never knew when he might be asked to stay overnight with a client. He even had a little sample tube of cologne that he sprayed on, and while this made him feel better, he remained uneasy as he continued his drive. In the future, he'd make sure this didn't happen again. Going straight from a client to the guy he was dating didn't sit right with him.

When his truck rumbled up to the apartment complex, Noah was twenty-seven minutes late. He was just about to get out when he saw a slight figure appear out of a glowing rectangle of light and stomp toward him. Noah remained in the driver's seat, watching to see if the expression matched the tense body language. When Felix passed beneath one of the parking lot's orange lights, Noah had his confirmation. Even with the shadows cast by the baseball cap that Felix wore, he clearly wasn't happy. At least he went to the passenger door and climbed in. That was better than him coming to the window and telling Noah to go away.

"Sorry—" he began.

Felix cut him off. "Let's get out of here. I'm so sick of my family!"

Noah didn't reach for the ignition. "You're not angry at me?"

"I wish you had gotten here sooner," Felix said tersely. Then his shoulders slumped. "But only because I needed rescuing."

"So you're happy to see me," Noah said, leaning over.

The grumpy expression melted away, those dark eyes darting over to him bashfully. "Very."

"Good." Noah stretched farther and stole a kiss. His forehead bumped against the brim of the baseball cap. "What's with the hat? It's cute on you, but… I'm going to need to see your ID again."

Felix blushed. "My sister always says this hat makes me look like Short Round from *The Temple of Doom*. Ever seen it?"

"The Indiana Jones flick?" Noah nodded. "Yeah." He had watched the entire series at a friend's house in secrecy, since his parents would never have approved of such movies. "Short Round was the little kid, right? You don't look *that* young!"

"I hope not!"

"And you're way cuter." Noah was leaning in for another kiss when he noticed something else. The sideburns poking out from the hat weren't as dark as before. "Did you—"

"Oh god!" Felix said, attention on the parking lot. "Here comes my sister. Let's go!"

Noah shrugged and did as requested. He waited until they were safely away from the apartment complex before he asked his next question. "I thought you and your sister were close?"

"We are," Felix said with a sigh. "A little too close." They rode in silence before he expounded on this. "All I suggested to her is that we go back to sharing a room. We could figure out a schedule for private hours, or we could set up a divider. I know that sounds lame, but I want my mom to have her own room again."

"Very noble of you," Noah said while nodding. "And I agree. I take it your sister doesn't?"

"She doesn't want to be in a room with all my junk. I told her I could get a storage unit or sell some of it on eBay. I need to downsize, I know, but she also— Never mind."

"Oh, okay," Noah said casually. "We can end the conversation there. I'm not dying of curiosity or anything. I'm perfectly fine with the cliffhanger ending."

Felix laughed. "I hate it when people do that too. I just didn't want to hurt your feelings, because it really has nothing to do with you. Mostly."

"I'm all ears," Noah said.

Felix grinned. "Actually, I'm the one who's all ears."

Noah was tempted to pull over, just to kiss him again. Why not? He gave in to the urge, not explaining his actions and refusing to stop, even when Felix was laughing too hard to kiss him back properly. Eventually he was pushed away, Felix's hat askew.

"Would you just drive?"

"I don't know where I'm going," Noah responded. "Although I'm getting more ideas by the second."

"Like what?" Felix asked, face rapt.

Noah settled into the driver's seat again. "I thought we'd start with dinner. Have you eaten yet?"

"No."

"Perfect. I know of a seafood place on Congress Avenue that has never failed to—" He noticed Felix's grimace. "Oh, right. You must be sick of seafood."

"All restaurants. No matter how different the food is, I'll still be watching the waiters and feeling like I'll get in trouble for slacking off. My mom took me out as a special treat last week, and I was itching to refill the drinks on the table next to ours. I'm not saying we can never go out, but maybe we could cook something at your place instead. Together! I don't expect you to do all the work."

Noah thought of his pantry, which was empty aside from instant oatmeal and coffee. The only things in the fridge were a gallon of juice, some carrots, and hummus to dip them in. "We'll have to hit the store," he said. He looked over at his date. "Then again, you don't look like you eat much. How about a bowl of oatmeal?"

"Only if it's cinnamon and spice. Let's go shopping. I'm hoping to impress you with my cooking skills."

"You know how?"

"No. That's why I was hoping."

Noah chuckled. "Then we'll figure it out together." He had helped his mother in the kitchen enough that he wouldn't be completely lost. He put the truck in drive again.

They didn't have far to go. Two blocks later they were parked and walking toward a bright red sign above automatic doors. After entering, they were faced with stacked pyramids of fresh produce. "Where do we start?" he asked, turning to find that Felix had procured a shopping cart.

"I dunno. What are we making?"

"Pasta," Noah said, since that was difficult to ruin. "How do you feel about zucchini?"

"Love it!" Felix declared. "Especially the yellow kind."

Then he knew what to do. Roasted vegetables tossed with pasta and butter. They would need fresh Parmesan cheese, red onions, and whatever else they found along the way that appealed to them. He looked over and saw Felix holding a pack of dried tomatoes. After seeking his approval for this potential ingredient, Felix picked up another brand and squinted at the prices, trying to find the best deal. All of this was so domestic! This is how normal lives worked: going on trips to the grocery store together, worrying about budgets, planning cozy nights at home… Noah loved it!

Felix noticed him staring and pulled down his baseball cap self-consciously. He couldn't hide the truth though, not in the stark light of a grocery store. The hat failed to conceal the blue hair. The bluest of blues! "What else do we need?" Felix asked, perhaps wanting to distract him. "Garlic? Or maybe not. It'll give us bad breath."

"It's fine so long as we both eat it," Noah said, attention still on his hair. "Do you like blueberries? How about blue corn tortilla chips? Or if you're in the mood to drink, we could buy some Curaçao liqueur. You know, the blue kind."

Felix groaned. "You noticed!"

"It's hard not to," Noah said, reaching for the cap to remove it.

Felix pulled away before he could. "Leave it! You don't want to see. It's a disaster. I was just going to do streaks, like I said, but then my sister talked me into going for it. I think because she messed up with the bleach and— It'll grow out. When it does and just the tips are blue, it'll look cool, I swear!"

"I think it's fun." Noah said, reaching for the cap again. "Redheads don't judge people by their hair color. We know how that feels. Show me."

Felix steeled himself. He didn't resist when Noah placed his hand on the brim and pulled off the cap. The hair beneath sprang up from its confinement, sticking up in multiple directions while still flat down the middle. Felix resembled a mad scientist after a particularly bad lab experiment, but this new look did nothing to diminish his adorableness. When styled properly, Noah had no doubt the punky hair color would add to his sex appeal.

"I'm dead at work," Felix moaned. "I don't know what I was thinking!"

"You'll probably get a raise. You look great!"

"I don't," Felix said, trying to smoosh his hair down before donning the cap again.

"You do," Noah insisted. "You just have to own it. Wear it with pride. Hey, maybe we should dye mine primary red so we make a better pair. Contrasting and yet the same."

This pep talk gave Felix shiny eyes and had Noah eager to get him somewhere private. He turned his attention back to finding the right ingredients, continuing the conversation as they shopped. "Is that what triggered your feud with your sister?"

"No, it really was the room thing. It started with my mom actually because, well, you woke her up the morning you left."

Noah spotted a pack of mushrooms and grabbed it just in case. "Are you sure? I was extra quiet when I left."

"My mom is so polite that she would have pretended to be asleep, even if she wasn't. It's not a big deal. She's in the middle of the living room during the day. What does she expect? That's why I want to change things, but my sister doesn't like the idea of sharing. Especially the bed."

"Can't say that I blame her."

"I know, but neither of our rooms are big enough for two beds. If we bought smaller ones then maybe, but we can't afford that, so I suggested we sleep in shifts. Turns out she was fine having to share a bed with me. We did that enough when we were growing up, but, um..."

Noah looked away from rows of produce to see that two red apples had replaced Felix's cheeks. "Oh."

"Yeah. I'd have to wash the sheets anytime you and I did it. *If* you and I did it! Theoretically speaking. Um."

Noah laughed. "So basically, this is all my fault. I woke up your mom, and your sister doesn't want to get my cooties."

"It's not your fault!" Felix said, but then he laughed himself. "I guess it's silly. You know what? I'll sell enough of my collection to buy us two twin beds. Or bunk beds! Problem solved."

Except that Noah couldn't imagine squeezing into such a small bed with Felix, especially when his sister was in the same room, but that was all right. Such things could take place at his own apartment. Perhaps even tonight.

"What else?" Noah asked, wanting to be done with shopping. How much more could they really need?

A lot, as it turned out. When first moving into the apartment, Noah had optimistically bought pots, pans, and dishes. He rarely used them, and when he did, it was never enough to justify running the dishwasher. Instead he did it all by hand. He was eager to finally make good use of the kitchen tonight. Felix was his first official guest! Not counting clients.

"Is your hair blue?" asked the cashier as they were checking out. "That's so cool!"

"Told you so," Noah whispered after they paid and were rolling the cart toward the truck. "This is Austin. You'll fit right in. They might even make you mayor!"

Felix tittered happily and Noah sighed contentedly. Whatever they got up to tonight, he was certain they were in for a good time.

Felix wasn't kidding when he said that he couldn't cook. Noah didn't know how either, but he meant it in the way most people did: He wasn't very skilled. He could still chop an onion and knew to spread oil at the bottom of a pan before heating it. He could boil pasta and possessed a few tricks, like adding salt to the rolling water to enhance the pasta's flavor. Felix was a complete novice. He wasn't a bad cook because he had never cooked at all. Still, teaching him the basics *was* kind of fun. Felix kept looking at him in wonder, like he was working magic. Soon he was making his own because Felix wasn't just a bystander. He wanted to learn and did so in leaps and bounds.

"Maybe we should slice the zucchini thicker," he said at one point before taking over. "I like it better when it still has bite. It gets too oily and limp when thin."

"Admit it," Noah said, taking a step back to supervise. "You've done this before. You've probably been on MasterChef and won."

Felix gasped in faux surprise. "There's a TV show you've actually heard of?"

"I like cooking shows," Noah countered. Mostly because it gave him something nicer to imagine while gnawing on raw carrots at night.

He wasn't watching his calories this evening! The pasta turned out great, considering their combined lack of skill. In fact, it was better than anything he had ever made on his own. Felix was a natural, and during dinner Noah kept encouraging him to explore this newfound talent further. By the end of the meal, food became an unappealing subject, so their focus shifted.

"I love your apartment!" Felix said, despite the minimal surroundings. The rooms were spacious enough, but a decorative touch was still missing. "You promised me a tour."

When first arriving, Noah had been too hungry for such a thing. "There isn't much to see." He rose and tried to find interesting details to comment on anyway. "You've seen enough of the kitchen. That's the living room over there, in case you hadn't noticed."

"You don't have a Blu-ray or DVD player?" Felix asked, inspecting the setup, which consisted of a television and decoder box. "You should at least get an Apple TV or a Roku. I love mine, although I guess this TV is new enough to be smart. Does it have built-in Wi-Fi?"

"I have cable," Noah said lamely. "That's already a big step up for me. When I was a kid, the only channels we got were through the antenna."

"Antenna?" Felix repeated. "Like those things on cars? I'm

going to need to see your ID, because I'm starting to think you're way older than twenty-three!"

"I will be soon," Noah said without thinking.

"You have a birthday coming up?" Felix said, already excited. "When?"

"Anyway," Noah said, walking away from the room and the conversation, "over here is where I do my laundry. Yes, that is a washer *and* a dryer, which is great, because when I was a kid we had to go down to the river and bang our clothes against the rocks." Felix didn't ask if he was serious, thankfully. "Here's the bathroom. One of them. I think it's ridiculous that this place has two. That's not something I need. Feel free to take photos, by the way. I know you must find this fascinating."

Felix pulled out his phone and took one. With a straight face. He wasn't really going to keep that, was he?

"And over here is my bedroom."

Felix made a choking noise. Then he coughed. "Sorry. Swallowed wrong. Oh, is that your bed?"

"Yes, sir, it is." Noah's mornings were slow enough that it was made. The sheets were freshly laundered too. Just in case. "I've got another bathroom over there. No photos of that one. The public isn't allowed to see it. Strictly confidential."

"Ha ha ha!" Felix said, sounding a little manic. "So..."

So indeed. Noah felt stuffed from their dinner, and he still hoped to take a shower before anything intimate happened. "The tour's not over yet," he said, returning to the hallway to lead them to a closed door. "I really should have gotten a smaller place. This was supposed to be an office. Don't ask me for what. I just like the idea of sitting behind a big desk and getting things done. Probably because I've never had a job like that."

He opened the door to reveal the empty room. He expected to close it again after a brief glimpse, but Felix walked inside to inspect the space in awe, even though there was nothing to see but blank walls and carpet. Noah realized how greedy all of this must seem. Felix and his family didn't have enough personal space to be truly comfortable, and here Noah had more square footage than he would ever likely need. "I really should get a roommate," he admitted.

"How much would rent be?" Felix asked, spinning around.

Noah stared in shock. Then he laughed. "I see what all this

is about. How many customers have you gone home with in the hope that they have a spare room for you?"

"I got lucky on my first try," Felix said, grinning at him. "Don't worry, I'm only joking."

Noah wanted to invite him to stay there. Why not? People on the streets shared with each other. Not always, but on some nights at the shelter when someone had gotten a large handout—fifty bucks on one occasion—the lucky recipient had brought back treats for them and the staff to share. Candy bars and chips. Junk food that anyone with healthy eating habits would turn their nose up at, but to them it had felt like a fine feast. Noah hadn't forgotten that gesture, and he had tried to do the same when he could, buying donuts on one occasion, and on his last night at Jerusalem, ordering pizza and soda for everyone. Right now he had more than he needed, and he felt like sharing.

All that stopped him was his occupation. Sometimes he hosted. That would be uncomfortable, if not downright disastrous with Felix around. Still, there might be something he could do.

"If you end up sharing a room with your sister and don't have enough space for your things, you can bring them here."

Felix brightened up. Then he shook his head. "I couldn't."

"Nothing's stopping you. Also, I know a guy who owns a used furniture store. I'm sure he would be willing to trade the bed you have for a set of twins."

"Are you serious?"

"I'll call him tomorrow and ask." In truth, the client of his dealt in new furniture as well, and that's what Felix would get, even if it meant paying more. Noah would take care of the difference. He wanted to help without appearing to be a sugar daddy or anything questionable like that.

"You're the best," Felix said, slamming into Noah to give him a hug. "I love you!" He pulled away just as suddenly. "I guess that sounds crazy, doesn't it? I'm moving too fast." His chin raised defiantly. "I don't care. It's the truth!"

Noah chose his response carefully. "There's nothing wrong with saying how you feel. Not if it's something positive."

Felix's features hardened with determination. "In that case, I wish we were still in your bedroom."

Wow! He definitely moved fast! "It's been a long day. Do you mind if I take a quick shower?"

"Okay," Felix replied, eyes searching his.

He might not have asked the question, but he still wanted an answer. Confessing feelings took bravery, sure, but sticking around to hear how the other person felt in return required nerves of steel. Noah took off the baseball cap, rubbed the messy blue hair affectionately, and kissed Felix to reassure him. Then he donned the cap. "I won't be long. I promise."

He left the room as casually as they had entered, even though he was eager for privacy to figure out how he felt. Was this venturing into unhealthy territory? Should he lecture Felix about leaping before he looked? Then again, as he undressed in the privacy of the master bathroom and pulled the shower curtain shut, he remembered falling even faster. That party when he had first met Ryan, by the end of it, Noah had been convinced he was in love. His heart had started beating faster that day and kept on pounding into the next. That's all it had taken, one night of talking to a complete stranger. Youth was either more capable of love, or perhaps more honest about expressing such feelings, no matter how quickly they developed. Noah wondered if he was holding back on his own emotions now. He cared about Felix. A lot. He wanted to take care of him, guide him, ensure that he was happy. He received much in return because the admiration was flattering, and getting to participate in Felix's life made Noah's feel more grounded. They could give a lot to each other. That was a positive thing no matter what words they used to describe it, or how little time had gone by since they met.

Noah had soaped up and was rinsing off beneath a hot spray of water when he heard the shower curtain rings jostle together. He wiped the water from his eyes and saw Felix stepping into the tub. His nude body was lithe and mostly hairless, but it was his expression that endeared Noah most, since he was clearly fighting against the terror he felt. He could almost imagine Felix pacing the bedroom, trying to work up the guts to abandon his clothes and join him like this. Noah wouldn't let him down.

"Come here," he said.

Noah took the slender body into his arms and pulled him beneath the water to warm up. They kissed, the blue hair appearing darker when wet and clinging to the sides of his face. This only made the ears stick out more. Noah moved his attention to them, licking, nibbling, and not letting Felix escape his grasp, no matter how much he squirmed. In fact, that felt pretty good. Noah finally released him so their bodies could part. They stepped back and eyed each other.

One of them gasped. The other laughed.

Felix's equipment was fine. Noah wasn't concerned with size, maybe since he was used to being bigger than most guys. The saluting dick was straight and earnest, just like the person it was attached to. What was above it though…

"You dyed your pubes?" Noah said.

"Seemed like a good idea at the time," Felix murmured distractedly, still hypnotized by what he saw. Then he moved his attention upward to meet his gaze. "My sister did *not* help me with that, by the way!"

"That's good to know, although I could use a hand."

"To dye your— Oooh!"

Noah grinned and flexed, causing his cock to bounce. He never had trouble with repeat performances. He moved forward for more kisses, but Felix dropped to his knees. Noah was used to that too, and in this situation understood perfectly, because it had probably been awhile since Felix had anyone to play with except himself. Still, blow jobs never felt as good in the shower, for whatever reason.

"Let's get out of here," he suggested. "We don't want to slip and break anything."

"Especially this," Felix said, still gripping his cock with one fist and staring up at him with hungry eyes.

Noah laughed and helped him to his feet. Then he shut off the water and opened the curtain. "Only one towel," he said, grabbing it from the rack. "Lucky for us, I bought the biggest one they had."

He wrapped it around them both in demonstration, drawing their bodies close. They resumed kissing, their hips shifting back and forth. Noah opened the towel and used it to dry Felix's hair, then his own. He was about to lead them to the bedroom when Felix's eyes went wide.

"Oh no! I hope that isn't permanent!"

Noah noticed his concern. The beige towel was now streaked with blue.

"It's always like that the first few days," Felix stammered. "I'll buy you a new one if it stains."

"I'm sure it's fine. I wanted blue towels when I bought this one but they were out. I also wanted blue sheets... and a blue dong. I might have to slap you around with this thing."

Felix squealed and ran for the bedroom. Noah gave chase and tackled him after leaping into bed. They wrestled, Felix not putting up much of a fight. Noah soon had him pinned. After making out, he slid downward to show what he was capable of. He didn't get much of an opportunity because Felix started to shiver, and not from pleasure.

"Do you want to get beneath the blankets?" Noah asked.

"Yes!" Felix said. "It's cold in here."

"I'll turn down the air conditioning." He darted from the room to adjust the thermostat in the hall. When he returned, all he saw was a large lump beneath the blankets. Felix was somewhere beneath them, head and all. "You can come out now."

"I don't want to," was the muffled reply.

"I see." Noah sauntered over to the bed, already understanding how this was going to play out. He slid between the sheets and made no effort to duck his head beneath them. Instead he stretched out on his back, put his arms behind his head, and let Felix have his fun. The kid had more than one natural talent! Stamina too! Noah lost himself in pleasure as time flew by, but Felix never seemed to tire. Noah was on the brink when he decided to take control again. He pulled the covers over his head, meeting Felix beneath them like children playing in a blanket fort.

"I wasn't finished," Felix said, sounding naughty.

"Neither was I," Noah replied, "but you got me very close."

He forced Felix onto his back, kissing his neck and moving down to the reddish-brown nipples. The little gasps were nice, but he was after moans, so Noah moved farther down and took the rock-hard dick into his mouth, already tasting precum as he worked his way down to the base.

"I don't want to—" Felix started to say. "Not yet!"

That was quick. They had other options, so Noah rolled Felix over, then shoved his face between cheeks that were pert and round. God he loved a bubble butt!

"Um," Felix said, clearly unsure of the situation.

Noah bit one of the cheeks to make him yelp, then let his tongue dart into the crack. He had managed to get Felix moaning while going down on him, but the sound that came out of his lungs next was more like a heavenly sigh. He knew the feeling. On paper, rimming seemed like a very bad idea, but in reality, the sensation was off the charts. Noah kept this up until it sounded like Felix was about to have a stroke. Then he rolled him over again and made his way upward, a knee to either side of Felix's torso.

"Wanna finish this off for me?"

"Yes please!" Felix responded, looking mesmerized again. Then he went to work.

Noah groped behind him to return the favor. He let himself reach the brink and held himself there, waiting until Felix started whimpering. They came at the same time, Noah mentally giving himself a high five. He had a few talents himself! His pride vanished as pleasure threatened to overwhelm him. Felix was still sucking like his life depended on it.

"Okay, okay!" Noah said with a chuckle. "Save some for later!"

"Sorry," Felix said, looking anything but. "Can we do it again?"

"Yes," Noah said. "Not now though. This is the best part."

"What is?"

"Spooning!"

"Oh." Felix still didn't seem to get it.

Did the idea not appeal to him? Then it clicked into place. The ex-boyfriend—whatever his name was—the undeserving jerk had never held him! His loss. Noah moved into position, lying next to Felix and pulling his hips near until shoulder blades were pressed against chest. He wrapped an arm around the narrow torso and kissed Felix on the back of his neck. How could anyone not want to do this with such a sweet person?

"I love you too," he said, determined to give Felix the sort of relationship he deserved. Whatever Noah's true feelings might be, they were close enough to love to make this claim. "Anyone would be crazy not to."

Felix sighed, as if in the midst of a pleasant dream. "Can I stay the night?"

He could stay this night and the next and the next, as far as Noah was concerned. Then he remembered again the reason why that wouldn't work. His job. For the first time since it had all begun, he felt a pang of regret. "Of course you can stay," he said, dismissing any potential consequences. The rest they could figure out later. For now, all that mattered was making this special person feel loved.

Chapter Sixteen

Noah awoke to find himself being used as a body pillow. Felix's arms and legs were draped over him, his head resting in the nook between arm and chest. That was cute, except that Felix was a drooler. Noah's armpit was so wet that he expected it to squelch as he methodically moved away one limb after the other so he could slip free. He soon realized that Felix was a heavy sleeper and therefore he didn't need to be so cautious. Noah gently rolled him to one side. This caused some incoherent mumbling, but for the most part, Felix remained unconscious. The lucky dog. Noah remembered sleeping that well before life on the streets made him jumpy.

In the gentle light of a new morning, those dark days seemed far behind. Noah used the restroom, went to the kitchen to make coffee, and wondered if his guest would like one as well. While waiting for the coffee to brew, he worked on cleaning up the mess they had made the night before. During all of this, he couldn't help sneaking back down the hall a few times, just to check on the slender body with a tangle of blue hair. Gosh he was cute!

After the third such trip, he returned to the kitchen and heard his phone pulse. He hurried to answer it and barely had time to read the caller's name. Tim Wyman. The voice on the other end didn't wait for him to say hello.

"We either do this today, or we don't do it at all."

Noah looked at his coffee longingly and wished he'd had time to drink more. "What?"

"The visit with Ryan," Tim replied. "I know it's a bad idea but I've talked myself into it. So if you really want this to happen, it has to be now."

"Okay," Noah said. His groggy mind scrabbled to remember what day it was. They couldn't just show up at the prison anytime they liked, but he was pretty sure it was the weekend, so they should be okay. "It's a two-hour drive. When do you want to head out?"

"Now."

"Like, right now?"

"Yeah. I'm ready. Are you?"

"Sure," Noah lied. Judging from Tim's tone of voice, he barely had this fish hooked. It was either reel him in now or let him get away. They haggled over who would drive, Noah agreeing that Tim should pick him up just to buy himself time. Evidently he lived outside of Austin, which helped. Noah disconnected the call and dashed for the shower.

Five minutes later, he was out and wearing a towel around his waist. He had nearly forgotten about Felix until he returned to the bedroom. Felix was awake now and sitting up, squinting against the light of the morning, one eye remaining shut. Then he noticed Noah, smiled, and reached out his arms. "Come back to bed!"

"I can't," Noah said, inching toward the closet. "Work called. Well, not exactly. I'll explain later, but right now, I need to get ready and go. I'll be out of town for most of the day."

Felix put on a pouty expression. Then another idea occurred to him and he smiled. "Do you have time for a quickie?"

"I really don't. Sorry!"

"Oh. Can I at least see you naked again?"

Noah laughed and let the towel drop. Felix looked him over and sighed. Then he squirmed deeper into the covers. "What if I'm still here when you get back?"

Noah chuckled. "I'd love that!" Of course he might have a client, meaning it would be even later. As he ducked into the closet, he debated calling Marcello to cancel. Then again, he wasn't on his boss's best side right now. Not with the whole Ryan situation.

"I should probably go home," Felix said when Noah emerged again. "Make up with my sister. In my family, we never stay mad at each other for long. None of us can stomach it."

"Sounds like a good idea," Noah said, wishing his family was the same. "Just let yourself out when you're ready to go. There's coffee if you want any. Oatmeal too. Not cinnamon and spice, but I'll grab some on the way home. For next time."

Felix grinned and clutched a pillow to his chest. "I like the sound of that."

"So do I." Noah meant to leave. He even made it to the door, but when he turned around to say goodbye, he struggled to tear his eyes away from the welcome scene. Forget about Ryan! Noah would call Tim and tell him the deal was off. Then he would get back in bed and spend the rest of the day there. He had always liked this apartment, but with Felix here, Noah loved it. "Just a second. I'll be right back."

He went to the kitchen and opened one of the drawers, then another, searching each and trying to remember where he had left the spare keys. When moving in he had been presented with three sets, despite only needing one. The tips of his fingers touched a cold ring. Noah grabbed it, identified the right key, and worked it free. Then he returned to the bedroom, slowing on the way.

This was a big step. He and Felix were still getting to know each other. More dates needed to happen before they could even consider cohabitating. Then again, he wanted this. Felix made him happy, and this was a surefire way of giving back some of that joy.

Noah entered the bedroom and tossed the key on the bed.

"What's that?" Felix asked.

"So you can lock the door on your way out. And unlock it on the way back in. The spare room is yours. Store your stuff there or move in permanently. It's up to you."

Felix stared, his mouth agape. Then his eyes watered up, but before he could speak, the buzzer rang.

"Sorry," Noah said. "That's my ride. I'll see you later."

He left the room, then doubled back for a quick kiss. He couldn't be sure, but he thought he felt Felix's hands trembling as they grabbed the back of his neck to draw him in closer.

"I really gotta go!" Noah said with a chuckle. After one more peck, he pulled away. He was still grinning when he answered the intercom by the front door. "I'll be right down."

His good mood lasted during the elevator ride. Not even seeing Tim again could shake it, although he was reminded of the awkwardness of the situation, starting with their travel plans. Tim drove a polished black sports car, a Dodge Challenger, the kind of vehicle that young people wished to own but almost never did and that older people owned while wishing they were younger. Tim was somewhere in the middle, so Noah wasn't sure what the vehicle said about him. He grudgingly had to admit it was a sexy car, and in that way, matched the driver perfectly.

Conversation on the way out of town consisted of logistics. What was the best way of getting to Gatesville? How did the process work when arriving? Noah asked if they could stop by a bank to get quarters, although he pretended it was for their benefit so they could use the vending machines while there. "You can't bring Starbucks with you," he explained, "and you'll want something to focus on."

"That bad?" Tim asked, eyes on the road.

"It's like visiting the hospital. Nobody wants to be there. A short visit is enough, but you'll feel guilty if you leave too soon, because you know the other person doesn't have that freedom."

Tim was quiet, but he stopped at the bank that Noah said he preferred. When they were on the highway again, he asked another question.

"Does he look different?"

"Ryan?" Noah shrugged. "He's skinnier. At least the last time I saw him. It's been a year."

"I'm picturing a lot of tattoos," Tim said without humor. "On his hands and face. A shaved head too."

Noah snorted. "Not even prison could make Ryan cut his precious golden locks. I used to tease him about how often he would check his hair."

"So did I!" Tim said. "Half an hour in the shower and then twice as long in front of the mirror. I guess it wasn't *that* bad, but some days it felt like it."

Noah eyed Tim discreetly, trying to imagine what his life with Ryan had been like. He couldn't, despite knowing so many details. He knew Tim had a big house, or used to, and that he had found Ryan on the streets and taken him in almost instantly. Noah thought of Felix and wondered if he was making the same mistake. He didn't have to search himself long to decide that he wasn't. Maybe he was rushing things, but Felix was sweet. Noah had seen none of the venom that would regularly seep out of Ryan to poison their time together.

"What made you change your mind?"

Tim glanced over at him briefly, hands flexing on the steering wheel. "I loved him. Once."

"So did I," Noah said, not needing further explanation. They shared the same obligation, borne out of a few good memories tucked in between all the bad ones. "You're lucky. At least Ryan loved you back."

"Lucky? When we're not driving, remind me to show you the scar the bullet made."

"That wasn't the same Ryan. You know it wasn't."

"Don't blame the drugs!" Tim shot back. "They might have brought that side out of him, but it's still part of who he is. And he's still responsible for his actions."

"I guess," Noah said. Then he exhaled. "Sorry, this is just really weird for me. In my mind you'll always be, I don't know, the other man. The one I could never compete with. Tim Wyman, the living legend. Ryan was constantly mentioning you. *Constantly.* I don't think he did it to be mean. Maybe he didn't even realize he was hurting me. I'd have my arm around him, and just when I thought things were nice and cozy, he'd mention how much he liked your muscles, or how everyone was jealous when the two of you went out. I wanted to make him feel that way. I kept waiting for him to say those things about me, but he never did."

"That sucks," Tim said, his brow furrowing. "I know how it is when you feel like you can't compete."

Noah scoffed. "Yeah, right."

"I do! Not everyone is impressed by muscles or good looks. Some guys aren't won over so easily."

If he was telling the truth, Noah couldn't imagine the man who had made Tim Wyman feel inadequate. He must really be something. They rode in silence as their tempers cooled. Noah wanted to steer the conversation toward the positive, because if they showed up at the prison feeling angry and hurt, it would result in disaster. "Do you ever miss him?"

Tim thought about it before answering. "Not anymore. I got lonely enough a few times that I thought it would be worth putting up with his shit again, just to have someone around. Ryan could be fun. When he got into a good mood, he could light up a room. We went to this big dinner with a friend of mine once. Your boss, actually, and Ryan was like a politician's wife, eager to charm everyone and win them over. He did too. People were jealous of me that night, but only because he was mine." He grimaced. "Sorry. I'm not trying to rub salt in the wound."

"I've moved on," Noah assured him. "I still get a little butthurt from time to time, but it's easier when you find someone who loves you the right way."

"Yeah," Tim said, a smile tugging at his cheek. "It is."

Noah noticed the wedding ring. Rather than it filling his stomach with warmth, he felt guilt sloshing around instead. "I'm really sorry for what happened. I had no idea what Ryan was going to do. I don't think he planned it. We lost touch before the shooting happened and—"

"It's not your fault," Tim interrupted. "If I seem crabby, it's just because I'm nervous as hell. Part of me wants to see him again, but the rest—most of me actually—never wants to. Ever."

"I appreciate what you're doing today. He will too."

The silence between them was suffocating, and it was Tim who chose to break it. "So you've moved on, huh? Found a guy who appreciates you?"

"Yeah! Sure looks that way." Noah thought of a sunlit bed and wished they were already on the way back. "He acts like I'm... Well, he acts like I'm you!"

Tim laughed. "I hope for his sake that you aren't. At least not how I was at your age. So I'm guessing he's also a, uh... Tell me about him."

"He's a few years younger than me," Noah said, unable to contain his smile. "You know how puppies are when they're halfway to becoming adult dogs? They're all gangly legs and oversized paws, and they barge into your life and knock everything over, but you can't help but love them because they're so adorably enthusiastic. That's what he's like."

"Sounds nice," Tim said. "What's he do for a living?"

"He's a waiter. And a college student."

"Oh. That makes it especially cool that he's so cool." Tim laughed. "You know what I mean."

Except he didn't. "Huh?"

"With your line of work. Relationships must be tricky."

Noah was quiet.

Enough that Tim looked over and cringed. "Sorry. I should mind my own business."

"No, you're right," Noah said with a sigh. "It is tricky."

"But he knows."

"We're not in a committed relationship, and he's said that he doesn't want to know if I do anything with other guys."

Tim shrugged. "Fair enough. If my husband got a job as an escort, I wouldn't want to know the details either."

That would be fine and dandy if Felix was aware of his true occupation. Noah had been intentionally dancing around that information so far. "Would you stay with him? Say you found out your husband started working as an escort because that's what he needed to do to survive. Would you still want to be with him?"

"Ben? Man... We're doing okay financially, so it's not like he would ever need to. But if for some weird reason he did, I wouldn't stop loving him. I'd probably try to get him away from that sort of work somehow. No offense."

"None taken," Noah said.

"Ryan cheated on me," Tim continued. "I don't know if he ever told you that. When it happened, the worst part was that I felt like I didn't really know him anymore. If he wasn't the person I thought he was, then who the hell did I fall in love with? Someone I made up in my own head? That's the lesson I had to learn with him. Ryan kept on betraying me, and I took freaking forever to finally leave him. Even then I couldn't do it on my own. I needed help."

Noah wasn't sure what he meant by help and didn't ask, because he was still fixated on one phrase Tim had spoken. *Who the hell did I fall in love with?* Noah knew how that felt. The same sensation had overtaken him on the day Ryan broke into a house and shot the man currently sitting next to him in the driver's seat.

"Maybe it's like that with everyone," Noah said. "We meet someone, make a bunch of assumptions, then feel hurt when it turns out we got it wrong."

"True," Tim conceded, "But when you're in a relationship with someone, when you share everything with them including your home, there shouldn't be any big surprises. Not like that."

Noah focused on the landscape whizzing by outside. Tim was right. When entering a serious relationship, the other person should gently place bombshells on the table for inspection instead of carelessly dropping them at some later date. "Felix doesn't know."

"That's your boyfriend?" Tim asked.

"Yeah. When we first met, I was trying to be discrete. Marcello wants us to because..."

"I get it," Tim said. "And you can trust me, especially when it comes to Marcello. We're close. I've got his back."

"Oh. Yeah, so when Felix and I went on our first date, I didn't know him very well. I didn't feel like I could tell him, and of course part of me didn't want to scare him away. When he acted like he didn't want to know, I leapt on that because—" Noah swallowed, the realization making his throat ache. "It's hard to say how I felt at the time, but now, I don't want him to be disappointed in me."

Tim considered this in silence. Then he laughed, which seemed cold, until he explained himself. "You *are* like me when I was your age. Want some advice?"

Noah nodded. "Sure."

"Don't play games with people. No matter how good your intentions. It always comes back to bite you in the ass."

Noah wasn't playing games or trying to lie to anyone, unless being willfully vague counted. Regardless, he recognized the truth in Tim's words. The situation with Felix was delicate, and he needed to decide—and soon—how he was going to deal with it.

He was lost in thought for the remainder of the trip, Tim eventually asking if he could put music on. Noah agreed, agitated when so many of the songs focused on the woes of love, but the more positive aspects were increasingly difficult to remember as they neared their destination.

"Jesus," Tim breathed when they pulled up to the prison. "So that's it, huh?"

"Yeah." Despite how often Noah had been there, he too felt a sense of dread upon every arrival. He was reminded of his first visit while watching Tim struggle with each step of the process, like when the car was searched. Not just the interior but the trunk and under the hood too. Going inside the building and through the metal detectors felt upsettingly close to being processed as a new inmate. Tim's mouth was a flat line, his face flushed, when he was pulled aside and subjected to a thorough frisking.

"I'm never coming back here," he muttered once they were sitting in the large open visitor area and waiting for prisoners to arrive.

"Can't blame you," Noah said. "I hate it here too, but just think how Ryan feels. This is his home now."

Tim stared at him from across the small metal table. "I hope I can trust you. You're supposed to be my witness, but you're on his side, aren't you?"

"I'm not on anyone's side!" Noah shot back.

Tim continued to scrutinize him, then he exhaled. "I hope Nathaniel was right."

Noah shook his head, not understanding. "Right about what?"

"He said that you're a good kid."

Noah stared back. "He did?"

Tim nodded. "I wouldn't be here if not for him. He said you have integrity. Nathaniel is big on that kind of thing. Integrity, honesty, and man does he hate laziness. He told me that you're a hard worker, that you never ask for anything you haven't earned."

That was flattering! Noah had always wanted to prove himself to Marcello, but he hadn't realized he was making an impression on someone else instead.

"Then again," Tim continued, "he also said that you follow your heart around like a carrot dangling from a stick."

The mental image made him laugh. "Really? He said that?"

"Yeah," Tim replied, not sharing his mirth. "I took that as a good sign, like you're too loving of a person to stab me in the back. But now I'm thinking—"

"I'm just trying to help Ryan move on. Seriously. I know you don't have much reason to, but you really can trust me."

A harsh buzz cut through the room before Tim could reply. All eyes turned toward a far door where prisoners were ushered in, one small group at a time. Noah watched tearful reunions, the most depressing of which involved children who didn't seem to know their own father, or weren't comfortable in their presence. Even the greetings that began with embraces and giggles were difficult to witness, considering that those families would soon be separated again.

Noah waited for the next group to enter. Then he stood and raised a hand. "There he is."

Tim stood too. What were his thoughts as Ryan was brought toward them and the two former lovers sized each other up? Noah wasn't sure. Tim's face was expressionless and his body rigid. When the guard left them and Ryan hugged Tim, his arms remained at his sides, not even lifting for a platonic pat on the back.

Ryan was getting teary when he turned to Noah, giving him the same treatment. "Thank you," he whispered before pulling away.

Noah took the chance to check him out. He wasn't as gaunt

as he had been a year ago. He seemed to be at a healthy weight, but the lines under his eyes were darker, as if he hadn't been sleeping well. He was still pretty, like an elegant antique chair that someone had forgotten by the curb, the rain and sun ruining the fabric and bleaching the wood.

"Something to eat?" Noah asked, holding up the bag of quarters. "Or drink? Better get it now before the lines start to form."

"Yes!" Ryan said, his smile bright. He looked to Tim. "Can we?"

Tim seemed to wrestle with a number of responses, but in the end he only shrugged. Okay. Noah led the way to the vending machines. Ryan picked out what he wanted and Noah did the same, his stomach rumbling with hunger. Tim just shook his head when offered. So far he hadn't spoken a word. When they sat at the table again, they did so on opposite ends, Noah between them like a mediator. He didn't need to prod a conversation into life. Ryan took the initiative.

"It's so good to see you," he said, eyes sparkling as he stared across the table. "You look amazing! Even better than before."

Tim opened his mouth. Then he shut it.

Ryan tried again. "How have you been?"

"Fine," Tim said at last. He seemed to struggle with himself before he added, "You?"

"I'm doing better." Ryan's eyes darted to the side. "I'm not alone in here anymore. I've made a few friends."

"That's great!" Noah said encouragingly.

Ryan's smile was tight. "Yeah. I still hate it here though. This is hell, and I know I deserve it but…" He slid his hand across the table toward Tim, who recoiled visibly. "Oh god! Look what I've done to you. I am so, *so* sorry! That's the first thing I need to say, because what I did was unforgiveable. I know that. But I need you to understand that the person in your house that day wasn't me."

"He sure looked like you," Tim grumbled.

"Of course! I'm not trying to say it was someone else, but that wasn't who I am inside." Ryan withdrew his hand to place it over his heart. "You know that! Even at my worst, I never tried to hurt you. I should have listened. When I overdosed and you pleaded with me to stop, I should have quit, but I didn't know any other way to numb the pain I felt inside. I missed you so bad, and I knew I had ruined it all. The drugs helped. Heroin, crack, whatever I could get. I just wanted to stop myself feeling, and I guess I succeeded because I never would have hurt you otherwise. I love you too much."

Tim looked at Noah for guidance. Or maybe to say, *this is what you brought me here for?* Either way, Noah felt the need to intervene, so he addressed Ryan. "In your letters, you often talk about wanting to explain what happened that day. From your perspective."

Ryan leapt on this. "I wasn't there to shoot you or anyone else!"

"Then why did you have a gun?" Tim demanded.

"I was in trouble. I owed money to some very bad people. Worse than that. I stole from them."

Tim glowered. "Like you did from me."

"Yes. I was an idiot then too, and I'm sorry. If I had it all to do over again, I never would have taken you for granted. I would have—"

Noah cleared his throat, wanting to keep the story on track. "What did you steal from the people you were in trouble with?"

"Drugs," Ryan said. "And money. I was supposed to be selling most of what I was using. I managed to move some, but then I got robbed. Just the cash, thank god. The thief didn't find the drugs, but I knew I was in trouble, so when a customer couldn't pay and offered me a gun instead, I took it. I only wanted to defend myself."

Tim crossed his arms over his chest. "You showed up at my house, and you didn't even knock. You crept through the back—"

"I knew you wouldn't answer the door! I needed to talk to you."

"—and when you found my husband and son in the kitchen, you pulled the gun on them. Was that in self-defense? Because I don't think they attacked you. Not until you threatened their lives."

Ryan had his hands up now. "Please, slow down. I was desperate to find you. I needed help—"

"You needed money."

"Yes! What else could I do, tell the police I used all the heroin I was supposed to be selling? Ask them to arrest the drug cartel so I could feel safe when sleeping on the streets at night? I was a nobody, and I was desperate!"

Tim didn't argue this point. He simply stared at Ryan in stony silence.

Ryan pressed on anyway. "I was trying to find you because I knew you were the only person on this miserable planet who ever loved me, and the only one who would be willing to help."

"I would have," Tim said. "Had you done things right. Had you come to me and explained everything—"

"That's what I was trying to do! I know it seems crazy and it was. I was half-mad from fear, starvation, and withdrawal. I wasn't myself, and when I saw him…" Ryan shook his head. "All the pain came back. Ben was the reason we broke up and I was still hurting—"

"Ben is *not* the reason we broke up," Tim said, his voice a low growl. "He and I weren't together then. I never cheated on you. We only made you believe that so you would get the hell out of my life, and for the record, I take the blame, because I should have been man enough to get rid of you myself."

"But you couldn't," Ryan said softly. "Because you love me."

"*Loved*," Tim said.

"You love me," Ryan repeated. "Some part of you must or you wouldn't be here today."

Tim stood. "Nice seeing you again."

Ryan was on his feet too. "You're not perfect either! Don't act like you were a saint in our relationship. The bruises might have healed, but I still feel them inside!"

Tim spared Noah a glance, his jaw clenching. He was ashamed, that much was obvious. A guard had noticed the commotion and was approaching, so Noah suggested they sit. He didn't think Tim would agree, but he did, having more he needed to say.

"I messed up," Tim began. "I'll never deny that, but you did too, and when we broke up, we were equally guilty. That should have been the end of it."

Ryan shook his head. "I don't agree."

"Of course you don't! Somehow it was always my fault."

"That's not what I mean," Ryan said, "I don't agree that it should have been the end."

Tim spluttered laughter. "Are you kidding me? We're toxic together! It never would have worked!"

"Because you never gave us a fair chance."

"I gave you everything!"

"Not emotionally, you didn't. You were always holding back. I just didn't realize why."

Tim ground his teeth. "I'll tell you why. It's because you were a spoiled little shit! I took you in, I fed you, I clothed you, and yeah, I loved you, and all you gave me in return was— What?"

Ryan was shaking his head, expression amused. "You think dating you is easy? You have no idea."

"Fine," Tim said, glaring openly. "Explain it to me. That's what we're here for, right?"

"You *were* cheating on me," Ryan said. "Maybe you didn't realize it, but your head was always somewhere else. You were dead emotionally. Do you realize that? That's why I used to push you, just to get a reaction. It was the only time I could tell you felt *anything* for me. When that stopped working, I pulled away instead. Yes, I ran around on you and hurt myself just to see if you would care, but you would have done the same thing in my shoes. Ben got to your heart first. Eric took whatever was left. I got nothing."

"I gave you everything."

"Scraps," Ryan said dismissively. "Leftovers."

"I fucking loved you!" Tim snarled.

"Calm down," Noah interjected. "Both of you. Please. Ryan, you didn't ask Tim here so you could argue. Right?"

Ryan rested his elbows on the table and pinched the bridge of his nose. "You're right. Maybe I was wrong. I probably was. You really did love me, and I was too messed up to see it. That's what I need you to understand. I was screwed up, and it only got worse. And I really am sorry. The one good thing about being in here is that I'm finally clean. I've had time to work through my issues. I've even found God."

"That doesn't make it okay," Tim muttered. "People do horrible things, go to prison, and act like reading the Bible makes up for it all. Well guess what? It doesn't change a thing. You still shot someone."

Ryan sighed and shook his head. "I hate that you've grown so bitter. I realize I'm partly to blame for that."

"I'm not bitter," Tim said, sounding drained. "Usually I'm annoyingly happy these days. I love my life. I just don't like my past."

"Then we still have something in common," Ryan said. "A past that we both regret, and an upbringing that neither of us can change. It could have been you in here. Do you realize that? If things had played out differently, if you hadn't inherited that money from Eric—"

"I wouldn't have shot anyone," Tim said. "Ever."

Ryan sniffed. "No. You're right. You always were the better half. That's why I looked up to you. That's why I'm turning to you now."

"I'm exhausted," Tim said. "Just tell me what it is that you want."

"For you to understand, because maybe then you'll find it in your heart to forgive me."

"Fine," Tim said. "I forgive you."

He didn't sound very convincing.

"You gave me so many chances," Ryan said. "I know it's greedy to ask for one more, but that's what I need."

"We're not going to be together again," Tim said, laughing humorlessly. "Ever."

Ryan appeared slighted. "I know. I hate that it's true, but I can accept it."

"Good." Tim took a deep breath and exhaled. "Listen, I can't be part of your life. Like I said, we're toxic, but I'll do one last thing for you. Remember the painting I made? The one of you in your bathrobe?"

"The pink one," Ryan said, smiling at the memory. "You barely let me see it before you hid it away."

"Because you bitched about your nose looking too big and—"

"It was a beautiful painting," Ryan interrupted. "That's all I remember."

Tim eyed him and nodded. "I finally sold it. Believe it or not, people actually like my work these days."

"You're a famous artist now?"

Tim shrugged. "I'm big in Japan."

Ryan laughed. "I love that song! That might be what I miss the most. The music. You don't get much of it in here. Hey, they should put a jukebox next to the vending machines! Do you remember when we would hit the clubs and I'd beg you to dance with me? You never did. Not unless you were wasted."

"I sold the painting," Tim said, refusing to be sidetracked, "and I put the money in an account with your name on it for when you get out. You won't be rich, but it's enough for a deposit on an apartment and a few months' rent. That'll give you enough time to find a job and get back on your feet."

"Thank you," Ryan breathed. "You have no idea how much that means to me. I want out so bad, but I'm also scared, because I don't want to be on my own. This will help. I have a hearing coming up soon."

Noah blanched. He saw that Tim did too. This was news to them both!

"A hearing?" Tim said. "You mean like parole?"

"Yes." Ryan noticed their expressions. "Don't all cheer at once! I'm ready for this. I promise. I've completed an anger management course, my behavior here has been spotless for nearly two years, and I don't feel the need to numb myself with drugs anymore. I'm ready."

Tim's response was guarded. "How much of a chance do you have?"

"Of making parole? That's what I'm worried about. I had a hearing years back, and it didn't go well. All they see is a junkie and a criminal. Why would they believe anything I say? They would listen to you though. If the victim of the crime steps forward and says he thinks I deserve leniency, then maybe they'll—"

"No." Tim's tone was steady, the word final, his voice quaking with rage as he continued. "You'll stay here until the judges or whoever decide to release you. When that happens, you'll get your money, but you stay the hell away from me. And if you come *anywhere* near the people I love—my son, my husband, even my friends—I will fucking kill you. Do you understand? I'll do it with my bare hands if I have to, so you go somewhere else. Not Austin, not Texas. Somewhere far away. No matter what you might think in that twisted little heart of yours, you do *not* want to see me again. Don't write, don't call, don't even whisper my goddamn name at night, because we are through! Understand?"

Ryan was too shocked to respond. He didn't have much of a chance because Tim stood and tromped toward the exit. Ryan was on his feet like he wanted to give chase, but Noah stood and blocked his path. "Let him go. Please. Nothing you can say or do will bring him back."

Ryan looked at him and blinked, like he barely remembered that Noah was there. This didn't come as a surprise, and Noah didn't take it as personally as he once would have.

"Sit," he urged.

Ryan did so, eyes still on the exit until, presumably, Tim was lost from sight. Noah didn't dare glance back, wanting to make sure Ryan wouldn't try anything crazy. Maybe he really had taken courses and was working on improving himself because he didn't shout or even launch into an angry rant.

Ryan only sighed. "I'm going to be in here forever, aren't I?"

"I don't know," Noah said, "but I'll start putting money in your account again. You can write me if you want, but not about Tim. Think how you felt about him and Ben. That's what it was like dating you. I hated hearing about this perfect guy I could never compete with. I can be your friend, but only on the condition that you never mention Tim to me again. I'll even come visit on occasion. That's all I can do. I've got my own life now. I've moved on."

Ryan looked him over for the first time since he had arrived. "You're doing well. I can tell you're no longer on the streets."

"I'm doing better, yeah."

Ryan nodded. "I'm glad. Thank you for trying."

"No problem. I'm sorry to do this, but he's my ride, and I'm worried that he'll forget about me."

"I know the feeling," Ryan said as they stood. "Will you come to my hearing?"

Noah could picture Marcello's face if he did, red with indignation and veins swelling with rage. Noah would probably be fired and put on some sort of blacklist that would make it impossible for him to work in Austin again. That would suck. Not being able to live with himself would be worse. He knew that now. "Yeah. I'll be there."

"Thank you," Ryan said, hugging him and not letting go. "For everything. I'm sorry I made you feel that way when we were together. I was too blind to realize what I had in front of me. I loved you, but I should have loved you more."

"It's all in the past now," Noah said, taking a step back. "I'd rather focus on the future. You should too. Some of the guys in here are kind of hot." He nodded to a muscular guy with long dreads at a nearby table. "What about him?"

Ryan looked over and snorted. "Total bottom. Not my type at all. But yeah, there are some gorgeous guys here, and you wouldn't believe how hot the setting makes it. I'm a notorious soap dropper."

Noah laughed and shook his head. "I don't want to know. Actually, I do. Next time, okay?"

Ryan's lip trembled but he bit down on it and nodded. "Next time."

The interior of the car was even stuffier now on the ride back. Tim didn't speak, he just glowered, his scowl increasing with the vehicle's speed. Then he would notice he was driving too fast and force himself to slow down. This cycle kept repeating. Noah had attempted conversation at the start of the drive, mentioning that maybe they should stop and get something to eat. Tim brought them to a fast food drive thru. After getting their food from the window, he parked and began chomping his way through a burger like he was sinking his teeth into Ryan's flesh. In surprisingly few bites he finished and resumed driving. Since then, silence.

Noah leaned the seat back and waited, figuring Tim would talk when he was ready to. This happened an hour outside of Austin.

"I fucked up," Tim said, sounding miserable. "I promised myself I wouldn't lose my temper and I did anyway."

"I get it." Noah adjusted his seat to be upright again. "I'd be angry with anyone who shot me. That's a given."

"But those things I said…"

"What things?"

Tim glanced over. "At the end, when I threatened to kill him. I asked you to come with me so Ryan couldn't lie about what I said. Now he won't have to."

"Still no idea what you're talking about," Noah replied, affecting disinterest. "I didn't hear anything like that."

Tim scoffed. "Were you paying attention?"

"Yup. To every single word. I definitely didn't hear you threaten him."

Tim finally caught on, his expression hopeful. "You won't say anything?"

Noah shook his head. "No, and honestly, I don't think he will either. He doesn't have much to gain aside from petty revenge, and whether you believe his story or not, I don't think he was ever after that. He was a crazed junkie. Still, even when sober, he has a lot of issues, and I totally understand why someone—theoretically, of course—might get defensive about him being around their friends and family."

"I'd do anything for them," Tim said. "Ben especially. It's a dark thought, but when you get attacked in your own home, you ask yourself what you'd do if it happened again. The answer is whatever it takes. I'd die for Ben if I had to. I wouldn't hesitate. Not for a second."

"Wow," Noah said. "I wish someone felt that way about me."

"What about, uh… What was his name?"

"Felix," Noah said with a smile. "He's convinced himself that he's in love with me, but we don't really know each other well enough yet."

"You could change that."

"I'm working on it. We keep going on dates and— Oh. You mean the escort thing."

"I thought that's what you were talking about."

"No, but I guess it should be. I'm dreading how he'll react." Noah groaned. "I should have told him from the beginning. Sometimes I wish I'd never taken this job."

"You could switch." Tim looked over at him, silver eyes sizing him up. "How long were you planning on doing this, anyway? You're still young, but you'd be surprised how fast the years start whizzing by."

"I don't have a plan for what comes after," Noah admitted.

"You could ask Marcello for a new position." Tim shook his head. "Actually, don't phrase it that way. I know exactly what he'll say. Ask him for a different job. No! Too easy. Ask him for another line of employment. That should be safe. Probably."

Noah laughed, but his amusement was short-lived. "I don't think Marcello will be in the mood to do me any favors. Come to think of it, I've got nothing to worry about because when he hears how it went today, I won't have a job. He never liked me anyway."

"Marcello?" Tim made a face. "He likes you."

"I'm pretty sure he doesn't."

"Why do you say that?"

"Because he's been giving me hell since day one. He set me up with the worst clients imaginable to scare me off, and lately he can't say my name without gritting his teeth."

Tim laughed. "Reminds me of when I worked for him."

"Oh. I didn't know that you were also an—"

"I was a model," Tim said quickly. "For fashion. I had clothes on. Not much sometimes, and it was only for a weekend, but he busted my balls every chance he got. He's acted like we're best friends ever since. I mean, we are, but at the beginning we weren't. He just likes to surround himself with people who take their work seriously. I've seen him do the same with another model of his. Nathaniel too. When he first started working for the studio, Marcello had him doing all sorts of ridiculous jobs. I guess it's his screening process. Once you make it through, you're golden."

"I may have been golden, but trust me, now I'm dirt again."

"You're not," Tim said, sounding confident. "Marcello doesn't drop people so easily. Not once he's decided to keep you around. Just ask him for a new job. If that's really what you want. It's none of my business."

Noah thought about it during the remainder of the drive. He still liked his work and especially the pay, but maybe he should consider alternatives. If not for himself then for the guy who might be living with him soon. When they pulled up to his apartment building, Noah looked up through the windshield to the higher floors, wondering if he would find anyone waiting for him there. Then he turned his attention back to the driver.

"Thanks again for doing this," Noah said. "At the very least, I think Ryan will finally move on."

Tim sounded exasperated. "Here's hoping."

What else was there left to say? "I guess this is it for me and you."

Tim grinned, which was a stunning sight to behold. "Don't be so sure. I think we'll see each other again someday. Maybe at one of Marcello's parties, or somewhere out in public. A restaurant! I can picture it now. You'll catch a glimpse of me, I'll notice you staring, and I'll raise my beer in salute. When that happens, you come say hello. Okay?"

Noah laughed. "It's a deal. See you around. Say hi to Ben for me."

Tim nodded. "Will do. Take care of yourself."

Noah was at the entrance to his apartment building before he looked back. He saw Tim's black sports car pick up speed and blow through a yellow light just before it changed to red. Then he was gone. Noah now had a better understanding of why Ryan had become so fixated on him. Tim seemed like a special guy. Unforgettable.

Chapter Seventeen

The apartment was unoccupied when Noah returned inside. Only a handwritten note left on the kitchen counter awaited him. Anyone else would have sent a text, but Felix had found scrap paper—the back of a junk-mail envelope—and purple ink. Noah didn't recall owning a purple pen, or Felix carrying one. Had he gone door to door to the neighbors, winning each one over with his adorableness until he found a colorful-enough instrument to write with? The note was just as charming as the imagined scenario.

Thank you for an amazing night! You're the best boyfriend ever. Literally. I checked online just to be sure and it's a fact. Is it okay if I come over again tonight? I love you!

Felix had signed his name along with a cartoonish self-portrait—as a human this time—with hearts for eyes.

"Of course you can come over," Noah said to the empty kitchen. "I told you that you could move in!"

He chuckled to himself, then grew more somber when remembering his recent conversation with Tim. Felix needed to know the truth about Noah's work. Deciding how to approach the subject was as simple as putting himself in Felix's place: young, idealistic, and innocent. Noah pictured himself as a teenager, as his life would have been if his parents hadn't found out about his sexuality, and his life in Fort Stockton had continued at the same slow and simple pace. Maybe, after graduating from high school, he would have met a man with more experience. Harold was the natural choice, so Noah went with it. He imagined developing a crush, getting intimate with his new boyfriend, and then being told the truth: Harold was an escort.

Noah filled a glass of water from the tap and frowned while drinking. His small-town self would have been devastated. Never before had he struggled to understand why people looked down on his occupation. Even those who weren't judgmental still took pity, which he didn't want because he hadn't felt forced into this occupation. Not exactly. For him, escorting was a way out that didn't involve begging or getting wasted. Noah had been willing to work hard and had done so. He felt proud of that, and not at all guilty for being on the streets in the first place because it wasn't the result of bad decisions. Instead it was—

Noah blinked. Then he nearly laughed, the solution having presented itself. He simply needed to tell Felix his story in the right order. Noah thought about how this would best be done and grabbed his phone to send a text.

I'm taking you to dinner tonight. Dress casual and don't worry, there aren't any waiters. You won't be reminded of your work.

He didn't get a response for nearly twenty minutes. When it came, it wasn't as enthusiastic as he was expecting.

Just promise me nobody will throw a cheese biscuit at my head.

Noah needed a moment to interpret this. *You're at work?*

Yup.

And someone is pelting you with biscuits?

Just one, Felix wrote back. *A toddler with impressive aim. Got me right in the ear. Then again, how could he miss?*

Noah laughed. *Don't wash that ear. I want to lick it clean tonight. I'll pick you up at five? Is that too early?*

Yes! I mean no, that's not too early. The yes is to everything else. Tonight!

Noah grinned. *I'll see you then.*

He checked his phone, still not finding a client for the evening. That was unusual for a Saturday, confirming his suspicions: Marcello wasn't happy with him. He decided to ignore this and catch up on his reading. Noah sat on the couch, picked up a book, and had turned three pages before realizing he hadn't taken in any of the words. He was still too distracted. Was he unemployed now? What if Marcello was only searching for an appropriately terrible client to punish him with, like the guy who enjoyed slapping his lovers a little too much? Not enough to bruise or hurt, but enough to get *really* annoying. That would also wreck his plans for the evening, so he chose to stop wondering and find out. A text wouldn't cut it. He called instead, tense as the fifth ring was interrupted by a voice.

"Ten minutes," Marcello said before hanging up again.

He supposed that was better than a simple "fuck off." Noah closed his book and waited, trying to imagine a variety of scenarios and appropriate responses. He was caught off guard anyway, because when the call was returned, it was of the video variety. Marcello wanted to see his face as they spoke, probably to assess if he was telling the truth. Or to watch him squirm.

"Did you enjoy your trip?" Marcello asked. The scene was the studio's top floor office, his boss seated behind a desk covered with stacks of papers and photos. Marcello meant business. Had he been relaxing on one of the couches, that would have implied a more amiable temperament. The desk *always* meant business.

Noah chose his answer carefully. "The visit with Ryan was... productive."

"How so?"

"He just needed to get it out of his system. Ryan's waited years to talk to Tim, and not only that, but he's doing good in other ways. He's clean, a lot less angry, and he says he's found God."

"Congratulations," Marcello said. "Perhaps Ryan would be so kind as to inform God that the rest of the world is wondering where he went."

"My point is that Ryan is doing a lot better."

"I care not for his feelings," Marcello said dismissively.

"I do," Noah shot back, "and he needed this. Tim did too, since he also got a few things off his chest."

"I heard." Marcello didn't seem interested in the conversation. Instead he shuffled a stack of checks into order and set them aside. "Mr. Wyman just left. He had some very nice things to say about you."

"Really?"

"Yes." Marcello looked directly into the camera. "I place an exceedingly high value on discretion."

Did he mean a bribe to stay silent? Or a reward for already agreeing to not mention the death threat? Either way... "I've always been a big fan of forgiveness myself."

Marcello considered these words and nodded. "Forgiveness it shall be. Some of us need it more than others, myself included, although I'm afraid I still can't extend my sympathies to Ryan."

"I don't expect you to," Noah said.

"How was his demeanor after Tim stormed out of the prison?"

Noah took a deep breath. "He gets it. Ryan finally accepts that he and Tim have severed all ties."

"And what of your relationship with Ryan?"

"I'll be there for him," Noah said firmly. "As his friend."

Marcello cocked an eyebrow. "Do you think that wise?"

"Someone needs to keep tabs on him. Just in case."

A flicker of amusement was quickly suppressed as Marcello resumed organizing his desk. "I see. Then it's business as usual for you and me."

That sounded good! Noah wasn't fired, and he would be free to do what he felt was right. Might as well cash in completely on the goodwill between them. "I could use the night off. I have a date. A *real* one."

"With a certain waiter?" Marcello inquired.

Noah grinned. He couldn't help it. "Yeah."

"Then I wish you the most pleasant of evenings." Marcello was reaching for his phone to end the call, but before a chubby finger poked the screen he added, "Well done, Mr. Westwood. Well done indeed."

The image froze and was replaced by a list of recent calls. Noah exhaled and willed his muscles to relax. Feeling a lot less stressed about his livelihood, he turned his attention instead to the evening, and all the ways it could end in disaster.

"What is this place?"

They stood on a street corner downtown, Felix nibbling on a knuckle and glancing at the people loitering there. Many were in rough condition. Some were loud or mentally ill. A few were drunk.

"It's a homeless shelter," Noah explained. "Jerusalem. We're going to help serve meals."

"Oh." Felix reassessed their surroundings and put on a brave face. "Okay."

"Good." Noah reached out to playfully tug on the drawstring of Felix's hoodie. "Don't worry, you'll be fed too. I won't make you starve."

"I'm fine. I eat so much at work, and being here makes me feel—" His expression hardened with determination. "Doesn't matter. Let's get to work!"

When they entered, the front desk was manned by two people Noah didn't recognize. He could hear Edith's voice shouting orders from the kitchen. Noah had called her earlier to make sure he could not only volunteer, but also bring someone with him. He had only done so out of politeness. The shelter always needed help, and as each mealtime neared, the effort to get everyone served became more of a scramble.

"I never did work in the kitchens much," Noah said, leading

the way, "and I definitely haven't cooked a meal big enough for hundreds of people. We both have a lot to learn tonight."

"But you've done this before?" Felix asked.

"Oh yeah," Noah said with a nod. "Tons of times."

He didn't have time to explain because the kitchen was filled with the sounds of steam hissing and pans clanking. A giant soup pot had just started to boil over, so Noah rushed over to lower the heat and stir its contents back to a simmer.

"Thank goodness you are here!" Edith said, having noticed him. As she approached, she saw Felix and focused on him instead. "And here is the waiter you can't stop speaking about!"

"Only good things," Noah stage-whispered to Felix. "I promise."

Edith looked his boyfriend over. "I love the hair! Very cheerful. It reminds me of my punk rock days. I couldn't get enough of the Buzzcocks."

"Who?" Felix asked.

"Before your time," Edith said, patting him on the arm. "You're younger, and that means you have energy. Do you know how to peel potatoes?"

"No," Felix admitted.

"Good! It's much more tedious once you've mastered the technique. Over here, I'll show you. Noah, can you start on the rolls?"

Noah had imagined them working side by side, but they weren't here to socialize. Hungry people needed to be fed. He still checked on Felix and was pleased to see him taking the work in stride, even an hour later when the meal was ready to be served. Noah hadn't considered how close that would be to Felix's normal job, but he didn't complain once. Felix stood next to him and slopped food onto plates, even joking about it.

"I always wanted to be a lunch lady," he said.

Noah laughed. "The hairnet *is* a good look for you."

"I mean it! I was picked on a lot in grade school, but the ladies in the cafeteria were always nice to me. They'd sneak me an extra chocolate milk or a second cookie for free."

"They were probably trying to fatten you up."

"Excuse me," said an older man with a nicotine-tinged beard and very few teeth. He raised his tray. "Will eating this do *that* to my hair? If so, I don't want it."

"Food didn't do this," Felix said reaching up to touch his blue mane. "I was struck by lightning. I used to be blonde. I also used to be a white guy!"

The old man cackled and went on his way.

"Don't listen to him," Noah said. "You're gorgeous."

"You make me feel that way," Felix said. Then he turned to the next person in line, a little more spring in his step. Another hour passed before everyone had been served, but their work wasn't done. Someone needed to start in on the dirty dishes that were piling up. A row of dishwashers took care of the smaller items, but the really big pots and pans wouldn't fit inside and had to be washed by hand.

"You sure know how to make a gal feel special," Felix said when they were done. The front of his shirt was soaked with water and he looked exhausted, but he smiled to show he was only teasing.

"Follow me," Noah said. "We'll get that shirt dry."

He led them to the laundry room, which was calm compared to the kitchen, and had Felix strip off his shirt and hoodie. Noah had fared better in terms of avoiding water. He threw the clothes into one of the dryers and grabbed a clean blanket from a nearby stack. He wrapped this around the narrow shoulders and slender torso. Then he kissed Felix on the nose, making him giggle.

"I used to come down here at night sometimes," Noah said. "Just to read."

"I guess there isn't a breakroom," Felix responded, missing the point as he pulled the blanket tighter around himself.

Perhaps this wasn't the best place to tell his story. "Come on. I want to show you something."

Noah walked them to one of the large dorm-type rooms. Some of the beds had already been claimed, but for the most part, people socialized elsewhere after eating. He sat on the nearest bed and patted the mattress so Felix would do the same. With the blanket wrapped around him and after working so much, he looked as though he had just been rescued from some natural disaster.

"This was my favorite bed," Noah explained. "It's close to the door, which is good if you need to pee at night. There's light from the hall, so it's not as dark, and the open doorway also helps ventilation. You don't want to be deep in this room on chili night!"

Felix looked around, then over at him. "You used to stay here?"

Noah nodded. "That's why I brought you tonight. Seeing it for yourself is different than just hearing about it. I told you my parents weren't crazy about me being gay. The truth is they threw me out when I was sixteen. This is where I ended up. Eventually."

"That's terrible!" Felix said. His eyes went wide and he covered his mouth. "Sorry," he whispered. "I don't mean anything bad about this shelter, it's just—"

"Nobody wants to be here," Noah assured him. "Before it happened to me, I assumed homeless people were all drunks and that any misfortune was their own fault. I was wrong. I wasn't the only teenager abandoned by their parents. I've seen every age—people from all walks of life—on the street, and for more reasons than you could imagine."

"And your parents knew? They were okay with this?"

"I don't think they care. But no, I never told them. It wasn't just a rough patch. I was homeless for years and had to do a lot of crazy things to survive. I stole, I begged, and… Yeah. It was rough."

Felix chewed his bottom lip, mulling it over. Then his eyebrows came together. "I'm selling my stuff. It's wrong that I have so much when these people have so little! I felt guilty enough when we first got here, and now that I know what you went through, I'm selling it all."

Noah laughed, but not mockingly. "I've had similar thoughts, but you still have a right to be happy. You work hard and study hard. If you don't blow off steam and indulge yourself somehow, you'll snap and end up here. It's great that you want to help. I'm just getting back into volunteering. We could do this together."

"Yes," Felix said instantly. "I'm in."

"Good." Noah leaned close for a kiss.

Felix reciprocated, but he pulled away sooner than he usually did. "I feel wrong for even saying this, but I'm starving!"

"Oh, right!" In all the commotion, they hadn't been able to stop and eat. Nor were there any leftovers. "What are you in the mood for? I'll get you anything you want."

"Pizza," Felix answered immediately.

"Okay. There's a place down on Congress that everyone raves about."

"I was thinking delivery," Felix said coyly.

Noah grinned. "You want to go home. Is that what I'm hearing?"

Felix nodded eagerly.

"You've been a very good boy tonight," Noah said, pausing to steal another kiss. "You'll get your pizza, and I'll let you stay up late enough to watch an extra show, but after that it's straight to bed, young man. Understood?"

"Yeah, but maybe we should go to bed early." Felix pantomimed a yawn. "I'm awfully tired!"

He no longer looked it! Noah had a feeling that—by the time they fell asleep—he was going to be the exhausted one.

Noah awoke the next day in a blissful state. Felix's back was pressed against him, the sun was shining through the window, and they were closer than ever. Physically and emotionally. Last night they had stayed up talking, Noah opening up about the difficult years behind him. He still hadn't explained the finer details of his modern life, aside from crediting his current job as being what finally returned stability to his life. One step at a time. Felix had a lot to assimilate, and Noah still hoped that he could change careers before they had that talk.

He remained in bed, enjoying the simple tranquility. Then he rose and repeated his usual morning rituals. Restroom, coffee, phone. He had switched off the ringer last night, not wanting their evening to be disturbed, so he wasn't surprised to find messages awaiting him. Only the sender troubled him. The texts were all from Harold Franklin. Noah let his eyes run down the sequence.

What time should we head out tomorrow?

Still thinking about it? It's a big decision, I know.

Okay, you're obviously busy. We'll figure it out tomorrow. Don't sleep in too long. All the good stuff will be gone!

I'm up. Are you up? Let's do this.

Hello? I want my date!

Date? Of course! The flea market or whatever they were supposed to do. So much had happened in such a short period that the charity auction seemed like ages ago. Noah swore under his breath, then texted back.

Sorry. It's been crazy lately. Maybe we should do this next weekend instead.

The response was swift. *I either get my promised date today or I want my four grand back.*

He couldn't help smiling, knowing that Harold wasn't really serious. Was he? *Do you want that in small bills or large?*

The only response was a sad face, but it wasn't an emoji. Harold had sent a photo of himself making puppy dog eyes. Noah stared long and hard at that image, a number of emotions stirring from slumber. *Okay. Fine. Give me an hour and I'll be right over.*

Harold texted back, this time with a photo of him looking happy. Noah pressed on the screen to bring up options, intending to delete the image from their conversation. Instead he changed his mind and hit the save button. Then he rolled his eyes, opened his photos, and deleted it for real. Take that! He also rebelled by showering slowly, as if he had no plans, although he chose to dress in one of his better outfits. He wanted Harold to see what he was missing. Only when fully clothed did Noah hurry, getting into his truck and driving to the nearest store for the cinnamon and spice oatmeal he had promised Felix. He returned to the apartment just in time to find a hungry boy lurking in his kitchen. Felix looked at him with questioning eyes that lit up when he took the box of oatmeal from its bag.

"You really are the best," he breathed.

"I try," Noah said, shooting him a wink. "I just hope you still think so when you find out I'll be busy all day."

"I have to work anyway," Felix said, opening a cabinet. He took out a bowl and turned around, seeming a little apprehensive. "I also thought I might start packing some things. Is that okay?"

"Stop asking that," Noah said warmly. "I meant what I said. Come live here if you want."

"But what do *you* want?"

"For you to stop fishing for compliments and to get some food in your stomach."

"I wasn't fishing!" Felix protested.

"You were. Everyone knows that cats love fish. If you need a ride anywhere, you better hurry because I'm already late. Hey, how did you get home yesterday?"

"My sister," Felix said, adding water to his oatmeal. "I called and she picked me up. Having me at her mercy always makes Darli happy. She loves being able to lord over me, so we're friends again."

"In that case I'm glad I'm an only child. You'll be okay if I leave now?"

Felix nodded. "Where are you going?"

"A date," Noah said without thinking. "A charity date," he amended quickly. "We had one of those auctions at work, you know what I mean? It isn't serious."

Felix shrugged. "Yesterday I found out that you grew up on the streets and that your ex-boyfriend is a murderer. Nothing can shock me now."

Noah only wished that were true. "He isn't a murderer and I didn't— You're messing with me, aren't you?"

"A little," Felix said with a mischievous expression. "When will you be home?"

"Late. Because of work, not the wanna-be date." He still needed to earn money, especially now, when he might be taking a different position that paid less. Besides, weekends were usually the busiest, and he didn't want to let Marcello down, not when they were finally getting along again.

"I'll see you tomorrow then," Felix said amiably.

Noah took his time with the goodbye kiss anyway, just to be sure. Then he was out the door, in his truck, and trying not to think about his destination. He didn't want to get nervous. Or excited. Still, pulling up to a certain house in an old neighborhood brought back treasured memories and expired dreams.

"Hey!" Harold said, throwing open the door before he could knock. He looked great. Harold always looked great, but clearly he was trying. The brown button-up shirt was a little too dressy for a flea market. "I thought you would never get here."

"I couldn't remember the way," he lied. Then he jerked his head toward the truck. "Ready to go?"

"I thought we'd take a taxi," Harold replied, eyes remaining on him. "Wanna come in for a sec while I call one?"

"Why would we need a taxi?"

"Because they sell booze at this thing, and that makes it way more fun. You're going to love it. Come on in."

Noah remained where he was. "I'm not drinking." If they got drunk and he started feeling mopey about how things had ended between them, it wouldn't be pretty. "I'll drive."

"You sure?" Harold asked, his face falling.

"Yeah. Ready?"

Harold patted himself down, checking for the essentials. "I guess so. Hey, is that your truck?"

"No, but if we're lucky, the police won't catch us."

Harold laughed as he shut the door behind him. He didn't lock it. Noah had almost forgotten about that quirk. "It's a nice ride! Fits your image well. I bet the clients love it."

Noah sighed dramatically. "You have no idea. This one guy wanted to watch me work on the engine. That got him all riled up. Good thing he knows even less about cars than me, because all I did was open caps and screw them back on. Oh, and I checked the oil. At least I know how to do that."

"Sounds like Stan Knutson."

"Yeah! That's exactly who it was!"

Harold nodded knowingly. "He's into handymen. Had me take apart a VHS player while he watched and whacked it. One of the weirder things I've ever done."

"A VHS player?" Noah asked, opening the passenger door out of habit. He always did so for clients.

"Yup. I guess he figured it would never work again, and that's why I wasn't given a PlayStation 4 instead. Hey, thanks! This truck rocks!"

The smile on Noah's face froze in place as he shut the door. He wasn't supposed to be enjoying this. Then again, if he acted miserable, they both would have a crappy day, so he decided to have fun. Harold already knew Noah was seeing someone. He wouldn't have any false expectations.

Conversation came easily on the drive to the flea market. They talked about work, naming their worst clients and their favorites, comparing notes and laughing a lot.

"Who sneezes while they're coming?" Harold said as they pulled into the parking lot.

"Not just one sneeze," Noah said. "He goes into a fit! The first time it happened, I thought he was having a seizure."

Harold nodded. "It's pretty intense. I swear he ripped one once."

"He farted too?"

"Yup! Hard to be sure because there's so much going on. I always feel kind of bad, like I don't know what to do for him."

"Grab some tissues," Noah replied. "I figured that covers both needs." After a beat, he added. "Or all three if it's a messy fart."

"That's disgusting!" Harold said, clutching at his sides. "I won't be able to keep a straight face next time!"

Noah put the car in park. "This job can be so gross."

"Or hot. If you had to marry one of your clients..."

"Tough one!"

This conversation carried them into the flea market. The smell of fried food was in the air and a live band was playing music, but neither of them stopped to look at any of the wares for long.

"I remember it being better," Harold commented as they walked beneath a long aluminum roof. Different vendors were set up on either side, shelves and tables acting as barriers between them. "It's been years since I was out here. Not since the fire. My parents used to be crazy about this place." They paused in front of a booth full of T-shirts with almost-but-not-quite-right logos. "I'm starting to see why they don't come here anymore."

Noah shrugged, not bothered by their surroundings. Sure, it all seemed like bootlegs and knockoffs, but he didn't know what else to expect. "What were you hoping to find?"

"Vintage stuff," Harold said. He noticed another vendor and perked up. "Like that one!"

He led the way. Tables and boxes were filled with old junk that wouldn't be out of place at a garage sale. Harold was grinning as he moved things aside, picking up various items for him to see. "Mickey Mouse phone? He'd be worth money if the ears weren't missing. New Kids on the Block lunchbox! I bet that makes your sandwiches taste extra funky. Get it?"

"Yes. Unfortunately."

"Hey, is that a Pee-wee Herman doll? If the pull-string is still there, I might bite. My mom loves Pee-wee, and I know she was looking for one of these."

Noah started searching too, wondering if he could find some special item that would impress Felix. He scoured the tables and was too overwhelmed to choose anything, so he turned to Harold again, who was holding something small in his hand. Noah moved closer to see. It was the kind of button people used to pin on their jackets, this one with a political theme, judging from the red and blue stars.

"What's that?"

"Nothing," Harold said, closing his fingers around it. Then he opened them again. "A reminder. You ever hear of Angela Brandt? She ran for governor last year."

"I don't follow politics much," Noah admitted.

"I don't either, but I used to date her son."

"Really?" Noah said casually, when in truth, he felt slighted. He wasn't even sure why until he chased down the feeling. Harold had refused to give them a chance, so of course it hurt to hear about the people he *had* deemed worthy of dating. "Want me to buy that for you as a souvenir?"

"It's not funny." Harold tossed the button onto a junk-filled table and left the booth.

Noah followed, feeling confused about what had just happened. "Not a good memory, I take it."

"No. Not at all. In fact, it's only gotten worse." Harold turned around to face him. "I wanted to talk to you about all of this anyway. I guess finding that button is a sign that I should. You sure you don't want to get a drink?"

Noah shook his head. "I could use something to eat. I skipped breakfast."

Harold nodded and together they walked away from the live music to the far end of the flea market. There they found a food vendor selling homemade tamales, and while the scent in the air was mouth-watering, the scattered tables and stools were worn and permanently stained. The kitchen equipment behind the counter was equally scorched and dirty. Noah didn't care. He wasn't picky, and right now he was hungry enough to eat just about anything. As they carried their orders to a table, his date didn't seem to share this indifference.

"Sorry." Harold glanced at their surroundings with a frown. "Like I said, I haven't been here for ages. I wanted our date to be nice! This isn't how I imagined it."

Noah hadn't given any forethought to this day at all and was surprised Harold had looked forward to it so much. "I like it here," he said generously. "It's the sort of place our clients would never take us, and that makes it feel like vacation." To demonstrate, he took a swig from his soda bottle and gasped like he was in a commercial. Then he peered at the label. "No corn syrup. This is the real stuff with actual sugar! That alone is worth the trip."

Harold smiled. "You're the best. You know that?"

The phrase was a little too close to something Felix would say, so Noah shifted the conversation back to a previous topic. "Tell me about the governor's son."

"She didn't become governor," Harold said. "I guess she did better because now she's a—" He shook his head and started again. "His name was Calvin. Is. He's not dead. I've stalked his Facebook page enough to know that. You could use one, by the way."

"I'd need to get friends first," Noah joked from around a bite of tamale. "How'd you two meet?"

"I was just starting out as an escort and was meeting a new client. Not just new to me, but to the GAC as well. When I got to the party, my date already had a hot guy hanging out with him."

"Calvin?"

Harold nodded. "I couldn't figure out what he was doing there. Calvin mostly ignored me to focus on my client, and he seemed to really care about him. The best theory I could come up with then is that the client was Calvin's uncle. Or maybe his dad. I was confused, but I still couldn't tear my eyes away."

"From his dad? I didn't know you were into older guys."

"From Calvin," Harold said, threatening to throw a plastic fork at him like a dart. He set it down again and continued. "I figured it out eventually. The client wanted two of us. Not so unusual, as you know, but normally that only happens in the bedroom. This guy wanted us both as dates too. Calvin kept ignoring me, except when our client was distracted. Then the weird faces started. At first I thought he was making fun of me. Calvin would glance over and go cross-eyed or puff up his cheeks. One time, after really twisting up his face like he smelled something bad, I started laughing so hard I about died. You know how it is when you can't stop and you're practically crying?"

Noah nodded, mouth full of food.

"I later found out that my nervousness was showing, and that Calvin was trying to distract me. It worked. He got me into a silly mood, which the client seemed to like. From then on, whenever the client was distracted, I stole every moment I could, like I was hungry—no, *starving* to talk to Calvin. By the end of the night, I had to keep reminding myself that we weren't alone. Lucky for us, the client only wanted to watch us have sex together. I didn't have to get myself into the mood for that one!" Harold's smile slowly faded as events caught up with him. "I don't regret any of that. We should have stopped there though. We shouldn't have dated, or maybe he should have quit and—" Harold sighed. "Hindsight, am I right?"

"Depends how far back you look," Noah replied. "When I was younger, I would have given anything just to kiss another boy. Love seemed impossible. Turns out it's not, which still feels like a miracle. I've dated a few heartbreakers, but I don't regret any of them."

"Even me?"

"We never dated."

Harold looked him straight in the eye. "We should have."

Noah held his gaze for as long as he could. Then he focused on his food. "You were in the middle of a story. Keep going."

"Oh. Okay. Calvin and I were together for a couple of years. I loved every minute of it. The job was an adventure and gave me everything I needed physically and financially. He took care of the rest. My happiness and my relationship with him were the same thing. Inseparable. Things were good. Great! I couldn't imagine better. All that was left was to make it official."

Noah nearly choked on his food. He managed to swallow and asked, "Marriage?"

Harold nodded. "I thought I was ready."

"What happened?"

Harold shrugged. "He wasn't. I tried not to blame him at first. He was under a lot of pressure from his mom. Politicians aren't the only ones in the public eye. Their families are too. It's crazy that he even worked as an escort. He used a fake name with clients, but still."

Noah shook his head. "So wait, you wanted to marry him and he wasn't into that, so then what happened?"

Harold swallowed and looked skyward. "That was it. He broke it off."

"Because you proposed?"

"Because of a lot of reasons. His family, this line of work, and maybe because of me. He couldn't have really loved me. If he did, it wouldn't have ended like that. Or at all."

"Then he's an idiot," Noah said before he could help himself. He didn't take it back either. Instead he steeled himself and pressed on. "Seriously. I know you loved him, but something was broken in his brain. The next time you propose, I promise you the answer will be yes." When he saw how Harold's face lit up at this statement, he quickly backpedaled. "I don't mean me! Or that you would even want that. Or that I'm hoping you'll propose. All I'm saying is that—"

Harold interrupted him with laughter. "I've missed you. For real."

Noah smiled. "We always had fun together."

"I hate that I screwed it up. All that stuff with Calvin, it wasn't ancient history. When you and I met, it had only been a year since he and I split. Long enough that I felt like my old self again, but I guess I wasn't done healing, because when we started getting close..." Harold glared, clearly angry with himself. "I'm sorry. It's lame, but that's all I can say. It had nothing to do with you. You're perfect. I hate that I missed my chance."

Noah wasn't sure what to think. He still needed to digest it all, but he was already confident enough to draw one conclusion. "I forgive you. And I meant what I said about needing friends."

"I'll take what I can get," Harold said, flashing a smile that seemed genuine. "Enough about me. How are things with you? You've got a home now. I was so freaking happy when Marcello told me."

"You and me both," Noah said. "You should come over sometime and check out the place."

"Yeah! So you've got the white picket fence and you're working on a wife and kids. Who's the lucky guy?"

"Felix."

"Nice. Things serious between you two?"

"Well, he's moving in."

"Awesome." Harold kept bobbing his head. "Super cool. I'm so pumped for you, man. Really. I mean it."

"Keep going," Noah joked. "I'm not quite convinced yet."

Harold swallowed. "I'm trying to be supportive. I know it's the right thing to do. Selfishly, maybe I wish you were still single." He managed a smile. "But only maybe."

Noah studied him. "There must be a slew of guys trying to win your heart. Be honest."

Harold grinned. "Just one. Ruben. He's all right."

"Just all right?" Noah wiped his fingers on a napkin and gestured with them. "Let's see a photo. I need to approve of this guy or you're calling it off."

Harold laughed and pulled out his phone. After browsing briefly, he handed it over. The man in the image was their age. His hair was tight black curls against olive skin. Maybe he was Greek or Italian. His face was both handsome and kind.

"Nope," Noah said, handing the phone back. "Not good enough. Want me to call him and explain that it's over?"

Harold chuckled. "Nah. We're not even official yet. He keeps pushing though, so I need to make a decision soon."

"Might be worth a shot."

Harold considered the image. Then he raised his eyes to Noah instead and that's where they lingered. "Maybe. How are things with your parents?"

"I wouldn't know."

"You haven't heard from them lately?"

Noah snorted. "Are you forgetting that I'm dead to them?"

"I thought you guys talked on the phone sometimes. I remember you saying that."

"My mom, yeah." Noah leaned back, trying to think of when the last time had been. "I haven't spoken to them since you and I went our separate ways."

"That was a year ago!"

Noah shrugged. "I know."

"They won't answer or..."

"I stopped calling. I'll try it again the next time I'm drunk and need a good laugh."

Harold's expression was earnest. "A lot has changed in the past year. Not just marriage equality, but tons of churches welcome gay people now."

"I refuse to get my hopes up."

"Okay, but you could still test the waters. Maybe they're sorry."

Noah raised an eyebrow. "You remember our trip out there, right?"

"I do," Harold said. "I think about it a lot. Especially the motel."

The night they had slept together. It should have been the beginning. Instead it had been the end.

"I liked the drive too," Harold said quickly. "Just us cruising down the road and talking. It was a good time. I wish it had been different with your parents, but I liked the rest."

"Me too," Noah admitted.

"Then let's do it again. Right now. We'll take a road trip somewhere. Maybe not Fort Stockton, but we could pick a direction and just go. See what we can find. This place is a bust."

Noah was tempted. As much as he tried not to care, he still had feelings for Harold, and he wasn't sure he could steer them towards friendship. Then again, he had to make an attempt. All this time, Noah had been angry with Harold for not giving them a chance. In a way, he was just as guilty. Noah could have tried being friends like Harold wanted. That was the least he could do now. If it got too hard, he would say so and they would go their separate ways again.

"I need your help with something. If you don't mind."

Harold perked up. "Anything! You name it!"

Noah studied him, reminded of the first time they had met—him standing nude in Harold's apartment, simultaneously scared out of his wits and horny as the devil himself. That had been the beginning of a wild ride but now... "I want out."

Puzzlement gave way to understanding. "You don't want to be an escort anymore."

Noah nodded.

Harold shook his head. "Why?"

"Because Felix doesn't know, and I'm worried that if he finds out, it'll break his heart."

Harold leaned back and exhaled. "Jesus, you must really love him."

"I'm starting to. It's more than that. He's shown me a life that I thought I'd never have again. He's reminded me of how the real world works, and I miss it. What we're doing isn't normal."

"That's why I like it!" Harold said defensively. "I'm proud of my work."

"I like it too," Noah said. "I'm not sure I'm proud though, because if I was, I wouldn't have such a hard time telling him."

"If people weren't so closed-minded, you would have already!" Harold's face was flushed. He turned his head, continuing to shake it as he stared into the distance. After a clench of the jaw, he returned his attention to Noah again. "Are you sure?"

About wanting to change careers? Or about Felix? Maybe he was asking if Noah was sure that he and Harold couldn't be together. No matter the intended question, Noah realized that the answers were all the same. "No. I'm not sure, but this is what I'm going to do anyway."

Harold's eyes bored into his soul. Then he nodded. "Okay. I don't see why you need my help. Marcello won't be angry if you quit. He might be disappointed, but he won't try to hold you back. Much."

"That's the thing," Noah said, licking his lips nervously. "I've been smart with my money. I have a lot saved up, but finding a new job is going to be hard because I didn't even graduate from high school, and all I can put on my résumé is the Gentlemen's Agreement Club. How am I supposed to explain what my job duties were? Customer service is my default response, but a potential employer will want details."

"Make something up and Marcello will go along with it." Harold snapped his fingers. "Or maybe he could find you some other position in the company!"

"Do you think so?"

Harold nodded. "Sure! He likes you. Even if he didn't, he owes me a favor."

"Really? How come?"

Harold didn't answer, already busy with his phone. He pushed a few buttons and set it flat on the table. Noah glanced at the screen and saw that he was calling their boss.

"I told you never to call me here," Marcello said, his voice loud and clear over the speaker. "What would my wife and children think if they discovered I was having an affair with a younger man?"

Harold rolled his eyes and grinned. "They'd worry more if you were having an affair with an older man. That would make him what? Ninety? At least."

"Short conversations are the sweetest," Marcello replied. "Goodbye!"

"Wait!" Harold said, leaning over the table. "You're the hottest man I've ever laid eyes on and I want you inside me. Repeatedly. I don't even want you to pull out between rounds."

"You always knew how to beguile me with poetry," Marcello said, sounding pleased. "What can I do for you?"

"I could use a paper bag to put over my head," Noah muttered, eyeing a nearby table of oblivious children and two concerned parents. "Could you two keep it down? We're in public!"

"Ah!" Marcello declared. "Is that Mr. Westwood I hear? Given your line of work, I always thought it a shame your name wasn't Northwood instead. Or perhaps Longwood, considering certain attributes. Oh, I think I've got it! Redwood!"

"I hate you," Noah said, burying his face in his palms.

Harold laughed. "It's his career we were hoping to talk about."

"I see," Marcello said. There was a pause, in which they heard the distinct sound of burbling water. "I'm much too busy at the moment. My desk is covered in invoices and unanswered correspondences."

Noah dropped his hands, relieved that the family had gotten up to leave. "It sounds like you're boiling pasta."

"That would be my noisemaker," Marcello replied. "Helps keep me calm in these troubled times."

Could he get any weirder? "Why are you working on the weekend?"

"Why aren't you?" Marcello retorted. "I really must go."

"Wait," Harold said, picking the phone up to hold it near. "Isn't it time for our yearly evaluations?"

"Noah already had his."

"But I haven't."

"You're doing great," Marcello said hurriedly. "Five stars. Areas of improvement? In the future, try not to harass your employer so much, particularly in regard to telephone calls. Goodbye!"

They heard the sloshing of water, then muted swearing and something that sounded like "Damned prunes!" before the call finally ended.

Noah looked at Harold. "I'm lost. You?"

"Nope, I've got him pegged." Harold's eyes darted up from his phone. "Not like that." He poked at the screen a few more times, grinned, and held it up for Noah to see. "Busted!"

The screen showed a map, a little icon with Marcello's image pointing to a location, but it wasn't the studio he owned and worked at. Instead it was a house in West Lake Hills, one that Noah had visited recently for a charity fundraiser.

"He's at home?"

Harold nodded in confirmation. "Yup! I know a hot tub when I hear one. A couple more years at this job and you will too!" His grin faltered. "Or would have. You're really sure?"

"Yeah," Noah said.

"Okay then." Harold stood. "Let's go see the man who makes wishes come true!"

Chapter Eighteen

"Pull over here."

Noah turned the wheel, bringing the truck to the side of the road where Harold had indicated he should park. After doing so, he turned his attention to the property outside the window. An iron gate blocked the drive to the mansion. Attached to this and stretching as far as he could see was a brick wall at least seven feet high.

"How good are you at climbing?" Harold asked from the passenger seat.

Noah laughed. Then he saw the serious expression. "Can't we just ring the buzzer?"

Harold shook his head. "Marcello is in one of his moods. He won't make this easy for us."

"Then maybe it's not the right time to bother him."

"Or," Harold said, fingers already gripping the door handle, "maybe he'll be impressed by our initiative."

"We could at least try the buzzer first," Noah said, but it was too late.

Harold got out of the truck, shut the door, and started sizing up the wall. Noah joined him. Up close, the wall appeared even taller. Eight feet? Or nine?

"Give me a boost," Harold said, rubbing his hands together and rolling his shoulders. "I'll go first."

"Then who's going to give me a boost?"

"I'll pull you up after me."

Noah snorted. "I'd like to see you try!"

"Then give me a boost!"

He sighed and assumed the classic position, linking his fingers together to form a stirrup of sorts and crouching so Harold could put his foot in it.

"On the count of three," Harold said.

"Just do it now," Noah said.

"Okay. Ready? Go!"

Harold leapt and Noah lifted with all his strength. As soon as Harold's tennis shoe left his hands, he winced and pulled away, worried that the foot would hit him in the face. He should have expected worse, because an entire body crashed into him and knocked him to the ground.

"You all right?" Harold asked, lying not far away.

"Yeah. You?"

"Uh, I think so. Harder than it looks."

"Your head or the jump?" Noah stood and brushed himself off. "Now can we try the buzzer?"

"He won't let us in," Harold said. He sat up and pulled out his phone. "I saw a different technique once. Let's see… Yeah! Here!"

He stood and held out the phone. Noah took it and watched a short video clip. In it, one person braced himself against the wall like he was about to be frisked. Then another ran up from behind, jumped onto his shoulders, and leapt again to grab the top of the wall to pull himself up.

"Uh-uh," Noah said, handing the phone back. "No way!"

"At least try it once!" Harold pleaded.

"Fine. Assume the position."

"I need to go first."

"I bet you do!"

"I'm serious," Harold said, unbuttoning the sleeves of his dress shirt to roll them up. "I'm stronger than you. Have I mentioned that I've been working out?"

"Multiple times."

"That means I have the muscle to pull you up after me. Don't make me beg. I will if I have to."

Noah shrugged. "Go ahead."

Harold walked closer. Much closer! Then he dropped to his knees and looked up at him with big brown eyes. "Please? I'll do anything. Anything at all!"

"You motherfucker," Noah said, laughing and shaking his head. "Fine. One try! If that doesn't work, we—"

"Ring the buzzer, I know." Harold remained on his knees. That was hot, but when he lifted one leg to put his foot on the ground, Noah thought of another scenario that wasn't at all sexual. Harold was down on one knee. And it made him want to cry.

"Get up," he said, taking a step back. "I mean it."

"Okay," Harold said easily. He stood and turned back to the wall. "We can do this."

"You're paying for any medical bills," Noah retorted.

"Yeah, yeah. Hit the wall and spread 'em."

Noah placed his palms against the wall and stood with his butt jutted out, his legs splayed to each side to help brace for impact. It really did feel like they were attempting something out of the Kama Sutra. The advanced edition. Then he heard footsteps running toward him and closed his eyes. In the video clip, the jumping man's feet had touched down on his friend's shoulders. In reality, Harold landed in the middle of Noah's back before leaping again. That hurt, but the pain was brief, and Noah was more interested in the results.

It worked! Harold managed to grab the top of the wall and pull himself up the rest of the way. He turned around and squatted, looking like the world's handsomest gargoyle as he grinned.

"You okay?"

"Yeah," Noah said, rubbing his back. "I can't feel my legs anymore, but that's normal, right?"

"Pretty sure it is. Ready to join me?"

"How?"

Harold draped himself over the wall like a wet towel, his stomach against the very top, his arms dangling over the edge. He twiddled his fingers in invitation. "You just gotta run, jump, and grab my hands."

"And you'll pull me up, Hercules?"

"I'll pull while you walk up the wall."

Noah thought it over. "That might work!"

"That's what I've been tellin' ya! Hurry up. The blood is rushing to my head."

Noah didn't hesitate, knowing that doubt would seep back in if he let it. He got a running start and leapt. The world seemed to slow as their hands neared. His aim was a little off, but Harold managed to grab one hand and a wrist. The physical contact felt good. Noah didn't need extra motivation to kick his feet against the wall as Harold pulled, bringing them closer. Any amorous thoughts fled his mind when he realized that he didn't know what to do next. Keep on wall-walking right over Harold and the wall itself? That would hurt them both—Harold as he got stepped on, and Noah as he toppled over the other side.

Harold seemed to share his concern and tried to shimmy backward while still pulling. If that kept up, they'd both fall. Noah still had one hand free, sort of, so he used it to reach for the wall next to Harold. This meant fighting against him. Harold really was strong, but he was also quick and seemed to understand. He stopped pulling on that arm while still holding onto Noah's other hand. This let Noah grab hold of the wall, and with another kick, get his arm over the top to secure himself.

It wasn't painless. He heard his shirt rip and felt the skin beneath scrape against stone, the burning sensation replaced by moisture. He was bleeding, but he didn't think it was a serious injury. After a little more struggle, he managed to pull himself up. Harold released his hand to grab the back of Noah's shirt and didn't let go until he was safe.

After panting—from adrenaline more than exertion—they both pushed themselves up into a sitting position, legs straddling the wall.

"Odd place for a picnic," Harold joked.

"Bad news," Noah replied. "I left the food in the truck. Wanna go get it?"

They laughed, then looked around. Noah felt like they had climbed the peak of a mountain together and were now able to enjoy the view. Their surroundings *were* very nice. Marcello's home was an impressive sight, the yard landscaped into a generous slice of luxury.

"You hurt yourself!" Harold said, noticing the way that Noah cradled his arm against himself.

"I'm fine. It's just a scrape. It's barely bleeding."

"You're bleeding?" Harold sounded concerned. "Here." He started unbuttoning his shirt.

"What are you doing?"

"I'm going to tie this around your arm like a tourniquet."

"It's just a scrape!"

"Better safe than sorry." The top two buttons were undone, a third soon joining them.

Noah could already see tan skin and toned muscles beneath. "Stop. I mean it! We're not doing this."

Harold's fingers paused. "Doing what?"

"You know what I mean. Don't play the gentleman, don't show off your body, and most of all, don't make me regret my decision."

"I'm the only one who should regret anything," Harold said, but after locking eyes with him, he buttoned up his shirt again.

He stopped just before the last one. "Just one pec? I've been working really hard on them."

Noah laughed. He couldn't help it. "No. In fact, if we ever hang out again, I want you in a turtleneck sweater. A really poofy one that hides any lines."

"Fine," Harold said in mock exasperation. "Ready to continue the mission, Agent Redwood?"

"After you, double oh five."

"Double oh five?"

"As in five inches."

Harold glared. "Hey! It's bigger than that!"

"Really? Because my uncle was an old-school carpenter and he taught me how to measure with my hands."

Harold's shoulders slumped. "It's a little bigger than five. Emphasis on the little."

Noah grinned. "Don't worry. I like you just the way you are."

"Do you?"

"Yeah. Now go first. I want someone to fall on if I slip. You owe me that much."

"Deal!"

Getting down was much easier than getting up. Marcello's security measures seemed to end with the wall. No barking hounds appeared to snap at their heels, nor did an army of guards pour from the building. They were able to walk around the house without interruption and arrive on the back patio. The same one where Noah had pleaded with Tim to visit Ryan, except this time, daylight instead of LEDs illuminated the pool. Noah hadn't noticed the hot tub that night, but his attention was drawn away from it to a deck chair and the man reclining in it.

Marcello wore the skimpiest of swimsuits, his entire body glistening with oil, large belly catching the sun. He held some sort of tropical drink in one hand and his phone in the other. His head turned as they approached, an eyebrow rising above the dark sunglasses.

"An impressive demonstration of acrobatic skills, but next time, save yourself the trouble and use the buzzer."

Noah shot an I-told-you-so expression at Harold before returning his attention to his boss. "Sorry for interrupting your weekend, but I really need to talk to you."

"That seems to be a running theme," Marcello said, pausing

to sip from his drink. Then he held it out. "While you're here, you might as well make yourself useful. You'll find a blender on the kitchen counter with more. Oh, and I feel uncomfortable being so exposed. Do something about it."

"Should I bring you a robe?" Noah asked.

"You should return with less on. Both of you. Seems only fair. Off you go!"

Noah exchanged a glance with Harold. Then they went into the house together. Noah focused on finding the blender and pouring another drink. Harold was already undressing while fighting down a smile.

"Looks like you'll have to see me naked anyway. Don't worry, I'm only kidding. I can stay behind you at all times. Sure it'll be awkward, but I don't want my hotness to haunt you at night."

Harold wasn't vain enough to be serious, but he might not be wrong.

"Fine," Noah said, setting down the blender and walking over to face him. "Let's see what you've got."

"This brings back memories," Harold said, unfastening the last button of his shirt. "Remember the first day at my house?"

"Nope," Noah said, crossing his arms over his chest. "Ancient history. Is that all you've got?"

Harold was shaking the shirt off his shoulders, and yeah, it was a beautiful sight. His body was meatier than before, the muscles more trained, but as always it was his face that caught Noah's attention, a hint of insecurity and maybe disappointment appearing as he started working on his jeans.

"You're gorgeous," Noah said with a sigh. "That was never the problem."

"I know," Harold said. "About the real problem, I mean. It was my fault and no amount of bench presses can change that or make up for what I did. I just like to tease you."

"I remember," Noah said softly. "I always liked joking around with you. I still do."

Harold's hands were on the front of his jeans, but they were no longer moving. Instead he nodded to the kitchen counter. "Better get undressed and grab that drink. Marcello is feeling ornerier than usual."

"Ornerier or hornier?" Noah said, but the joke did nothing to dispel the tension between them. He felt a tug of sorrow as he stripped down to his underwear, glancing over to see that Harold had done the same, but lustful thoughts were far from his mind. Instead he made himself think of Felix, some of the joy returning to the day. Then, together, they returned outside.

"Wonderful!" Marcello said, clapping a few times. "Now that's what I call a memorable presentation. You know, in all the years I've been using shirtless waiters, I never thought to have them go pantless as well. What do you think the reaction would be?"

"More money from your donors," Harold said.

"And fewer waiters willing to work for you," Noah added.

"I suspect you are both right." Marcello accepted his drink. "Now then, why don't you stand there and block the sun with your youthful brilliance while telling me why you've gone to such extremes. Was it lust that drove you to see me? Or love?"

"Business, actually," Harold said.

"Greed then," Marcello said, removing his sunglasses and setting them aside. "How predictable."

"It's not about money!" Noah shot back. "I need out." He regretted the words the second they slipped free. Harold surely knew a better way of broaching the subject, but Marcello had managed to strike a nerve and probably not by chance.

"Not quite so predictable then," his boss said, "but highly disappointing. Shall we skip past your reasons and discuss how I can change your mind? A good number of clients count you amongst their favorites."

That was flattering! But not enough. "The reason is important."

Marcello took a sip of his drink. "Love always seems that way at the beginning, although few manage to keep it a priority. How long have you and Felix been together now?"

Not long at all, but then again, Romeo and Juliet's relationship and subsequent tragedy had taken place over the span of four days. Compared to them, he and Felix were an old married couple. That's how love worked. It exploded into existence. The only challenge was protecting that flame so it wouldn't go out, and that's what he intended to do. "Long enough," Noah said. "I don't want to lose him. I'm also thinking of my own future. I can't do this forever."

Marcello nodded as if approving, but his words remained

critical. "And what would you do? Some menial task for an impersonal corporate machine?"

"You can offer him something," Harold interjected. "We both like him and don't want to see him go, right? There's gotta be a job he can do at the studio."

"Perhaps," Marcello said, sizing Noah up. "I'm sure we could make use of your ceaseless energy if you'd care to join the production crew."

"What's that?" Noah asked, but Harold reacted before their boss could answer.

"You want him to haul equipment around for one of your photographers? He's worth more than that! Those guys have terrible egos! They're worse than any of our clients!"

"It's honest work," Marcello replied. "Isn't that what he's seeking?"

As the sun warmed his skin, Noah thought of Pete, manning the front desk of a homeless shelter and checking people in and out. Not thrilling or glamorous, but Marcello was right: It was honest work. The kind he wouldn't have to hide from Felix. "That would be fine."

"No," Harold said, turning to him. "Trust me, I've worked for these guys. Even as a model, they still give you hell. I wouldn't want to be on their crew."

"You'll discover that photographers have a variety of temperaments," Marcello countered. "I simply had you work with my best, and yes, he is a diva."

"Wait," Noah said, shaking his head. He addressed Harold first. "You were a model?"

"Yeah."

"Like for fashion magazines?"

"Yeah. It wasn't for me." Harold perked up and turned to Marcello. "Hey, how about that? Noah is hot, and the pay would be way better. Enough to put up with big egos."

"I'm afraid I have more than enough talent in that regard," Marcello said. "In fact, I may have to thin the herd to maintain the delicate balance."

Harold wouldn't let it go. Another idea had occurred to him because he punched the air victoriously. "Got it! Give him the job you offered me."

Marcello scoffed. Then he narrowed his eyes, looking between them. "You have an odd sense of humor, Mr. Franklin."

"I'm dead serious," Harold pressed. "You want out, Noah wants out. It's perfect!"

"I don't follow," Noah said.

Marcello took a long swig of his drink and set it on the table. "Nathaniel has been pressuring me to jettison the Gentlemen's Agreement Club for years. Lately, I find myself concurring. I've worked hard my entire life. I deserve to have the occasional weekend off where I'm not disturbed by deranged young men. At least not in this regard. And yet, I would prefer to see my legacy live on."

"And who better to take over than him?" Harold said, gesturing to Noah.

"I don't know anything about running a business," Noah admitted.

"Precisely," Marcello said with a curt nod.

Noah scrunched up his face at Harold. "I don't get why you would turn that down. You need to think about your future too."

Harold rubbed the back of his neck. "I like to keep things simple. Between clients and training, I've got enough to do. I don't want to sign paychecks and worry about balancing books. That's not who I am."

"And yet," Marcello said, "you possess an intimate knowledge of the club's innermost workings."

"And it pays nothing," Harold countered.

"It isn't a profitable enterprise," Marcello admitted. "That's true."

"You aren't making any money from the GAC?" Noah asked, not hiding his surprise.

Marcello reached for a bottle of oil to squirt some on his arms, then began rubbing it in. "For me, it's more of a moral conviction than a successful business model. Taking a cut of any undocumented activities would be illegal, and demanding a higher hourly rate from our clients would lead them to paying the escorts less."

"But you could include more legal activities," Noah insisted. "Webcam sites are really popular right now, and the viewers are always hoping to find someone in their area. That could be good advertising. Or if you keep it limited to the GAC, you can charge a monthly access fee. Escorts could work from home in rotating shifts to earn tips, and it doesn't even have to get sexual. Sometimes keeping it in your pants can be hotter."

"Indeed," Marcello said, letting his eyes travel over their bodies. "Although I'm skeptical that membership fees would be enough to provide anyone with a salary."

"Then how about courses too?" Noah said. "A lot of these guys have really good hearts. They just lack the skills needed to date successfully. Escorts have enough experience to teach them a trick or two. Or you could charge a higher hourly rate for mystery dates. If you set up that database I was talking about, it would be easier to find a guy they hadn't met before who could meet their exact needs. The perfect date! A fantasy service would be cool too, where we help them enact more complicated scenarios. We always meet them as ourselves, but being an escort requires *some* acting ability. Roleplaying, complete with costumes, characters, and maybe even the right setting, like a locker room. That would be worth a higher hourly rate."

"You're just full of ideas," Marcello said, clearly amused.

Noah wouldn't be discouraged. He turned to Harold again. "You should do it. You'll need a different job eventually. Turning a profit wouldn't be that difficult."

"I'm not a businessman," Harold said, shaking his head. "You do it!"

"He hasn't been offered the job," Marcello pointed out. "While I admire his creativity, he still lacks practical knowledge."

Noah didn't take that personally. He was fine with hauling around equipment. He wanted Harold to have a better option for his future though, because eventually that stunning face would wrinkle and those muscles would start to sag, no matter how much he fought against time. "You should do it," Noah urged. "I know you can."

"I'm not good at stuff like that." Harold shook his head. "I'd mess it up. Trust me."

"What a shame," Marcello said after tsking. "One of you has the necessary experience, the other the ambition. If only there was some way of combining you together. An idea occurs to me, as do a few positions, but they have very little to do with business."

"You're already training every new employee," Noah said, attention still on Harold. "You know all the clients and they love you. I'm sure the escorts do too. That idea about playing characters comes from you. Why do you think I'm driving a rusty old truck around? It fits my image. You were right about that from the start. You've got a good instinct for these things. All you'd need to do is a little paperwork and some reinventing."

"I'd psych myself out," Harold said. "That's way too much responsibility for one person."

"Getting warmer," Marcello said, shaking the bottle of oil. "Who wants to do my back?"

"We could team up," Noah said. "Marcello is right. We each have half of what's needed. I know we could do it together."

"I like how simple my life is," Harold repeated, expression pained. "I really do."

"Right," Noah said. "Sorry. I get that it's not for you." He turned to his boss. "I'll take the crew job. Thank you."

"Wait!" Harold said. His head was hung, but when he looked up again, his expression was determined. "I'll do it."

"Really?" Marcello said. He pursed his lips thoughtfully. "It's an intriguing idea, but I'm even less certain this enterprise could generate enough to support two salaries."

"I'll go on my dates," Harold said. "During the day, I'll do the office stuff, and at night, I'll make my money how I do now."

Except it was clear that the idea didn't appeal to him. Not the daytime work, anyway. "That's sweet of you," Noah said. "You don't have to do this though. Seriously."

"Yes, I do," Harold said, jutting out his chin. "Seriously."

Noah's heart swelled with gratitude, but he tried to keep it in check. "Are you absolutely sure?"

Harold locked eyes with him. Then he nodded.

"I always thought you would make a beautiful pair," Marcello said cheerfully. "Perhaps not quite like this, but I'm very pleased nonetheless."

"So he's got the job?" Harold asked.

Marcello smiled. "You both do! Now then, how shall we celebrate? Oh, I know! Allow me to rub oil on your backs. And your fronts."

Noah barely heard him. His attention was still on Harold, who seemed miserable until he noticed Noah staring. Then he forced an upbeat expression, his tone matching it.

"Actually," he said. "I'm starving. All we had to eat were soggy tamales, and I barely touched mine."

"Excellent!" Marcello said. "If it's Mexican food you crave, I know just the place." He reached for his phone. "Agreed?"

They nodded, Noah moving over to talk to Harold in a low whisper while Marcello made his call.

"Thank you," he said. "I know this is outside your comfort zone, but I swear I'll make it as painless for you as possible."

Harold managed to muster some enthusiasm. "I know you'll do your best. I just hope I won't let you down. I'll try, but don't be disappointed, okay?"

"You're the only one who's worried," Noah said. "Marcello believes in you and so do I. Time to join us."

"I'll work on it." Harold's stomach growled just as the call came to an end. Louder he said, "Where are we eating anyway?"

"As I said," Marcello answered, "we're going to have Mexican food. None of this Tex-Mex nonsense. There's only one place for it. We're going straight to the source! The plane will be on the runway and ready for us. All we need do is get dressed." He tapped a finger on his lips thoughtfully. "Although, do we *really* need to wear clothes?"

"Yes," Noah said with a laugh. "We do!"

He couldn't help grinning as they all returned inside. A new challenge awaited him, they would soon be celebrating in Mexico, and he could expect years spent with a guy he truly admired. Maybe not in the way he had once dreamed, but he was looking forward to it regardless.

They landed in Austin again at three in the morning. Marcello was so drunk that they had to help him to his front door, a big arm draped around each of their necks.

"Where are your keys?" Noah asked as they stood on the patio.

"Pocket," Marcello slurred. "Pants pocket."

Noah looked to Harold. "Think he means the front or—"

"Of course he means the front. You take your side, I'll take mine."

They spent a good minute digging around before they gave up.

"You must have left them on the plane," Noah said. "Do you have a spare key hidden somewhere?"

Marcello stood upright, no longer needing their support.

When he spoke, he sounded perfectly sober. "Oh, silly me! They're in my jacket pocket. And you call that a search? You barely gave me a thrill at all!"

Noah rolled his eyes.

Harold laughed, patting down Marcello until he found the keys. Then he pulled them out and handed them over. "In you go, old man!"

"Won't you join me? You're both too inebriated to drive. Stay the night. I'll even give you a room with a lock on the door, although I can't promise on which side it will be."

"Sure!" Harold said instantly.

Noah hesitated. "I should get home. Felix is probably worried." Noah had texted him earlier in the day to say he would be late, but his boyfriend might still be up and increasingly concerned.

"I'll call another taxi then," Marcello said. "You aren't driving in my condition. Or in yours."

"Good idea," Noah said. "Thank you."

Harold was staring at him again. He had done so occasionally throughout the night, as if haunted. "I'll, uh… I'll wait with you until it arrives."

"Very well," Marcello said. "I wish you both a pleasant evening. Harold, you know your way around?"

"Yeah. Thanks."

Marcello had a twinkle in his eye before he turned away and left them alone. Together they walked down the drive, the gates still open. They stopped where the old pickup was parked. Noah kicked at the ground, praying this wouldn't turn awkward.

"There's something I need to tell you," Harold said.

Damn it!

"You really don't need to explain," Noah responded.

"I do. I'll feel guilty if I don't get it off my chest."

Guilty? For still having feelings? Noah looked up. "Okay. Do what you've gotta do."

Harold took a deep breath. "I'm not sure if Felix will like my plan. You wanted to move on because of him, and I wanted you to have the best job possible. I still do! But he might not like that you're—I don't know—the madam of a brothel."

Noah laughed. "I'll have an easier time getting him to accept that than me being an escort."

"Yeah, but he'll have no trouble with you working on a production crew. That's guaranteed. You wouldn't have to tell him about the escort stuff at all."

"I do," Noah said, "because if he's going to love me, he needs to know who I really am."

"You're more than your job," Harold said, eyes watering up. "Especially to me." He shook his head and leaned against the truck, head downturned and features lost to shadow. "If you don't want to lose him, maybe you should think about the crew position instead. I'm not saying that because I'm nervous about taking over the business. I'm saying it because I don't want you to think I'm trying to sabotage what you've got with Felix. Just think about it, okay?"

"I will," Noah said. The night was quiet. Few cars drove along this road, especially at such a late hour. It was easy to pretend that they would always be alone like this. Would that be such a terrible fate? "That guy who's after you, Ruben, you should give him a chance. You deserve to be loved."

Harold looked over at him, already shaking his head. "He can't compare to—"

"Just think about it," Noah said. "Okay?"

Harold's chest rose and fell a few times, air rushing through his nostrils. Then he nodded. "Okay."

"Tell me about him."

Harold did so, reluctantly at first, but as he kept going, his fondness for the guy became clear. Eventually they heard an engine as headlights cut through the gloom.

"Okay," Harold said, pushing away from the truck. "Um… Goodnight."

Harold started to walk toward the house, but Noah grabbed his shoulder and spun him around for a hug.

"No matter what I decide," Noah said, "I hope we'll still be in each other's lives."

Harold nodded. "Yeah. Me too." He took a step back, biting his lower lip. Then he walked through the gateway, pausing once to look back, before it began to close. Noah stared after him. Then he climbed inside the taxi and was whisked away, wishing he could be two places at once.

Chapter Nineteen

Noah stood outside of Studio Maltese and wondered if he should see a doctor about his perpetual grin. Then again, he didn't mind it so much. He would still be able to talk and eat. Drinking would be trickier, although he could probably squeeze a straw between his teeth. Kissing Felix would be a lot harder, and that wouldn't do at all, so despite how happy he felt, Noah forced his lips together into a pleased smile instead.

His happiness didn't only stem from having a wonderful boyfriend. Noah had just signed his contract, taking possession of half the Gentlemen's Agreement Club. This wasn't a decision he rushed into. Harold was right. There could still be consequences, but after considering the opportunity from every angle—taking five days to do so—he found himself reaching the same conclusion repeatedly: Noah wanted this. The challenge appealed to him, and he had a number of ideas on legitimizing the business.

His first trial would be explaining it all to Felix. Ever since the trip to Mexico, Noah hadn't seen any clients. He was officially out of commission. Permanently. This made a tremendous difference to their relationship. Noah had more drive and appetite sexually, but the real change came emotionally. He hadn't realized just how much energy his near-nightly dates had taken. His clients had often needed more than just the physical, and he'd been happy to give it to them. Now that he was able to focus on one person instead...

The grin returned. Noah was still dancing around the great big "L" word. He said it without hesitation to make Felix happy, but in his own mind, he was reluctant to admit the truth, worrying that it would somehow jinx what still felt like a miracle. He simply couldn't believe that someone so adorable and sweet, so grounded and yet downright weird at times, continued to offer his heart unconditionally.

At least Noah hoped that's how Felix felt. He pulled out his phone, noticing a text message that must have arrived while he was signing papers in Marcello's office.

Dinner tonight?

Noah walked to his truck while composing his reply. *Just you and me? Sounds perfect. I'll take breakfast that way too. And brunch. And lunch!*

Felix sent an emoji of a laughing cat. The text that came next was more subdued. *Don't be mad, but I sort of promised my mom that we would eat with her tonight. She's worried about me moving in with you.*

Noah stopped next to his truck. *That's fine. Why is she worried?*

She just needs to get to know you, Felix sent back. *Mom stuff. Sorry!*

Noah chuckled to himself. *Don't be! I'd love to meet her. For real this time. When?*

Is six okay?

I'll be there!

That he could agree so readily felt good. No more working nights. No more uncertain hours. Everything was changing! Noah placed his hand on the truck, wondering if it should go too. He no longer needed it to maintain his image. Then again, he had grown fond of the rusty old thing, and it would come in handy as they continued moving in Felix's possessions. Noah had plans for that spare room. They wouldn't need separate beds, so his original plan to make it an office was on again. His desk would be surrounded by Felix's possessions, shelves upon shelves of toys and collectibles acting as motivation to make this new enterprise a success. Felix would be his muse, his inspiration. Noah wanted to give them the best life possible, and maybe it was just the bright August day making him feel optimistic, but he saw very few obstacles standing in the way of their happiness. Just one, in fact, and he was ready to deal with it. Tonight, he would tell Felix the full truth about his past.

Felix met him at the door to his family's apartment, quivering with excitement. He practically leapt to wrap his arms around Noah's neck, and as good as that felt, Noah politely disentangled himself, having noticed two people watching them from deeper inside the home.

Felix's sister, Darli, seemed amused by this display. The older woman who must be their mother appeared puzzled, or perhaps concerned. Noah made sure to focus on her as he was ushered inside. She was short, like her son, although her hair was butterscotch brown instead of black, and long instead of the shorter styles preferred by her children. Noah offered his hand and his name.

"I'm Bianca," she responded. "It's nice to finally meet you."

He noticed a slight strain on the word "finally" and decided to address the issue. "I wish it could have happened sooner," he said. "And it would have, if my job wasn't so demanding."

"Understandable," Bianca said, her smile reserved. "Still, I would have thought we'd meet before any talk of moving in began."

"Mom!" Darli complained. "Stop grilling him! Not on his special day."

"Shut up!" Felix hissed at his sister.

Noah was thoroughly confused, especially when Felix grabbed his hand and dragged him toward the dining area. The table had already been set, which wasn't surprising. The colorful paper streamers that looped from the ceiling to the walls, along with clusters of balloons, gave him pause.

"What's this?" he laughed.

Felix squeezed his hand. "Happy birthday."

Noah looked at him, feeling a mixture of emotions that he had trouble separating. Sorrow was there. Of course he knew what today was, but he had grown accustomed to ignoring it. His first birthday out on the streets had been one of the most depressing experiences of his life. Noah had accepted then that such things were for other more fortunate people. Aside from that emotion, he also felt hope that simple pleasures like a cake and candles were within his reach again. Mostly he felt a surge of affection for the guy still clinging to his hand.

Noah remained puzzled though, because he normally avoided the topic of his birthday. "How did you know?"

"I went through your wallet," Felix confessed. "I had to pretend to be sleeping and wait until you really were." He shot a glare behind him. "I wanted it to be a surprise!"

Darli rolled her eyes. "And I gave it away a whole ten seconds before he would have seen it anyway. Crucify me, why don't you?"

"Enough, you two!" Bianca scolded. Her expression was softer when turning to Noah. "We're very happy that you've chosen to celebrate with us."

"Well, I'm thrilled to be here! Thank you for having me."

This earned him a smile. Bianca gestured to the table. "Please. Sit."

He did so gladly, Felix pulling out a chair to show him which to use before taking the one next to his.

Darli sat across from her brother, sticking out her tongue at him. Then she turned a mischievous expression on Noah. "How old are you, anyway?"

"Twenty-four," he answered.

Darli raised her eyebrows. "Robbing the cradle, eh?"

Noah laughed. "Can you blame me when the baby is so cute?"

"I'm not a baby!" Felix pouted, making him sound younger than he really was.

"You're still a teenager," Darli retorted, gleefully twisting the knife.

Noah shook his head and made sure his tone was just as teasing. "If this is what sisters are like, you make me glad I'm an only child."

Darli grinned in approval. "I know, right? You lucked out." She addressed her brother next. "So did you. Older guys are the hottest."

"No talking for the rest of the meal," Bianca said, reappearing with a steaming baking dish held between two oven mitts. "I've heard enough out of you both to last me a lifetime."

Noah stood to help her, even though he couldn't do much aside from creating a little more room on the table. She seemed to appreciate the gesture anyway. The scent that greeted his nose as he sat again made his mouth water.

"Is that tuna noodle casserole?" he asked.

"Yup!" Felix said, beaming proudly. "I made it. With some help."

"With a lot of help," Bianca said as she sat. "Felix tells me it's your favorite."

"He's right." Now he understood why they'd had a conversation about their favorite meals earlier in the week. "Should I serve?"

"No no," Bianca said, picking up the spatula and holding it out to her son. "Plating is just an important part of cooking as the rest."

"Better do it right," Darli chided. "Otherwise it's pack-your-knives-and-go time." She looked at Noah and must have seen his puzzled expression because she explained. "Mom is crazy about *Top Chef*."

"He doesn't know what that is," Felix said, standing to get a better angle on the casserole. "His parents were too religious to have a TV."

"We had one," Noah said. "They just never let me watch anything good on it."

"Did you hear from them today?" Bianca asked, features crinkling with concern. "I understand that they aren't as accepting as they should be."

"We don't really talk anymore," Noah admitted.

"Do you mind me asking why?"

"Because he's gay," Darli interjected.

"That's no reason!" Bianca said to her daughter. "There's nothing you children could do—*nothing*—that would make me turn my back on you." She addressed Noah again. "If you think it would help, I could talk to them for you. Explain how I felt when—"

"Mom!" Felix said, slopping a rectangle of casserole on her plate. "We're supposed to be celebrating."

"Of course," Bianca said. "I'm sorry."

"Don't be," Noah replied. "You're what every parent should be. I would always be there for my kids too. If I had any."

"You've got Felix," Darli said. "Close enough."

For a second, her brother seemed to consider using the spatula like a catapult to bombard her with casserole. Instead he whispered something that sounded like, "I will have my revenge!"

Bianca ignored this exchange to continue a conversation with Noah. "Do you mind if I ask what faith you are? Felix wasn't sure."

Because they hadn't had that conversation yet. Noah wondered what most people in the Philippines believed and assumed it was an Eastern religion he knew little about, so after admitting that he was raised Baptist, he was surprised by her response.

"This family is Catholic, which isn't so different really. Again, if you ever want me to speak with your parents—"

"Mom!" Felix and Darli said in unison.

Bianca pursed her lips. "Maybe I should go eat in the other room. Would that make you happy?"

"Yes," Darli said.

"Let's just eat," Felix said. "I'm hungry."

Bianca nodded and folded her hands. Noah recognized the motion from his childhood and quickly did the same. When the blessing began, he was familiar with it and was able to join in. This earned him brownie points, but at the moment, he was more in the mood for tuna points. They dug in, Noah not having to fake his enthusiasm because the food was delicious. Conversation flowed nicely as they ate, Noah asking polite questions about the work Bianca did and how often she visited the Philippines to see family.

"Not as often as I'd like," she admitted. "It's easier now that the children are old enough to stay behind. Those flights are expensive! Felix hasn't been since—how old were you?"

"Twelve," Felix said.

"So just a couple of years ago," Darli teased.

Felix ignored her. "It was amazing! You have to go sometime."

"I'd love to," Noah said. He hadn't been as lucky as some escorts when it came to traveling and still hadn't ventured outside the country except for Mexico. He would love to take that trip with Felix, maybe when his birthday rolled around. That would make a nice present. Hell, he wouldn't mind bringing the whole family along! Even though Darli could be a brat, she clearly loved her brother. The same was true of Bianca's love for her son, or she wouldn't be so concerned about his wellbeing. They were good people.

When the meal was finished, Noah helped clear the plates. Then he was asked to sit again. He knew what was coming next, but he still felt moved when a cake dancing with tiny flames was set before him and three voices sang in unison. Noah didn't bother making a wish when blowing out the candles, feeling all of the most important ones had already come true.

"Yum," Felix said around a mouth full of cake. "I've been watching my figure lately."

"Yes, because you're *so* fat," Darli said, shoving some frosting to the side of her plate.

"You're all gorgeous," Noah said. "I vote we have seconds. Then we'll bring the tuna casserole back for another round."

"You'll have plenty to take home with you," Bianca said, an extra crinkle or two appearing on her forehead. She was reassured, but still not convinced they should be living together so soon.

"You're welcome to stop by anytime you like," Noah said. "You too, Darli. In fact, we'll have to do this again soon at our place." He looked at Felix. "Right?"

His boyfriend wasn't quite as thrilled with the idea, but he nodded.

Bianca seemed relieved. "I'd like that very much." She set down her fork and patted her mouth with a napkin. "Tell me about the work you do," she said. "Felix wasn't able to explain it well."

"It's one of those jobs that people have a hard time understanding," Noah said. Wasn't that the truth! He felt like patting himself with a napkin too, but to dab at his increasingly sweaty forehead instead of his mouth. "I work with a number of clients, and my job is to keep them happy."

Bianca nodded along. "What company is this?"

"Studio Maltese." That was true. Sort of. Soon enough the Gentlemen's Agreement Club would sever all ties with the studio, but for now, it wasn't a lie. "They deal in photography and have some really high-profile clients." He mentioned a few of the more impressive names.

"Well!" Bianca said in awe. "I'll have to pay more attention to the ads in my magazines! I still don't understand exactly what you do though. How do you keep these clients happy?"

Three sets of eyes turned to him. "Wining and dining," Noah said, grasping for something more substantial. "I try to be a good listener too. That's important."

Bianca continued to nod, but her expression remained confused. "Is this a full-time position?"

"Absolutely." It had been just about any position imaginable! "It's a hard job to describe. On that front, I have some good news. I signed a contract today and am embarking on a new position. I'll be a manager now!"

"Really?" Felix said, already proud.

That made Noah feel guilty, but he would clear the air just as soon as they were alone again. "Yeah! I start first thing on Monday."

"Manager of the entire studio?" Bianca asked.

"No." He shook his head and came up with the perfect description. "Manager of human resources."

If people could be considered a resource, he would certainly be managing what they did. This explanation seemed to satisfy them.

"Then we have twice the reason to celebrate," Bianca said. "That's quite the promotion. And what great timing!"

"It's the perfect birthday present," Noah agreed.

"Don't you want to give him yours?" Darli asked her brother.

"Yeah," Felix said bashfully. "I'll wait until we're alone."

This didn't seem intended as a racy comment, but Darli snorted anyway. Then she groaned when her mother insisted that she help clear the table.

"You two just relax," Bianca said. "I insist."

Noah thanked her, then turned to Felix, who had flushed cheeks. "You didn't have to get me anything. Or do any of this."

"I wanted to! Are you ready for your present?"

Noah nodded. "Sure."

Felix glared at his sister, who had come back for more plates. "Let's go outside."

"Outside?"

"There's no privacy in here."

"Oooooh!" Darli said. "I didn't realize that trucks had backseats."

"I'm not sure," Felix shot back. "Why don't you ask Toby?"

Darli went rigid. Then she leaned over, kissed Felix on the cheek, and said, "You're the best brother in the world, you know that? I love you with all my heart. I'll make sure Mom doesn't come outside. Deal?"

"That would be nice," Felix said smugly.

Noah waited until they were outside before he asked the burning question. "What just happened and who's Toby?"

"Toby is her boyfriend. He's a year older than you."

Noah sucked in air through his teeth. "So she really does like older guys!"

"Yup!"

They were walking toward his truck out of habit more than anything. "Aren't you worried?"

Felix scoffed. "Worried about Darli? She's always made good

decisions. Better than me. Sometimes she feels more like my older sister. Besides, I've met Toby. He's quiet and sweet. And he's her dance instructor. The best part is that everyone thinks Toby is gay. I was heartbroken when she told me he's not."

"Hey!" Noah said, pretending to be jealous.

"He *is* really cute," Felix said. "But I'm more into handsome guys. Like you."

"That's better." They reached the truck, Noah opening the passenger side door and eyeing the present that Felix had grabbed on the way out and tucked under one arm. Noah honestly couldn't remember the last time he had gotten a birthday present. He was excited enough that instead of going around to the driver's side, he made Felix scoot over so he could climb in after him.

"It's nothing big," Felix said, spotting how eager he was. "If I was rich, I'd buy you a lot more. Starting with a Blu-ray player. One of the cool hacked ones that are region-free."

"You lost me again," Noah said. "I was raised by cavemen, remember?"

Felix laughed and handed over the wrapped present. It was square and firm, convincing Noah that it was a book of some sort. He carefully tore away the paper, noticing how nervous Felix was and paused to give him a reassuring kiss on the nose. "I love it already," he said.

"You don't even know what it is!"

"Yeah, but it's from you, and that makes it perfect."

Felix looked like he would be in need of oxygen soon if he didn't hurry, so Noah focused on the present. It was indeed a book, but without title or cover art. He knew what it was, because he had often flipped through something similar as a child. "A photo album?" he asked.

Felix shook his head. "A memory book. Open it."

Noah did so, a yearning filling his chest. In the center of the first page was a photo of him and Felix, standing in front of Bottoms 1UP. It was the first photo they had taken together. Felix had insisted after leaving the barcade, wanting to prove that he had been there. In the photo he was pointing upward at the bar's sign behind them. Noah was next to him, grinning in amusement. A simple image, but it had special significance now, because that had been their first date. Other souvenirs surrounded this photo.

An arcade token was glued to the page, as was a cocktail napkin with the bar's logo on it, a ring-shaped stain revealing where one of them had set their drink. The popped-off tab from a can of soda confused him until he remembered drinking one that same night, when Felix had invited him home. Noah always popped off the tabs, out of habit mostly, a childhood friend having collected them for luck. What really surprised him was the receipt from the seafood place where Felix worked, complete with the cartoon drawing of a cat with a fish in its mouth.

"Hey!" Noah said, looking up at him. "That was in my wallet!"

"I stole it," Felix said shamelessly. "I was happy that you kept it."

"It looks like you kept everything else," Noah said, turning the pages to find more photos of them together, notes they had written each other, and more subtle reminders like an empty packet of the instant oatmeal Noah had bought him, or a dried flower from when they had driven outside the city, spotted a hill, and pulled over to race each other to the top. "Is there anything you don't collect?"

"Don't you like it?" Felix asked, worried eyes fixated on the book.

"I adore it!" Noah said. "This is my favorite part." He flipped through the empty pages, which was most of the album. "These are for us to fill, aren't they?"

Felix smiled. "I knew you would get it."

"You get me," Noah said, leaning close for a kiss, "and I love you for it." The words felt truer than ever before, but one giant obstacle remained, and he knew they would never reach their full potential together until it was removed. "I don't suppose we can leave already? There's something I need to talk to you about."

"Mom wants us all to play Scrabble together," Felix said. "Be warned, she always wins. If you want to stay on her good side…"

Noah laughed. "I'll make sure to throw the fight."

"What did you want to talk about?"

He looked over, Felix's face illuminated by the orange light of a setting sun, the deepening shadows hinting at how handsome he would be when older. Noah hoped he was still around to witness that for himself. "It can wait. For now, just remember this moment, okay? If you ever have any doubts about us, think back to now, because this is real. What we feel for each other is pure. The world can't touch it, and nothing that happens will ever change it."

Felix studied him, a number of questions poised on his lips before he pressed them against Noah's own. He tasted like birthday cake, and when they had privacy again, Felix would be the best present he'd ever unwrapped. For now, Noah leaned back and pulled Felix with him, their embrace tightening as they kissed. They would keep holding on to each other. They had to. If God hadn't abandoned him completely, Noah prayed for understanding, because the person wrapped in his arms was quickly becoming his everything.

Noah needed his birthday wish back. He shouldn't have dismissed it so easily, especially now. Getting what you want didn't guarantee it would remain there. Noah was very much aware of all he might lose. He stood in the space between kitchen and living room, watching as Felix put away leftovers and raved about how successful the evening had been.

"I know she likes you! You should have seen her with Marcus. It was baaaad! They couldn't stand each other. His fault really, since he didn't even try. Ever. In retrospect, he was a terrible boyfriend." Felix shut the refrigerator door and spun around. "Hey, would you mind if we 'accidentally' run into him sometime? He works at Best Buy, and I want him to see how much hotter and cooler my new boyfriend is." His cheeks flushed. "Sorry, I know I shouldn't call you that."

Noah cocked his head. "Why not?"

Felix busied himself with refolding the dishtowel hanging on the oven handle, even though it ended up more wrinkled than before. "Because we're not committed."

"That's what I wanted to talk to you about."

Felix's head shot up like a dog called to dinner. He must have known they weren't about to break up. As insecure as he could be, their relationship was too good right now for any dark turns. That only left room for one possibility, the idea alone causing Felix to prance from the kitchen and crash straight into his arms. "I'm ready!" he cried. "Let's talk."

"Easy now," Noah said with a chuckle. He wished the conversation could be that simple. Noah would say he was ready to settle down, Felix would kiss him, and they would celebrate by cuddling up on the couch to watch a movie, or better yet, by leaving the television off and stretching out to make entertainment of their own. He was tempted to give in to this urge. After all, it was his birthday, but an even bigger gift would be banishing the specter hanging over their relationship. "There are things you don't know about me."

The words were ominous enough to make Felix pull back, but then he shook his head. "I don't care. I want this. I love you!"

"I love you too." Noah hoped it wouldn't be the last opportunity to say so. "Come sit down with me."

He led them to the couch, placing Felix on one end and leaving a cushion empty between them so they could face each other. He noticed the socked feet, patterned with some sort of superhero symbol he didn't recognize, but it looked like a W. From there his eyes moved up the skinny black jeans and hip-hugging dress shirt almost the same hue as the blue tufted hair. Then he settled on the face. Felix was biting his bottom lip, the only sign of nervousness on an otherwise eager expression, like he was already determined to accept whatever Noah had to say.

"I've told you a lot about my life on the streets," he began. "Keep in mind that I was sixteen at the time. I should have been in school. Instead I was sleeping in my car and—" Noah shook his head. "What *was* I doing? Partying? That's probably how it looked from the outside, but I suppose I was also trying to find myself. I'd grown up thinking my life would play out a certain way, and when that didn't happen… Well, it was a big adjustment."

"You found yourself though."

"Yes," Noah said grudgingly, "but at a price, and that's what you need to hear about."

Felix nodded encouragingly. "I'm listening."

"I never graduated from high school. We can start there. I've always been a reader, and I like to think that I was blessed with brains, so I honestly don't feel like I'm missing anything. Although I guess an accounting course would have been useful."

"You can take one at the community college I go to! And you can get your GED. I have a friend who did that. She said it was easy."

"Yeah," Noah said. "Both good ideas. The point I'm trying to make is that not having a high school diploma, or a bank account, or even a mailing address, made it hard to find a real job. I didn't have much luck. Nothing that lasted, or that I could put on a résumé, since a lot of it was under the table. None of it paid well. The shelters are great, but two meals a day wasn't always enough, or I would be too busy trying to take care of Ryan while he was high and—" He sighed. "It sucked. You get the picture, right?"

"Yes," Felix said, but he no longer looked so certain.

"You probably see where this is going," Noah continued, heart pounding and mouth increasingly dry. He should have brought a glass of water with him, but he didn't dare back away from this conversation lest he never again find the courage to continue it. "Just imagine being desperate and scared. Then you discover a solution that's really easy, so you take it, even though it's something most people would look down on."

Felix's eyebrows came together in confusion before they shot up in realization. "Oh."

"Yeah," Noah said, still tense. "Ryan did it first. I didn't like it, but we needed the money. Or he needed it. For drugs. When he saw how unhappy it made me, he took me out for a burger and told me to get whatever I wanted. As much as I could eat. I stuffed myself. By the end of that meal, I had already forgiven him. God that sounds sad, but you'd be surprised what hunger can do to you. I was starving, and he made a sacrifice to feed me. I still couldn't bring myself to do the same. Not until he was locked up and I was on my own. I had seen Ryan get ripped off, so I demanded the fifty bucks up front." Noah shook his head. "Fifty bucks. Jesus! What a stupid kid I was."

"What happened?" Felix croaked. "What did he make you do?"

"To be honest, once the guy started groping me, I pretended I needed to pee. The second I was out of his car, I freaked and ran off. That's the only time I stole. I'm not proud of it."

Felix exhaled, visibly relieved. "So you never actually had to sleep with anyone."

Noah's stomach sank, but he forced himself to press on. "Not that night. And not in those conditions. Keep in mind that I was on the streets for years, stuck in the same vicious circle. Then I saw a way out. An escort service." He paused, letting that sink in while wishing he didn't need to say more. But he did. "That's what I've been doing for the past year."

Felix moved his mouth, trying to find the right question or maybe just settle on one. "But that's just going on dates. You're not actually... You know."

"I sleep with people for money," Noah said, refusing to dance around it any longer. "Yes, it begins as a date. It isn't as cold as you might imagine. For the most part, these are really nice guys who are lonely. The work isn't heartless, but yeah, when you break it down, I get paid to have sex."

Felix scooted back, recoiling from him. He made sounds, fragments of incomprehensible words, before he gave up completely and shook his head, as if wanting to deny what he'd just heard.

"I was hungry," Noah reminded him. "I was desperate! Escorting was the only way out of my predicament I could see. And it worked! I turned my life around in less than a year. Not just this apartment or the full pantry. I actually have money in the bank, and like I said, the work isn't as grim as you might imagine. But that's all changing. I really did get the promotion I told your mother about. I have a new job now and—"

"How many?"

Noah's mouth clamped shut. He wished he could keep it that way, because he knew what was being asked, and how upsetting Felix would find the answer. Still, in the off chance that he was wrong... "How many what?"

"Um." Felix resumed nibbling on his bottom lip, struggling to get the words out. "How many guys— People? Was it just... How many have you slept with?"

"It was only guys," Noah confirmed. "I don't know how many."

"Okay, but do you just have one or two that you see regularly? I saw this movie once about a hustler, and the guy just slept with the same clients every week. I think he had five?" Felix looked hopeful. "Is that how it is with you?"

"I have regulars," Noah said carefully. "Some guys want variety, so I only see them once or twice."

"But how many?"

"Does it matter?" Noah snapped. Then he exhaled and forced himself to be patient. "I don't keep count, but it's dozens. Even if it's over a hundred, I still—"

"Is it?" Felix said, looking shocked.

"Maybe. Listen, when you love someone, sex isn't the same. It's the difference between hearing music on the radio, and buying an album that you play over and over again because you can't get enough and it's better each time."

Felix's face, already strained with hurt, crumpled before disappearing behind his hands. The sobbing noises that followed left no room for doubt. He was devastated.

"Please," Noah said, pulling at his arms and wanting to look him in the eye. "I didn't love those guys. It's just a stupid job! It's just sex!"

Felix moved his hands away, face wet and questioning. "Did you… Since we met. Since we started dating?"

Noah leaned back and sighed. "Yeah."

Felix was on his feet and heading toward the door. Noah barely had time to react. He scurried to catch up, one word on his lips that he kept repeating because this was the last thing he wanted. "No no no no!" He sprinted ahead and slammed his back against the front door to prevent Felix from leaving. "No! Please! Just talk to me!"

Felix bared his teeth, but the anger didn't last. His features fell and he started crying again, pawing at Noah ineffectually in an effort to get him to move. Even though Felix was small, he still could have summoned enough force to hurt him. He could have balled his fists and started swinging or kicked Noah's shins until he moved out of the way, but even so deeply hurt, he was still too gentle to resort to violence.

Noah tried to grip his shoulders to calm him. When Felix pulled away, he realized that words were his last chance for salvation. "I quit that job. For you! I'm not an escort anymore. I only want us to be together. I didn't cheat! You know that, right? I never lied. We weren't monogamous."

"I know," Felix said, arms wrapped around himself, like he was trying to hold his intestines in after being gutted. He kept sniffing too, Noah not daring to move from the door to fetch him tissues. "I figured there might be someone else and that's why you were so busy but I didn't think—" Felix squeezed his eyes shut and shook his head. Then he stooped to pick up his shoes. "I need to go."

"Stay here," Noah pleaded, taking the shoes from him. His

throat ached with the effort to hold back tears of his own. "If you need time to think, do it here. This is your home. I'll go."

Felix kept shaking his head. "No."

"Yes! Please. For me. If you love me, do this one last thing. I need to know that you're safe. Stay here. Think about it. I'll come back in the morning and we can talk."

Felix spun around and took a few paces down the hall, shoulders shaking as more tears racked his body. Noah wiped away a few of his own, because he hadn't expected it to be this bad. He needed to make it better. He let the shoes drop to the floor and walked down the hall to place a hand on Felix's shoulder, but his boyfriend flinched at his touch. Noah retreated. If he pushed his luck now, Felix really would leave, and Noah wasn't sure he'd ever see him again. He took his keys from the hook by the door, grabbed his own shoes this time, and looked back down the hall. Felix still had his back to him, but at least he had stopped crying.

"I'll be back in the morning. Please be here."

No response.

"I meant what I said in the truck earlier. Nothing I've done in the past can touch what I feel in my heart. That's my sanctuary. That's where I love you."

His hand was on the door knob when the response came, faint and trembling.

"I love you too."

Noah took little comfort in the words, knowing that this wasn't always enough. Sometimes, not even love could make the pain worth staying for.

The truck rumbled through Austin, its path just as aimless as the driver's thoughts. Noah needed guidance, someone to turn to for reassurance and advice. His parents were next to useless, and while he had made plenty of friends in the previous year, none of them seemed qualified to help. Marcello held the world in his hands, but his personal fulfilment revolved around business conquests and financial success. Edith wasn't so different, having once said that she couldn't imagine a romantic relationship as satisfying as the work she did. Harold was no stranger to heartbreak, but turning to him now would be incredibly unfair, maybe even tempting, so Noah scratched him off his mental list. That didn't leave him much to work with. His clients? Too unprofessional, especially now that he was taking over the business. Tim had a successful marriage, but Noah had meddled in his life enough. Who was left? Ryan? Ha! Pete the bouncer? Noah knew little about him and would probably be better off talking to a complete stranger. Not a bad idea, actually. Maybe he should hire some sort of therapist or marriage counsellor. Then again, a therapist would probably find his past just as abhorrent as Felix did.

Noah noticed the stop sign just as he blew past it. He slammed on the brakes, coming to a halt in the middle of an intersection. Headlights blinded him and a blaring horn sent adrenaline shooting through his system. When he squinted through the windshield, he saw that the other car had barely managed to stop in time. He was shaken but okay, and clearly in no state to be driving.

Noah ignored more angry honks as he eased his foot off the brakes, hands shaky as he cruised a block away and pulled over into a metered parking spot. He wasn't sure if he needed to put in coins this late and didn't care if he got a ticket. All that mattered was keeping himself in motion, because this seemed to help him think. He left the truck behind, still desperate to find a solution. Felix was too special, too sweet, to lose over something that—frankly—wasn't a big deal. Noah hadn't cheated. He hadn't been forthcoming, but he hadn't lied either, and he still wasn't ashamed of the work he had done.

It's just sex.

The toe of Noah's foot hit an uneven slab in the sidewalk, causing him to stumble. He barely noticed, his mind racing back to a night where he had stood huddled with Ryan, a car parked not far away. Inside was a guy with big hairy arms and a smile that put him in mind of a leering wolf.

"I don't like this," Noah had whispered, quivering even though the evening air held only the mildest of chills.

Ryan shook too, but out of need rather than from the temperature. "He'll probably blow his load in two minutes flat. Easy money. It's not a big deal! It's just sex."

It wasn't "just" anything! Sex was special, an expression of their love. That's why it was a big deal. And now Ryan wanted to sell part of that love to a complete stranger. "Please don't!"

"I'll be fine," Ryan had said in patient tones reserved for the exceptionally naïve. "You're sweet for worrying." Then he had given him a peck on the lips and went to use them on another man. Noah had stood there in the cold and continued to tremble, each second that passed adding another small crack to his heart until it broke completely.

Noah blinked, returning to the present. *Sweet*. That's how Ryan had described him, and how Noah so often thought of Felix. Innocent, inexperienced, and yes, maybe a little naïve. Noah played the opposite role now. He had become Ryan in this scenario, the guy with a complicated past that he used to explain away any behavior that others found unsettling. The one who had exposed another to the unsavory truth that bodies could be bought and sold. That's life. No big deal. It's just sex.

Noah shook his head as he continued walking down the street, drawing more parallels, like the divided heart. Ryan had been unable to stop longing for Tim. Noah had done the same, never quite sure if he was ready to let go of Harold completely. Thank god he'd had the decency to keep those uncertainties from Felix. He hadn't talked about Harold all the time like Ryan had Tim, but he was still guilty of having feelings for more than one person.

Noah checked his surroundings and found himself in the past again. His own, and during a much simpler time, because he had been alone. No friends, no boyfriend. The park he currently stood outside of had been one of his favorites to sleep in. Noah opened the waist-high gate to let himself in, checking for any police nearby out of habit, although these days they were less likely to harass him. Noah had a home he could return to, and a wallet full of plastic cards and paper cash that proved he was a respectable person.

If only he still felt that way. Then again, why shouldn't he?

Noah tried to get angry. How dare Felix make him feel ashamed for doing what was needed to survive! This didn't work, because he imagined Ryan expressing the same indignation. *It's not a big deal!* To him maybe it wasn't, and perhaps not to Noah these days, but the issue still mattered to Felix, and that made it important.

What could he do? The damage had been done. Noah approached the problem from a new angle and tried to imagine how Ryan could have made it up to him. No longer sleeping with others would have been a start, as would Ryan finally giving him the entirety of his heart, but that's what Noah had tried to do. He had quit working as an escort. He had been steadily falling in love with Felix. What more could be done?

He didn't know. Despite repeatedly pacing the length of the park, he didn't have any ideas, short of begging Felix to forgive him. Noah would try that, but somehow he didn't think it would be enough. Eventually his body and mind felt just as exhausted as his heart. No closer to finding a solution, he longed for sleep and decided if he couldn't share a bed with Felix, he didn't want a bed at all. He located a cluster of bushes that he had used to hide in long ago. Not as nice or secluded as the reeds he had once shown Harold, nor was there an angel to watch over him, but it would have to do. A sleeping bag would have been nice, or even just a coat.

Noah crawled into the brush and twisted and turned, trying to find a position that didn't involve being poked by branches or bruised by hard stones. He found one eventually. Curled up on his side, he listened to sirens in the distance and heard drunk revelers shouting to each other. Noah felt strangely at home. Here he could pretend that the previous year had been a feverish hallucination, a self-induced fantasy of the life he longed for. When he woke up and returned to the reality of his homeless life, Noah wouldn't feel sad. He would feel relieved that none of it had happened. Not for his own sake. Winding back the clock was the only way he could avoid breaking the heart of an innocent person, one that he would do anything to protect, even at his own expense.

Chapter Twenty

Noah's first thought upon waking was that he had a hangover. His entire body ached, and he still felt remnants of the stress headache that had begun last night. Then he remembered his promise: He would be back in the morning so he and Felix could talk. Noah scurried to his feet and shoved his way out of the bushes. His timing wasn't great, since a woman with a shocked expression stood not far away. The little boy whose hand she held found it amusing, pointing at Noah and giggling.

"I lost my Frisbee," Noah said lamely before hurrying away.

More like he'd lost his marbles! Noah could have gotten a hotel room last night. He supposed he had a flair for the dramatic. Or maybe he had wanted to punish himself. If so, it hadn't worked, because sleeping rough had reinforced his opinion that getting off the streets by any means necessary had been the right thing to do. Now he needed to convince Felix of that.

Noah hurried back to where he had parked his truck the night before. No ticket or wheel clamp. He accepted that as a belated birthday present from the universe and hoped a few more were in store as he drove back to his apartment. He called Felix's name the second the door was open and listened for a response. None. It was only eight in the morning, so Noah checked the bed. Empty, but he could tell it had been slept in and made again, since Felix never got as many wrinkles smoothed out as he did. The kitchen was his last hope, but Noah had already accepted that it would be unoccupied. A note was on the counter.

I have work and school today. I'll be sleeping at a friend's house tonight, so the apartment is yours. I'm sorry I can't get over this. I'm lame, I know. Sorry.

I love you,

Felix

No cute cartoon drawings this time. Just handwriting that grew increasingly shaky as the note went on. Noah reread it and groaned, hating how Felix had turned this around on himself. At least he had tried to set the issue behind him and still purported to love Noah. And yet, he hadn't been able to find the solution either. Time? Did they need to spend a year apart like he and Harold had done? Or did Felix need to be set free so he could have more sexual exploits of his own, evening the playing field?

Noah didn't like either idea, but it was better than saying goodbye permanently.

The phone in his pocket vibrated, Noah practically clawing through his jeans to get at it. He was disappointed. The text message was from Marcello, not Felix, and mentioned yet another paper that Noah needed to sign at the studio. He wasn't in the mood. He set aside the phone and went to take a shower, missing how Felix usually shared that activity with him. Noah had even bought special tubes of soap that acted as body paints, but they hadn't had a chance to try them yet. Now they might not ever. He left the shower and dressed. Then he had breakfast, eating two packets of the cinnamon and spice oatmeal that Felix liked so much. Yeah, Noah definitely had a flair for the dramatic, but he didn't find it very amusing at the moment. Instead he was starting to despair.

He didn't have the answer. Felix didn't seem to either. Who did? Marcello might be worth a shot after all. Noah had to go there anyway. First he washed his dishes and left a note for Felix, just in case he stopped by, saying that he hoped they could talk soon. A text message would have been more efficient, but Felix hadn't chosen to send one, and if he needed his space, this was the best way of respecting that.

The drive to the studio passed in a blur, Noah lost in thought, but he wasn't so distracted that he couldn't drive. Not like last night. He worried that Felix might be in a similar state. Hopefully he didn't have the car today and had to rely on his sister, a bus, or any type of transportation that didn't have him behind the wheel. This concern was still on his mind when he entered Marcello's office, a place where it was impossible to remain distracted. The occupant made sure of that.

"Mr. Westwood!" Marcello declared. "What an impressively prompt reply. Few men come so quickly when I call, although I can think of one who could do so on command. Really! Be it ten seconds or ten hours, all I needed was to give the word. An amazing feat of self-control, although I eventually found myself missing spontaneity."

This was the person he hoped could provide relationship advice? Noah dismissed the idea and approached the desk to sit, turning his attention to the paperwork Marcello pushed toward him. The letterhead was that of a bank.

"Nathaniel feels it's too much of a paper trail to transfer the account to you, so we've closed it and opened another in your name. A joint account between you and Harold, of course." Marcello was pointing to where he was supposed to sign, but his eyes remained on him. "There isn't much of a balance, but I did manage to secure an account with a decent interest rate. If you'd care to look over the details first, or if you're having second thoughts..."

"It's fine," Noah said, scribbling his name. "Thanks."

"I'm the one indebted to you," Marcello responded. "Speaking of which, is there any way I can be of service? Yesterday you were a ray of sunshine! Today you have me reaching for my umbrella. What troubles you?"

Noah exhaled. "Relationship problems."

"The two words are synonymous. I take it Felix isn't pleased with your choice of career?"

"Exactly. He just found out last night and took it pretty hard. Don't you dare make that into a joke!"

Marcello fixed him with a steady gaze. "Am I so without credit in your eyes?"

"No. Sorry. I'm just a mess right now. I feel terrible for putting him through this."

"Nonsense," Marcello said. "I know you to be a man of integrity. You've demonstrated that repeatedly. I don't believe for a second that you've deceived him in any way. Am I mistaken? Did you promise Felix a monogamous relationship despite the demands of your work?"

"No," Noah said. "I didn't."

"And do you now question the morality of a mutually beneficial exchange between adults?"

"Not at all," Noah said.

"Good. In that case, the flawed viewpoint isn't your own."

"Then why is he so hurt? It's not like he got angry and called me a slut. He wasn't mean about it. But when he found out how many guys I've been with..." Noah shook his head, too emotional to continue.

"I've never been the jealous type," Marcello said musingly. "With one exception. The conclusion I reached then is that I was the one at fault. His name was Tolga, and we first met when—"

"Felix isn't at fault," Noah said, cutting him off. "He's hurt, and I don't know what to do about it."

"We *always* hurt the ones we love," Marcello said. "I'm afraid that comes with the territory. To be capable of love, a heart must be open, and that leaves it exposed. There is no other way."

"I guess not," Noah said as he stood. "I better go."

"Just a moment!" Marcello said. "I need one more favor from you."

Noah watched as Marcello wrote a note on a piece of paper that was then folded, placed into an envelope, and sealed. This was held out so he could take it.

"Would you mind delivering this to Nathaniel on your way down?"

Noah resisted an eyeroll. "Sure."

"Excellent. Thank you. Oh, and please don't leave before getting his response."

Noah stared long enough to be sure that Marcello was serious. Then he nodded and took the elevator to the second floor. Once standing before Nathaniel's office, he was tempted to slide the letter beneath the door and leave, but Marcello had described him as a man of integrity. Noah wanted to live up to that, so he knocked instead.

"Yeah," a voice grunted in response.

Much to his surprise, the tone was friendlier when he opened the door and stepped inside.

"Hey! Noah!" Nathaniel rose from his desk. "How's it going?"

"Okay," he replied. "You?"

"Not bad. Come in. Do you want something to drink? It's either water or coffee."

"I'm okay." Noah walked forward and held out the envelope. "Marcello wanted me to give you this." When he saw that Nathaniel was going to set it on his desk, he added, "You should read it now. I'm supposed to wait for your response."

Nathaniel raised an eyebrow, Noah finally free to roll his eyes. Then they both laughed.

"You think I'd be used to it by now," Nathaniel said. "Working for a madman."

"How long has it been?"

"Since I started here?" Nathaniel puffed up his cheeks and blew out, eyes scanning the letter he unfolded. Then he looked up. "About ten years now. Amazing how time flies."

"Yeah," Noah said. He nodded to the letter. "What's he want?"

"I'll give him my response in person," Nathaniel said tersely, folding the note and putting it back inside the envelope. "Do you have a few minutes? Please, sit down. We didn't get much of a chance to talk yesterday."

They had talked plenty while Noah filled out form after form, but he didn't want to be rude, so he sat.

Nathaniel settled into the chair behind his desk, turning back and forth slightly as he too seemed to search for a topic. "I've been meaning to thank you," he said at last.

"Thank me?"

"Yeah. For taking over the Gentlemen's Agreement Club. I didn't want to, and in my opinion, it's been hanging over Marcello's head like a sword since the day I met him."

Noah laughed nervously. "You're making me regret my decision."

"You'll do fine," Nathaniel said. "Marcello has more to lose than either of us do, and that makes him a target. Not just from his enemies. When you've got that much money, even friends can turn on you. If they get desperate enough. Know what I mean?"

Noah nodded. "I could see that."

"Still, you should be careful. You know I'm here if you need any advice. I'm not a lawyer, but I have plenty I can call, and if there's anything about running a company that trips you up, bookkeeping especially, then just say the word."

Noah nodded again. "Thanks."

Nathaniel drummed agitated fingers against the desk's surface. "We can talk about anything you need to."

Noah finally understood. "That letter from Marcello..."

Nathaniel leaned forward, grabbed the envelope, and tossed it toward him. Noah managed to catch it and pulled out the letter to read the content.

I believe that Noah could use a sympathetic ear for a matter outside my realm of expertise. A rare occurrence, I know, but one of the many reasons I appreciate you so. Please do what you can for him. And don't let him see this letter! Heaven knows his pride will get the better of him and he'll go stomping off rather than listen to anything you have to say.

Noah clenched his jaw and stood. "Sorry to waste your time." He was turning toward the door when he hesitated, because leaving now would prove Marcello right. Instead he faced Nathaniel again. "Goddamn it!"

"I'm guessing he knew I would show you the letter," Nathaniel said with a sigh. "I gave up trying to outthink him years ago. It's easier just to give in. Sit down."

Noah did so. "You don't want to hear about my relationship problems."

Nathaniel shrugged. "Beats invoicing."

He clearly wasn't going to get any more encouragement than that, so he started talking, trying to keep it brief for Nathaniel's sake. "So basically that's it," he finished. "Felix is hurt, and I don't blame him, but I also don't know what to do."

Nathaniel scowled, hopefully in concentration. Then he did something much rarer and laughed. "Now I see why he sent you to me. I *am* the jealous type!"

"Really?" Noah said, feeling slightly more optimistic. "Any advice?"

Nathaniel leaned back, eyes moving to the framed photo on his desk. Then he reached out and spun it around so Noah could see. In it, Nathaniel and a handsome guy were both sitting on their knees, most likely to accommodate the Siberian Husky in front of them. The dog's head was cocked, attention on where the camera must have been, but what really stood out is how one of Nathaniel's large hands was splayed across the furry body. His other arm was wrapped tightly around the man at his side. The image was simple, and not out of the ordinary, and yet it still communicated a surprising amount of love and happiness that Noah wanted to find his way back to.

"Kelly took that photo," Nathaniel said. "He had to drape lunch meat over an expensive camera to hold the dog's attention, but he didn't complain once. Not until after the photo was taken and Zero launched himself at the tripod like it was an attack dummy."

Noah laughed and tore his eyes away from the happy scene. "You're very lucky."

"Yeah," Nathaniel said, but he didn't sound boastful. "I came really close to messing it up though. A few times. Once was because some guy tried to kiss Kelly. That was the worst, and it took being without him for a long time for me to get over my jealousy."

"I don't want that," Noah said.

"I don't recommend it," Nathaniel said. "The other occasion might be closer to what you're going through. Kelly and I had finally gotten back together and were doing great. Then he mentions some guy he dated while we were apart and it felt terrible. I honestly thought I was past feeling that way and tried to keep quiet, but it ate at me until I couldn't stand it anymore, so I asked him how many guys there had been while we were apart. I didn't like the answer."

"That many?"

Nathaniel shook his head. "No, but a handful was more than enough. Like I said, I'm the jealous type. I kept obsessing over these nameless men, like when we were out in public and someone would catch Kelly's eye. I'm not *that* jealous. I understand there's a biological imperative that drives such behavior, but I started imagining him with those guys, which didn't help."

"So what did you do?"

"Held it all in, started making veiled comments, and behaved like an ass until Kelly called me out on it. Then we talked, and that made everything better."

Noah resisted the urge to grab paper and pen to take notes. "What did you talk about?"

"The guys he was with. Kelly went into detail, which sounds like the last thing he should have done, but it helped. In my head, these guys were like porn stars. All I imagined was muscled bodies, handsome faces, and oversized…"

"Egos?" Noah supplied helpfully.

Nathaniel nodded in gratitude. "The reality was different. Kelly gave them names, showed me photos, and talked about who they were as people. He told me their stories. One guy was still in the closet when he met Kelly and came out because of their time together. Another was really political and was always dragging him out to protests, which Kelly hated. He explained the good along with the bad, not pulling any punches. In the end, I had a better understanding of who he'd been with, and why he wasn't with them anymore."

"I've been with a lot of people," Noah said carefully. "Even if it wouldn't take forever to tell Felix about them all, I'm not sure I remember the details. And anyway, if Kelly told you he'd had sex for money instead, wouldn't that have been harder for you to get over?"

Nathaniel held up a hand. "I try not to judge. I did when I first started here, but I've seen over the years that the GAC isn't as sleazy as I imagined it to be. I've met a lot of your clients through the fundraisers Marcello hosts, and they aren't so bad. That's what I think you should do—the same thing Kelly did for me. Felix needs to see these people as the human beings they are. If you can do that, then maybe he'll have an easier time coming to terms."

"That's not a bad idea," Noah said.

He still worried the sheer number of clients bothered Felix most, but that was something he'd never be able to change. Not unless he got his hands on a time machine. He stayed a little longer to ask Nathaniel more about his personal life, out of interest rather than a need for further advice. When Noah did leave, he felt more hopeful than when he arrived because at least now he had a plan. He just wasn't sure how to execute it. Not alone, anyway.

Noah waited until he was outside in the parking lot. Then he pulled out his phone and placed a call.

Harold sounded happy when he answered. "Hey! How's it going?"

"That depends on you," Noah replied. "I need your help."

Noah paced the interior of a bar, faced on all sides by temptation. Alcohol called to him the most. Not beer or wine as he usually preferred, but the strong stuff he never messed with. Rum, vodka, whisky. The taste didn't matter. He just wanted to numb his thoughts. Before giving into this urge, he turned away from the bar to be faced by other distractions, like the arcade cabinets lining the wall. He might not be a gamer, but he knew he could get lost in a digital world for a while. What better way to ignore reality? Of course that would be rude to his guests. Guest.

Noah looked to the table where three people should be sitting. Only one was there, an old man who raised his wine glass in toast before taking a sip. If anything good had come from this situation, reconciling with Chester was it. Noah had called him to apologize and to ask a favor. Not the best combination, but it was a testament to Chester's generosity that he hadn't dragged

Noah over the coals. Instead he simply agreed to be wherever and whenever required. Sitting down with him for an entertaining conversation would be a welcome diversion too, but Noah wasn't quite ready to give up yet.

He held up a finger, indicating to Chester that he would need another second. Then he went to the front door of Bottoms 1UP to speak with the bouncer. Again. "My friend should be here soon," he said. "He's short, has—"

"Blue hair," the bouncer said as if reading from a script. "Although it might be different now because you haven't seen him in a few days."

"Right," Noah said, face burning. "Just wanted to make sure you were paying attention."

The bouncer turned toward the street, probably hoping for a group of teenagers with fake IDs or any other nuisance that would demand his attention. Noah decided to leave him be. After looking up and down the street for any sign of Felix, he returned inside with a heavy heart. He had hoped the good memories here would be enough to lure Felix in. They needed the perfect spot. After an awkward conversation on the phone and a few half-hearted text messages, he realized they would have to make amends in person. Felix was still hurt, and Noah was reluctant to say the really important things unless they were together. He wanted Felix to look him in the eye and see his sincerity. One more chance. That's all he needed.

From all appearances, he might not get that chance. He took a seat across from Chester, wishing again for a stiff drink.

"No luck?" Chester said.

Noah shook his head. "What little I was born with ran out years ago."

"I was raised to believe that we make our own luck," Chester said, "although I've had enough bad times to know life isn't so simple. Goodness no! However, I do believe it's possible to make luck for other people."

Noah blinked. "What do you mean?"

"Well, if someone is on the street and starving, it's up to the man with money in his pocket to decide how lucky the hungry person will be that day. Do you see what I mean? If we go through life being kind to other people, we're spreading luck around. Assuming the other person benefits from our actions. I had a neighbor who baked me a cake every week. Very charming, but my lord did I put on weight! I'm not sure how lucky that was."

"Sounds good to me," Noah said. "I've barely eaten for days."

"I'd be happy to buy you—" Chester stopped, having picked up on his meaning. "Ah. Being lovesick will do that. Of course it can also make you eat like a pig. That old neighbor of mine moved, but I'm sure it wouldn't be so hard to look her up. We'll have you sitting in front of an entire carrot cake within the hour."

"I might need it," Noah said with a sigh, "although I prefer German chocolate."

"You definitely won't need it," Chester said. "He'll be here."

"I hope so."

"I know so! If I were his age, or even mine, and you had asked me here tonight… Well, I suppose you did and I am!"

"Thank you," Noah said. "I mean it. You've always been kind, but you being here is more than I deserve. Especially considering the way I behaved toward you."

"Think nothing of it," Chester said, waving away his concern. "People are allowed to have shortcomings. Friends especially."

"Well, I've got plenty of shortcomings," Noah said. "I might not have as many friends as I thought I did." He looked over his shoulder toward the door. "There was supposed to be another—"

The words caught in his throat because Felix was standing by the entrance and considering the bar interior, his eyes lingering on an arcade cabinet or two. This gave Noah plenty of time to notice the freshly cut hair and the skin-tight thermal shirt that he hadn't seen before. He would have recognized how complementary the olive green fabric looked against light brown skin. The gray jeans weren't new, since Noah vividly remembered undoing the button and zipper during one lazy afternoon last week.

Felix looked good. Intentionally. Noah wasn't sure how to take that. The fresh appearance could either be intended as a "see what you're missing?" or a much more humble "I wanna look my best in case we get back together." All he knew for sure was how nice it was to see him again. Even a mere handful of days was too long for them to be apart.

Noah was on his feet and walking across the room while still lost in these thoughts. His brain ceased functioning when Felix noticed him at last, the usual joy in his eyes making a welcome reappearance before clouds of uncertainty returned.

"Hey," Noah said, opening his arms for a hug. "Thanks for coming."

Felix hesitated before accepting, but as soon as their arms were wrapped around each other, he squeezed with need. Noah was unsure how to interpret this. Did Felix recognize how good it felt to touch again and not want to stop? Or was this the last time, and that's why it felt so intense? Noah took a step back to find out.

"You chose the one place I couldn't resist," Felix said, eyes darting around the room again.

"I've got a pocket full of tokens to keep you here too," Noah replied.

They smiled at each other, which felt good, until Felix started searching the room again. "You said you wanted me to meet some people."

"Yeah!" Noah turned and gestured to the table where Chester sat. "Just one person for now. Um. Come on. I'll introduce you."

Felix remained where he was, still staring at the table. "Who's that?"

"Come find out," Noah said, putting a hand on his back to gently guide him forward. "Do you want something to drink?"

Felix shook his head, still fixated on the table. "He's one of them, isn't he?"

"He's a lot of things," Noah said. "I'll let him speak for himself. Try to be open, okay? For me?"

Felix nodded. At least he was still willing to trust, if only a little. They sat at the table, side by side, both facing Chester, and Noah made the introductions. First names only. He didn't dare put a title on his relationship with Felix, and he didn't want Chester being pigeonholed.

"I'm told you enjoy video games," Chester said. "So did Raymond. That's my late husband. He loved his gadgets! I thought he was crazy when he brought home a video game for the first time. I don't mean a Nintendo or a PlayStation either. This was in the early seventies, you see."

"Pong?" Felix asked, already hooked.

"No, it was a Magnavox… Let's see."

"A Magnavox Odyssey?" Felix guessed. "Did it have overlays you had to put on the TV screen?"

"Yes!" Chester chuckled. "That's it exactly."

"Those are amazing!" Felix enthused.

"They were terrible," Chester said with good humor. "And expensive. I was furious when Raymond brought it home, but he insisted we play together. He thought I would be impressed! I wasn't, but after seeing him behave like a little boy with a new toy, I couldn't stay angry."

Noah risked a glance at Felix, who seemed interested in the conversation. That was good. Maybe he already saw Chester as the gentle and friendly person he was. "You should tell him more about Raymond," Noah suggested. "It's a beautiful story."

"I'd hate to bore him," Chester said with a twinkle in his eye, "although I did see someone walk by with nachos. I'd feel a lot better about droning on and on if you both had something to occupy yourselves with."

"Nachos *do* sound good," Noah said innocently. "And a few Cokes to go with them?"

"I am kind of thirsty," Felix admitted.

"Then it's a deal!" Noah hopped up to take care of their order. By the time he returned to the table, Felix was enthralled by the story Chester was telling. He laughed at all the funny parts, but what mattered more was the emotional ending—how deeply affected Chester was by the loss of his greatest love, and how the Gentlemen's Agreement Club provided him with a brief respite from the isolation he sometimes felt.

Chester was in the middle of explaining this when a handsome guy walked over to the table. Noah didn't recognize him at first, having only seen a photo before. The dark curly hair and fine features were even more impressive in person. Ruben was handsome, his style refined and yet casual. He wore a thin V-neck sweater and faded blue jeans. The expensive watch on his wrist implied he could afford whatever he chose to wear. His grooming was impeccable too. Judging from the cultivated way he spoke, he either took his education seriously or came from an intellectual household.

"Sorry, gentlemen," Ruben said as he took a seat next to Chester. "I'm rarely late, but when I am, I make it count. Are we discussing Raymond?"

"Indeed we are," Chester said.

"Then there will be time for introductions later," Ruben said, looking at Felix and Noah. "I don't want to interrupt. I'm too fond of this story. I've been looking for my own Raymond ever since I first heard it."

"If only they had made more than one," Chester said wistfully before resuming his tale.

Noah checked on Felix, who was distracted by the newcomer. Or maybe attracted to him, which wouldn't be difficult to imagine. Harder to understand was why Harold would ever hesitate. Assuming that Ruben's personality matched the rest of him, he seemed like a good catch.

Chester was a good enough storyteller to compete with handsome faces and soon had the table's full attention again. "Nothing is more important than spending time together," he said, eyes wet with emotion. "I wish I had realized that sooner. When I remember Raymond, it's not the exotic vacations we took or life's big events I think of. It's us sitting at the kitchen table in the morning, or driving up to Oklahoma to visit family. Quiet moments where it was just the two of us, and all we had for entertainment was the pleasure of each other's company. Human connections matter most. That's what I've carried with me over the years. Possessions are a welcome luxury, but nothing soothes the soul like good companionship. I feel honored to have made the acquaintance of many charming young men. I've enjoyed the camaraderie and had the pleasure of hearing their stories while sharing my own. Why, two of my favorite young men just happen to be sitting at this table!"

"We're the lucky ones," Ruben said. "We all adore spending time with you, and I meant what I said earlier. Your story is what finally got me looking for love."

"I can't imagine that you'll have to look far!" Chester said. He turned next to Felix. "Do you have any questions for me?"

Felix most likely did, but he seemed hesitant.

"You can ask him anything," Noah said. "I've tried making him blush before. It's impossible."

"He made me blush once," Ruben said teasingly. "You don't want to know how."

"Ignore him," Chester said. "I really am an open book. Go ahead. Please."

Felix swallowed. "Okay. Um... Do you ever feel—I don't know—bad? Do you worry that Raymond wouldn't like what you're doing? At least when it happened before, you were together."

"When he brought other guys home." Chester nodded. "That's a fair question. And yes, there are times I worry that I'm disgracing his memory, or that his ghost is hovering over my bed with hurt feelings. Then I remind myself that I knew him better than anyone. When you're together as long as we were, you barely need to ask the other person a question, let alone permission, because you already know what the answer will be. I can speak with confidence when I say that he wouldn't want me to be lonely. I bear the pain as long as I can sometimes, just to see if I can go without, but I need human contact. I may be old, but I still want intimacy. I know Raymond wouldn't deny me that. He might worry about my safety, but that's not an issue with the Gentlemen's Agreement Club. These aren't street hustlers looking to rip me off. They're good people!"

"Sounds like an opportune time to introduce myself," Ruben said, extending a hand to Felix. "I'm one of those purportedly good people. And you're my new boss, right?"

Noah had never met Ruben before, but he probably knew that Felix wasn't his new boss, if only going by age. It was a charming gesture regardless and helped break the ice.

"No!" Felix said. "I'm just…" He freed his hand to point a thumb at Noah, but he seemed unable to find the right words, probably because that's what they were here to resolve. What exactly were they to each other now?

"His name is Felix Ramos," Noah said, "and your new boss's happiness hinges on him, so pray he's in a forgiving mood. Otherwise you won't like working for me very much."

He didn't bother gauging Ruben's reaction to this, choosing instead to fix Felix with a gaze that showed how serious he was.

"Then you must be Noah," Ruben said, offering his hand until it was accepted. "I've heard a lot of good things about you!"

From Harold, most likely. Noah had contacted him with two requests. The first was for a client who embodied the most positive aspect of their work. They hadn't needed long to settle on Chester. Demonstrating the human side of their clients was only half the challenge. Noah also wanted to prove how beneficial the work could be to escorts, and that's what he had needed help with. Harold knew the other guys and was able to select the best representative. Ruben just happened to be the one, which had taken Noah aback. He was beginning to understand his choice because Ruben was charismatic.

"I've heard good things about you too," Noah said, "and I'm open to hearing more. How'd you get started in this business?"

"Oh that," Ruben said with a sly smile. "I guess it all began when I was eight years old and I broke my arm. How? I fell out of a tree. A born genius, wouldn't you agree? My aunt rushed me to the hospital, which I despised every second of, until they put the cast on me. Then I became fascinated. My arm was broken, and all it needed to heal was some plaster? I needed to know more! First I tried sealing one of my broken action figures in plaster. Admittedly, it was only papier-mâché, but that's the best I could manage. My toy didn't heal—obviously—so I got serious and checked out a book on bones from the school library. Fast forward past years of me diagnosing playground injuries and uh—performing a few examinations on the neighborhood boys—and I entered high school knowing I wanted to be a doctor. The only hurdle was that my parents don't have an excess of money, and I have terrible luck when it comes to scholarships. I was about to settle for a nursing program when I met a girl at a party, and she explained how she put herself through college."

"She was an escort?" Felix asked.

"Yes," Ruben answered, "an occupation that I never seriously considered, but she made a good case for it, and I decided it was worth a try. The first few times were disastrous. I advertised online, and the requests I got were very *very* strange. I made decent cash regardless, and I've always been stubborn, so I stuck with it. Then one of my clients tipped me off to the GAC and… I don't intend this to sound like propaganda, but that's when my life really started to improve. The work was demanding, but I graduated, and guess how much I still owe in student loans?"

"Not much?" Felix wagered.

"Not anything!" Ruben replied. "Part of that is thanks to a few generous souls who make sure I'm taken care of, but don't misunderstand me. Escort work is demanding, and I gave it all the energy I could spare. If I had put those same hours into a traditional occupation, I wouldn't have earned as much. Had I worked longer hours at a normal job, my grades would have suffered. Without escorting, I'm not sure I would have gotten my doctorate. Ever. I won't pretend it's all been pancakes and maple syrup. I've had some hideous nights because of my occupation, but as with any job, you'll have good days and you'll have bad. For me it's been mostly positive. This will sound like I'm trying to be witty, but I'm also more familiar with people's bodies than my colleagues. I've had experience with adults of every age and build you can imagine, which should prove useful in my future career."

"I've had doctors who try not to look!" Chester interjected. "It's hard to trust someone with your health when they're uncomfortable with a little nudity."

"Prostate exams," Ruben said with a nod. "Everyone in my class was squeamish about learning those, but I was the star pupil that week. You reach a point in this work where you're comfortable with other people's bodies, and that has many advantages, especially in the medical field. STD screening will be a cinch for me."

Ruben kept talking. Chester joined in. They did a commendable job of describing both the pros and cons from their points of view. Felix really seemed to be listening too, and nodding as though he sympathized. By the time Ruben challenged Chester to a race on one of the simulators, Noah was feeling optimistic that his plan had worked. He waited until they were alone at the table. Then he angled his chair so he was facing Felix and began.

"Before I started working as an escort, I had this picture in my mind about how it would be. Bad, mostly, because all I focused on was the physical. I thought it would be creepy guys making me do gross things. Sometimes it was. Mostly it's just very normal people who found an easy way to get what they need while giving something back in return."

"I like them," Felix said, looking to where Chester and Ruben were competing across the room.

"And what about me?" Noah asked, lungs feeling weak. "Do you still like me?"

Felix's lip began to tremble before he nodded. "Yes."

"I need us to be okay," Noah said. "I know I hurt you and I'm sorry. I never wanted to, but I'm glad you know the truth. I don't regret telling you. I need you to understand who I am, and now that you've come here today and seen that things might not be as bad as you imagined…" He shook his head, at a loss for words. Another idea occurred to him, one that just might be dumb enough to work, so he leaned back, reached into his front pocket, and plunked down the contents. A fistful of cheap golden coins shifted and settled on the table's surface.

Felix stared. Then he laughed. "You weren't joking!"

"I'm a desperate man," Noah said, shoving the tokens forward. "I don't suppose you accept bribes?"

Felix ignored the tokens, his hand reaching past them and settling on top of Noah's, thumb stroking in quick succession. Almost as quick as the breath shooting through Felix's nostrils as he struggled to keep his emotions in check, the battle lost when a tear slipped free.

"I'm sorry," Felix said, the words accompanied by a shake of his head. He opened his mouth, a squeak coming out before he tried again. "I'm sorry, but I can't."

"Can't what?" Noah asked, already dreading the answer.

"Stop hurting?" Felix said. "I don't know how to describe it. I don't want to feel this way. I want to go back to when all I could think about was how much I love you. Now all I can think about is them."

"The guys I've been with."

"I know I shouldn't," Felix said. "You must think I'm a stupid baby for—"

"You're perfect the way you are!"

"I'm not! If I was, I would just feel the good things and let go of the rest because I'm ruining it!" Felix pulled his hand away to wipe at his eyes. Then he stood unsteadily. "I don't know what's wrong with me. I'm sorry."

Noah stood too, but only because Felix was hurrying toward the exit while choking back sobs. Noah almost chased after him. He almost refused to give up. Then he imagined how Felix would go home, cry himself to sleep, and wake up feeling a little more callous the next day. He would report to work, go to school, and after enough weeks and months, the events that now haunted him would retreat into the distance. Eventually a handsome young guy with a healthier past would notice him, and Noah would take his place in history as the difficult lesson that Felix had needed to learn. So instead of chasing after him, Noah watched Felix go, telling himself it would be a final sacrifice borne out of love. The kindest thing he could do.

He went to the bar, ready to obliterate his tortured thoughts. Noah ordered a beer. While he waited for it to be poured, his eyes moved to a drained drink on the counter, the ice cubes at the bottom slowly melting. Then he heard cheering and turned around to see Ruben celebrating his racing victory. Chester stood next to him, laughing at his antics. A college graduate without debt and an old man who refused to be lonely. Noah still believed in the Gentlemen's Agreement Club, despite what it had cost him. And he still believed in love, regardless of how often it had burnt him. Most of all, he still believed in a future where he came home every night to a sweet guy with way too many interests and never enough room to store them all.

Noah slapped a ten dollar bill on the counter, then ran for the exit. Once outside, he looked up and down the sidewalk, not finding who he was searching for, but spotting a familiar figure near the cars parked out front. The man was leaning against a maroon convertible and stood upright when he noticed Noah there.

"Harold?" Noah said disbelievingly. Then he shook his head to clear it. "Did you happen to see—"

"That way," Harold said, pointing to the left. "Seemed like he was in a hurry."

Noah peered in the indicated direction. He could see far enough to know that he was too late. Felix could have gone down any of the side streets, or already gotten into a car and driven away.

"Are you okay?"

Noah looked back to Harold. "No. Not really."

"I'm sorry," Harold said, taking a step closer. "I guess it didn't go so well."

"It went fine," Noah said wearily. "Ruben was great. He's inside. Go see him if you want. I'm okay. I'll be in after a little while."

"I'm here for you."

"Thanks," Noah said, looking down the street again. "It was nice of you to bring Ruben. Seriously though, go see him. You don't have to hide out here. Especially now."

"I didn't give him a ride and I'm not hiding," Harold said. "I'm here for you."

Noah looked over at him in surprise. He had misunderstood the meaning of the words, but there was no misinterpreting that expression. Harold appeared vulnerable, like he'd just spoken a confession.

"Just in case you need me," he added. "Or want me."

"What about Ruben?" Noah asked.

Harold shrugged. "He's got an internship lined up in Arizona. He wants me to go with him, but we both know I won't. I'm too much of an Austin boy."

"So you're not together?"

"We're letting it play out to the end. That's what we agreed on." Harold lowered his head and seemed lost in thought. Then he raised it again and took a couple more steps forward. "It just seems to me that we're both looking for second chances, you know? And neither one of us is having much luck, but maybe that could change."

Because while it wasn't possible to make your own luck, you could make it for another person. Noah could give Harold the luck he yearned for, and in return, maybe he could finally let himself continue feeling what they had—

Footsteps. Noah had been aware of them on the edge of his perception, but it was the thud and cry of pain that finally drew his attention. He glanced over and saw someone pushing himself up from the sidewalk. When he noticed the blue hair, he broke into a run. Felix was half a block down, looking more embarrassed than hurt. Noah helped him to his feet and checked his hands. They were indented where they had slammed into small stones. The skin along the meaty part of the palms was scraped, tiny droplets of blood rising to the surface.

"I'm fine," Felix said, pulling away his hands. He sucked on one of them, eyes searching Noah's, until he let his arms drop. "It helped."

Noah shook his head, not understanding. "What?"

"Meeting Chester helped," Felix said, his chest heaving. "Ruben too. I want to meet more of them."

Noah felt lightheaded. "Are you serious?"

Felix nodded, eyes still wet with tears. "I think I can get over it. I love you too much for—"

Noah kissed him, reveling in the sensation, even though his aim was off and the result was clumsy. All that mattered was how Felix kissed him back. With warmth and forgiveness.

"We'll take it slow," Noah said, pulling away. "We'll ease into it, and this time, I won't hide anything from you. And if somehow you still manage to love me despite knowing all the facts, we'll take it straight to the altar. No hesitation!"

Felix laughed, the sound a blissful melody, because it meant that Noah hadn't broken him. He was still sweet and wonderful and innocent.

"Let me see those hands again," Noah said, turning the palms upright. "I know a doctor who might be able to help you. He just graduated. I don't think he has any real experience, but maybe he can help anyway. We'll talk to him, and if he gives you the all-clear, we can play some video games together. Sound good?"

Felix nodded, the joy in his eyes moving toward a more tender emotion. When another apology started to form on his lips, Noah kissed it away. All was forgiven. Everything was right.

He remembered that wasn't quite the case when they began the walk back to the barcade. A convertible pulled away from the curb, turned in the middle of the street, and drove away in the opposite direction. The tires didn't screech. The speed was respectable. Noah already knew that if asked about it later, Harold would claim he had wanted to give them their space. Maybe he had even convinced himself of that reason, when in truth, it always hurt to see someone else be given the luck that you had so badly longed for.

"I know I said we would take it slow," Noah said as he stood up from the couch. They were in his apartment again, which felt much more like a home with Felix there. The evening had gone well. They had played arcade games and spent more time with Chester and Ruben. Enough that it felt like a double date, although sometimes he struggled to remember that anyone besides Felix was there. Noah celebrated every touch between them, every shared glance brimming with emotion, although he did occasionally think of Harold and feel guilty. Then again, he only had one heart to give, and he felt like he had finally done so. Nothing stood in the way of his relationship with Felix. Except semantics. "You living here is definitely rushing things," he continued, "but I don't want that to change. Even though your mother probably thinks I'm a monster by now."

"Because of our big dramatic misunderstanding?" Felix shook his head. "She has no idea. I've been staying with a different friend every night."

Noah didn't show his relief, deciding to test the waters with a little humor. "Just how many friends have you stayed with? Ten? Twenty? Over a hundred?"

"I lost count a long time ago," Felix said coolly. "Deal with it."

"I'll try," Noah said, leaning over to nuzzle their noses together. "I'd like to meet some of them. For real. I'll keep showing you off to mine, and you start introducing me to yours."

"Okay!" Felix said. "Just warning you though. Some of them are kind of nerdy."

"Nerdier than you?"

Felix thought about it. "Ever heard of cosplay?"

"No, but I look forward to being educated." Noah kissed him and stood upright again. "We're getting off track. What I'm trying to say is that, even though we're taking it slow, I still want you to consider this your home. So you take the bedroom. I'll sleep on the couch."

"That doesn't seem fair," Felix said, stretching out across the cushions and clutching a plush animal to his chest. Whatever it was looked like the lovechild between a platypus and a bison. "Appa and I will take the couch."

"*That* doesn't seem fair," Noah said. "There's two of you and only one of me. You guys take the bed."

"I'm too tired to move," Felix said, shaking his head. "Appa is especially exhausted. Will you get us some blankets? Oh! And a juice?"

Noah made a face like he was annoyed. Of course the second he turned away, he allowed himself a smile, because this exactly what he had missed and wanted more of. When he returned with a blanket and a drink, he saw that Felix had his eyes closed and was breathing softly. An earlier conversation had revealed that neither one of them had slept much lately. Noah draped the blanket over Felix, tucked him in, and left the juice on the coffee table. Then he shut off all the lights except the one above the stove.

Once in the privacy of his bedroom, he stripped down, cherishing the fuzzy contentment he felt inside. Only when he slid between the sheets did he think of Harold, wishing that things had worked out better for him. Noah might have a word with Ruben to see if they couldn't keep that relationship going, even long distance. Part of him still loved Harold and always would, meaning Noah wanted the best for him. Ruben might be just the thing. If not him, then some other willing heart.

Noah was just drifting off when a gentle whisper stirred him from sleep.

"Hey."

He rolled over and found Felix standing in the doorway. "You okay?"

Felix shook his head. "Appa is hogging the covers. And he drank all my juice."

"That's terrible!" Noah said. "I guess you'll have to sleep on the floor."

"I'm pretty sure I heard burglars too," Felix said, trying again. "Oh, and I'm allergic to carpet. If I sleep on it, I break out into really gross sores with lots of pus."

"I understand," Noah said as he sat up. "I'll sleep on the floor in the living room. You take the bed."

"Too late!" Felix said, shutting the door behind him and locking it. "The burglars have broken in. Appa is our last hope. We better stay in here until morning."

Noah grinned. "Then I guess you better get over here so I can protect you. Just in case they break down the door."

"Good idea," Felix said, hurrying over.

"Uh, you might want to leave your clothes on," Noah said a minute later. "What if we have to make a run for it?"

"They'll have a harder time catching us if we're nude," Felix said, tossing aside his shirt and working on his jeans. "This way there's less clothes they can snag hold of. Are you…"

"Ready to run naked down the street?" Noah threw the covers open. "What do you think?"

"The underwear needs to go," Felix said critically.

"Yours first," Noah retorted, but then he grabbed and pulled him into bed to do the deed himself. Felix yelped and laughed during this, occasionally silenced by a kiss. After enough wrestling, and once they were both completely undressed, he scooted close to Felix, pressing their bodies together chest to chest, stomach to stomach. Noah rolled over onto his back, clinging to the most precious treasure he had ever discovered and swearing to never let go again. Not so long as he had the strength in his body or the will in his heart.

Epilogue

"It's official. I'm single again."

Noah turned around in his office chair. The extra bedroom with its blank walls had been transformed over the previous months. Shelves were grouped in pairs, each with different displays and themes. On a good day, Noah had little trouble identifying what action figures belonged to which franchise, or what books were manga and meant to be read from back to front versus the rows of Western graphic novels, which were colorful and not as confusing to him. Enough free space still remained for the desk where he sat and a couple of chairs off to each side, for when he had visitors. Such as now. Standing in the middle of the room was Harold, his partner, his colleague, his friend.

At times—usually, in fact—this seemed to be enough. He and Harold worked well together. Awkward moments or any sort of tension between them was nonexistent. Almost. Judging from the emotion in Harold's eyes, they might be due for a relapse.

"You and Ruben?" Noah asked.

Harold nodded, but before he could say more, someone else bounced into the room. The dyed hair had grown out, only the tips remaining blue. The rest of Felix's hair was shiny, black, and worn loose these days—no product—since Noah liked being able to run his fingers through it.

"I'm saying goodbye!" Felix declared. He spotted Harold, who was over often enough that neither of them were surprised to see each other. They got along just fine too. Felix hugged Harold in greeting, then skipped over to where Noah sat to give him a quick smooch. "I've got class right after work, so no doggie bags. Unless you want fish that has been stuck in a hot car all afternoon."

"I'll pass," Noah said with a chuckle. He appreciated how many meals Felix brought home from work these days. Money was a lot tighter than it had been. "Will you be late?"

"Probably," Felix admitted. "Darli texted to say that Mom misses me, which is code for my sister wanting to hang out. She's just too cool to admit it. I thought I'd swing by after class and let them pamper me. Do you want to come along?"

Noah glanced over at his laptop. "I've got a lot of work to do. Free-for-all?"

"Free-for-all," Felix repeated, offering him a fist bump.

Noah complied, then watched him leave the room, unable to force down his grin.

"Free-for-all?" Harold asked from one of the side chairs. "Are you guys part of some sort of fight club?"

Noah laughed. "That's just what we call it when we each get to do whatever we want."

"Cute," Harold said. He seemed to mean it too. "You guys remind me of the first guy I dated in high school. He was my fairy-tale prince. Or king, I guess I should say, since this was junior year."

"When you were prom king?" Noah asked. "Your boyfriend was too?"

Harold grinned. "It was a very good year for me."

"I can imagine!"

"Not just because of prom. Everything was perfect and sweet. The first date, the first kiss, and especially the first time. Everyone should have that. When you get stuck in a crappy relationship, it's good to be reminded of how love is supposed to be."

"Surely you don't mean Ruben."

"No," Harold said, shaking his head. "He was one of the better ones."

Was. Past tense, although this hadn't come as a surprise to either of them. Harold and Ruben had continued dating, knowing that it would end when one of them moved away.

"So that's it?" Noah said. "Ruben is in Phoenix now?"

Harold's chest rose. Then it fell again. "Yup."

"How are you doing?"

"Okay. I guess."

Noah studied him, recognizing that he was handsome, personable, and still had a touch of sweetness of his own. "Did you love him?"

Harold looked away. Then he smiled, his brown eyes moving back to lock onto his. "Not as much as I've loved some people."

Noah's mouth went dry. He turned toward his desk, heart thudding in his chest as he sought a distraction. "The new system is working well," he said. "Chester has somehow managed to create four separate accounts for himself, but besides that, everyone seems to be adjusting well to The Menu."

Noah's idea for a database had developed into much more.

Now it was a system that their clients could sign into. One of the most popular features was a list of services that went beyond the usual dinner date scheme. Now clients could choose a companion for lunch, shopping, or travel. Clients could also request various forms of training, including the services of a fitness coach or a primer on relationships. They even had a few specialists, like a mechanic who could actually do repairs. While shirtless, of course, and far oilier than necessary, but real auto work regardless. Marcello had always accommodated unusual requests, but Noah had discovered that most clients didn't realize how many options were available to them, or weren't comfortable asking for anything out of the ordinary. With the new system—nicknamed The Menu—all they had to do was click a button. The clients were happy, but…

"How are the guys adjusting?"

"They love it!" Harold said. "You and I weren't the only ones getting sick of eating out every night. The variety is nice. I've got an afternoon appointment with George today. Wants me to take him shopping for some stylish duds. I guess there's a new foreman on one of his construction sites that he's hoping to impress."

"Let's hope the foreman likes pineapple juice," Noah said. Then he snapped his fingers. "Hey! Try signing him up for our dating course!"

"Will do," Harold said. "I had an idea of my own. Just hear me out, because I know this sounds stupid, but what about pet-sitting? The Colemans have that yappy dog who hates everyone but me."

"The biter," Noah said, rubbing his ankle while grimacing.

"Yeah. I've heard he can be a real nightmare, but for whatever reason, he's butter in my hands."

"Like most guys are."

Harold grinned. "Thanks! But what if we offer pet-sitting services too? We'll take selfies with their dogs when people are out of town. We can make those sexy or cute and send them with texts to update the owners."

"Sexy dog photos?" Noah asked. "That's pushing the limits of good taste, don't you think?"

"Shut up," Harold said with a chuckle. "I just mean that I'll be shirtless and snuggling up with their dog. Nothing more than that. Or maybe we could take some of the more energetic dogs out jogging and capture video."

"I bet people would be into that," Noah said, grabbing a pen to scribble some notes. "Really, most services are improved by having a cute guy do them. Marcello had it right with the shirtless waiters."

"Yeah, except we'll offer shirtless *everything*. Plumbing, housekeeping, cable installation…"

"Lawn mowing," Noah suggested.

"Taxes," Harold said, lifting his arms to flex. "These twin beauties will take care of your ten forties!"

"That's good! You might be on to something. We'll be the ultimate problem solvers. Call the GAC no matter your needs and we'll send a hot guy over to help you out."

Harold nodded musingly. "If anyone can make it work, you can."

"I'm not doing this without you," Noah said, jotting down more notes. When there wasn't a response, he looked over to see a familiar longing on Harold's face. The last time he had seen it was outside Bottoms 1UP, an evening that neither of them had spoken of since.

"I'll always be here," Harold said hoarsely. "If you need me."

"Thanks," Noah replied, grasping for a subject they could switch to.

"I really like Felix," Harold continued. "But if it doesn't work out—"

Noah didn't let him get any further than that. "I really like Felix too," he said pointedly.

Harold nodded his understanding. "Sorry. It's just been a rougher day than I was expecting. I guess I'm still raw."

"Who could blame you?" Noah said. His pulse was racing. He didn't think it would stop unless he spoke his mind too. "No matter what happens, I'll always need you in my life."

"One way or another?" Harold asked.

Noah swallowed and nodded. "One way or another."

That was all the promise he could give. For now he was too content with where things stood. He had the sweetest boyfriend imaginable in Felix, a guiding light in Marcello, a mixture of family and friends in people like Chester and Edith, and when it came to Harold… He supposed "partners" summed it up best. Partners in business now, and for one unforgettable night over a year ago, partners in love. There was no telling what else they might be to each other eventually, for if Noah had learned one thing, it's that life always chose the most surprising path and challenged him at every turn, but not without reward. As they settled down to turn their dreams into reality—Harold a reassuring presence at his side—Noah marveled at how far he had come, a beggar now spoiled by riches of the heart.

The story continues—

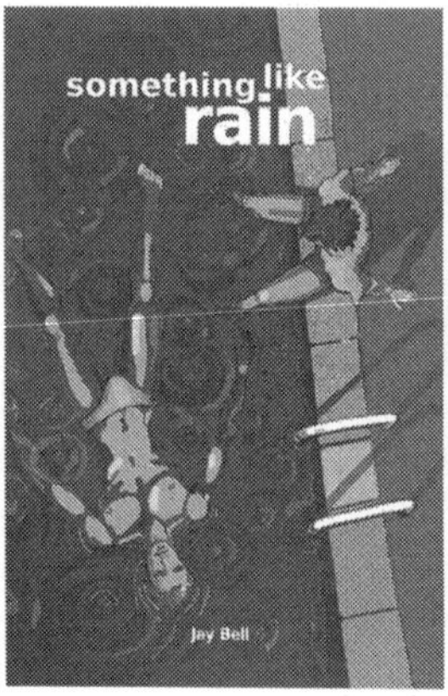

—in the Something Like… series, each book written from a different character's perspective, the plots intertwining at key points while also venturing off in new directions. The quest for love takes many different forms, changing like the seasons. Which is your favorite?

Current books in the series:

#1: *Something Like Summer*
#2: *Something Like Autumn*
#3: *Something Like Winter*
#4: *Something Like Spring*
#5: *Something Like Lightning*
#6: *Something Like Thunder*
#7: *Something Like Stories – Volume One*
#8: *Something Like Hail*
#9: *Something Like Rain*
#10: *Something Like Stories – Volume Two*
#11 *Something Like Forever*

Learn who each book is about and where to buy at:
www.somethinglikeseries.com

Also by Jay Bell

Something Like Rain

Nice guys finish last, but that doesn't mean they give up the fight. Sometimes it's necessary to keep trudging through the rain in the hopes of finding a break in the clouds.

William Townson is a good person. He's kind, considerate, and the last thing he ever wanted was to hurt anyone. Accidents happen though, and when they do, all that can be done is to pick up the pieces. For William, this means trying to hold together a stagnant relationship while resisting the temptation of Jason Grant, a young man with eyes just as intense as his love. Only the future can promise redemption for mistakes of the past, forcing William to choose between the Coast Guard and the needs of his heart. Can he find his way through the downpour to somewhere warm and dry?

Also by Jay Bell

Something Like Stories – Volume Two

The Something Like… series is drawing to a close! Before it ends, reunite with favorite characters and meet others for the first time in this special collection of fourteen stories. Highlights include Something Like Champagne, in which Marcello searches for the truth behind a drunken vision. In Something Like Bunnies, a young Jace Holden struggles with his first crush. Ben and Tim return in Something Like Memories as they debate when exactly they should celebrate their anniversary, and Jason finally makes an important decision about his future with William in Something Like Sun. Joyful reunions and tearful goodbyes await you, as do many affirmations of love, in this second volume of short stories.

For more information, please see:
www.jaybellbooks.com

Something Like Summer **has been reimagined as an ongoing web comic series! Join us on this colorful new adventure at** **www.gaywebcomics.com**

Also by Jay Bell
Straight Boy

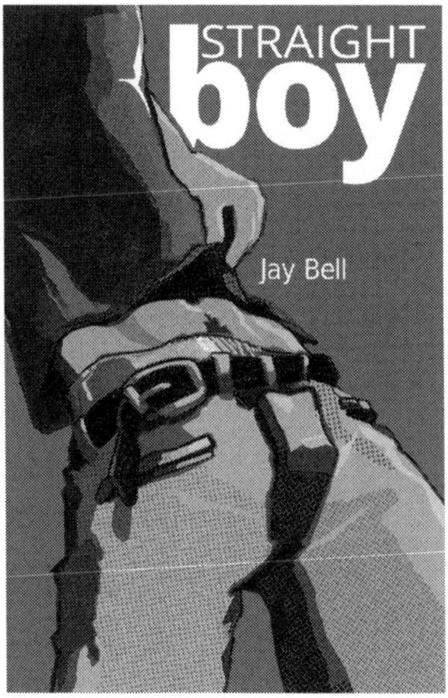

I love him. And I'm pretty sure he loves me back... even though he's straight.

When I first met Carter King, I knew he was something special. I imagined us being together, and we are, but only as friends. Best friends! I'm trying to be cool with that, even though I know he has secrets, and there have definitely been mixed signals. I don't want a crush to ruin what we already have. Then again, if there's any chance that we can be together, it's worth the risk, because Carter could be the love of my life. Or he might be the boy who breaks my heart.

Straight Boy is Jay Bell's emotional successor to his critically acclaimed Something Like... series. This full-length novel tells a story of friendship and love while skating the blurry line that often divides the two.

Made in the USA
Monee, IL
12 May 2024

58358653R10224